MURDER ON AIR FORCE ONE

Murder on Air Force One

A Kate Dawson Mystery

John L. Flynn

OPEN ROAD

INTEGRATED MEDIA
NEW YORK

ISBN: 978-1-5040-8422-2

This edition published in 2023 by Open Road Integrated Media, Inc.
180 Maiden Lane
New York, NY 10038
www.openroadmedia.com

To John, Beloved of God, and the rest of my Madoni family, with love

MURDER ON AIR FORCE ONE

PROLOGUE

Thirty-three-year-old Meghan Kendrick slid gingerly out of her seat on Air Force One and slipped into the restroom near the rear of the plane without any of her fellow reporters in the Press Corps noticing that she was gone. She was direct, purposeful in her movements, with none of the awkward, hobbled carelessness that may have characterized someone who was more likely to get caught. She was beautiful, poised, and self-assured.

Without a second glance, she moved swiftly into the darkened room, no larger than a closet, and latched the door securely behind her. Then Meghan stepped into the arms of a man who was waiting for her in the shadows. She had no way of knowing that her life had dwindled down to a matter of minutes.

The popular reporter for Fox News had spent the last ten years of her life in front of the cameras, reporting with a distinctly conservative slant that made her a favorite of both Republicans and Tea Party Activists. Democrats dismissed her as just another pretty face that lacked any kind of substance. Neither Party would have disagreed that Meghan Kendrick was a gorgeous woman. She was tall and slender with short blonde hair that made her seem even taller. Her eyes were blue; her mouth, full luscious red lips. Her posture was perfectly erect, with long legs and an athletic look that made her seem like an All-American girl. And while she had captained her cheer-leading squad in high school, her law degree from Syracuse University had given Meghan a distinct advantage over the other pretty reporters who covered the news of the day. In fact, her insightful comments about the judicial system during the live coverage of the confirmation hearings for U.S. Supreme Court Justice Samuel Alito had boosted the ratings at Fox News over rivals CNN and MSNBC nearly ten-fold. She cemented her reputation as the blonde with brains, reporting on some of the top stories of the day, including the death of Chief Justice William H. Rehnquist, the trial of George Zimmerman in the fatal shooting of Travon Martin, the Benghazi embassy attacks in Libya, and the Presidential Election of 2012. Meghan Kendrick was destined for an anchor desk or an hour-long show of her own, that is until she drew an assignment with the Presidential Press Corps . . . and met him.

At first, he was just another politician to her. Maybe a bit more polished and handsome than most, but still a political figure whose ready smile and charming wit cloaked a personal agenda that was really all about the accumulation of wealth and power. In her years as a reporter, she had met more than her fair share of silver-tongued politicians like him. They told her everything they thought she wanted to hear and answered none of the hard questions she tried to ask them. Clearly, Meghan was attracted to him. He had the charm and charisma of Jack Kennedy and the sex appeal and "lingering eye-contact" of Bill Clinton, but she still didn't trust him. When he resigned his seat in Congress to support his wife's run for the Presidency, he surprised her. She started following his career more closely, and soon the only thing she wanted to do was hold him in her arms.

Since scandal was the last thing that either of them wanted, they kept their relationship quiet and private.

Meghan Kendrick knew fully well what she was doing. She understood that revelations about an affair between her and the First Man, if they were ever made public, would touch off a constitutional firestorm that might weaken the Presidency, distract the federal government from essential business, undermine the rule of law, and embitter American politics for years to come. She was bound and determined to see that never happened, even if it cost her career. Meghan thought about that and a myriad of other things as she embraced and kissed him passionately, undulating in his arms until she was curled all around him.

The man kissed her deeply, then moving his kisses around to her right side, he whispered in her ear, "You're late."

"You're lucky I came at all," she whispered.

"You'd better be nice to me, Meghan, or I'll have one of my Secret Service agents escort you off this plane."

"At 40,000 feet? I hardly think it's likely." She drew him even harder to her breasts.

The man tried to pull away from her embrace, but Meghan held onto him tightly, with a passionate, almost violent sensuality that he had never found in any other woman. Her eyes burned into him, red-rimmed and horrible, and yet somehow . . . soft. Yes, soft and wanting. She wanted him more than any other man she had ever known, and she would have done almost anything to possess him, short of triggering a public scandal, but she had already taken reasonable steps to make sure that didn't happen.

Meghan brought her hands up to his face and gently stroked the coarse bristles of his five-o'clock-shadow. "Besides, when have I ever not been nice to you? Now stop talking and show me what you've got, big boy."

Kissing her deeply, urgently, his hands moved up her dress on each side, raising the edge of her skirt until it was nearly around her waist, squeezing the cheeks of her ass. Meghan Kendrick pressed her firm, bountiful breasts against his finely-tailored Brooks Brothers suit, clawing at his chest with her meticulously sculptured nails. Their embrace was intense, like two wild jungle animals in heat. His mouth slipped away from Meghan's lips, and started kissing her neck, then shoulders as he tried to move around behind her. She reached down to rub his crotch, breathing deeply as she writhed under his touch. Her skirt was bunched up around her waist, a frilly pair of lace panties the only thing that covered her ass. Bending her forward over the wash basin, he seized the panties with his left hand, but Meghan suddenly protested, pushing him away.

The man stepped back, red-faced, with the look of confusion slowly spreading across his handsome features. He was about to say, 'What the fuck?' when she put a finger to his lips to silence him. They had already discussed the ground rules for their intimate encounter. No talking and no noise. And even though they had already broken the first rule, she was determined they were not going to break the second. The last thing that either of them wanted to explain to a nosy Press Corps was the reason why the two of them were alone in a small, confined restroom on Air Force One.

As soon as he had stepped back, Meghan Kendrick smiled playfully. She reached for her lace panties, and with slow, methodical precision, she pulled them down her long legs and stepped out, one leg at a time, then bent back over the sink, with the palms of her hands flat on the counter for support. As she stretched and twisted her body, she felt his manhood swelling, pressing the cheeks of her ass. The feeling was electrifying as he grew longer and larger. He leaned his weight on her body, holding her in place. She reached between her legs, and fumbled with his zipper, freeing the large bulge growing in his pants. Teasingly, he slapped her ass several times, grabbed her tightly, and pulled her onto his crotch, thrusting forward. She spread her legs wide and rolled her hips in response to the sensation that grew stronger and quickly intensified. Finally, no more delicate teasing, it was time to bring it on hard. Meghan pushed against the counter and arched her back as she ground down on his crotch.

For an instant, the man stopped and straightened up, listening in breathless silence to a sound he thought he heard outside the room.

"What is it, my love?" she whispered, looking up at his reflection in the mirror.

"I thought I heard something."

"Just your imagination."

"I suppose," he acquiesced, leaning over and kissing her neck.

The man took hold of her hips and moved slowly towards her. She seemed to be accepting, moving her ass back to meet him. Then he made one quick movement between their bodies, and at once, they were joined. Slowly almost methodically, he began pumping her from behind. She moved and twisted her body with him, trying to keep pace. Silhouetted by the light that shined through the crack at the base of the door, shadows of the two lovers danced against the dark wall of the restroom as they merged and separated, then came back together again. Graceful and elegant, they appeared like revelers dancing the waltz at a grand ball.

Without warning, the man stopped his rhythmic pumping and the expression on his face changed. He reached into the pocket of his suit and produced a clear plastic bag, not unlike the ones drycleaners used to protect laundered shirts. Then, with one lightning-fast movement, he placed the bag over her head and tied it off at her neck. She glanced up at him in the mirror with a look of surprise. She had wanted him to be more spontaneous with his sex play, had even encouraged him to add some of the kinkier elements that she enjoyed, but this had caught her completely off guard. As she reached instinctively to adjust the bag, he grabbed her hands, pinning them to the counter. She fought back, playfully, assuming the role of the victim. But when he pushed her back down so roughly, she was concerned whether he knew the difference between play-acting and actual rape.

As the man leaned back into her, Meghan Kendrick arched her head back, gasping for air, struggling to free his grasp, her long luscious legs wildly kicking the air. But again, he shoved her back down, his weight more than twice that of hers. This time, he held her down firmly, and continued to thrust himself in and out, while her legs flailed and her body twisted back and forth. Even though Meghan continued to go through the motions, she had no real desire to push him away. He might have been stronger than she was, but she could have easily broken free if she had really wanted to. She was trying to enjoy the rough sex play. Then, as she gagged unrelentingly on the plastic bag, she began making little guttural sounds that had originated deep in her throat, sounds that could only have been mistaken for extreme pleasure.

Each thrust penetrated her deeply, driving her body forward with the force of a jackhammer, slamming her head against the restroom mirror. She was crying out again with each jab of his cock, but this time it was more of a choked orgasm as she twisted and struggled to maintain her connection with him. He grabbed her hips and redoubled his speed, driving home his rigid member faster and faster. Furiously, she was sucking the plastic in and out of her mouth, growing faint from the lack of oxygen to her body, struggling before she lost consciousness. But as she became passive, almost liquid in his arms, he continued to pound away at her ass with his furious thrusts. Finally, the man slowed his pumping and grew rigid as an orgasm began to overtake him. He made one final thrust and pushed all the way into her. The last thing she felt was him exploding inside of her as she passed out.

A few heartbeats later, the man climbed off, zipped up the fly to his trousers, and adjusted himself, looking in the mirror with a smug sense of satisfaction, as he straightened the lines of his suit. Tightening his tie, he turned his attention back to her.

Beneath him, Meghan's body had gone completely limp. Her hands and arms had slid away from the counter, and she'd dropped to the floor, her legs sprawled out on either side of her body.

Awkwardly, he removed the plastic bag from around her head and patted her cheek to rouse her. "Meghan, you've got to wake up," he said softly into her left ear. "Meghan . . ." He patted her cheeks again, but when she failed to respond, he started shaking her more vigorously. She was truly out cold, *or dead*. Panicking, the man reached for her neck and pressed his fingertips against the side of her windpipe, feeling for a pulse. When he felt the familiar thumping of blood coursing through her veins, he breathed a deep sigh of relief. He remained there for maybe thirty seconds, then slipped away from her side.

With the look of utter disbelief on his face, the man shuffled around the tight room, moving very slowly, occasionally glancing down at her body. He stopped in the center of the room to look up at the ceiling. *What the hell am I supposed to do now?* he asked himself, a cold sweat washing over his body.

Overhead, he heard the familiar whine of the plane's flaps as they extended. Next, he imagined, the grinding and whirring of the plane's hydraulics signaling the landing gear as it thumped down and locked into place. And finally, he pictured in his mind as the plane reaching its outer marker and beginning its slow, inexorable descent to the runway below. *Ten minutes, maybe twelve at the outside. Not enough time to revive her and get her back to her seat, unnoticed.* He felt like a rat caught in the proverbial trap as he realized there was nothing that he could do to prevent the plane from landing.

Staring at the door, his mind began rifling through several possible scenarios. He stood frozen for a moment, then resolutely made up his mind. Nothing must look unusual or out of place. The restroom must look exactly like it did before he arrived. So, he went into action, moving methodically around the small room, cleaning up after himself. He scooped up her panties from the floor and shoved them into his pants pocket, then crumpled up the plastic bag and pushed it to the bottom of the trash bin. Lastly, he bent briefly over Meghan's body and pulled the skirt that was up around her waist down over her bare ass. He reasoned that if anyone found her collapsed over the sink, they would have assumed she'd taken ill during the landing and sought out the restroom as a private refuge.

The man stood straight and regarded his reflection in the mirror, a satisfied look settling on his face. Moving across the room, he listened momentarily at the door, took a deep breath, and raced out the door without a backwards glance.

He failed to notice Meghan stirring, coming back to life.

At 9:06 P.M., fifteen minutes later, the Secret Service reported finding Meghan Kendrick's body in the rear restroom of Air Force One. Dead.

CHAPTER ONE

Kate Dawson was sitting up in bed in her small, studio apartment at Bayside Village, watching the television with the volume turned off while her boyfriend, John Prescott, slumbered next to her, snoring softly, when the call from the dispatcher came in.

They had spent the day sightseeing at Alcatraz Island, sampling chocolates at Ghirardelli Square, and riding cable cars before returning home to eat Chinese takeout from cardboard boxes, and making love. It was yet another fast-paced weekend for Kate, one that had come to typify her long-distance relationship with John. After nearly a year together, she had come to accept the fact that he would never leave his job at the Department of Justice to move in with her. So, once a month, she'd pick him up at San Francisco International Airport after his five-hour direct flight from Reagan-National, spend a few pleasant days together, then pack him off on his red-eye flight back home to D.C. She hated to see the weekend end and would often sit up in bed next to him mindlessly flipping through channels with the remote just so she could have a few more hours, feeling him next to her. She didn't even mind his snoring as long as she could look over at the lovely man that lay beside her.

The phone rang, and it rang again. Kate swung her legs over the edge of the bed and picked up her iPhone from the night stand.

"This is Dawson," she answered, then paused to hear the news. "Okay, I'll be there in about an hour." She hung up weary.

For a long moment, Dawson just sat there, staring off into space. Officially, she was on duty that night as the senior member of the Homicide Bureau. It had been a quiet Sunday night; hadn't expected much action. In fact, she had hoped to spend the last couple of hours with John before his flight, but now it looked like she was going to have to go to work.

"Is everything all right, honey?" John asked, rolling over.

"No, I have to go in." She rubbed his back. "Do you mind terribly if I drop you off at the airport earlier than usual?"

"Don't worry about me," he responded groggily. "I'll just take a cab."

Kate climbed back into bed and pinned him down on the mattress, taking hold of each of his hands in hers. "Not on your life," she said playfully, leaning over and kissing him. "You're not going to rob me of one of my great pleasures . . . spending the last few minutes of my weekend with you."

"Okay, okay, but we'd better get moving then."

"Not necessarily," she replied, naughtily. "We've still got a couple of minutes. The crime scene is out at the airport."

"Homicide?" Prescott asked, almost indifferent, rubbing the sleep from his eyes.

"Yep, Caucasian female, approximately thirty-three years old, apparent 6-0-1. I understand they found her body lying flat on the floor of the rear restroom, no panties. The real kicker is that the plane is Air Force One."

"Air Force One? Are you serious?" he queried, suddenly quite awake. "Listen, Kate, I think you might want some help on this one."

"Why is that?"

"Because it sounds like you got a homicide that may involve the President or a member of her detail aboard Air Force Once. It may be sticky. Have you ever worked with the Secret Service before?"

"No, but a homicide is a homicide."

"Kate, you don't realize what you're up against," he said, scrambling into his clothes.

"Well, we've got about fifty-five minutes until I'm supposed to be there," she said, heading for the bathroom. "Why don't you explain it to me?"

By the time Kate and John got dressed and out the door, ten minutes' time had passed. She stepped on the gas of her BMW 5.25i, laying tread out of her apartment complex. She wasted little time picking up Highway 101, the Bayshore Freeway, and cut south and west across the city. San Francisco International Airport was located thirteen miles south of downtown area, near Millbrae and San Bruno in the unincorporated County of San Mateo. Technically, the airport was not even within ten miles of the city limits, but SFO was still owned and policed by the City of San Francisco. Since most of those who lived and worked in the Bay Area relied on Highway 101 to get them to and from the airport, the traffic was always heavy, especially near San Bruno where it almost always came to a crawl. Dawson made a left turn onto Aviation Boulevard to get around some of the traffic, then took the ramp to the commercial hangars that served UPS and FedEx.

Up ahead they saw the lights from the main terminal building. The place was lit up like Christmas with lights flashing from row upon rows of mobile news trucks that surrounded the Arrival and Departure gates like an occupation army. Reporters from

CNN, Fox, MSNBC, ABC and other cable television networks stood just outside the gates on the cement curb talking into their news cameras. The media feeding frenzy had already started.

Dawson drove to the bottom of the ramp and stopped so they could get their bearings. The flat expanse of the airport runways was laid out ahead of them. She turned right towards the hangars and crisscrossed the back roads until they reached the hangar where Air Force One had been stored temporarily. A uniformed patrolman who recognized Kate pulled aside a makeshift barrier and waved her through the labyrinth of police cruisers parked in front and on the opposite side of the street from the hangar. She pulled into the first available spot and stared out of the windshield with John at the usual crime-scene carnival.

Dozens of uniformed police officers and plain-clothed detectives moved in and out of the hangar in a random but orderly fashion. Several of the crime-scene boys were gathering their equipment from an unmarked van, while, at the same time, Doctor Edgar Brogan had formed his techs from the ME's office into a small detail and were about to process through the Secret Service screening. A police spokesman was talking with some interested bystanders. In addition to members of the San Francisco Police Department, she counted several military types, a handful of TSA cops, and suits from Homeland Security, the F.B.I., and, of course, the Secret Service. On top of all that, soldiers with M-16 rifles formed a secure perimeter. She wasn't really surprised by the huge turnout of law enforcement officials and military personnel, considering the multi-jurisdictional aspects of the crime. After all, a homicide had taken place onboard the President's plane, a first in the history of Air Force One. Kate just thought it was a little bit of an overkill to think they needed so many people to catch a single perpetrator when there were likely multiple homicides happening on the streets of San Francisco tonight that would go unsolved because of a lack of manpower.

Inspector Dawson climbed out and stood with John Prescott on the pavement in front of the hangar, looking up in awe at the plane. With the large hangar doors open, Air Force One towered above them. Almost as tall as a six-story building and as long as a city block, the aircraft with the familiar white and blue markings that ran the length of the plane's fuselage just barely fit in the largest hangar at San Francisco International Airport. The "flying oval office," as it was known in political circles, had been produced by the Boeing Aircraft Company, customized from the highly popular Boeing 747-200B transport. Designated VC-25A by the military, the four-engine jet plane included a Presidential Suite, which was comprised of a conference/dining room, lounge/bedroom, and office space for senior staff members. A second conference room, which could easily be converted into a medical facility, dominated the middle section of the plane in addition to a rest area for the flight crew. The rest of the interior contained work and rest areas for a small presidential staff, while the rear of the aircraft had been transformed into first class seating and work space for the few media representatives who traveled with the President. Normally, the plane carried the four members of the flight crew (including two pilots, navigator and flight engineer), twenty-three additional crew members, and seventy passengers.

As she admired the huge aircraft, emblazoned with the words "United States of America," the American flag, and the Seal of the President of the United States, Dawson couldn't help but feel an undeniable presence. It was an impressive achievement in modern aviation. She was just surprised when her boyfriend corrected her use of the term "Air Force One." Like most people, she thought that Air Force One referred to the two, highly-customized, Boeing 747-200B transports that operated solely for presidential travel by the United States Air Force. But in actuality, Air Force One was the radio call sign for any Air Force plane carrying the President.

"That's really interesting. I never knew that," Dawson declared, walking slowly along the pavement.

Prescott looked over at the metal detector, then back at Kate. "Have you decided how you are going to deal with the Secret Service? You're probably going to find them to be very irritating, especially tonight."

"Not really, no."

Prescott said politely, "Then perhaps I can suggest a strategy that we should follow."

"That's fine with me. I'd be grateful for your help. You seem to know these guys better than me."

"All right. Since you're the senior member of Homicide on call, it's probably best if you take charge of the crime scene right off the bat."

"Okay."

"Don't bother to introduce me, or refer to me in any way. Don't even look in my direction," he instructed her. "They'll know who I am from my identification, but won't know my significance here."

"I think I understand."

"Officially, I don't even exist. I'm a nonentity. You, alone, are in charge of the investigation. Besides it's doubtful that anyone at the Justice Department, other than the Attorney General, even knows."

"All right."

"It'll help to be formal. Stand straight. Wear your badge on the outside of your suit jacket and keep the jacket buttoned.

Give clear, concise orders to your men, and show them that you expect results from their forensics work. Stay focused. Never look around. Never appear distracted. Keep your voice calm and even. Keep your thoughts and personal comments to yourself."

"I have done this before, John," she said, a little annoyed.

"You and I both know that, but they don't. They're going to be testing you, probing for your weaknesses, trying to trip you up. Remember, they don't want your investigation to succeed. They'd prefer to keep everything in house and private. But since they don't have any other choice but to cooperate with local law enforcement, they're going to do everything in their power to see that you fail. Handle it as best you can. But whatever happens, don't lose your temper."

"I never lose my temper," Dawson blatantly lied.

"Is that right, Kate?"

"Well, almost never."

Prescott smiled warmly. "I'm sure you'll do just fine. You probably won't need my help at all. But if you find yourself in a bind, you'll hear me say 'Perhaps I can be of assistance.' That will be the signal that I'm formally asserting the power of the Attorney General. From that point on, it will be the clash of two Cabinet-level titans—the Department of Justice and the Department of Homeland Security—and it's anyone's guess who will win. But at the very least, the pressure will be off you, and I suspect the Secret Service will be much more eager to help with your investigation rather than give everything up to Justice. Okay?"

"You make it sound as if we're just pieces on a very large chess board," Kate said, a strange, almost bewildered, look upon her face.

"Pawns, actually, but I am glad you're starting to come to grips with the reality of this homicide. The woman that was found dead on Air Force One wasn't murdered by some ordinary perpetrator. There were some very powerful and influential people on that flight, and everyone who boarded that plane at Andrews Air Force Base had a security clearance, even the members of the Press. Make no mistake, she was killed for a reason, and that reason is at least as important as the identity of the person who killed her."

"Gee, thanks."

Prescott took her by the arm, peering deep into her eyes. "Would you rather I lie to you about what you're facing?"

Dawson stared back at him. "No, but I'm just wondering now what would have happened if I'd told you to take that cab."

"You're going to be just fine, Kate."

"From your lips to God's ears," she said under her breath, barely audible.

"What?" he asked, with a puzzled glance.

"It's an expression my father used to say. 'From your lips to God's ears' is a phrase that literally means all desires spoken aloud will be heard by God and answered," she remembered fondly.

"I'll be right there with you," John reassured her.

"Okay, then, let's get this show on the road."

Dawson walked with Prescott the length of the pavement in front of the hangar, stopping at the checkpoint that had been set up by the Secret Service to screen all visitors to Air Force One. Several men in black suits with noticeable earpieces were milling about, while a soldier holding an M16 rifle stood guard. Three other suits were stationed at the metal detector.

"Kate Dawson, Homicide," she said, holding her badge out in front of her.

One of the men at the metal detector looked at her badge and police identification card, and closely compared the ID photo against her face. Satisfied, he said, "Inspector Dawson, come right on through."

But no sooner had Dawson stepped through the gate-like structure than the security alarm sounded, indicating the detection of a concealed weapon. All at once, she was encircled by Secret Service agents with their guns drawn. As a homicide detective, Kate Dawson had carried a twelve-shot .9mm Beretta in a triple-draw holster under her left arm nearly every day of her life for the last ten years. It had become such a familiar part of her daily wardrobe, like a belt or a pair of shoes, she had completely forgotten to mention it to them. Carefully, she raised her right hand in the air, and with her left hand, slowly pulled back the lapel of her Versace jacket to reveal her service weapon. The men in black suits maintained their ground.

"Your weapon," the lead agent said, with his hand out, "is not permitted on Air Force One, but you'll get it back when you leave."

Dawson acknowledged, slipped the gun out of her shoulder holster, and handed it over to him. Without a word, the second man took it, and routinely removed the magazine and cleared the chamber. He passed the Beretta onto a third man who, in turn, entered the make and serial number in a logbook. He then locked it and the magazine into a small portable vault on the screening table. With the weapon finally secured, the men in black suits sheathed their guns, and went back to milling about.

Kate Dawson let out a deep sigh between clenched teeth.

Next Prescott stepped through the metal detector, without alarm, and came up behind her. "They're just trying to intimidate you, Kate," he whispered. "Whatever you do, don't let them see you sweat."

"I'm afraid it's too late for that," she said under her breath, feeling a wave of cold perspiration wash over her body.

Firmly, the lead agent said, "This way, please."

The three of them walked up a rolling staircase, which had been pulled up to the plane's rear cabin door, stepped onto the aircraft, then climbed a staircase to the middle deck. After passing through heavy drapes that had been drawn shut, they entered the press area. The Press Lounge looked very much like the first-class section of an ordinary jetliner, with large, comfortable leather seats and flat-panel monitors. Four work tables with docking bays for laptop computers were positioned at each of the four corners of the cabin. The soothing pastel colors of tan and light green made the lounge feel even more comfortable and luxurious. Towards the rear of the cabin, Kate could see a narrow corridor and several restrooms where her technicians and forensics people were gathering their samples.

"Inspector Dawson," the agent said flatly, without emotion. "You and your investigative team are restricted to this deck, in particular, the press lounge and the rear restrooms. The rest of the plane is off-limits to you. Please be mindful of the fact that you are a guest here."

"Thank you, agent. . . ?"

"Smith."

"Thank you, Agent Smith," she repeated and started towards the crime scene, but stopped dead in her tracks.

"It's about fuckin' time you got here," Matt Balardi said to her, sidling up. He was wearing a checkered, polyester jacket, a thin leather tie, and skin-tight corduroy jeans that barely covered the flab around his waist.

Kate Dawson gritted her teeth when she saw him. Balardi looked uptight and tense, irritable from the wait for the duty officer to arrive. She took some solace in the knowledge that every department had one; the guy nobody wanted to work with. She hated the fact that he had been assigned to her detail. From what she knew about Balardi, he had been transferred from one division after another, never staying very long in one precinct or with one partner. No one ever had the courage to come right out and give a reason why. He just rubbed people the wrong way. At all times outspoken, Balardi had made enemies in every department he had ever worked, including a few in the chief's office. At forty-six years of age, his career was over. Now an embittered, middle-aged detective, with few prospects and further advancement unlikely, he was just there to put in his time. He didn't really care whether he was liked or not. Personal integrity meant nothing to him; it was just a big joke. If he kept his nose clean, Balardi figured the union would protect him until he could retire and collect his pension.

"You know, this is all bullshit, Dawson," Balardi said, with venom. "We can't even take a piss without asking one of them for permission. I really hate these fuckin' Secret Service guys!"

"What have you got to report, Balardi?" she asked.

He continued ranting, "They're nothing but pussies. You should arrest the lot of them for obstruction of justice, so we can conduct a proper investigation."

"*Your report*?" She cocked her eyebrow.

Balardi inhaled and exhaled sharply in retaliation. "The woman's name was Meghan Kendrick," he said, reading from notes that he had scribbled on the back of his bill from Pacific Gas and Electric. "Thirty-three years-old, five-foot-nine inches tall, blonde hair, blue eyes. A real beauty. Apparently, she was a star reporter on the Fox News Channel, attached to the President's Press Corps."

"Okay, that's a start. Now I want you to find out everything you can about her: boyfriends, co-workers, rivals, anyone that would want to see her dead. You know, beat the grass and see what crawls out."

"Shit! That could take hours!"

"Yeah, it's called police work," Dawson said with a grin, as she headed towards the rear section of the plane.

Slowly, almost deliberately, she moved through the cabin, observing everything, using her eyes to take a photographic record of the crime scene. She made special note of the security cameras embedded in the walls and ceiling. Prescott and Balardi followed closely behind. She then walked past the forensics team, who was unpacking a small piece of electronic equipment, acknowledging each of them, and side-stepped several plain-clothes detectives conferring with members of the Secret Service, but kept moving. Finally, she came upon two crime scene boys who were working the room for trace evidence.

"How's it going, boys?" she asked, crouching down next to them.

"Not bad," one replied, with a ticked expression. "I'd be doing a lot better without all the interference from the feds."

"Yeah," the other one answered. "These Secret Service guys are a real pain in the ass."

Dawson peered closer. "Say, what have you got there?" she asked, spotting what looked like a woman's handbag in their evidence kit.

"The victim's purse," the first one said.

"I found it," the second added, handing it over to her.

Pulling on a pair of latex gloves, Kate Dawson took the purse in hand and searched through its contents: a cell phone, a wallet with credit cards and a reporter's identification card, a compact, breath mints, a nail file, sunglasses, stamps, a hair brush, Purell, a tampon, and roughly twenty dollars in cash. Through years working Homicide, Dawson had developed a theory that the contents of a woman's purse revealed a lot about her personality. Was the woman organized and always prepared for the unexpected, or was she a scatter-brained free spirit? She concluded that Meghan Kendrick was not only well-organized and detail-oriented, but had a place and purpose for everything. The only thing Meghan seemed to be missing was lipstick, which seemed odd for a television personality who was often called upon, at a moment's notice, to report news live on camera.

Dawson was still thinking about the missing lipstick when she handed the victim's purse back to the crime scene investigator. "See that forensics gets her cell phone so that we can have a record of her calls."

"Okay, Inspector," the second one acknowledged.

"Hey, Dawson!" the police photographer called, running over to her side.

"Ritchie, what's wrong? What's going on?" she asked, standing up.

"They've just confiscated all of my film."

"What?"

"Yeah!" Ritchie was visibly upset. "No sooner had I shot all the pictures of the crime scene, this big guy in a black suit comes over, takes the camera right out of my hands, and removes the SD card."

"Which guy? Where?" Kate said, searching the area.

The police photographer scanned the room, then pointed at a man who was just coming through the closed drapes. "That's him!"

"Excuse me, Inspector," Agent Smith said, politely, suddenly standing at her side, "but all film stays in-house. Orders."

"Whose orders?"

"I'm not at liberty to say."

Smith's evasiveness was beginning to piss her off. Dawson said, "Well then, once your superiors have reviewed it and determined the photographs don't break any of your security protocols, I will expect its return."

Prescott shot her a look, but remained silent.

"I'm not sure that I can make that promise, Inspector."

"That was not a request, Agent Smith," she said firmly. The look she gave him said it all. Dawson was done with playing his infantile games and was prepared to take things to the next level should she be forced to do so.

"But Inspector—"

"Oh, and one more thing," Kate said, cutting him off. "See that Detective Balardi gets a copy of the plane's manifest. Until they're cleared, everyone who was on board Air Force One is a suspect."

"Except the First Family." Agent Smith interjected.

"Especially the First Family."

Abruptly, she turned away, left him standing there with his mouth open, and moved into the narrow corridor at the rear of the plane. Flanked by Prescott on one side and Balardi on the other, Dawson leaned into the restroom, and regarded the victim's model face.

"How long has she been dead, Doctor Brogan?" she asked.

"Two to three hours is my guess," the Medical Examiner replied, hunched down over the body. "You see, rigor mortis is progressive. After a person dies, the muscles in the arms and legs become rigid in a couple of hours; in twelve to eighteen hours the body is, as the saying goes, stiff as a board. Given the temperature on board the aircraft and the state of the body, I would guess death occurred two to three hours ago."

"Do you think you could be any more precise?"

Doctor Brogan looked down at the dial on the thermometer he had placed in the victim's abdomen and checked his watch. "Ninety-six degrees. Give or take an hour for each degree, I would place the time of death around 9:00 P.M., plus or minus a couple of minutes."

"Cause of death?" Dawson asked.

"Maybe strangulation," Brogan answered, as he pointed at the victim's throat. "The redness, swelling, and bruising on the neck is usually a clear indication that a person has been strangled. But I also look for fingernail marks, handprints, pronounced red spots on the whites of the eyes or on the cheeks and face. Blood red eyes or subconjunctival hemorrhages are usually a dead giveaway for severe trauma to the neck in cases of strangulation."

"What is this world coming to?" Balardi cynically.

Kate Dawson bent down and took one of Meghan's hands in her gloved hand, examining her manicured nails. "Doesn't look like she put up much of a struggle."

Brogan shook his head. "No, but that's not the only thing bothering me." He reached for a clear plastic bag he had tucked inside his evidence kit. "The boys found this stuffed deep in the trash bin."

"What is it?" she asked, taking the plastic bag from the Medical Examiner's hands.

"An ordinary plastic bag. You know, just like the kind drycleaners use, only this one has smudges of her make-up and lipstick and hair fibers on the inside."

"So, what did he do?" Balardi interrupted, breaking Dawson's line of inquiry. "Try to suffocate her with the bag, and when he realized that wasn't working, he decides to strangle her instead?"

"Or maybe he strangled her first," Brogan proposed, "and put the bag over her head to make sure she was truly dead. There's enough evidence here to suggest that she's been strangled before. Some of the bruises and lacerations on her neck are much older than the ones from tonight. In fact, you can see where she's tried to hide them with make-up."

Balardi surmised, "Okay, maybe she was just a battered woman? We see a couple of dozen a month down at the precinct."

"No, she *wasn't* a battered woman," Kate Dawson said matter-of-factly. "Just look at her clothes, her make-up, her grooming. Meghan Kendrick lived a pampered life! She wasn't beaten up by a jealous boyfriend or an enraged husband. Something else happened to her. Something that we're just not seeing."

"Maybe she OD'd on coke?" Balardi said, pulling a small wooden toothpick out of his pocket and lodging it between his teeth. "Wouldn't be the first time one of those show-biz types snorted a little too much blow."

"I don't think so," Dawson said, scouring the area with her eyes.

Brogan offered, "We did find trace elements of a white, powdery substance on the restroom counter, and Meghan's nostrils had traces as well. I'll have a much better idea once I run a complete toxicology screen down at the lab."

"See, what did I tell you?" Balardi added like a smart ass.

Kate Dawson turned away from her fellow detective. "Is there any evidence that she was sexually assaulted, Doctor?"

The Medical Examiner adjusted the glasses on his face with his right index finger. "The external genitals are pretty raw, and there's some seminal fluid down there, but it doesn't look like forced intercourse. She had sex with someone, but I'm not sure she was murdered. At least, not by him. I'll need to conduct a complete autopsy of the body and run some more tests before I know for certain."

"Come on, Doc, you gotta be kidding me," Balardi said.

"Are you saying this wasn't a murder?" Dawson added.

"I'm saying that I don't know," Doctor Brogan replied. With much effort, the portly man climbed to his feet, extreme pain from the arthritis in his knees causing the features in his face to squeeze temporarily out of shape. Once the discomfort had passed, he pulled out a white handkerchief from his pocket and mopped his brow with it. "She was strangled all right, and may have even suffocated to death, but I believe those were actions she initiated or willingly took part in."

John Prescott listened closely, but didn't say anything. He kept his eyes on Dawson, but her face was a complete blank.

"I think she may have been a 'gasper,'" the Medical Examiner said.

"A gasper? What the fuck is that?" Balardi asked.

"A person who is sexually aroused by asphyxiation or the sudden loss of oxygen to the brain through strangulation or suffocation," Brogan explained.

Balardi was struck dumb. "Get the fuck out 'a here."

Kate Dawson backed him up. "No, I've heard of this before. When the brain is deprived of oxygen, it induces a lucid, semi-hallucinogenic state that increases feelings of giddiness and pleasure. Combined with orgasm, the rush is said to be more powerful than cocaine, and highly addictive."

"The state is called hypoxia, but in conventional circles it's referred to as erotic asphyxiation or breath control play," Brogan added.

"And with fuckin' six, you get egg-roll," Matt Balardi broke in. "You're not buying all this crap he's selling, are you, Dawson?"

"Why not?" She put her hands on her hips and cocked her head.

"I'll put together my report and have it to you no later than Monday afternoon, Inspector," the Medical Examiner said.

"Thank you." Kate felt as if she was on a roll. She then made eye contact with Agent Smith. "Now I'd like to talk with the agent who found the body. Where can we find your friend, Smith?"

He didn't answer immediately, but stared hard at her. Dawson could almost see the wheels turning in his head, plotting his next move, figuring out how to best protect himself and his fellow agent. But then again, Smith seemed to be the kind of person who rarely did his own thinking. When he was asked something that didn't conform to any standardized instructions, his basic programming seemed to break down. He was slow to respond because he simply didn't know what to say.

"You gonna tell me?" asked Kate. "I'd like to ask him a few routine questions about how he found the body."

Smith hesitated a moment longer, then gave in. "I'm afraid that he's not here. He's been assigned to protect the First Family."

"And where's the First Family?"

"The First Family—" Smith started to say, but was cut off by a deep, operatic voice that bellowed, like a great pagan god issuing commands to his subjects, throughout the small cabin. The words themselves seemed to hang out there—grand, theatrical, larger than life.

"—is of no concern to this investigation!"

Harlan Reinhardt, a tall, chunky figure of a man dressed all in black, pushed his way through the closed drapes. He was perhaps fifty or fifty-five, with the broad shoulders of an NFL half-back. His complexion was very pale; looked like a man who had spent a lifetime living in the shadows. It was likely that he had not seen the direct rays of the sun in decades. His hair was mostly white, peppered with a few darker strands, and his eyes were gray but appeared milky white. He was breathing hard as he stormed into the Press Lounge.

Dawson wasted little time in walking over to him. She stood toe-to-toe with the big, hulking man who towered over her, like some giant, mythical behemoth. "As long as this is my investigation, I'll make the determination of what is or is not relevant to it."

Smith said, "Sir, this is Inspector Dawson with the San Francisco Police—"

"I know who she is," he interjected.

"Then you have me at a disadvantage," she said, flatly. "You know who I am, but I don't know who you are."

He looked down at her, like a puny bug under a microscope. "Harlan Reinhardt. I'm in charge of the President's security."

"Excellent! Just the man that I should be talking to," Dawson said, standing her ground. "Now, if you'll provide me with the name of the agent who found the body, I have a few questions for him."

Reinhardt acted as if Kate's questions were too boring, too basic to bother to answer. "The agent's real name is classified, but you can refer to him as "Jones." Right now, he is part of the detail protecting the First Family." His body language said, "end of story."

Dawson asked, "Where's the First Family?"

"Classified."

"Classified?"

"That information is on a need-to-know basis only, and, at this time, you don't need to know."

She stared at him a moment, disbelieving, all cordiality evaporating instantly. "You mean, you're not going to tell me what I need to know as the lead investigator."

He looked back at her without a reply, deadpan eyes, expressionless.

"I noticed there are a number of surveillance cameras in this cabin," Kate Dawson persisted, pointing at one directly over Reinhardt's shoulder. "What would it take for me to see the video from earlier tonight?"

"Not much," he answered monotoned, "just an act of Congress."

Son-of-a-bitch! Dawson's thoughts belied an outward exterior of calm, as a feeling of rage burning deep within her began to bubble up to the surface and reach the boiling point. She bit down hard, clenching her teeth together in an attempt to keep it together, having had her fill of bullshit for one night from the Secret Service. What she really wanted to do was grab Reinhardt by his balls, slam him up against the bulkhead of the plane, and clamp him in irons for obstruction of justice, but she thought better of it. "Maybe you didn't understand my request? I'm asking to see the surveillance tapes," she said, repeating herself a second time.

"Not a chance, Inspector."

Dawson finally lost her temper. "That's it! I've had enough of your bullshit!" she exploded, reaching for her nonexistent side arm. When she remembered she didn't have her sidearm, she reached for her cuffs. "Harlan Reinhardt, I'm putting you under arrest for obstruction of justice."

Reinhardt made no effort to resist, just stood his ground. His agents took flanking positions, with their weapons drawn. "You have no authority here," he said calmly. "May I remind you that as long as you are aboard this aircraft, you are a guest of the Federal Government?"

"This is still my city and my investigation," she said, unyielding.

For an instant, the temperature in the cabin turned icy cold, as everyone froze solid in place. Doctor Brogan and the detail of crime scene investigators did not move a muscle, even though several were in the middle of deploying a portable three-dimensional laser scanner. A couple of the cops paused in mid stride as their counterparts in the dark suits stood, holding their guns out in front of them, in a combat stance. Even the hands on the clock seemed to stop moving, as if they were somehow trapped between the tic and the tock of that instant in time.

"Dawson!" Balardi yelled, from the back of the cabin. "Will you just fuckin' cuff this asshole!"

Kate Dawson heard his words, but her expression didn't change and no one moved. She seemed to be blind to everything except the smug, self-righteous face in front of her. For a fleeting moment, she imagined what she could do to alter those features. The cabin and the other men in it were miles away. All that mattered to Kate was wiping that smug look off Reinhardt's face. It was then she noticed it, a single drop of perspiration on his brow.

"Let it go, Kate. He's not worth it," John whispered.

At that, Dawson relaxed her shoulders a tad, took a deep, tortured breath, and let it out through clenched teeth. Kate was upset with herself that she had lost her temper, particularly in front of her boyfriend, but felt justified that she had made her point. "I've had it with this fucker," she cursed under her breath. Dawson turned and started to walk calmly away him, ignoring the blunt snouts of the pistols still trained on her.

"Perhaps I can be of assistance, Inspector," Prescott said, holding his identification up in the air. With a slow, almost deliberate pace, he stepped forward, moving between the two combatants, and waited for the tension to subside before identifying himself to the Secret Service chief.

Indignant, Reinhardt motioned for his men to put away their guns. "I wasn't aware that anyone from Justice had been called."

"Let's just say that I'm an interested third party. I happened to be at the airport catching a plane back to D.C. and these officers were good enough to invite me along to the crime scene."

"I'm sorry they wasted your time. There was no crime committed here tonight." Reinhardt stood with his hands crossed in front of him in defiance.

Prescott looked at him, his eyebrows raised, silent question marks. "Well, if I'm not mistaken, what I see over there is a homicide."

"You are mistaken," Reinhardt corrected him. "Meghan Kendrick died of an apparent overdose."

"Overdose? What about the marks around her neck?"

"Self-inflicted."

"Self-inflicted?" Prescott was astonished.

"Yes, that's what I said, self-inflicted," Reinhardt insisted. He looked from face to face, then back at Prescott. "It's unfortunate her death was reported as a homicide, but then what do you expect from the media. A sensational murder makes for far better ratings than a simple drug overdose."

For a moment, John Prescott thought about this. Something didn't seem to make sense to him. He continued to puzzle over it, until all at once, the answer came to him. He looked deeply offended.

"You son-of-a-bitch," he swore under his breath.

"I'm only thinking about the good of the country, particularly at this critical juncture in history when we stand locked with the Iranians over their plans to build a nuclear arsenal."

"And what happens to Meghan Kendrick? You just sweep her body under the rug and pretend she never existed."

"Believe me, it's for her own good."

"She was one of *them*," John protested, pointing out towards the flashing lights and vans. "The media will never accept this as a simple drug overdose. Never."

The Secret Service chief said, "If you tell a lie that's big enough, and you tell it often enough, people are going to believe you're telling the truth, even when what you are saying is total bullshit."

"You can call it whatever you like, Reinhardt, but we both know this was a homicide. Meghan Kendrick was murdered by someone on this plane."

Reinhardt snorted. "A man of integrity . . ."

Kate Dawson grew weary of listening to their banter and

turned back to the crime scene. She couldn't seem to get over the feeling that they were missing something. She asked, "Agent Smith, during the last hour or so of the flight, can you give me a sense of what members of the press corps were doing?"

"Yes, ma'am," he replied respectfully. "We had had a great deal of turbulence during the flight and nearly everyone spent the whole time buckled in their seats watching movies."

"Movies?"

"Air Force One has its own internal audio-video system, and there are fifteen movies available, which Press Secretary Nora O'Donnell usually selects prior to the flight. The movies include: *The American President*, *Diabolique*, *Skyfall*, *Independence Day*, *Waiting to Go Home*, *Kill Bill Again*, *Stress Test*, and *Fargo*," Agent Smith reported. "As always, the reporters in the press cabin voted to see *Fargo*. *Fargo* has become the *Rocky Horror Picture Show* of the White House Press Corps, and the reporters kept requesting it again and again. And as soon as the movie was finished playing, the technicians would start it over, so that after a long flight, it was very possible to have seen *Fargo* several times."

"Is that right?" Dawson queried.

"Yes, ma'am. In fact, many of the reporters left their headsets off and shouted the dialogue at the screen."

Changing subject, she asked, "Would you mind showing me where Ms. Kendrick was seated on the plane?"

The Secret Service agent indicated with his hand. "She sat in the first seat in the last row, usually by herself."

"Ok," she said, as if Smith had confirmed something she had already suspected was true. "Thank you. You've been very helpful, Agent Smith. I'll let you know if I have any further questions."

"Right you are, ma'am."

Kate moved down the aisle and sat in Meghan Kendrick's seat, inspecting everything within reach. She tried the seatbelt, raised and lowered the seatback, and searched through the pocket in front of her, finding the usual assortment of magazines and passenger information about the Boeing 747-200B's safety features. She felt on the sides and beneath the seat cushion. Nothing.

Dawson hesitated a moment, as if on the verge of giving up, when she reached over to the seat next to her and patted it several times. She felt something hard beneath the leather seat cover.

With a surprised look on her face, she had a quick look around to see if anyone was watching her, but they were either involved in their work or had taken a break to listen to the two men talk. Kate Dawson craned her neck to overhear their conversation, but she only caught the occasional word or phrase. Once she thought she heard Reinhardt refer to her as a "bitch," and several times, she heard the word "sorry" as Prescott pretended to be a remorseful parent. It seemed like he was apologizing for the way in which she had been conducting the investigation.

Cautiously, Dawson reached over to the seat next to her, and pulled out an elegant shiny black lipstick container with a pretty silver collar from under the leather seat cover. She was certain it was the missing lipstick from Meghan Kendrick's purse. She palmed it in her hand long enough to slip it into her pocket without alerting the Secret Service agents who were all around her. Dawson then stood up and brushed out the wrinkles in her Versace suit.

Twenty-three minutes later, Kate Dawson was escorting John to his departure gate. The DC-bound flight was scheduled to take off at 11:41 P.M., and they had to hurry their pace to get through the media circus that had snarled traffic and doubled the lines at the check-in counters. As they worked their way through the lights and television cameras, Dawson listened to the reporters tell their story, but failed to hear the words "woman" and "murder" in the same sentence. Instead, she heard a lot of them saying "the investigation is ongoing" or "all information will be forthcoming."

"I don't know about you, but I'm sick of the way the media sensationalizes every news item," Kate said, glancing over her shoulder. "So many stories involve violence, celebrities, sex, or "shocking surprises." It's not bad enough that they emphasize these stories, but they often mislead us as well. Call it fake news."

Prescott patted her back. "It's all about ratings, love."

"Last week, I heard a 'tease' on the news that said, 'Mitt Romney makes an important announcement about running for President in 2020.' Of course, when they returned from the commercial, I learned that the 'announcement' was that he had not changed his mind and still had no plans to run again in 2020."

"Yeah, I heard that report, too."

Dawson continued, "In print, they use these big, bold letters to catch our eye because most people who don't have time to read the entire article just skim the bold print. But those are just teasers, too. Look at the way they've been treating this crisis with Iran! It's all got to stop."

Jokingly, John stopped and half-turned toward his girlfriend. "So, what do we do? Throw out the First Amendment, and kill the next reporter who says something we don't like."

"Yeah, something like that."

"Honey, you can't be serious?"

For a moment, Kate Dawson seemed to be a million miles

away as she wrestled with her thoughts and fears about Meghan Kendrick. More important than *who* killed her was the answer to *why* the news reporter had been killed. Long before she realized it, the woman's murder was under her skin, gnawing at something deep within her soul. She squared her shoulders. "Of course not."

John squeezed her hand. "You had me a bit concerned."

"Sorry."

"No need to apologize. We've all got a dark side."

Dawson stared at him, unblinking. "You know, that's something John Munroe used to say. He was convinced that every one of us was capable of murder because of the mindless primitive that we keep all bottled up inside. He thought that one day we'd lose control and the beast would run amuck."

"I really wouldn't worry about that, Kate."

"I don't. It used to bother me, though," she confessed. "I'd wake up nights in a cold sweat, imagining Munroe had come back from the dead. But I haven't thought about that in over a year."

Prescott never took his eyes off her. "Good, I'm glad. Old wounds can take a long time to heal."

"You're damned right!" she exclaimed, inhaling deeply. "But it's more than just that, John."

"So why don't you tell me what's really on your mind."

"Okay." Kate hooked her arm into his, a warm and affectionate gesture, and continued with him to his departure gate. They passed by several fellow travelers as they maintained a fast pace. "For the last couple of hours, I've been wondering why anyone would kill a member of the press."

"You're talking about motive now, or superstition?"

"Motive."

"Well, you just said it yourself," he explained. "Maybe

not in so many words, but you agreed to a comment I made earlier in jest about killing journalists who report a story you don't like."

Suddenly, the proverbial light bulb came on over her head. "I see! The reason why Meghan was murdered was for something she said . . ."

". . . or had planned to say . . ."

". . . or had planned to say," she repeated his words.

"Discover the motive, and you'll find your killer."

They stopped walking just short of the gate, and he turned to look into her eyes. "Everything's gonna be all right, Kate. You're a very competent detective. I have every confidence that you can solve this case *and* bring Meghan's killer to justice."

Kate looked down at her feet. "I just wish you weren't going home right now. I could really use your help."

Lifting her chin, he said, "You'll do just fine on your own. But if you do run into any trouble, please don't hesitate to call me."

"Don't worry. I've got your number on speed-dial."

John Prescott reached for her, and gathered her into his arms. She melted into them, peering into his dreamy blue eyes. He placed his right hand under the back of her neck and kissed her deeply. She responded, her tongue meeting his, dancing happily in place; their bodies pressed firmly together as if they were meant to be forever joined into one form. But just as quickly as they had come together, they parted. His left hand reached up and stroked her cheek as she leaned forward and kissed him one last time.

"I love you," she said, breathless.

"I know," he replied playfully.

As he turned to board his plane, Prescott paused on the gateway, the other passengers moving around him. He looked back at her, saying, "The First Family always stays at the

InterContinental Hotel when they're in San Francisco. It's located at Fifth and Howard streets."

Dawson shot him a look of surprise. "And when were you going to tell me that?"

"I think you'll also find Madam President has several events planned throughout her four-day stay, including a speech in Pacific Heights this morning and several private fundraisers with Democratic donors scheduled to keep her busy in the afternoon and evenings," he added, then hurried down the ramp.

After a moment or two, Kate Dawson walked away from the gate, smiling.

CHAPTER TWO

Several hours later, as a heavy fog began rolling over the San Francisco Bay area, Kate Dawson drove towards South Beach, taking Highway 101 north until it merged with Route 80. She then followed the Bayshore Freeway to Bryant Street, and turned right at Beale. But as she rounded the corner at Delancey Street, she screeched to a stop. Police cruisers were everywhere and uniformed police officers were moving in and out of her apartment building. She rolled down the driver's side window and looked up towards the third floor.

"Ma'am, I'm afraid you can't stop there," a policeman said, shining a flashlight in her face. "You're blocking traffic."

Dawson held up her badge to block the light. "That's okay, officer. I'm a detective from Homicide."

"Sorry, Inspector," he apologized, after checking her identification. The policeman inspected the row of cruisers, then added, "I'll get one of the boys to pull up, and you can park right over there."

"Thanks," she replied, idling her car's engine.

Within a few moments, they had cleared the bottleneck of police cruisers, and Dawson pulled into a parking spot across the street from her building. She rolled to a stop at the curb and killed the engine. It struck Kate that they might be there waiting for her; a thought that sent a chill down her spine and caused her to shiver.

She scurried across the sidewalk and climbed the steps to the third floor of her apartment building. Kate lived in a small, studio apartment at Bayside Village on the south side of town, near San Francisco's hip, trendy neighborhood of South Beach. She had always dreamt of living there, a few steps from the Embarcadero and nearby AT&T Park. So, when her marriage ended so tragically with her daughter's death, she decided to make her dream a reality and moved into the only apartment she could afford on a civil servant's salary. But soon she realized that dreams of a better life and a brand-new start could not replace the sense of loss she suffered. No matter how hard Dawson tried to enjoy her strolls along the water's edge, gazing dreamily at the sailboats on the Bay, she felt very empty. Nearly three years later, she still struggled with feelings of guilt amplified by her partner's death at the hands of the serial killer she later brought to justice. The site of police cruisers and the usual crime-scene carnival outside her apartment building dredged up all those thoughts and feelings.

When she rounded the corner of the third floor, Dawson breathed a sigh of relief to see her apartment undisturbed by the SFPD. But as she looked closer, she saw uniformed policemen going in and out of her neighbor's front door. Dawson approached Lenny Provolone's apartment, and paused for a moment outside. She had not seen him in a couple of weeks, but had chalked up his fourteen-day long sabbatical to the new woman in his life. She hoped that he was all right.

Dawson pulled out her badge and, with it in hand, pushed her way past the police at the front door. As she entered the apartment, she gagged on a pungent odor that was tinged with a mild seasoning of sweetness. Immediately, she put a handkerchief to her nose. The smell in the apartment was one that she had encountered many times before. Dawson knew that a dead and decomposing body smelled like nothing else in this world. When she tried to describe it once to a friend, she said, "Try to imagine a piece of rotting meat over which someone has sprinkled a few drops of cheap perfume." And that was exactly the odor she smelled in her friend's apartment. She prayed that she wasn't going to turn the corner and find Lenny's dead body on the floor.

In its place, she found the kitchen had been turned into a dumpster. The CSI boys were picking through rotted food, slices of week-old pizza, half-eaten tins of sardines, cardboard containers of sushi, fast food bags, leftover French fries, empty soda bottles, discarded newspapers, and all manner of trash. They seemed to be searching for something that was not immediately apparent to her, but their probe had spilled over into Lenny's bathroom which smelled worse than a public toilet. She peeked around the door, and saw two technicians from forensics scooping up the dead carcass of a skunk, its entrails spilling over their gloves as they shoved it into an evidence bag. The scene might have been laughable if it hadn't been so morbidly repulsive. *What on earth had Lenny been doing these last two weeks?*

Dawson walked into the living room, and watched as more police officials combed through Lenny's personal belongings. Boxes and bags, and even his personal computer was being searched. Two guys wearing ATF jackets from the Bureau of Alcohol, Tobacco, Firearms, and Explosives were carefully going through several of his collectable props from *Star Wars*. His prized Obi-Wan Kenobi lightsaber was among them. At the front door, a couple of uniformed cops stood around, talking and taking in the sights. It was like a policemen's convention.

Lieutenant Emmanuel Ramos folded his arms across his chest as his eyes swept over the room, a commander of men. "Search every room and closet in the apartment, and make sure you do a thorough check of his storage space in the basement," he barked out orders.

"Yes, sir," one man responded.

"I'm on it, Lieutenant," another one answered.

Dawson watched as the two policemen snapped to attention, then marched off to complete their tasks. She asked, "Are you in charge here?"

"Yes, I am. And just who are you?"

"I'm Kate Dawson. I live in the apartment next door."

"This doesn't concern you," the Lieutenant said, all business. "Keep your nose out of this, lady."

"It's *Inspector*," she corrected him, flashing her badge. "I work in Homicide. I'm also Mr. Provolone's friend."

Ramos didn't reply right away. He stood there, looking everywhere but at Dawson, refusing to make eye contact. "I've seen you around."

"Yeah, as I have you," she said, trying to be polite. "Would you mind telling me what this is all about?"

"What's it to you, Inspector?"

"Occasionally, Mr. Provolone works as a consultant for the Homicide Bureau and, as I mentioned, he's also a friend."

"Well, 'your friend' threatened to kill a young woman, nearly half his age, if she didn't submit to having sexual intercourse with him," the Lieutenant reported, dead serious. "A protective order has been issued, instructing him to stay away from her and not to contact her in any way. The Court has also instructed him to turn over any firearms and ammunition to the police."

"I presume you have a warrant?" she inquired, with her hand out.

Ramos took out what looked like an official document from the chest pocket of his jacket, and handed it to her. "Warrant is signed by a judge. Everything is in order."

Dawson read the warrant. "Hardly, this doesn't give you permission to go through his trash or disrupt his household. This warrant just permits you to confiscate any weapons he has. Anything else you've done or taken far exceeds the parameters of this document."

"You sound like an attorney," said Ramos, as he threw his head back and guffawed. "I *hate* fuckin' attorneys."

"I demand that you and your men leave these premises immediately."

"Or what?"

"Or I will be forced to press charges of criminal trespass . . ." Dawson said, as she watched hopelessly as the men under the Lieutenant's command stumbled through the apartment, knocking over Lenny's precious collectables. A bull in a China shop might have done less damage. ". . . *and* vandalism."

One of the ATF agents took Lenny's prized Obi-Wan Kenobi lightsaber from the shelf, and threw it carelessly into an evidence bag.

"Hey, will you be careful with that," she said, reprimanding him. She then reached into the bag, attempting to rescue the priceless prop. Unfortunately, the plastic lightsaber blade had broken off from its metal hilt. She held the two pieces in her hands, addressing the ATF agent, "There was nothing deadly about this lightsaber. It was a prop from a fuckin' movie. But now you've broken it, asshole."

"Looked real enough to me," he said, remorseless.

"It was a movie prop. It was supposed to look real."

Emmanuel Ramos smirked. "Perhaps I should arrest you for obstructing an official investigation."

"An investigation into what, exactly," she countered shrewdly. "I thought you were here serving a warrant?"

"It's all right, Kate," said a familiar voice. Lenny Provolone appeared at his bedroom door in his moth-eaten, dingy gray t-shirt and briefs from Fruit of the Loom, and shuffled across the floor, like a dead man walking. "I've already informed the Lieutenant that he and his men are free to inspect anything they like. I don't have anything to hide."

Dawson walked over to his side and handed him the two pieces of his lightsaber. "Lenny, I don't think you understand," she said. "They have a warrant that empowers them to take any firearms or ammunition you may have. However, the warrant does not give them permission to conduct a search of your apartment."

"What difference does it make? My life is over!"

"It makes a big difference, my friend. They could impound everything you own, including your assets, and those could stay tied up in the courts for years. I've seen it happen. You could find yourself out on the street, or worse."

"I don't care. My life is over," he repeated.

"Well, you better start caring, or the next intimate relationship you're going to have is with some hairy beast named Bubba behind bars."

"You might as well let them shoot me; put me out of my misery."

Kate shot him a sideways glance. "You've had worse ideas," she said, with a hint of sarcasm, "but right now, you're going to pick yourself up out of this muddle of self-pity you're trying to drown in, and act like a man. You're going to put on a pair of pants and grab your toothbrush, then we're going over to my place and you're going to sleep it off."

"Will you have sex with me?" he pleaded.

"No! You're sleeping on the couch."

"I'm such a pathetic loser," Lenny said, feeling sorry for himself, as he shuffled back to his bedroom.

Dawson turned back to Lieutenant Ramos, glowering at him. The look in her face said it all: *You'd better not piss me off.* "Your investigation is over. I want your men out of here immediately."

"I've already given them the word. 'Fraid they won't have time to clean up that mess in the kitchen."

"Right now, that's the least of my problems."

The police lieutenant walked over to the door, but stopped short of leaving. "I work a lot of domestic violence cases in the span of a year," he said, speaking over his shoulder. "In about half of those cases, abusers violate their restraining orders and perpetrate even worse forms of abuse on their victims."

"What's your point, Ramos?"

"I'll be keeping a close eye on your friend," he said, turning with a bitter expression written across his face. "Creeps like him who prey on little girls half his age belong behind bars, with the other perverts and wackos."

"You've got the wrong idea about Lenny," she protested.

"Right, that's what they all say. But I've got a protective order from a little girl who's frightened out of her mind that says different."

Dawson could not believe it. "Everyone knows that restraining orders and orders to vacate are granted to virtually all who apply. The low burden of proof has led to a great deal of misuse, with a large percentage of allegations being thrown out of the court for lack of proof."

"How typical! Blame the victim for everything."

"I was just saying—"

"I'll make it easy for you," he said, walking out the door. "You just keep him away from her, and everything will be fine."

"Good night, Lieutenant," Dawson said, closing the door behind him.

The next morning, when Kate climbed out of bed, Lenny was still sound asleep on the couch. She decided to let him sleep it off and tiptoed around her apartment so that she wouldn't wake him. In less than fifteen minutes, she had showered, dressed, put on her make-up, and was heading out the door when he heard him beginning to stir. Kate stood at the door, with her arms folded across her chest, and looked down at her houseguest. The last thing that she wanted to do was wake him; she didn't have time for a long conversation. She was also concerned that, in his present state of mind, he might do something to himself or his ex-girlfriend Rebecca that he'd later regret. It was a sticky situation, and the longer she stood there, the more she realized she was going to have to make a choice.

With a delicate, almost maternal touch, Kate pulled the comforter up over his shoulder, then leaned over and whispered in his ear, "Lenny, we'll talk about what happened later tonight. Just get some rest and lock up when you leave. Whatever you do, stay away from Rebecca! If you're feeling energetic, you may want to clean up your apartment." Satisfied, she walked out the front door.

Minutes later, Dawson was making the right from Delancey Street onto Brannan when her cell phone rang. The caller ID on her car's Bluetooth device identified John Prescott as the caller. She pressed the 'talk' button on her steering wheel and was instantly connected with him through her car stereo. The convenient, built-in, hands-free link allowed her to talk while she continued to drive, a feature she liked a lot.

"How was your flight?" she asked.

"Uneventful." It sounded like he was seated in her back seat. "How about you? How are you holding up, Love?"

She thought about it a moment. "Okay, I guess. I had an unexpected wrinkle come up, but it's really not worth discussing."

"I understand. Things are actually pretty crazy here for me. There's a lot of concern that we may be going to war with Iran over the nuclear arms stand-off. People are just scared."

"Well, you be careful . . . please, John."

Prescott was silent for a moment. "Listen, Kate, I sent a couple of agents to check out Meghan Kendrick's residence this morning. The apartment was completely empty. Wiped clean. Other than some furniture, there wasn't any evidence that she had ever lived there. When they questioned the building superintendent, he told them the Secret Service had taken everything, including her garbage. This morning. Just after midnight."

"Wait a minute," Dawson said, stomping on the brakes. Coming to a complete stop, she reached for her briefcase on the back seat and pulled out a small notebook. The vehicle directly behind her and several others in the lane started honking their horns as she thumbed furiously through the pages. Finally, she reached a page she had scribbled a few notes on.

"Kate, are you still there?"

Dawson threw the car into gear and stepped on the gas. It lurched ahead, like a dragster on nitrous oxide out of the starting gate. She left the other vehicles behind her in a cloud of smoke.

"Kate, answer me!"

Glancing at her notes, she said, "Meghan's body was found just after 9:00 P.M. With the three-hour time difference, between the East Coast and our Pacific Time, the Feds would have gotten to her place just a few minutes later."

"How is that possible?" John asked, confused.

"I don't know, but I am beginning to smell a cover-up."

"Well then, you're not going to like this any better. Her Capitol Hill apartment is registered in the name of McMillan & Associates."

"The name doesn't mean anything to me."

"I don't know why I expected you to know that," he apologized. "Maybe it's just an inside-the-beltway kind of thing, but McMillan & Associates are huge contributors to the Democratic Party."

"The Democratic Party? Why would they be holding the lease to an apartment that a Fox News reporter is using?"

"That's exactly what I was thinking."

Dawson turned the corner at Sixth Street and pulled into a parking spot opposite police headquarters on Bryant Street. "I just got to work, and I'm running a few minutes late."

"No problem, Kate. We'll talk later on tonight."

"Do you think you could do me a big favor?" she asked.

"Sure. Anything. Whatever you want."

"I need a list of everybody who was on board that plane. I asked Agent Smith for it last night, but now I'm thinking he may only give me a partial list or none at all. I need the original manifest that was filed at Andrews Air Force Base before Air Force One took off."

For an instant Prescott was silent, then said, "I'll see what I can do. In the meantime, you be very careful."

"I will."

Kate Dawson scrambled into the conference room at police headquarters, grabbing a cup of coffee, a couple of sugars, and a donut as she passed the cantina. She sat down at the conference table, directly across from Lieutenant James Roberts, who was standing there glaring at her, nostrils flaring. Rather than return her boss's look, she took headcount around the room. Most of the detectives from the Homicide Bureau were assembled at the table, including William Clark, Mikhail Jawara, Matt Balardi, and several others she didn't know well. Her partner Jorge Ramirez was noticeably absent. As she mixed the sugar in her coffee, Kate sifted through the pile of photocopied materials in front of her, and listened to the detective who was talking to the group.

". . . and once we obtained the subpoenaed records from his Internet Service Provider, we were able to link his IP address with the emails he sent to the contract killer," reported William Clark, reading from his notebook. "When we confronted him with the evidence, he confessed to taking out the hit on his wife. In fact, we couldn't shut him up once he started talking."

"Cried like a baby is more like it," Mikhail Jawara corrected his partner.

Clark looked down at his notes. "We've referred everything over to the D.A. We're just waiting for a court date."

"I still say that rich boy would've done better on *Divorce Court*," Jawara joked, sparking a round of snickers and laughs from his fellow detectives. "I'd take my chances against a roulette wheel any day of the week. Now he's going to spend the rest of his life in jail, then what good is all that money going to do him."

"The point is," Clark said, trying to correct him, "he didn't think he was going to get caught."

The African-American had the final word. "No, partner. He just didn't *think*."

"Great. Good job, Clark, Jawara," the Lieutenant said. "Corcoran, Farris, where are you guys on your case."

"Crime scene is clean. No weapons, no prints, no witnesses," Farris reported.

"The couple was shot at point-blank range by an assailant

who probably hid out in the house and waited for them to come home," Corcoran added. "The family thinks they were killed by a crazy ex-wife who's had a history of stalking the ex-husband, but her alibi is solid. She was a thousand miles away in Colorado."

"We're following up on other leads," Farris said.

The Lieutenant put his hands on his hips, pushing back his blazer, in a commanding stance. "Okay, keep on it and see what you can do about getting me an update by Friday."

"Yes, sir," they replied in unison.

"All right, what about you, Dawson?" Roberts said, turning to glare at the female detective. The look of irritation on his face fixed her right in place. "What have you and Balardi got to report?"

Fumbling with the notes from her briefcase, Dawson finally said, "Last night, shortly after 9 P.M., a Secret Service agent attached to the President's security detail aboard Air Force One reported finding a woman's body in the rear restroom of the plane. Apparently, she had been strangled, although that is now being disputed. Her name was Meghan Kendrick, a thirty-three-year-old reporter for Fox News attached to the Presidential Press Corps."

Jawara perked up at his seat. "Are we talking about *the* Meghan Kendrick? The 'fair and balanced girl' from Fox News?"

"The one and only," Kate replied.

"Oh, man! I've had a hard-on for her longer than I can remember."

"She *was* a real beauty," Balardi added.

"Do you remember the *GQ* spread she did?" Jawara asked, with a faraway look in his eyes. "She was wearing that skimpy black dress. Barely. Man, that was some serious ass skin. Made you want to join the Republican Party."

"I cut that picture out of the magazine and had it pinned up over my desk for over a year," Balardi reminded them.

"Yeah, I remember."

"So much for family values," Clark interjected, with an eyebrow raised.

"Maybe she figured it worked for Sarah Palin, so why not give it a shot," Jawara defended her.

"She certainly gave 'stiffies' to a lot of conservatives across the country."

Clark added, "Maybe a few to Democrats as well."

"I'd wager she caught the First Man's eye," Jawara joked. "He's got an eye for tall blondes just like her."

"He'd be *my* first suspect," Balardi said, grinning.

"When you're finished being rhapsodic about your favorite celebrity crush, we can get back to some real police work," Roberts demanded as he sat down hands folded, leaning forward in his chair at the end of the table. Then he turned to Dawson. "You referred to the woman's death as a homicide, but you also said that was now being disputed. By whom?"

Dawson looked back in her notes. "Harlan Reinhardt. He's in charge of the President's security."

"Let me guess. The woman's injuries were self-inflicted?"

"That's right, Lieutenant," Dawson acknowledged. "The thing of it is, when I first received the call, they said it was a homicide, but then Reinhardt started saying that it wasn't."

"I'm really not surprised," the Lieutenant said. "No doubt cooler heads prevailed, and that's when they started to evolve this rather elaborate story of their own. I think you'll find the man who reported it as a homicide will be guarding an igloo in Alaska for his next duty assignment."

Dawson took a sip of her coffee. "I just don't understand why they don't want to cooperate with us."

Roberts explained, "The Secret Service just doesn't want to risk a full investigation that might expose the President, her husband, or any one of the officials on board to allegations of murder, particularly on day thirty-four of this nuclear arms stand-off with Iran. They'd rather sweep it under the rug now and conduct their own investigation later, when the press has more important things to think about. Better a page-five story on the day when the front page announces an end to the crisis than a front-page story now while the President is trying to negotiate a peaceful resolution to the stand-off. I really can't blame them, but it's a shitty way to treat a woman's death."

"Agreed."

"What does Doctor Brogan think?"

"He plans on releasing his coroner's report this afternoon," she answered.

"Well, pending the results of his report, let's continue to treat Meghan Kendrick's death as a homicide," Roberts said, all business-like. "I want Clark and Jawara to do a complete work up on the plane's manifest and find out if there was anyone on the list that had it in for Meghan Kendrick. That includes members of the First Family, officials, press, stewards, and the flight crew—"

"Sir, I've already assigned that task to Detective Balardi," Dawson interrupted.

"I want you and Balardi to get the low-down on the coroner's report, then follow up with the person who initially filed the homicide report. Get him to talk. Find out why he thought Meghan was murdered."

"Yes, sir," she responded.

"With all due respect, Lieutenant, I don't want to work with Inspector Dawson," Balardi said, exchanging glances with her like the crossing of swords. "She's unlucky, sir. She has a way of getting her partners killed or seriously fucked up in the line of duty, and I don't want to be next on the list."

"We've been over this before," Dawson growled, swallowing her anger.

"C'mon, cool it, man," Jawara said, looking at Balardi.

"There's no point in opening old wounds," Clark added.

"Well, maybe I'm still not satisfied with her explanation," he taunted Kate, with a sing-song inflection in his voice.

"You know damn well that I had nothing to do with Frank Miller's death!" she shouted.

"You keep saying that," Balardi said, egging her on, "but I have a hard time understanding why you didn't have his back."

"How many times do I have to go over it? Frank Miller was my partner and my friend. We were chasing a suspect. We got separated. By the time I got back to him, he was dead, and the suspect was nowhere to be found."

"Yeah, right. Maybe if you'd spent less time boffing Monroe's brains out, you'd have seen him for the cold-blooded killer he was."

Red-faced, Dawson sprang to her feet, ready to reach across the table and rip out his throat, while Clark and Jawara struggled to pull her back down to her chair. "You son-of-a-bitch," she snarled.

Matt Balardi was on his feet. "C'mon, tough guy, hit me. Show me what kind of man you are."

Roberts shot the pair of them one of his patented steely looks. "All right, that's enough, Balardi, Dawson," he said, shaking his head with disgust. "I've warned you about this before. I'm not going to have two of my homicide detectives brawling in the conference room." Standing, his big, hulking form towered above them, like a giant over insects. "Look, I get the fact that the two of you don't like each other, but this isn't a Sunday social where you get to select your partner. This is the San Francisco Police Department, and as your superior, it's my prerogative to make the workforce assignments. The day that you can't live with that is the day I want to see your resignation on my desk. Is that understood?"

"Yes, sir," Kate said, grudgingly, finding her chair.

"Right you are, Lieutenant." Balardi smirked, cutting his eyes at Dawson, as he sat back down.

Roberts sat down in his chair and read the agenda. "Okay, we're moving onto the last item," he said, matter-of-factly. "Some of you may have heard already that Jorge Ramirez's wife went into premature labor last night around 8 P.M. and gave birth to a little girl."

Everyone looked surprised at that, but Dawson jumped as if she had just been given an electric shock. "Is she okay? What about the baby?"

"The mother and the baby are fine," he reported to the group. "Ramirez told me his wife, Angelina, was scheduled to be released today, but the Neonatal Intensive Care Unit at the hospital was going to be monitoring the baby's underdeveloped lungs for the next few weeks. He seemed very upbeat and positive, and wasn't concerned that his newborn still has a ways to go."

"Does she have a name?" Kate asked.

Roberts had notes. "Layla. Born 2lbs, 12oz. She's already become a celebrity on Facebook, thanks to the mug shots Ramirez took of her in the arms of the nurses in the NICU."

"Wasn't there a song from the 70's called 'Layla'?" Jawara asked.

Dawson told them, "Yeah, by Eric Clapton. My father loved that song, and I've always had a sweet spot for it myself."

"The song was inspired by Clapton's unrequited love for Pattie Boyd, the wife of his friend and fellow musician, George Harrison," Clark added.

"Thank you, Mr. Trivia," Jawara joked. "One of these days I'm going to harness that eidetic memory of yours, partner, and we're going to go to Las Vegas and make lots and lots of money."

"Promises, promises," Clark joked.

"Well, your trip to Las Vegas is going to have to wait just a bit longer," Roberts said, on a sour note. "Ramirez has asked for a few days off to be with his daughter in the hospital, and I've granted him family medical leave in accordance with union regulations. But that just means his current caseload has to be divided amongst the rest of you." He started handing out folders to the detectives around the table.

"Thanks a lot, Lieutenant," several of them grumbled aloud.

Jawara groaned when he picked up his stack of folders. "Just when I thought I was going to see the light of day."

"Look on the bright side, partner," Clark said, "with all this work, we'll never have to worry about standing in an unemployment line."

"Yeah, I guess we should be grateful that people keep killing other people."

William Clark chortled, "Think of it as job security."

"I don't know about you guys," Balardi complained, "but I'm hoping Ramirez was a better writer than speaker, or else we're all going to need a "Spick" dictionary to figure out what the fuck he's talking about."

Farris and Corcoran chuckled, but the other detectives regarded Matt Balardi's racial comments with disdain. Kate bit down hard on her lower lip, barely able to contain the anger smoldering deep within her.

Roberts finished doling out the folders. "Okay, that's the lot. Now I want you to take some time reading each case file and bringing yourselves up to speed on the facts in the case. If you have any questions or you're not sure about something, talk to me, and we'll figure it out. Oh, and one more thing, whatever you do, don't miss a court date. I don't want to get any complaints from the D.A.'s office."

"Hey, Lieutenant, what's the word 'wetbacks' used for in homicide?" Balardi joked.

James Roberts fixed on him like death daggers. "That'll be all," he said, dismissing his detectives.

Dawson gathered the case files into her arms, stood up, and pushed the chair back with her hip. As she headed towards the conference room door, she pushed by Balardi who was joking with his friends, Corcoran and Farris, and exchanged a momentary look full of anger and rage, worthy of Medusa, and by all rights should have turned the man to stone.

She returned to her office, collapsing at her desk, under a pile of work.

An hour and a half later, Kate Dawson was driving down Van Ness Avenue towards Lafayette Park; her partner sitting in the passenger seat with his elbow hanging out the window. Dawson would have never admitted it, not to Prescott, not to the department shrink, not even to herself, but John Monroe was right. Everyone had the capacity to commit murder, and right at that very moment, she was struggling with her own inner demons, trying not to reach for her weapon and fire a round right into the temple of Matt Balardi as he sat next to her. She hated the man with every fiber of her being. She regarded him as an arrogant, wise-cracking son-of-a-bitch who treated women like playthings and showed nothing but contempt for other ethnic groups. In fact, she could think of nothing the least bit redemptive about his character. She let her mind go for a second and imagined collecting a medal on the steps of City Hall for exterminating the vermin before he could reproduce. Her daydream was broken when she slowed for another car in front of City Hall and watched the normal foot traffic going in and out of the domed building.

They had ridden a few blocks from the Hall of Justice before Balardi finally broke the silence, saying, "This is bullshit, Dawson. You're not going to get within a mile of Lafayette Park. The place is going to be crawling with Feds protecting the President from John Q. Public."

"That's what I'm counting on," she replied, determined.

"Just what makes you think this joker is going to be there? For my money, he's in Alaska already, freezing his nuts off, guarding that igloo," Balardi huffed.

"A hunch," Kate said simply.

"I get hunches, too. And I've got a pretty good hemorrhoid cream that I can recommend for them. Ha-ha-ha-ha-ha."

"Besides," she added, ignoring his comment, "Reinhardt said the agent was assigned to the detail protecting the First Family."

"And you believe that asshole? Well, you're dumber than you look, Dawson."

Dawson thought about something Reinhardt had said. "I suppose if they're going to be telling this big lie about Meghan Kendrick, then some parts of it must be true."

"You're dreaming."

"We'll see."

They drove a few more miles on Van Ness, heading towards Pacific Heights, and just past Geary Boulevard, the traffic slowed to a standstill. This time, Kate broke the silence. "So, what do you think, Balardi? Cut over to Franklin Street, then make a left on Pine?"

"Doesn't really matter to me. I already told you we're not going to get within a mile of Lafayette Park."

"Christ, Balardi, you never give up, do you?"

"No, not when someone's being a jackass."

"Why don't you just shut that fuckin' hole of yours and let me drive!" Dawson snarled, as she made the turn at Franklin.

There was silence for some time, then Balardi spoke up, "This is a fool's errand, Inspector. Even if we do get close to the location where the President is speaking, how do you plan to identify Agent "Jones" from among all the other agents that are there? Let alone, talk to him?"

"Reinhardt's going to point him out for me."

"You're out of your frickin' mind. He's never going to give up one of his guys, especially to you."

Dawson made the left at Pine and stepped on the gas. "I happen to know that the Feds were all over Meghan's apartment last night."

"Big deal. I'd be surprised if they hadn't."

"Less than five minutes after she was reported dead?"

All of a sudden, Matt Balardi sat up in the passenger seat. "Are you shitting me? That would mean those assholes knew about it the whole time, *or* actually had planned to take her out."

"Let's not get ahead of ourselves," Dawson cautioned him.

"I suppose the guy you're humping at Justice told you."

"Yeah, he called me this morning, and told me all about it on my drive into work."

Balardi rubbed his hands together, giddy with anticipation. "I can't wait to see the look on that asshole's face when you confront him. Five will get you ten, he craps right in his pants."

"I'm sure he already knows."

"What? No fuckin' way," he disagreed with her.

"But it doesn't really matter," she said, pulling up to the curb, "he's still going to give me what I want."

They climbed out and studied the street barricade the police had erected to discourage motorists from driving through the

Pacific Heights neighborhood. A block away, the President stood on a make-shift platform that had been constructed on the grounds of Lafayette Park. On the platform sat an array of dignitaries from local and state government. Nearby, a handful of Secret Service agents stood on flanking sides of the wooden structure, watching and waiting, while others wearing black suits and sunglasses were strategically deployed around the rolling green hills of the park. Local police officers struggled to contain the crowd of about five hundred people who stood directly in front of the platform. Red, white, and blue bedecked cheerleaders, who made the event seem more like a political rally than a speech, knelt on one knee in the buffer zone between the President and her constituents. Meanwhile, protesters carrying signs, which read "NO TO U.S. WAR ON IRAN," "GIVE PEACE A CHANCE," and "END THIS CONFLICT," walked to and fro in the background, chanting slogans from a bygone era. They seemed to be aging hippies who had been bused in from Haight-Ashbury to add color to an otherwise colorless event, and they definitely caught the eye of the news reporters on hand.

At that distance, Dawson strained to hear the President's voice, which could be heard coming from a remote loudspeaker system. From what the detective could tell, the President sounded like an excellent speaker who drove hard toward her arguments and crashed down on each of her points. She certainly captured the attention of the crowd as her edgy voice rang with sincerity and angst, ". . . there is no higher priority than protecting the citizens of the United States of America from the tyranny of a rogue nation that has disobeyed international law and now seeks to intimidate the world with nuclear terrorism. By arming themselves with nuclear weapons and targeting cities in the Western hemisphere, they are defying several key resolutions that have been adopted by the United Nations Security Council."

The President paused briefly to drink in the adulation and applause, then launched into the next section of her speech with renewed vitality. "Some have sought to justify this belligerent behavior on the part of the leadership in Iran as a step to protect their own borders from the possibility of preemptive strikes launched against their nuclear arsenal by Israel or the United States. But that is simply a stratagem they are employing to turn public opinion to their side. Never in the history of this great nation has the United States launched a preemptive attack against a foreign government, nor do we have any plans to do so now. While we all agree that sovereign nations have every right to protect themselves and their borders against their enemies, they do not have the right to intimidate others with huge arsenals that threaten mass destruction among their neighbor nations. America is committed to a nuclear-free Iran and will do everything in its power to stop this nuclear proliferation."

As they searched for Harlan Reinhardt in the crowd, a policeman on foot patrol walked around their parked vehicle and came up from behind them. "Ma'am, you can't park here."

"It's okay, officer," Dawson said, turning around and handing her identification to him. "I'm a detective from Homicide."

The policeman checked her ID and handed it back. Politely, he said, "Sorry, Inspector, but I'm still going to ask you to move your car. In a few minutes, the Presidential motorcade will be coming this way, and we have orders to keep the street cleared."

"I understand. I was just hoping that I could have a brief word with the Secret Service agent in charge."

"I'll be happy to point him out to you, Inspector, but I must insist you move your car first."

"Hey, numb nuts, this is official business," Balardi shouted, flashing his badge.

"What did you say to me?" the policeman asked, straightening up and putting a protective hand on his service revolver.

"I called you numb nuts. You want to make something of it?"

Dawson shot her partner a look, then apologized to the patrolman. "Look, Officer, I'm sorry, but we're in somewhat of a hurry. My partner's a bit anxious, and sometimes gets ahead of himself. Would you mind directing us to the staging area for official vehicles?"

"Inspector, we're using the parking lot at the California Pacific Medical Center," he said courteously. "Use the entrance off Buchanan."

"Thank you, Officer."

"That's fuckin' two blocks away," Balardi cried, jumping into the passenger seat.

"Really?" Dawson asked sarcastically, slamming the door after she got back in. She started the engine, pulled away from the curb, squealing her tires, and made a U-turn, heading back to California Street.

"Shit, Dawson, I took you for someone with balls, but you're nothing but a fuckin' pussy. Who gives a fuck what his orders are? We're from Homicide. We've got the juice to do whatever the fuck we want to do."

"Can it, Balardi. I don't want to hear another word."

By the time Dawson had fought her way through traffic and other road closures and had parked at the Medical Center, the political rally was over. She and Matt Balardi hiked up to Lafayette Park and watched as the Presidential motorcade pulled out of the park and made the right onto Gough Street. Kate stood there on the grass as the people began to disperse, shaking her head.

"Shit!" she cursed.

Balardi went through the pockets in his jacket, found a cigarette, and lit it, exhaling luxuriantly. Like the asshole he was, he said, "Maybe next time, Dawson, you'll fuckin' listen to me."

"Yeah, next time."

At half-past twelve, after dropping Balardi off, Dawson stopped by the Medical Examiner's office to steal a look at his official report on Meghan Kendrick, but Brogan and most of his staff were nowhere to be found. The Assistant ME was there, working in the lab, processing a sample.

At thirty-two, Doctor Rosa Romano had worked the second shift at police headquarters for the last three-and-a-half years, and while she had had opportunities to distinguish herself with several high-profile cases, she still labored under the long shadow of her much more illustrious boss. Dawson considered her a friend on the very first night they went drinking together with a few of the other girls, and now counted her as one of her closest friends on the SFPD. Even though they hadn't spent as much time together in the last couple of years, due to the late hours that Romano put into the lab, Kate knew that she could always count on her for help.

"Hey, Kate, what brings you down here? Are you slumming again?" Romano asked, giving her a big hug.

"I'm here to get a look at the coroner's report," she said, returning the hug.

"I don't think it's ready. I know that Doctor Brogan and his team have spent most of the morning working to complete it, but as far as I know, he's not planning to release the report until this afternoon."

Dawson glanced at the watch on her wrist, a slim delicate slip of platinum she had found at the Treasure Island Flea Market for

$95, then looked around the lab to make sure the two women were alone. With her voice lowered, she said, "Well, actually, I've got a favor to ask."

"Sure, anything, Kate, but don't ask me about that damned report. Brogan would have my head if he found out I had leaked his report."

"That's not it at all."

Romano perked up. "Good. So, do you have some more cloak-and-dagger work for me to do?"

"No, not exactly."

"Too bad. The last time, we managed to flush out a professional assassin who had faked his own death in Afghanistan."

"I remember. That broke my case wide open."

Rosa Romano beamed. "What have you got for me this time?"

Dawson held out a plastic lunch bag containing an elegant, shiny-black container with a distinctive silver trim. "Lipstick. It belonged to the victim."

"Meghan Kendrick?"

"Yeah."

"Where did you get this?"

Dawson swallowed hard. "Rosa, you've got to promise me you won't say anything, but I took it from Doctor Brogan's crime scene."

"What? Why would you do that?" she asked, incredulous.

"It's a really long story that I don't have time to tell you now, but suffice it to say, there were others at the crime scene that I think were prepared to do anything, including murder, to possess it."

The Assistant Medical Examiner looked more closely, holding the baggie up to the light and turning the container a complete 360°. "Aren't you being just a bit melodramatic, girlfriend? It's not like you've just discovered the secret to Eternal Youth here."

"No, I'm not," Kate said, flatly.

"Okay, then, what's so important about it?"

"I don't know. I was hoping that you could tell me. But I know that it's important. Damned important."

Romano looked squarely at her friend, holding her gaze for an instant or two, then turned back to the lipstick container. "Well, if you think it's important, then that's good enough for me."

"Thanks, Rosa, I knew I could count on you."

"What should I be looking for? Fingerprints? Hair and fiber? Body fluids? DNA? Trace evidence?"

"I'm not really sure."

"Okey-doke," she said, bobbing her head up and down. "I'll run a full screening and analysis. How soon do you need it?"

"Right away?"

"Right away takes seventy-two hours."

"Is that the best you can do for me?"

Romano hesitated only a split second before responding. "Seventy-two hours, but you don't have seventy-two hours, so I'll do it for you in thirty-six."

"Doctor Romano," Dawson said, jovially, "have you always multiplied your work estimates by a factor of two?"

"Certainly, Kate. How else can I keep my reputation as a miracle worker?"

"Your reputation is secure, Rosa."

The two women shared a hearty laugh together and embraced each other as if they were long-lost sisters. When they came out of their embrace, Romano draped her arms across Dawson's slender shoulders, and gazed into her eyes. "You know, Kate, I really miss the old days when we used to go out to the local clubs, get drunk, and dance the night away."

Dawson returned her gaze. "I know what you mean. I miss them, too. When did life get to be so serious?"

Rosa Romano was closer now. She put her soft hand to Kate's cheek and stroked, as she might a cat. "I don't know, girlfriend, but when you figure it out, let me know," she said, her voice satiny smooth.

"Do you remember the time that you, me, Joan, and Gillian stumbled into that one club in the Mission District? We saw all those women dancing together? Cheek to cheek."

"The Lexington Club?"

"That was it," Kate said, recalling the name. "I was so embarrassed, but you and the others just took it in stride. We ended up having such a good time pretending to be lipstick mafia, and making fun of the whole scene."

"That was a fun night." She was close now. Kate could feel her breath on her face, smell it. It was sweet, like her perfume.

"I tried to find it recently because I thought John would get a kick out of it. I hadn't planned on telling him that it was a club that catered to lesbians. I just wanted to see his reaction. He can be so straight-laced at times."

Rosa broke free of Dawson. "So, you're still seeing that hunky lumberjack?"

"John and I have been dating for over a year now," Dawson reported. "Only he's not a lumberjack. That was the undercover identity he used to infiltrate the religious cult I brought down. He works for the Department of Justice in D.C., but we manage to get together every month for a long weekend. We've also shared holidays and vacations. It's not what I would call an ideal relationship because of the distance, but it beats being alone."

"The minute I saw him, I knew he was a keeper. I'm so glad that it's worked out for you."

"What about you, Rosa?"

"Well . . . They come and they go . . . Mostly go. You know it's really hard for women our age in a city like San Francisco where most of the men are either gay or married, or both."

"You'll find someone."

"I hope so," she said, wistfully, holding back the tears.

After a moment of awkward silence, Dawson said, "You know that project of mine? Can you also run it through CODIS for me?"

"Sure, Kate, no problem."

"Thanks, I really appreciate it."

"Any time."

"Listen, I'll see you later," Kate said, stumbling out of the ME's office. She was feeling a bit shaken, almost embarrassed, and didn't quite yet know how to classify all the conflicting emotions she was experiencing. In time, she would come to understand, feel even flattered by the gesture, but then pay it no additional mind. Right then, though, all she wanted to do was run.

CHAPTER THREE

Matt Balardi led the way downstairs to the morgue, with Dawson following close behind. But instead of stopping by the Medical Examiner's office, they went directly to the end of the basement corridor, and walked through a double set of doors into the county morgue. The strong odor of formaldehyde hung in the air like an eighth-grade biology class. Every time she walked into the morgue, Kate half expected to find a group of little boys hunched over tables dissecting frogs, but found Doctor Brogan hunched over a pile of papers, eating a roast beef sandwich on rye bread. His diener, a young African-American in his twenties, was sound asleep leaning on a corner table, his head propped up on one arm. Both were wearing white lab coats stained with blood and other fluids.

Brogan didn't look up, but acknowledged them with a hardy, "Good afternoon" as he chomped down on his lunch.

"Hey, Doc, how's it hanging?" Balardi asked.

"What's up, Doc?" Dawson added, with humor.

"I've got the report on Meghan Kendrick right here," he said, glancing over at the stainless-steel table where the victim's body lay. He took another bite of his sandwich, stood up, and carried it over to the table with him. "Sorry, detectives, I never had the chance to finish my lunch today."

"Enjoy." Balardi blanched and swallowed bile.

Dawson forced her own lump down hard. She couldn't imagine eating anything, let alone a roast beef sandwich, while there was a dead body less ten feet away, but then she wasn't a coroner either. She figured the Medical Examiner must have developed a strong stomach over the years.

"Oh, and you can just ignore William," Brogan added, pointing at his assistant. "He's been up all night working with me and just couldn't keep his eyes open any longer. I told him to take a forty-minute cat nap."

As she followed Brogan to the table, Dawson took a glimpse the diener, then looked down at poor Meghan Kendrick. She could see the dissection had already been done and the body was ready to be prepped for its short journey to the funeral home. The familiar Y-shaped incision, which started at the top of each shoulder and ran down the front of the woman's chest to her sternum, was there, with the chest flaps pulled back for easy access to the chest cavity. Meghan's internal organs had been removed and placed neatly in two rows on stainless steel trays. Divided into four groups on the table, they appeared to have been measured and weighed prior to any samples being cut for pathology. The body block, which had been used to elevate the chest cavity for dissection, now elevated the head. Incisions behind the ears and over the crown of the head were clearly visible where Brogan and his team had removed the brain and examined the skull. The brain was preserved in a large, glass container of formalin next to the other organs. There was very little left to remind anyone of the glamourous woman who dazzled millions of viewers on Fox News.

"So? What've you found?" Balardi asked, impatiently.

Dawson got right to the point. "Was she strangled, Doc? I need to know if this was a homicide, or something else."

The Chief Medical Examiner stared at them for a long moment. "Yes, Meghan Kendrick was strangled to death, Inspector, but that's really only half of the story."

"What are you talking about?" Dawson prodded.

"The redness, swelling, and bruising on her neck is consistent with that of a person who has been strangled," he reported, pointing to the victim's throat. "However, I also noticed that Meghan had applied a heavy amount of makeup to her neck to cover some recent contusions she had suffered. The bruises looked like they were from different periods of time. So, I ordered up a spectroscopic analysis of the hemoglobin breakdown at each of the bruise sites and discovered that some were up to three weeks old. Others even older. That also explains why I found evidence of repeated, chronic cervical trauma to the spine."

Dawson said, "Last night, you thought Meghan might be a 'gasper.' I guess your autopsy now pretty much validates that conclusion."

"Yes, that's right, but I don't think that's what killed her."

"You know, Doc, sometimes I can't tell shit from shinola unless I get my nose right up in it," Balardi said. "All this mumbo-jumbo is just giving me a headache. Why don't you lay it out straight for people like me?"

"Erotic asphyxiation involves temporarily cutting off a person's oxygen supply to heighten sexual sensations during climax. They ask their sexual partners to strangle or choke them or put a bag over their head to increase their sexual excitement. The lightheadedness, giddiness, and euphoria it creates have been likened to a cocaine high, and supposedly heighten orgasmic sensations as well. For some, greater sexual satisfaction results from the feelings of helplessness, lack of control, self-endangerment, or sense of control. Others are into the heightened sense of fantasy or altered states of consciousness that such sex promises," Brogan explained in simple laymen's terms for the detective. "The danger of such arousal, no matter how careful the two people are, is two-fold. You risk death or significant injury in one, cutting off blood to the brain, and two, cutting off oxygen for a period of time. Add this to other dangers, including loss of consciousness, and you've got a recipe for disaster."

"But you just said this isn't what killed her," Dawson repeated.

The Medical Examiner didn't answer immediately, but rather stared hard at the two detectives. They could almost see him thinking, running through the possible scenarios, as he tried to put together the right words and phrases to say. He seemed like an overly cautious man who preferred to have everything scripted for him, to have the correct response written down so that he would not later be accused of making a mistake. He had never liked talking "off the cuff," and preferred to stick to the facts that he could prove.

"You gonna tell us or do I have to go out and hire us a psychic?" demanded Balardi.

Brogan hesitated a moment longer, then finally gave in. "She was strangled all right, but I think the killer took advantage of Meghan Kendrick's fetish to make her murder look more like an accident."

The answer did not seem to surprise Dawson. "Then you must have a pretty good idea who's responsible for her death."

"Yes and no."

"C'mon, Doc," Balardi said, exactly what Kate was thinking. "Enough with all the games, just tell us what you know."

Doctor Brogan had a pained look on his face. "When I

examined the victim's vagina for evidence of sexual intercourse, I found a thick, whitish fluid which I initially thought was seminal fluid from her male partner. But upon closer examination, I discovered it was female ejaculate, fluid expelled by the paraurethral ducts through her urethra either during or just before an orgasm."

"You mean to say she was a 'squirter,' Doc?" Balardi asked crudely, with a renewed interest in his celebrity crush.

"That's quite impossible to say, detective," the Medical Examiner answered honestly, factually. "The research community has yet to make a distinction between female ejaculation and what is colloquially known as 'squirting' or 'gushing.' These terms are used by the public interchangeably, and therein lies part of the problem. However, recent research suggests that female ejaculation is the release of thick, whitish fluid from the structures called Skene's, or paraurethral glands, that are sometimes referred to as the female prostate, while the 'squirting' or 'gushing' shown frequently in pornography is a different phenomenon altogether."

Matt Balardi tilted his head to the ceiling in frustration. "Dammit! Why can't you just answer a simple question without making it so complicated?"

"I thought that's what I just did." The good doctor cut his eyes at Balardi.

Dawson asked, "Is there any evidence that she was sexually assaulted, Doc?"

"Yes and no, again." He held up a hand like a cop stopping traffic. "Now before you accuse me of being evasive, let me try to explain."

"Okay, I'm all ears."

"What did I just say?" Balardi added, with a smirk.

"Last night, when I first looked at Meghan Kendrick, I said

her external genitals were pretty raw," the Medical Examiner said slowly, taking his time to select each word carefully before he spoke. "During my examination today, I found abrasions and tearing on her external vaginal labia and vagina that are consistent in a woman who has had forced sexual intercourse. Unfortunately, I've seen it in dozens of rape victims. Without sufficient lubrication, rough intercourse wreaks havoc on the unprepared labia and—"

"So then, she *was* raped?" Dawson deduced.

"There's no question about it. She had forced sex with someone before she died."

"I hear the word 'but' in your voice, even though you haven't said it. There's still something you're not telling us," she surmised.

"Meghan Kendrick had sex with two men last night," Doctor Brogan said, finally. He paused to adjust the small, horn-rimmed glasses on the end of his nose, before referring to his report. "There's traces of lubricant in the vaginal tract and under her fingernails. When I ran a sample through the lab, I found it was nonoxynol-9, which is commonly used in spermicidally-lubricated condoms. Nonoxynol-9 is basically a type of detergent. It disrupts the plasma membranes of sperm and other cells and has been shown in the laboratory to be quite effective at killing many STD pathogens, including HIV, herpes, Chlamydia, and gonorrhea. It is also an excellent lubricant, but it also causes two types of damage to the vaginal epithelium. It causes inflammation of the vagina and cervix, and kills off layers of cells so that the skin becomes raw, irritated, and overly sensitive."

"Okay, so the perpetrator wore a condom," Dawson said. "I don't see how your evidence suggests the presence of two men?"

"Lubricants specially-lubricated condoms, are used to improve the comfort of sexual intercourse, for women, and to eliminate the risk of vaginal tearing and other abrasions to the vagina that might occur during sex," the Medical Examiner added. "I should not have found a single abrasion, let alone tearing, that is if Meghan and her partner had used a lubricated condom. The evidence suggests they did, but the evidence also shows Meghan suffered severe abrasions from forced sex. Both can't be right, unless there were two men who had sex with her last night."

The proverbial light bulb went on over Dawson's head. "I think I'm beginning to understand."

"Well, you damn well better explain it to me. I don't understand a fuckin' thing the doctor is saying," Balardi complained.

"There is one nagging question that I have to ask," she said, ignoring her partner. "Wouldn't there have been sufficient lubricant leftover from the victim's first sexual encounter to protect her vagina during a second?"

"No," Brogan said abruptly. "For nonoxynol-9 to be effective as a spermicide, it disrupts cellular membranes by penetrating the outer layer of sperm and skin cells. Most of it would have been dissolved and absorbed right into the cells, and the rest would have evaporated in a relatively short period of time. Besides, we're not talking about much more than a thin coating of lubricant over the condom."

"Of course, that makes sense," Dawson agreed.

"Also, let's not forget that, other than the bruises around her neck, there were no signs of a physical struggle at all," he said, taking another bite of his sandwich. The Medical Examiner swallowed it down with a beaker of liquid that was sitting next to the other samples from the autopsy. "I'm thinking that Meghan Kendrick was still out cold, or just stirring, as the result of the hypoxia of near-strangulation when the second man entered the scene. He saw her lying there, helpless, with obvious bruising and swelling around the throat, then made his move."

"But why would he rape her, Doc?" Dawson persisted, like a fighter trying to wear down her opponent. "And then, kill her?"

The phone rang, and as Doctor Brogan reached across the stainless-steel table to pick up the receiver, he said, "There are some questions that medical science simply can't answer." He held the receiver up to his ear and bobbed his head a couple of times before saying "Okay, send them down." After he had hung up the phone, he added, "Well, you're not going to believe this, but your Secret Service pal and a couple of his buddies are on their way down."

"Shit," Balardi cursed.

Dawson crossed her arms. "I wish I could say I was surprised."

"How did he know when we were planning to meet and go over the official report?" the Medical Examiner asked.

"He didn't, unless it was something he overheard last night," she replied.

"Don't be so fuckin' naïve, Dawson," Balardi said. "The Feds have been watching people for years. I wouldn't be surprised if they had each of our offices rigged with surveillance equipment right now."

Dawson did her best to hide the smirk on her face. "That sounds a little paranoid, Matt."

"Just because you're paranoid doesn't mean they ain't still out to get you," her partner said.

A moment later, Harlan Reinhardt entered the room, flanked by two of his Secret Service agents wearing black suits. He surveyed the morgue and the people in it with a cool, discerning eye. He was wearing a Visitor's Identification Badge, along with his two agents. He looked out of place, but if he felt it, Reinhardt didn't show it. Dawson could see that masking his emotions was second nature to the Secret Service chief, in much the same way that others would don a pair of sunglasses in the bright sunlight, making him all the more sinister.

Brogan put his sandwich down on the autopsy table as Reinhardt came in the door and thrust out his latex-gloved hand.

"I'm Doctor Brogan, the Chief Medical Examiner," he said, shaking hands with the newcomer, who slightly hesitated, seeing the glove. "I've been discussing my official report with these two detectives from Homicide—I believe you've already met them—but if you'd like me to stop and start over again, I'd be willing to do so."

"Just continue, Doctor," Reinhardt insisted. He took a handkerchief out of his pocket, sneezed, and wiped his nose with it. He noted the windows were sealed shut and it was very cold in the room.

Brogan continued, "In addition to the other physical evidence, I found several strands of pubic hair mingled with Meghan's own when I did a basic comb-through. They were definitely male, with a moderate curl and triangular cross section. A couple of gray hair fibers, and at least one with a brown, almost reddish tint. Since the victim was a true blonde, they stood out like a sore thumb."

"Did CODIS return a match?" Dawson asked, interested, leaning forward on the stainless-steel table.

"The results were inconclusive," Brogan reported, ignoring Reinhardt, his gaze fixed on Kate Dawson with something like admiration. She was asking all the right questions. "As you know, CODIS uses two indexes to generate investigative leads in crimes that contain biological evidence. The forensic index contains DNA profiles from biological evidence left at crime scenes, and the offender index contains DNA profiles of individuals who have been convicted of a violent crime."

Dawson had his attention. "But if they were never convicted

of a violent crime, then there would be no DNA profile in the offender index for them."

"Unfortunately, that's true." The doctor held up his index finger. "Inconclusive results indicate that DNA testing could neither include nor exclude an individual as the source of biological evidence."

"I still say she OD'd on coke," said Balardi to no one in particular.

Harlan Reinhardt coughed into his handkerchief, complaining, "This recycled air is not very good for my asthma. The chill always gives me a cold."

She looked at the Secret Service chief for a fleeting moment, engaging his eyes, then quickly looked away. "What about Matt's theory? Are there any indications that Meghan Kendrick died of a drug overdose?"

"We did find trace elements of a white, powdery substance on the restroom counter and inside Meghan's nostrils. But when I ran a complete toxicology screen on the victim, I found that her body chemistry was normal, other than the low oxygen content in her blood, which is consistent with her penchant for sexual asphyxia. She was a perfectly healthy woman."

"Whoever killed Meghan Kendrick planted evidence to make us think that she had suffered a drug overdose." Dawson looked straight at Reinhardt.

"That's about right. I concur," the doctor agreed.

"I just can't imagine the brass balls that would take," she commented.

Reinhardt listened closely, but didn't say anything. He kept his eyes focused on Dawson, watching her every move.

"So, the way I see it, we're looking for two men," Dawson said, putting it all together, poised, cool and in complete command of herself. She walked over to the white board where

Brogan and his team had earlier divided up assignments and scribbled down a few notes with the black marker. "The first man is older, maybe in his late fifties or early sixties, with gray hair. He is distinguished-looking, noteworthy, someone with great power and influence who would appeal to a jaded news reporter. The other man is younger, maybe in his thirties, with brown-to-reddish-brown hair. He's someone you wouldn't notice in a crowd. He's more of a follower, somewhat shy and reserved, with perhaps an inflated sense of his own importance."

"What makes you so certain?" Brogan asked. "Why couldn't it be just the other way around?"

She was unruffled by the question. "No, I don't think someone like Meghan Kendrick is going to be putting her career on the line for a 'nobody.' She's going to be attracted to a very powerful man. Perhaps a Senator? A Congressman? A political figure who is very well connected . . ."

"What about the First Man?" Balardi asked. "He'd be my first suspect. Hey, get it? First Man? First suspect?"

"Bill Harrison? He certainly fits the profile. He's tall, handsome, in his sixties with a beautiful head of gray hair. He's married to one of the most powerful women in the world and I seem to recall rumors of him dallying with other women when he was a Junior Congressman from the State of Arkansas."

"This is all very interesting, Inspector Dawson. But it is pure speculation, not fact," Reinhardt said, as he leaned forward, his cold, deadly eyes boring into her. "What would you say if I gave you the name of the second man? Would it help to move your investigation forward?"

She stood erect. "You know it would."

"Doctor Brogan, have you established the time of death?" Reinhardt asked, still staring at her.

The Medical Examiner reviewed his report. "Yes, I place the time of death between 9:05 P.M. and 9:15 P.M."

"That is consistent with our findings," he replied flatly.

Dawson's eyes never left his face. "I need a name, Reinhardt."

Their eyes were locked now, as if they were two gamblers sitting across a poker table trying to read each other's tell. Dawson stared at him, fighting the urge to blink, while he stared back at her expressionlessly. There was a moment, a long moment of silence, then he blinked.

"Carlos Ortega," he said.

"Carlos Ortega," she repeated. "And just who is he?"

"Mr. Ortega is a steward," Reinhardt said.

"Steward? What does a steward on Air Force One do?"

"Well, unlike flight attendants on a commercial flight who have the complete run of the plane's service to passengers," Reinhardt explained, "a steward has one job and one job only. He works in the galley, keeping the equipment clean, sanitary, and in good repair. During a single shift, the steward may be responsible for cleaning dishes, utensils, and the cooking equipment. Counters and work areas need attention as food preparation continues through the shift. The steward rarely leaves the galley, unless it is to make a delivery to the President or one of our onboard guests."

"What makes you think he was responsible for Meghan's death?" Dawson asked the question that they all wanted answered.

"No one from my staff can account for his whereabouts during the twenty-minute period when the woman was murdered. And just prior to when the Secret Service found Miss Kendrick's body, he was seen coming out of the Press cabin."

She was blasé, brushing off the information. "If that's all you got, Reinhardt, you've got nothing."

"Except this," said the Secret Service chief, snapping his fingers.

One of his agents came forward and handed Dawson a Ziploc bag containing a small metal object. She looked more closely, holding the baggie up to the light and determined it was a lapel pin with the Presidential seal. Kate handed it off to the Medical Examiner for closer examination.

"A lapel pin?" she asked, unimpressed.

"This lapel pin was found in the restroom. It has Meghan Kendrick's fingerprints on it, and it belongs to Carlos Ortega."

"There must be hundreds of these," Dawson commented. "What makes you think this lapel pin belongs to Mr. Ortega?"

Reinhardt sniffled, then explained, "In the beginning, there *were* hundreds of them. That was the problem. We'd issue them to personnel who worked for the President, then they'd turn around and sell them as a collectable on eBay and report the item lost. So, that's when we started numbering each one. This one bears the number forty-two, and, according to our records, it belongs to Carlos Ortega."

Dawson got the feeling that, right then, Harlan Reinhardt was telling the absolute truth. She wasn't sure if the lapel pin had been found in the rear restroom or if it even really had Meghan Kendrick's fingerprints on it, but she knew the collector's market and how valuable Presidential collectables were on eBay. Her fellow detective William Clark had amassed a small fortune in beer cans, Civil War medals, comic books, sports collectibles, toy trains and everything in between. In fact, he probably had enough junk to fill several warehouses. His estimated worth was well over $500,000. She made a mental note to confer with Clark over the validity of Reinhardt's statements, but she had the feeling that he was telling the truth.

Dawson looked squarely at Harlan Reinhardt, holding his gaze. "Why didn't you tell me any of this last night?"

"My investigation was still ongoing," he replied, blank-faced.

"All right, if Carlos Ortega is our chief suspect, where is he now?" Kate placed her hands on her hips. Everyone in the room could hear the determination in her voice. She wanted to get to the bottom of things.

"I've issued orders to my men to pick him up."

"Well, if the Secret Service doesn't mind, I'm still going to issue an APB for the suspect's arrest."

"That is your prerogative, Inspector."

"I could use some inter-agency help from you with a photo and some background information," she requested, politely.

"His complete dossier should already be in your e-mail's inbox," the Secret Service chief said as he turned to leave the morgue. His men in black suits were right behind him.

Dawson stopped him at the double doors. "I need the other man's name."

Reinhardt coughed again into his handkerchief. "It's getting chilly here and that's very bad for my asthma."

"You know something that you're not telling me," she said.

They pushed past her and continued down the corridor.

"Reinhardt!" Dawson shouted, as she trailed after him.

At that moment, one of the elevators from the bank of elevators chimed and its door whisked open. Reinhardt shuffled toward it, blowing his nose into his handkerchief. "You know all that you need to know," he said over his shoulder, stepping into the elevator right as the door was closing.

Dawson pounded her fist in anger on the elevator door. For only the second time in two days, she had lost her temper.

In the corridor, just beyond the bank of elevators, a figure stirred. He had been standing in the shadows, listening to the exchange between Dawson and Reinhardt with his ear to the wall. His face was completely obscured by shadows. In his right hand, he held a long, thin-bladed knife, but he simply stood there, watching and waiting and listening.

Swamped with the work her partner had left behind, Kate Dawson was the last one to reach the bar and order a couple of drinks. McGinty's Public House was the only bar on Bryant Street, and with its close proximity to the Hall of Justice and police headquarters, it was much favored by Dawson and other members of the San Francisco Police Department. Modeled after the traditional Irish pubs in Ireland, Scotland, and Wales, McGinty's sold hard drinks to the law-and-order crowd. The pub also specialized in hamburger sliders, deep-fried chicken wings, and greasy French fries. Johnnie O'Flynn, the third generation Irish-American owner, made no apologies for the pub's quaint, old-fashioned atmosphere. He wasn't about to change a thing to attract yuppie businessmen or wealthy tourists. He was content to pour drinks at the bar the same way his father and grandfather before him poured them. Straight up shots of bourbon and full-bodied beers filled the counter for the thirsty patrons.

Dawson would have been the first to admit that she was a two-fisted drinker as she picked up her shot of Wild Turkey and the beer chaser with both hands from the counter, and headed to the back of the pub. She slugged back half of the scotch before taking a deep gulp of beer. William Clark and Mikhail Jawara were seated at a back table, nursing their drinks and waiting for Kate. She hadn't told them that she'd be stopping by, but they knew she would show up eventually—everyone did—just like a fledgling bird returning to the nest.

Jawara started in on her, even before Kate had a chance to sit down. "Fuck, Dawson, what the hell have you gotten us involved in now? Those Secret Service guys are a really scary bunch."

"It took us the better part of three hours to get the plane's manifest and I'm not even certain if we got it all," Clark reported, handing her a sheet of paper.

Dawson scanned it. There were about sixty-one names on the list, including Carlos Ortega. The only name that was noticeably absent was Harland Reinhardt. She handed the list back to Clark, saying, "So, you've got a real mixed bag of political and entertainment types, the First Family, Secret Service agents, press, and crew."

"Does the Lieutenant really expect us to do a complete work-up of all the people on this list?" Jawara asked, knowing what the answer would be.

"I told you he did," Clark answered.

Jawara gave him a sullen look. "I just wanted to hear it from Kate."

"I punch the same clock that you do." She sipped her Scotch. "For what it's worth, that is what I heard him say."

Matt Balardi stumbled up to their table with a beer in his hand, slightly glassy-eyed from the spirited drinking he'd been doing, swaying as he stood over them. "San Francisco's finest," Balardi said, raising his glass to salute them and slugging down a deep gulp. "You do us proud."

"We're discussing the case, Matt," Clark said, politely.

Balardi tried to focus on each man's face, but settled on Dawson. "I know that. I had absolutely no doubt 'bout it. Please continue."

Dawson shot him an irritated look. "Balardi, you're drunk. You should go home and sleep it off."

"Okay, I don't mind if I do" he said, slapping his drink down on the table and pulling up a chair. "I don't usually drink with niggers, but since we're all working on the same murder case, I'll make an exception."

"That's awfully white of you, Balardi," Jawara rebuked him.

"Frankly, it never made any sense to me why the city started hiring niggers to be policemen," the detective continued to babble away, digging himself an even deeper grave. "I mean . . . you're just askin' for trouble puttin' a gun in the hands of a black man when we all know . . . most of them are heroin addicts or sexual deviants. But I s'pose there are bound to be 'ceptions to every rule."

"Can I shoot him?" Jawara asked the others, very calmly.

"I ask myself that every day," Dawson said, in a whisper.

"He's not worth it," Clark said.

Balardi put his two-cent's worth in, "Frank Miller. Now there was an 'ception to the rule. Finest cop I ever knew, even if he was a . . . nigger."

With that, Matt Balardi struggled to his feet, both hands pressed against the table to steady himself. But when he let go of the table, he started to sway back and forth, and collapsed to the floor. The three of them sat there for a moment, stunned. Then Dawson bent over and placed her right hand at the junction of Balardi's neck and shoulder to keep his head upright, but he sagged, like a Raggedy Andy doll. In a final attempt to rouse him, Kate gently slapped him on both cheeks, but he was out cold.

"Well, what do you think we should do?" Clark asked.

"Leave him. Let him sleep it off," Jawara said, with a smirk. "No, wait, I've got a better idea. Let's find an open dumpster!"

Dawson fixed Jawara with a glance. "We can't just leave him here."

"Do you know if he has any friends? Any family?"

"Yeah, he lives with his sister in Noe Valley." She pulled her cell out. "I'll look up the address on my iPhone."

Almost immediately, Clark and Jawara were at each side of the unconscious man. They grabbed him under both arms, hoisted him up, and took him out to the curb.

Ten minutes later, they had packed Balardi off in a cab home, and settled down at the table with a fresh round of drinks. Dawson took a sip of the bourbon before slugging back half of the beer in one gulp. "Ahhhhhhhhhhh," she exhaled in satisfaction, licking her lips. It tasted mighty good to her. Mighty good.

"Now, tell me again, Kate," Clark asked, nursing his ginger ale, "what Brogan said about our victim's sexual proclivities."

"Meghan Kendrick had a fetish for erotic asphyxiation. She was sexually aroused by asphyxiation or the sudden loss of oxygen to the brain through strangulation or suffocation."

Jawara protested, "Not my girl. She wasn't into that. She was too classy to be involved with something like that."

"Yeah, I'm afraid so, Mikhail."

"It's just hard for me to see how that would be a turn-on to her."

"Not at all," Clark objected. "The throat has long been a fascinating and sensitive erogenous zone."

"I've only got one erogenous zone. It's right here—" Jawara insisted, pointing to his crouch.

"That's a frightening thought," Kate mumbled, drinking down the rest of her beer.

Jawara said, "I still don't understand how it works."

"What's there to understand?" William Clark asked, with a painful look on his face. "When the brain gets robbed of oxygen, it starts to hallucinate, creating a lucid, dream-like state that heightens sensations of pleasure. Combined with an orgasm, the rush is like a drug-addled high."

"Doesn't sound *too* bad," Jawara said, taking a swig.

"The problem is that, if you go too far, you end up on a slab in the morgue, like our victim Meghan Kendrick," Dawson added.

"Hey, isn't that what happened to the actor David Carradine?"

"Yes, I'm afraid so," Clark said, recalling a newspaper article that he had read back in 2009. "Bangkok police found the seventy-two-year-old actor's naked body in a hotel closet, with one rope tied around his neck, another around his genitals. There was evidence of a recent orgasm. Two autopsies were conducted concluding that his death was not suicide, and the Thai forensic pathologist who examined the body stated that his death was likely due to autoerotic asphyxiation."

"What a tragic way to go for *Kung Fu's* Kane," she bemoaned.

Jawara joked, "And I always thought Uma Thurman killed him with Pai Mei's Five Point Palm Exploding Heart Technique."

"That was a movie, you jackass," Clark retorted.

"I know. I was just bustin' your chops, partner," the African-American said, pearly whites shining ear to ear. "Still, could you imagine standin' up in front of a judge, tryin' to justify your actions in a strangulation case? 'She asked me to choke her during sex, Your Honor, honest.'"

"That's not very funny." Clark swirled his ginger ale.

Dawson swallowed down the last of her strong, dark-brown beer and stood up, pushing her chair away from the table. "I need another round. Can I get anything for you guys while I'm up?"

"Nope," Jawara replied.

"No, thanks," Clark added.

She was just about to head to the bar when Johnnie O'Flynn, the bartender, raced up to the table all excited, "Inspector, there's breaking news on the TV. I thought you might want to know."

"Thanks, Johnnie. Be a pal and turn up the volume, would ya?"

"Sure thing, Kate."

Swiftly, Dawson followed him back to the bar and stared up

at the flat-screen that sat above the counter as the bartender adjusted the volume with the remote control. She was soon joined by Clark and Jawara and several other cops who happened to be standing close by.

The female news reporter said, "Police Officials are reporting tonight that they have identified a suspect in the tragic murder of Meghan Kendrick and are seeking him for questioning. His name is Carlos Ortega, a Latino male in his thirties who worked as a steward aboard Air Force One. He is considered armed and dangerous. If anyone has knowledge of the suspect's whereabouts, they should contact the San Francisco Police Department immediately. Repeating our top story at this hour, Police Officials have identified a suspect . . ."

"'Armed and dangerous,' my ass!" Dawson cursed out loud. "I was afraid this was gonna happen. Now every nutcase and gun-toting asshole in the Bay area is going to be out there tearing up restaurants, taquerias, bakeries, and produce markets along 24th Street looking for this guy. Goddamn media."

"Well, the shit just hit the fan," Jawara almost bellowed to his partner.

"Yeah, you're right," Clark said. "Be prepared to put in a long day tomorrow."

"Yep." Suddenly Kate looked tired, drained, older than her forty-one years. "I'm going home, boys. I need to get some sack time before the real circus begins."

"Good night, Kate," they said in unison.

"Good night. I'll see you in the morning."

At 1:17 A.M., Kate Dawson was struggling to keep warm, her head and body buried beneath several layers of blankets, shivering. She knew she had a big day in front of her, but she just couldn't get to sleep. She wished John was lying next to her for warmth, even if it meant she had to listen to him snore, but he was three thousand miles away. She was beginning to hate the cold winters they had had in San Francisco and tried to imagine a tropical beach in the Caribbean where it was warm. As she drifted in and out of consciousness, thinking about John and her day ahead, the shrill notes of Eric Clapton's "Layla," her ring tone on her iPhone, jolted her upright. She lunged for the cell on the night stand and pulled it with her under the covers.

"This is Dawson," she answered, barely audible. "Okay, okay, I'll get there as soon as I can."

She turned off the iPhone, shivering uncontrollably under her blankets for another five minutes before she got up. Running to the closet, she decided on a heavy, cable-knit sweater for warmth, climbed into her favorite pair of skinny jeans, and pulled her long hair back with a scrunchie.

"And I was just getting to sleep. Shit!" She grabbed her badge, gun, and wallet, locked her door and headed downstairs.

On her way to the Hall of Justice, she managed to draw on a pair of lips over her pale skin with lipstick. She parked on the street and crossed at the crosswalk to the brick and mortar building, locking her car on the fly, and rode the elevator down to Lock-Up. Her neighbor, Lenny Provolone, had been arrested for breaking the protective order against him and had used his "one call" to ask her for help. She made a mental note to block his number on her phone, but forgot about it almost as quickly as she thought of it.

When Dawson and the duty officer reached his cell, she didn't seem surprised to find Lenny behind bars. In fact, for a split second, the look on her face betrayed a touch of pleasure, as if she was thrilled that authorities had finally apprehended the notorious criminal mastermind. But while she stood there, staring at him like a caged animal at the zoo, her heart softened. She could tell from the red pupils of his eyes and his tear-stained cheeks that he was genuinely sorry for what he had done. She had warned him what would happen, but obviously, he hadn't listened to a word she said. She wondered why she even bothered to care.

The duty officer read her the short version. "Inspector Dawson, Mr. Provolone is being remanded into your custody as an officer of this court until such time that he is required to appear before a judge. Therefore, you will be held legally responsible for his actions. If he fails to appear in court or again violates the protective order, the court will issue a summons for you to appear and explain his actions. Do you understand these responsibilities as I have explained them to you?"

She stared at the policeman for a long moment, then said, "I'll personally kick his ass if he gets out of line again."

With a curt nod of his head, the duty officer unlocked the cell door and motioned for Lenny to come out.

"Thanks, Kate. I really appreciate your help," Lenny said, scrambling into the hall. The bars clanged behind him.

"Save it, buster," Dawson said, heading back to her car. "You've got a lot of explaining to do, and if I sense you're hiding anything from me, you'll be back here lickety-split."

They had driven a few blocks before Lenny finally broke the silence. He leaned forward in the passenger seat of her BMW and addressed her apologetically, meekly, "I'm really sorry, Kate . . . I honestly didn't know who else to call."

"Being sorry just doesn't cut it," she said, her eyes focused on the road.

"I just thought if I could talk with her—you know, reason things out—this would all be over," Lenny tried to explain.

"No, the problem is you just didn't *think*," Dawson scolded him like a child. "I read the provisions of the protective order to you. It clearly states that you are to stay away from Rebecca, her home and her workplace, and that you are not to contact her in any way. No flowers or gifts, no telephone calls, no text messages, no emails, faxes, or mail. No contact. Period."

Provolone looked down at his feet. "What do you want me to do?"

"I want you to start acting like a responsible adult and not some love-sick teenager, or you're going to end up back in the slammer."

"I'm such a pathetic loser," he muttered under his breath.

"No, you're not, and I don't want to hear talk like that anymore," she chastised. "You can feel sorry for yourself on your own time, but not when I'm trying to have a serious conversation with you."

"Okay."

Dawson got right to the point. "Lenny, you're one of the smartest people I've ever met. Honestly, I'd say you're a genius. That satellite surveillance system you built is truly spectacular. Ground-breaking. But when it comes right down to people and relationships, you don't know a damned thing. You're like a child in a great big candy store who doesn't know when to stop eating candy."

"Thanks a lot."

"It's true, and deep down inside, you know it's true," she said, striking a raw nerve. "The real reason why you don't like women your own age, and prefer to hit on young women like Rebecca, is that they wouldn't deal with your emotional immaturity for one second."

Lenny had a pained look on his face. "Now, you're just being cruel."

"No, I'm being honest with you, and don't you think it's time you started being honest with yourself?"

"I haven't got a clue as to what you're talking about," he mumbled, folding his arms across his chest. "I told you once before that I wasn't attracted to women my own age, and that should have been enough."

"Yeah, yeah, I know. Something about 'saggy tits and wrinkled skin,'" Dawson said, nearly quoting him verbatim.

"I can't help it if I prefer younger women, and I won't try to justify my choices to you or anybody else. Besides there are plenty of men out there who only date women younger than themselves."

Dawson slowed to a stop for the next red light and looked at her passenger in the adjacent seat. "Well, right now, my friend, there's a young woman out there who doesn't want to talk to you, who doesn't want to see you, and who feels like she needs protection from you."

"Nonsense," Lenny said, indignantly. "I wouldn't harm a single strand of hair on her head. I love her and she loves me."

"Apparently, she doesn't think so," Dawson persisted, pulling away as the light turned green. "Take it from me, most women don't stand up before a judge in court and swear out a protective order unless they're really worried about their safety."

"You know me, Kate. I couldn't harm a fly."

Dawson cocked her head to the side. "That's exactly what Ed Gein said during his arraignment in Plainfield, Wisconsin, after he was charged with murdering two women in cold blood."

"Kate, I never threatened her!"

"Lenny, think about it. You must have done something, or said something, that made Rebecca think she was in danger."

Provolone's shoulders slumped as fatigue and despair washed over him. "This is all just a big misunderstanding."

"Well, it may be," Kate was willing to give him the benefit of the doubt, "but it's not up to you to decide that. Right now, you must stay away from her. Forget that she even exists. And in time, when, if, she's ready to talk to you, she'll call and let you know."

"If only I could talk to her, reason with her . . ."

"That's her decision," Dawson emphasized.

"Why is it up to her? Why can't I just talk to her?"

"She's afraid of you! Don't you get it?!" she yelled at him. "And the court order protects *her* from *you*."

"But I'm not a threat to her."

"I can see we're not getting anywhere with this discussion," she said, taking a deep breath and letting it out between clenched teeth. "The bottom line is that until she is ready, if ever, to talk to you, you must stay away from her, or you're going to be back in that jail cell."

"But that's not fair!" he cried like a baby throwing a temper tantrum.

"Shit, Lenny, who ever said life was going to be fair?"

Lenny went silent, brooding.

They rode for a few more blocks before Dawson made the turn into their apartment complex. She parked near their building, climbed out of the driver's side, and grabbed her briefcase from the back seat, and all the while Lenny fumbled with the lock.

She looked at him with pity written all over her face. "Look, it's really late, and I've got a long day ahead of me tomorrow. We'll talk about this some more, and try to come up with some ideas of our own. In the meantime, you've got to promise me that you'll stay away from her."

"I promise," he said, stumbling out the door of the car.

"Maybe we can grab a hamburger one night this week, and you can tell me all about it. I'm sure there's quite a story to tell."

Lenny Provolone had tears pooling in the corners of his big, brown eyes. "I really do love her, Kate. She's the best thing that's ever happened to my life, and I mean that sincerely."

For an instant, Dawson was tempted to take him into her arms like an infant and comfort him with all the lies and half-truths that mothers often tell their children to stop them from crying, but then a cold wave of disdain washed over her and her face turned to stone. "I'm sure you do, Lenny."

"Kate, please tell me that everything's going to work out."

"I don't know that," she said sourly.

"I wish you'd—"

She turned her back on him, and headed towards the stairs. "Good night, Lenny. Try to get a good night's rest."

He stood there in the parking lot, looking anxiously at her for a moment longer, and when he realized that she wasn't coming back, he shuffled along to his apartment, like the walking dead.

CHAPTER FOUR

The next morning, Dawson found Matt Balardi outside his sister's small house on Alvarado Street. He was leaning against the crumpled fender of his classic '67 Cadillac Deville in the driveway, smoking a cigarette. The red and white pillared sedan, with its forward-thrusting front fenders and sleek sculpted body style, seemed out of place in the working-class neighborhood of Noe Valley. Somehow, she expected to see a car like that parked outside a mansion in Pacific Heights.

Carefully, she pulled up alongside the big, old car and hit the horn. Dawson then leaned over and opened the passenger-side door of her foreign import.

"Get in," she yelled to Balardi.

Balardi took another puff or two of his cigarette and stamped out the butt on the driveway. As he slid in next to his partner, he could tell from the look on Dawson's face that she wanted to reprimand him for his drunken behavior from the night before, but she never said a word.

Dawson side-stepped the subject, saying, "She's a real beauty. You must be very proud. How long have you had her?"

"The car was my father's." He adjusted himself in his seat. "It was the only thing he ever gave me, other than a beating with his belt now and then."

"You've kept it in great shape."

"I've got to fix the fender one of these days. My own fault. I got pretty wasted one night, drinking shots of bourbon, and I hit a lamppost coming home from the bar."

"I used to be a pretty good friend of Jack Daniel myself," Kate told him, as she backed out of the driveway and headed down the road.

"The old man really came unhinged that night. We had a real knock-down, drag-out fight," he said, taking his chin in hand and adjusting it back and forth. The jaw still hurt. "At eighty-four, he still packed quite a wallop. He died a few months later, but not because of the car. Heart attack. Who knew?"

"I'm sorry to hear that."

Matt Balardi was silent for a few blocks, but finally said, "Look, Dawson, I have a really hard time saying "thank you" to people. My father always thought it was a sign of weakness to be in someone's debt, and made it a point—sometimes at the end of his belt—to teach me self-reliance. So, I just never learned the right words to say."

"Don't mention it."

"The thing of it is," he stammered, struggling to find those right words, "my sister said that you called to make sure I got home okay last night. I've never had anybody check up on me like that."

"You would have done the same for me."

"Not a chance," Balardi replied, honestly.

Dawson thought about his response, then turned to her partner. "Balardi, it's not a big deal."

"I was just curious why you didn't just leave me there."

"C'mon, Balardi. You've heard Lieutenant Roberts say it a hundred times. 'In the SFPD, we never leave a fallen officer behind,'" she explained, quoting the boss with her tongue firmly planted in cheek. But Dawson felt compelled to say something more. "Despite our differences, Matt, I sense you're a decent cop who's more interested in getting results than collecting medals. And that decency is something you share with ninety-five percent of the men and women who work in this division."

She cut her eyes at Balardi, expecting to see him squirming in the bucket seat, ready with some smart-ass comeback, but he sat still, his face set in stone, like the famous faces carved on Mount Rushmore.

After about a mile, when Dawson failed to make the cut-off towards the Hall of Justice, he asked, "Where are we going?"

"The Lieutenant wants us to follow up on a lead," she said, turning the wheel of the car towards the Mission District. "Apparently, someone called in a tip last night or early this morning about Carlos Ortega. The tipster said she thought he was hiding out in some tenement apartment off skid row."

"A stakeout?" he groaned.

"Orders. What can you do?"

"I thought you wanted to corner that Secret Service thug and hammer him with some hard questions."

"I do," Dawson stated with a sense of determination. "We may still have time to do that later. The President's got three events today, including a posh luncheon with campaign donors late this afternoon."

"Must be nice to have somebody on the inside keeping an eye out for you."

"John's not really an 'insider,' she corrected him, turning left at the corner and driving north on Folsom Street, "but he manages to keep his eyes and ears open for the latest intel."

"If he lives and works inside the Beltway, he's an insider."

She hesitated for a moment. "I guess we'll just have to agree to disagree on that one, partner."

Dawson rolled to a stop at the curb and pulled the brake. Leaning out the window, she read the address. An old five-story Victorian home that had been converted into an apartment building for five or six families to reside in now housed more than a dozen. A great iron gate guarded the front entrance, where several smelly garbage cans, sad and leaning together, stood as silent sentries.

Deciding on a different approach, she released the brake, popped the clutch, and made a wide U-turn, wheeling to a halt in front of a building on the opposite side of the street. Both got out and walked across the street, opened the iron gate, and went into the house through the front door.

The foyer has been converted into a reception area, with a small desk and a key rack to one side. An older woman in curlers sat with her feet up on the desk, reading a copy of *People* magazine and smoking a cigarette. She was wearing a worn but clean gingham dress over sweat pants. She had whiskers, not unlike a cat, on her chin, and looked like she hadn't washed her face in weeks. When she opened her mouth to exhale, her crooked teeth were stained black from nicotine.

"Yeah, what do you want?" the woman growled, looking up from her magazine.

"You run this apartment building?" Dawson asked.

"Ten years, ever since my low-life husband ran off with my no-account sister. What's it to you?"

"I'm Inspector Dawson. This is Detective Balardi," Kate said, showing the woman her badge. "We'd like to ask you a few questions."

"I run a clean place here," she replied, hastily putting her feet down and rocking forward in her chair. "No prostitution. No drugs. If somebody tells you any different, they're lyin.'"

"We're not from Vice, ma'am," Balardi reassured her.

"You're not Vice cops?" she asked, looking from face to face.

"No, homicide. We're here investigating a murder," Dawson said, all business.

The woman stood up and leaned on the reception desk. "Well, get to the point then. I've got a lot of work to do."

From her jacket pocket, Dawson produced a photograph of Carlos Ortega, and shoved it in her face. "Have you seen this man before?"

"Yeah, what about it?"

"He's wanted by the SFPD for questioning," Dawson explained.

"Is there a reward?" she asked, taking another drag on her cigarette.

"No," they both replied in unison.

The woman looked again at the photograph. "He checked in yesterday. Didn't have any luggage with him, but he paid me in cash. I figure if a guy's going to pay me thirty days in advance I don't care whether he's got a toothbrush or a change of clothes. His money is the same as anybody else."

"What room is he in?" Balardi asked.

"Oh, he's not here now." The woman pointed to the key rack. "There, you see? His key is on the rack."

"When do you expect him back?" Dawson asked.

"I saw him leave about thirty minutes ago. Probably went out to get a bite to eat. No way to know when he'll be back."

"Can we get a look at his room?" Balardi inquired.

Dawson shot her partner a sideways glance, who responded by shrugging his shoulders.

"You got a warrant, detective?" the woman asked, with her hand out. "You know, this may seem like a run-down dump to the two of you, but my clients are entitled to their privacy. I don't think any of them would mind, really, but still I'd be responsible if any of their personal items went missing."

"C'mon, Matt, let's go," Dawson said, walking to the door.

"When Ortega comes back," he spoke directly to the woman, "don't say a word that we've been here."

"You got twenty bucks?" she asked.

For a moment, he simply stared at her, then reached in his trousers and pulled out a twenty. She snatched it from him and stuffed it down the front of her dress, with a wink. He tipped his head toward her, then scrambled to catch up to his partner who was already out the door.

"Big mistake," Dawson said.

"Maybe, but we pay informants all the time. What makes her so different from the rest?"

"Nothing, but somehow I get the feeling that woman would have sold her first born for a pack of smokes."

"I don't think so."

"Bet I'm right and you're wrong," she said confidently.

"That's a bet I'll take."

"Alright, your twenty bucks. If I'm right, you owe me twenty. But if I'm wrong, I'll pay you twenty."

"Deal."

They shook hands and walked back across the street to her car.

Like most cops, Kate Dawson did not care much for stake-outs, and after an hour and a half of staring at the tenement building, she was starting to get antsy. She looked over at her partner, and wasn't too surprised that he had fallen asleep. Balardi was far less disciplined and had less tolerance for boredom than she did. He would have easily slept the day away if she had allowed him, and thought nothing of it later when he awoke. She reached over to the passenger side and was about to shake him when she saw a quick flash out the back window, her suspect. He appeared to be walking down the sidewalk, but she really wasn't certain. It had been only a glimpse. Wondering exactly what she had seen, Kate looked at him again, engaging his eyes, but quickly turned away.

"Balardi, wake up," she said calmly, shaking him. "I think that's our boy."

Matt Balardi awoke with a start. "What's wrong?"

Dawson pointed out the window without a word. Her partner rubbed the sleep from his eyes, tracing an imaginary line from her finger to the opposite side of the street. It was their suspect all right.

Trying not to draw attention to themselves, they watched Carlos Ortega walking towards the hotel, carrying a bag of fast-food from In-and-Out Burger. A Latino, he seemed to blend easily into the flow of foot traffic on the sidewalk. Each time, he looked up, they turned away, and pretended to be engrossed in a private conversation. But the third time he looked up, they locked eyes with him, and were certain he had spotted them. Two plain-clothed detectives sitting in a BMW in the Latin neighborhood? Ya think? He did not give himself away immediately, but as he slowed to look in one of the shop windows, their images were reflected in the glass. Suddenly, he took off running in the opposite direction.

Dawson jumped out of the car and chased after him, followed closely by Balardi.

Three figures ran down the San Francisco street, along the busy thoroughfares filled with shoppers and merchants, dashing across traffic-filled streets. They ran into a bottleneck at the street fair and had to push their way through to the other side.

Dawson maintained an even pace, both breathing and running, while Matt Balardi sucked down deep gulps of air, his heart pumping fast, his legs burning to keep up with her. She was filled with an overwhelming urge to draw her weapon and end this grueling chase by wounding Ortega with one well-placed shot. But then she looked around . . . too many people milling about the street. Someone was likely to get hurt, or even killed, if they started shooting. Resolutely, she picked up the pace.

At Mission Street, she took the same turn that Ortega had made and plunged head-first into a crowd of people who were walking to-and-fro on the sidewalk. "Fuck! There he is!" The Latino always seemed to be one turn ahead of her, always one step in front. She pushed and shoved, thrusted people aside, ignoring their complaints and outcries. *Keep moving! Don't lose sight of him!*

Right before 16th Street, Ortega darted across the boulevard, skillfully dodging traffic in both directions, like a running back, jogging left and right through an all-star squad of defensive linemen. He ran right past Walgreen's, taking a left into a square lined with palm trees. Two old-timers sitting on a blue bench near Burger King looked up from their lunch and watched him run a complete circle around the square before he scrambled down the steps into the BART station. They gave each other a high-five as that was the least-productive run they had witnessed all day.

Dawson dashed across the street, maneuvering her way through traffic. On the other side, she crashed into two-day-old garbage cans and had to sidestep. It was then she saw the BART sign in big, bold letters, and pointed it out to Balardi. He acknowledged with a slight nod, and followed her across the street, huffing and puffing like a locomotive.

The Bay Area Rapid Transit was an advanced subway system that connected San Francisco with Oakland and most of the other major cities and suburbs in the areas. Sixteenth Street

Mission was one of forty-three stations in four counties. More than fifty-thousand passengers used the transportation system every day. She knew if Ortega managed to get on board one of the trains, they would lose him in the million miles of tracks.

She ran past the Walgreen's and scrambled down the escalator. The two old-timers cheered Kate, and then, moments later, Balardi, as they chased the Latino into the subway station. The excitement could not have been any more real to the two octogenarians.

At the bottom, just outside the Station Agent's kiosk, Dawson ran toward the automated ticket machines on the left and stopped briefly to see if Ortega was still there waiting to buy his pass. She pushed her way through the crowd of subway commuters, looking and listening; studied several lines of commuters as they waited to feed their tickets into the turnstiles. Satisfied that her suspect wasn't among them, she flashed her badge at the Station Agent and they went through the stainless-steel turnstile closest to the kiosk, then walked down the steps to the trains.

A train, heading north to Oakland, pulled into the station. Several passengers got off the train, while a few others boarded.

With their guns drawn, they sprinted down the platform, checking each cluster of passengers for some sign of Ortega, but he simply wasn't there. She continued running towards the front of the train, looking randomly in windows and open doors. But the only thing her actions managed to accomplish was to scare a handful of passengers who panicked at the site of her gun. These frightened commuters jumped off the train and joined others who were running away, waving their arms wildly at the crazy woman with the gun.

Dawson was about to move forward and shove her way through the congestion at the first car when she heard the familiar "ding-dong" commanding passengers to stay clear of the doors. Kate pushed her way onto the first car, with Balardi right behind her, just as the subway door hissed shut. The site of a dozen passengers either peacefully dosing or moping in their seats was enough for her to holster her weapon and find a seat. There was a blurred flash as the subway car raced out of the station and barreled down the tunnel towards Oakland.

As the BART slid smoothly underground, Dawson stood and began reading the advertisements on the walls of the car, walking to the rear. That's when she was recalled that he was a stranger; that he knew very little about the Bay area. She pointed out the schematic transit routes' map. "He doesn't know where he's going," she said loud enough for Balardi.

"Yeah, what would he know about the BART?"

Dawson traced the route on the schematic map. "There are four stops before we reach Oakland: Civic Center, Powell, Montgomery, and Embarcadero. We've got to stop him before he reaches Oakland or we're bound to lose him in that damned construction at the West Oakland station."

"Okay, so what's your plan?" Balardi asked, cycling his .38.

"I'm going to work my way to the end of the train, moving from car to car, to flush him out," she explained, talking in his ear.

"Check."

"Be the first to get out at each station, and wait for him on the platform. He'll be heading towards the exit. You should be able to cut him off. I'll be right behind him if he does make a break for it," Dawson said, confidently. "If he doesn't get out, wait until the last second and get back in the next car, always working towards the rear. We should converge on him in the last car by the time we reach Oakland."

"Then, you better get moving," he said, stealing a glance at his watch. "We'll be at Civic Center station in a matter of minutes."

"Good hunting," Kate said, with a determined look.

Balardi wearily said, "Let's nail this asshole already. I don't really want to go back to the station empty-handed."

"Neither do I!"

Dawson burst into the next car, her gun drawn, wild-eyed, walking quickly down the center of the car, examining each and every seat as she moved towards the rear. Several of the subway passengers panicked at the sight of her gun and began screaming. Some slinked down on the floor or tried to climb under their seats; other riders tucked their arms, legs, and head into a little ball, like a tortoise retreating into its shell. Violent acts on the BART system were all too common and no one wanted to be the next victim. At the first stop, everyone scrambled out of the car, stampeding into the station in terror, nearly knocking Balardi over.

At the end of the car, she waited in front of the connecting door and asked herself, "Where are you, Ortega?" She pushed her way into the next car, forcing the heavy door open, and continued her frantic examination, looking under seats and behind dividers at each of the exit doors. She had both hands on her .9mm, using the weapon like a divining rod to find her suspect. Her eyes had a determined, faraway look, which would have easily frightened all but the seasoned traveler.

In the second car, she drew the same reaction from the riders; screaming, hiding, trying to be inconspicuous. At the next station, as she moved to the rear door, they all ran out hysterical, arms flailing above their heads.

Stepping through the connecting door, Dawson was so focused on finding her suspect that she didn't notice a man tracking just behind her, following her; not until the man released the heavy, connecting door and it slammed shut. She caught a quick glimpse over her shoulder, swiveled around, and came face to face with the person she feared the most: some nut-case with a gun.

"Drop *it*, or I'll drop *you!*" she shouted, drawing a bead on him.

"I'm Captain Avenger," he spoke from beneath a dark sea-green mask. "Put your gun down on the floor and step back. I'm making a citizen's arrest as a duly deputized member of the Justice Federation."

Dawson stood her ground, regarding the nut-case wielding the gun before her with contempt. He was dressed in a woodland-camouflaged flight suit, black Ultra Force Jungle Boots, a webbed army belt, and a cape made from the Stars & Stripes.

Her heart was beating out of control.

Ever since Hollywood had started making realistic movies about comic book superheroes, the City of San Francisco had become haven to vigilantes donning superhero costumes who were determined to bring their own form of justice to the streets. She was surprised that Lenny and his sci-fi friends hadn't banded together to fight crime themselves. Dawson knew there were citizen superheroes who were content to volunteer at charity events and visit sick children, but the ones who carried guns represented a real threat to the city.

"I'm a cop, you asshole," Dawson said, slowly taking out her badge.

Captain Avenger stood his ground. "I've seen real badges before. Yours looks like it came out of a gumball machine."

"Look, I'm in pursuit of a suspect and if I lose him, I'm charging you with 'aiding and abetting a criminal.'"

"I didn't see a suspect. I just saw some crazy woman running through the train with a gun drawn," he said, pumping up his chest. "Now, if you'll be good enough to put your weapon down."

Dawson threw a glance deliberately over Captain Avenger's

left shoulder. As he jerked in that direction, Balardi came up on the right, and took him down with the brunt end of his service revolver. Captain Avenger shuddered, then hit the floor of the subway car like a sack of flour.

"You look like you needed some help," Balardi said, peeling the gun out of the costumed freak's hand.

"Thanks!" She turned and raced down the center aisle.

Passengers in the car were scrambling to get out of her way, most of them tucking their arms and legs in or moving to a window seat, giving her a clear, unobstructed path. She peered forward into the next car, just in time to see Ortega moving again.

The train flew down the tunnel, racing to the next stop.

Ahead, Carlos Ortega glanced over his shoulder as he ran, watching her through the glass in the connecting door. He bolted through the door in the next car and slammed it shut behind him, turning the lock.

Dawson made her way to the next car, leaving the connecting doors open as she went. She stormed toward him, her hand reaching out for the handle to the connecting door long before she could reach it. Locked. She shook it furiously, then aimed and blew the door handle to pieces—four shots, point-blank range. She charged the door.

By the time she entered the last car, Dawson had lost track of her suspect. Ortega had either disappeared or was hiding in plain sight. She crouched down and began a furious search of the car, looking underneath each seat. The subway riders didn't know what to make of the woman with the handgun, but each time she passed a row of passengers, they scrambled out of their seats and ran frantically for the safety of the previous car.

Balardi eventually caught up with Dawson, wheezing and gasping, the legacy of too much alcohol and far too many cigarettes. In between gulps of air, he screamed, "What the hell happened, Dawson? Where's Ortega?"

"I don't know!" she cried out, eyes darting here and there.

"Well, he must have gotten past you somehow. Doubled back?"

"Impossible. I've been working my way to the rear of the train, one car at a time. There's no way he could have gotten by me."

"Okay. Then, where is he?"

Dawson shot a worried glance at her partner and decided to have another look around. Besides the two of them, there were only five people still seated: an old man with a cane, a woman with a basket of groceries, a young couple holding onto each other in fear, and a black teenager with an enormous ghetto blaster. She could feel the train was beginning to slow; knew they would be reaching the West Oakland station in moments. Then she saw it. The rear door was open, maybe a quarter of an inch, but enough of a difference to cause it to swing freely when the car hit a bump on the tracks.

"The rear door," she shouted, pointing towards the back of the car.

Dawson hustled down the center aisle with Balardi right behind her right as the train came to a stop. She yanked the door open and hung off the back of the train, listening . . . *Footsteps down the tunnel! He'd been hanging off the back of the train!* She tucked the gun into her waistband and jumped from the train onto the tracks.

Further down the tunnel, she glimpsed a shadow.

"Freeze! Hold it right there!" Dawson yelled, drawing her gun and holding it in front of her in the combat stance. The muzzle of her .9mm was trained center mass. She couldn't miss at this distance.

For a fleeting moment, the suspect thought about running,

even as he came to a complete stop on the tracks. He could see the workman's platform and emergency exit just up ahead. But as he slowly turned and his face came into the light, Carlos Ortega saw the gun in her hand. His face blanched white with fear. The fresh, cool air from the tunnel licked away the sweat from his forehead.

"Put your hands up."

"Don't shoot. I'm unarmed," he said, staring down the muzzle. "I had nothing to do with that woman's death."

"Put your fuckin' hands up!" Dawson screamed.

Slowly, Ortega raised his hands above his head in surrender and intertwined his fingers behind his head.

"On your knees!" she commanded.

As he knelt, first on one knee, then the other, Dawson motioned for Balardi, who was standing close by with his own gun drawn on the suspect. Cautiously, she approached Ortega, swiftly handcuffed his hands behind his back, then reached under the right arm and helped him to his feet. With one hand holding him in place by the cuffs, she patted him down and Mirandized. Balardi holstered his .38 and, expecting another train, they herded him, one on either arm, to the emergency exit.

At the Oakland West station, after boarding a train going south, they seated Ortega between them, sitting at a ninety-degree angle to the suspect, so he wouldn't get any ideas about running. As Dawson eased back in her seat gratefully, ever so glad to be headed back to San Francisco, she looked out the window at another train, heading north, stopped beside them.

"Balardi, look!" she exclaimed.

Agent Smith sat in the northbound car. An old woman with groceries pushed her way through the crowded car to sit down next to him. He shifted closer to the window and looked away from her, out the window. His gaze locked with Dawson's. As her train pulled out going south, and his train pulled out heading north, he jumped up and stared after her with an expression of shock and anger.

Half an hour later, Carlos Ortega was sitting on his hands in the back of a police squad car, his wrists manacled behind him, his head bent down. One of the uniformed cops closed the back door, while the other walked around the front of the car and climbed into the driver's side. Dawson leaned against the patrol car and used the roof as a make-shift desk to scribble out a brief report as her partner stood nearby on the curb, finishing a smoke. She added her signature to the report before handing it through the window to the lead policeman.

"Thanks, guys. I really appreciate it," Dawson said, waving. "I'll see you back at the station."

Balardi flicked his cigarette butt into the dirt. "So, the Secret Service guys were right behind us the whole time."

"I'll bet you another twenty bucks, they wouldn't have taken him alive. Carlos Ortega has no idea how lucky he is that we got to him first. I have a feeling they would have shot him dead attempting to flee their custody. Case closed."

"You don't think he killed Meghan Kendrick, do you?"

"Nope." Kate walked towards her car. "I think he's nothing but a patsy to protect the real killer."

"Well, at least, that's one thing that we can agree on," he said, trailing slightly behind his partner.

Speeding off, they headed to the Hall of Justice.

When they reached police headquarters, the television mini-vans were lined up along Bryant Street, as well as several sedans with PRESS signs sitting in the window or propped up on the dashboard. A gauntlet of reporters stood outside the front door to the Hall of Justice and all along the street. Among the reporters, Dawson spotted representatives of the three major cable networks, in addition to some of the local newscasters and radio personalities. Now that they had arrested the lead suspect in the Meghan Kendrick murder case, the media circus had swung into full gear. Every reporter was anxious to scoop the competition.

"Keep driving, Dawson," Balardi said. "We'll go around the back of the building and enter through the rear doors."

"Good thinking! The last thing I want to do is answer any of their questions. I've had my fill of the Press."

"You'd hardly know it."

"Why is that?"

"I saw you on the Oprah show. You were a real rock star. Did the department a lot of credit. I especially liked what you had to say about Frank Miller. He would have been proud of you."

"That was over two years ago, and the only reason why she had me on the show was for bringing down John Monroe."

Dawson drove around the corner and slowed along the back street, looking for a parking place. She passed several squad cars and the sedan that belonged to Lieutenant Roberts, then pulled into a spot.

She and Balardi went up the rear stairs of police headquarters, avoiding the lethal press. They pushed their way through the usual bottleneck of civilians and police officers at the Information Desk, then climbed several flights of steps to the Homicide Bureau.

No sooner had Dawson reached her desk and put her briefcase down on the empty chair than Clark and Jawara were in her face, making demands. After a moment or two, she put both of her hands up in the air, like a referee calling a penalty in a football game, saying, "One at a time, please."

"We've put together a composite list now of those who were on board Air Force One when Meghan Kendrick was murdered," Clark said, reading from his notes. "The list is based on the official passenger manifest we got from Agent Smith and the one your boyfriend faxed us."

"Pop quiz. Whose name is missing from both lists?" Jawara asked.

"Harlan Reinhardt," she answered.

"How did you know?" they asked, sounding like a chorus.

"I think you'll find Reinhardt was traveling aboard a different plane," she stated, with a high degree of certainty. "The United States Air Force provides a C-5 Galaxy heavy cargo transport aircraft for carrying the President's bulletproof limousine, standby limo, and a fully-fitted ambulance. That plane usually arrives a few hours in advance of Air Force One. I think Reinhardt was already at San Francisco International Airport by the time the President's plane arrived."

William Clark looked at Dawson then his partner, raising an eyebrow, but continued working from his notes, "When we compared the two lists, we found that they were nearly identical. Smith's list has sixty-one names on it, while Prescott's list has sixty-two names. There's an unidentified Secret Service agent who got on the plane at Andrew's Air Force Base."

"Now he either took a stroll off the airplane while it was in flight or his name has been purposely expunged from Smith's list," Jawara said, completing his partner's point before he could finish it himself.

"My guess is he's our murderer," Kate said, looking from face to face.

They both nodded their heads in agreement.

"What about you, Mikhail? What have you got for me?" she asked.

"Well, first, I want to know, when was I appointed your personal secretary?" the African-American asked, his arms folded across his chest. "I've gotten four calls for you already this morning. Your boyfriend has called once and some other man has called here three times looking for you. Says he has information about Meghan Kendrick's death but will only speak to you."

Dawson looked at her iPhone. "Son-of-a-bitch! I turned my phone off during the stakeout! I guess I just forgot to turn it back on."

Jawara handed her three "While You Were Out" messages on pink note paper. "He wouldn't leave his name—they never do— but that's the number of your mystery serial caller. If you ask me, he's some nutcase who saw the TV coverage and decided to get in on the act."

"Thanks," she replied, reading the number.

"Second, I wanted to let you know that we've started processing the identities of those who were traveling aboard Air Force One. If we rule out the four-member flight crew and the staff of twenty-three additional crew members who routinely travel on board, that leaves us with thirty-five people."

"But," Clark interrupted, trying to one-up his partner, "I also think we can safely eliminate the President's doctor and her assistant, members of the White House staff, and the First Family, except for the First Man, who is our primary suspect. The rest of them never left the forward cabin area."

"We've also ruled out the military attaché who carries the nuclear football," Jawara said, now interrupting Clark. "Since the football is carried by a Presidential military aide, whose work schedule rotates among the five service branches, it was just a matter of chance that this guy was aboard the flight."

"Besides," Clark added, "he wouldn't have had much

freedom of movement being physically attached by his wrist to the briefcase."

Dawson added the numbers in her head. "That's still about two dozen people who need to be checked out."

"Yep, that number includes the Secret Service, the Press Corps, and six others who were traveling as "guests" of the President," said Jawara.

"Guests?"

"It's a pretty eclectic bunch," Clark said, reading from his notes. "We've got a pop singer and her traveling companion—"

"A pop singer? Are you kidding me?"

"The one and only Nikki Lynn," Jawara replied. "She's the first female contestant to win *American Idol* since Jordin Sparks took the crown back in 2007. She's had three Platinum albums and swept the Grammy's last month. She's also been front-lining some of the President's speeches lately."

"I've got to get out more," Dawson wiped her forehead with her palm.

"The list of guests also includes a couple of congressmen, a Republican senator, and an eighty-five-year-old physician who's possibly one of the oldest soldiers still on active duty: Colonel Bernard W. Goodine."

"I read about him in *Time* magazine," Jawara said, recognizing the name. "He's a tough old bird. He joined the Army Air Corps just after the Second World War, served as an adjutant to one of the Joint Chiefs, and became a flight surgeon when he was fifty-years-old. He still serves in a combat unit caring for pilots on flight status; conducting annual physicals, and taking care of the sick or injured."

Dawson raised her eyebrows. "Why does that name sound familiar?"

"The President plans to present him with the Congressional

Medal of Honor at a formal ceremony at the new VA Hospital in San Francisco later this week," Clark reported. "I'd hate to sound like a cynic, but I suspect her motivation is a selfish one. She's pinning a medal on him to show solidarity with the Armed Forces in the event we end up going to war with Iran."

"Sure, I know what you mean. There's never been much love between the First Family and the military."

"We'll follow up with him and the others," Clark promised.

"Yeah, if we find that any one of them shares a connection with Meghan Kendrick, we'll be sure to let you know," Jawara let her know.

After the two of them left, Dawson finally sat down at her desk. She stared at the three phone messages that Jawara had given her, then at the telephone on the edge of her desk. She picked up the receiver and started to dial the number but stopped short of the last digit. *Jawara was right*, Kate thought, as she hung up the phone. *It's just some whack-job who wants to feel important for five minutes.* She threw them down on her desk and headed to the vending machine for coffee.

Dawson walked straight into the Interrogation Room at the San Francisco Police Department headquarters and slapped a thick manila folder down on the table. The name on the file was "Ortega, Carlos A." She surveyed the room and the men in it with a cool eye. The Interrogation Room was as cold and somber as the morgue, with very few furnishings other than a metal table, several chairs upholstered in black vinyl, and a wastepaper basket from the Department of Public Works. Ortega was hand-cuffed to the metal table, facing a large two-way mirror and a video apparatus that was set up to record the interrogation. Matt Balardi, leaning back against the rear wall with his arms folded across his chest, seemed anxious to get the show on the road.

Unruffled, Dawson sat down across the table from her suspect and opened his folder. Paper rattle marked the silence as she flipped several pages, reading bits and pieces. After a few moments, she closed the file and looked at him.

"Mr. Ortega, my name is Inspector Dawson. I'm the lead detective on this case. My partner is Matt Balardi," she said, pointing to the back of the room. "I am required to inform you that this session is being recorded and that we are perfectly within our rights to do that."

"Just get on with it," he interrupted her.

"Sir, I must also ask you if you understood your Miranda rights as I said them to you," Dawson said, all business, as if reading from a prepared script. "And with these rights in mind, do you consent to speaking to us without a lawyer being present?"

"Yeah, what does it matter? I'm a dead man anyway."

She repeated, "You do have a constitutional right to an attorney, and if you cannot afford one, an attorney will be—"

"Stop wasting my time," Ortega demanded. "We all know that this is nothing but a big sham. So, get on with it, Inspector."

Dawson raised her eyebrows and sought Balardi for an answer, who sent it right back to her. She finally said, "Mr. Ortega, I have had the opportunity to review your personnel file that was provided to me by Harlan Reinhardt. There are a few inconsistencies that I was hoping you could clear up for me."

"Well, this ought to be good," he said with a smirk, shaking his head. "Go ahead. Fire away."

"It seems that you have been living two lives," Dawson said, tapping the police folder impatiently with the tips of her fingers. "In one life, you are Carlos Angelo Ortega, a steward who has served several presidents aboard Air Force One in the last ten years. You're also a veteran of the Second Gulf War. You have a social security number, you pay your taxes, you have a mortgage on a duplex, and you help your sister care for her two illegitimate children."

"That's right. What's your point?" He was all edgy.

"The other life is lived in the shadows where you dress in black leather like a biker and frequent gay bars in the D.C. area like the Banana Café, Cobalt & 30 Degrees, and the Black Rose."

"So what? I'm gay," said Ortega, not the least bit ashamed. He didn't look apologetic; his eyes ice daggers. "And for the record, I wore that biker outfit one time. Last Halloween. I was dressed as a "Leatherman," not that you would know shit about that, Snow White."

"You might be surprised." Kate recalled what John Monroe had taught her about the BDSM sub-culture of the Leathermen.

"Good for you," he snorted.

"Personally, I don't care what you do behind closed doors," she said, returning his gaze with an equally cold stare, "but in the court of public opinion, which is where your case is going to be tried and a verdict reached well before you go to trial, a man living a double life has no chance in hell of an acquittal. You may think you're living in a culture that respects diversity and espouses 'don't-ask, don't-tell' liberties, but you'd be wrong. The moment the media gets wind of your gay lifestyle, as a Leatherman, you're going to be convicted of murder, whether you did it or not."

"I didn't kill Meghan Kendrick," he said flatly.

Dawson pressed, leaning toward him. "Then tell me who did."

"I don't know."

"You don't know, or won't say?"

Ortega wagged his head back and forth. "I can't help you, Inspector. Even if I wanted to help you, I couldn't say."

Matt Balardi had grown tired of Dawson's line of questioning, and decided it was time to get the show on the road. "Did you have sex with Meghan Kendrick?" he asked, walking to the table.

"No, never!" Ortega watched the other detective's reaction.

"But you did come on to her, right?"

"No, I'm gay," he repeated, annoyed by the question. "But I saw plenty of other guys come on to her. I mean, she's hot. Even someone like me can appreciate a good-looking woman like Meghan."

"So, you *were* attracted to her?" Balardi asked.

"Yes, but not in the way you mean," Ortega answered, shifting uncomfortably in his chair. "Besides Meghan Kendrick was strictly hands-off."

The suspect had just confirmed something she half-expected to be true. "What do you mean, "hands-off?" she asked, breaking her partner's line of inquiry.

"I don't know." Ortega hung his head.

"C'mon, you know more than what you're telling us," she said, staring him straight in the face. "Help us out here."

Ortega returned her look. "No! You just don't understand the kind of powerful people that you're dealing with here."

"You see, my partner believes that I am wasting my time with you, but I believe you want to do the right thing." She interlocked her fingers in front of herself. "It is obvious that you are an intelligent man, Mr. Ortega, and that you are interested in getting back home to be with your family. That is why I believe you are ready to do the right thing. Tell me what I need to know."

"You don't understand these people, like I do," he said, adamantly.

Balardi butted in. "You'd better start cooperating—"

"Or what? There isn't a thing you can threaten me with that isn't worse than what they're going to do to me."

Balardi was on the verge of blowing his top. Deliberately, he walked over to the table, tipped the suspect's chair back, and got right in his face. "You're looking at first degree murder, pal. That's murder committed during a rape. You could spend the rest of your life in prison, with no possibility of parole. We're talking hard labor here. And when you're done putting in your ten-hour work day, you'll be taking it up the ass three or four times a night from Bubba and his lice-infected friends. But then, maybe you'd like that. Maybe you'd like having some ugly, smelling inmate fuck you like a bitch every night."

"What do you know about it?"

"But then again, Meghan Kendrick was a huge celebrity. So, instead of life in prison, you'd get the death penalty," added Balardi, his hot breath in the Ortega's face. "San Quentin. Death row. Spend the rest of your miserable life in a cell no bigger than a toilet, waiting for a lethal injection to put you down like some animal."

"Hey, I didn't kill anybody!"

"Then you'd better start fuckin' cooperating with us!" he yelled, breathing fire. "Or your life isn't going to be worth shit."

Balardi and Ortega held each other's eye for a moment, then Balardi released the suspect's chair and straightened up.

"I'm as good as dead anyway!" Ortega was clearly terrified. "If I don't roll over and play dead for them, they're going to target my sister and her kids. I'll not have their blood on my hands."

"Cooperate with us," Dawson said, hands flat on the table, "and I promise you that no harm will come to your sister or her kids. All I need to do is make one call to my friend in the Justice Department and they'll be in protective custody."

"You would do that for me?"

"Yes, but you've got to help us connect all the dots." She hoped to be convincing enough.

Carlos Ortega didn't react right away, but looked intently at them. Dawson and Balardi could almost see the wheels turning in his head, plotting his next move, figuring out how to best protect his three family members. There was an air of deep contemplation about Ortega that didn't quite match the portrait of a man accused of an impulsive act of murder. He seemed more like the kind of person who would have willingly sacrificed himself to protect the ones that he loved the most. He stared back at them, tightlipped, weighing his options.

"You gonna cooperate with us?" asked Balardi. "Or are you just going to make things tougher on yourself?"

Ortega hesitated a moment longer, then gave in. "Okay, in exchange for my family's safety, I'll tell you what you want to know."

"Why was Meghan Kendrick considered 'hands-off?'" Kate asked.

"Alright, I'll tell you." He leaned forward in his chair, his cuffed hands folded in front of him on the table, lowered his voice, and said, "She and the First Man were having an affair. It had been going on for about six months. Some of the Secret Service guys knew about it and kept other men away. They'd always refer to her around me and the rest of the staff as "hands off."

"Were they together the night she was murdered?" Dawson asked.

"Yeah."

"How do you know that?" she prodded him for more answers.

"We were running almost an hour late due to weather-related problems in the Midwest. People were hungry and Bill Harrison suggested that we could make our passengers a bit more comfortable with a lite snack. He instructed the galley staff to put together a couple of platters—you know, cheese and crackers, cakes and cookies—and take them around to our guests," Ortega explained. "I delivered the late snack, with tea and coffee, to the Press Lounge. He came with me; made the rounds chatting people up while I served. They had been watching some movie with the head-sets off, so they welcomed the break. After about twenty minutes, they all went back to their movie, and that's when I noticed the First Man had disappeared. I never actually saw him leave the cabin, so I just figured he really needed to use the john and went into the rear restroom. Only later did I start putting two-and-two together. That's when I realized that he had used the snack as a distraction to meet with Meghan Kendrick."

Dawson bobbed her head up and down. "So, that's why Reinhardt said that no one from his staff could account for your whereabouts during the twenty-minute period when she was murdered."

"Maybe, I don't know." His eyes darted from Dawson to Balardi and back several times.

"Did you see Harrison again after that?"

"Yeah, I had gone back to the Press Lounge to pick up anything I had missed," he added, his eyes with a faraway look. "We were starting our approach, and I had gotten waylaid by one of the Secret Service agents from fully busing the cabin. I knew that I would have caught hell if it wasn't clean on landing, so I got up out of my seat and ran into the room to finish up. I practically ran into him being escorted by two Secret Service agents out of the Lounge."

"Did anyone else notice the First Man leaving the cabin?"

"No, not really. Nearly all the reporters had left their headsets off and were shouting dialogue at the screen. I suppose if they did notice him, it wouldn't have been a big deal," he conceded. "Bill Harrison is a very friendly guy who often sits in the Press Lounge with friends and associates that he knows. I've seen him sit next to Ms. Kendrick several times. But not just her, other people as well."

Dawson thought about this a moment. Something still didn't make sense to her. "Have you misplaced a lapel pin recently? One with the Presidential seal?"

"Yeah, how did you know?" Ortega asked, surprised.

"Reinhardt told me that his men found a lapel pin in the restroom with Meghan Kendrick's fingerprints all over it," she revealed, gauging his reaction. "He said it was stamped with the number forty-two; that it belonged to you."

"The lapel pin is part of our uniform. I wear it on my steward's jacket. When I hung the jacket up in my locker on Sunday night to clean up the galley, it was there," he said, without a stumble. "Later, when I went to pick it up, the pin was missing. I thought it had fallen off in the locker. But after a thorough sweep, I couldn't find it. I was going to report it missing the next day, but then . . ."

She shot him a sideways glance. "Can you think of a reason why the Secret Service chief would try to pin this murder on you?"

"No, none whatsoever." Ortega was being honest.

"Well, that should do it for now," Dawson said, as she slid her chair back from the table and stood up.

Carlos Ortega looked up at her. "You won't forget our deal, will ya?"

"No, just as soon as I get back to my desk, I'll call my friend at Justice, and your sister and her children should be in protective custody by tonight."

"Thank you." He relaxed a bit.

The interrogation was over for the time being. Matt Balardi swept out of the room, with Dawson trailing behind in his wake. They passed a uniformed policeman who entered the room to take Ortega to lock-up. In the outer room, Balardi hesitated a moment, then said, "What do you say, Dawson, let's get some lunch. Nice big plate of old-fashioned police goulash; some meat stew, potatoes, vegetables. My treat."

"Thanks, Matt. That's a nice offer, but I've got to pass."

"Are you sure about that? It's just lunch."

"Lieutenant Roberts is expecting my report, but I'll take a rain check for tomorrow."

"Okay, tomorrow it is, but I'm still hungry. So, I guess I'll go buy a newspaper and see if I can choke down a plate of that Hungarian stew by myself." He shambled off, his shoulders slumped with fatigue. As she watched him go, Dawson thought he wasn't that bad a sort after all. The forty-six-year-old misfit had certainly proven his metal that day. At least, he had proved it to her.

Time to make that call to John.

At 1:25 P.M., Kate Dawson figured that the Lieutenant would be in his office at the Homicide Bureau.

Roberts frowned at her when she entered his office, carrying her briefcase. He was unshaved and the dark circles under each eye made him look like he had been in a prize fight the night before with a world heavyweight boxer. The glare on his face warned her to tread lightly.

"I think he's innocent, Lieutenant," Dawson said, briefing her superior about the interrogation of the suspect. "He has no motive and the evidence against him is mostly circumstantial. A lapel pin? I mean, good grief, you would've never let me hold Ortega on flimsy evidence like that."

James Roberts scratched the stubble of beard growing on his face, considering it. "All right, Inspector, let's say you're right. What's your next move?"

"I'm not sure." Surprised, Dawson wasn't used to her boss agreeing with her, and she paused for a moment to make sure that she hadn't missed something. She had spent so much time trying to document Ortega's innocence that the thought of a "next move" had never really occurred to her. "I am convinced that Reinhardt and his people are protecting one of their own, but I still don't know the reason why."

"Could this simply be about keeping the First Man's affair with a news reporter out of the headlines?" Roberts asked, playing devil's advocate. "You know, sometimes the simplest answer is often the correct answer. And we do have a precedent for this kind of thing with Bill Clinton and a White House intern."

"The thought had occurred to me, sir, but the two incidents are really quite different. Monica Lewinsky wasn't found dead after the President's blow job, whereas Meghan Kendrick was, and we're not even sure of the First Man's involvement in her death. All we know for certain is that the two of them were having an affair, *and* there is evidence of a second man."

Lieutenant Roberts shot a look at his female detective, then let his eyes drop to a report on his desk. The report looked like it had just been printed on a LaserJet printer as the ink was still fresh on the page. "Well, I'm sure you'll be thrilled to know that the Press is making up their own stories. This latest report from the AP suggests a love triangle between Ortega, Meghan Kendrick, and Harrison. Apparently, they had it out on board Air Force One and Kendrick died trying to keep the two men apart."

Kate leaned forward in her chair, reading the report. "You know that is total bullshit, sir. Fake news."

"Well, it is what it is," he said flatly. "You know, as well as I do, the Press never lets the facts get in the way of a sensationalized story."

"They'll have Ortega tried and convicted before we even finish our investigation."

"I wouldn't be surprised."

She gathered up her notebook and placed it inside her briefcase. Then, as she turned to go, Dawson said, "Do I have your permission, sir, to follow up on a few leads of my own?"

Roberts paused for half a second, then gave his approval. "All right, go take another crack at it. I'm allowed to keep Ortega in a holding cell for thirty-six hours before officially charging him with a crime, but be sure to leave your report with me before you go."

"Thank you, sir."

The Lieutenant shook a finger at her. "Just remember, when you're holding on for dear life over a precipice, you can't afford to go waving your arms around."

Dawson smiled close-lipped and walked out of his office door.

CHAPTER FIVE

Kokkari Estiatorio was one of the finest restaurants in Downtown San Francisco. It was favored by Politicos and the power elite for its incredible Greek cuisine, notably its impressive meats spit-roasted on an open fire and the "to-die-for" desserts. Sandwiched between Jackson Square to the west and the Financial District in the south, Kokkari Estiatorio had the warmth and coziness of a beloved tavern as well as the "grand" fine-dining experience that its wealthy patrons expected and felt they deserved. The restaurant had often played host to sitting presidents or presidential hopefuls who wanted to wine and dine their Democratic donors. The *Oenos* or "wine" room was favored for its small, intimate setting, which had seating for about thirty guests. The large, wood-framed, sliding glass doors that separated the private dining room from the main *Kouzina* allowed guests to feel as if they were part of the restaurant while still being in a space where they could enjoy private conversations. The key to booking the private room at Kokkari Estiatorio was being guaranteed that it would remain private.

When Kate Dawson and her partner arrived at the restaurant,

the luncheon had already started in the *Oenos* room just adjacent to the main dining hall. Secret Service agents were strategically placed at each of the main entrances, the kitchen, and on the street, along Jackson. It took every trick in Dawson's playbook, including bluffing her way through with her police badge, to get into the private dining hall. As they walked into the room, Balardi was impressed by the dramatic wall of wine racks that spanned floor to ceiling. Sunlight streamed in through the large, picture windows on the handful of people sitting on both sides of the "Chef's Table," an elegant twenty-foot-long, hand-carved wooden table covered with stark-white linens. The First Family, including the President and the First Man were seated at odd intervals next to the other dining guests. Nearly everyone had a Greek salad, while several others enjoyed traditional lentil soup.

Dawson and Balardi pushed by the male servers who wore elegant tuxedos with tails and approached the "Chef's Table." She had her badge out, ready to read them all their Miranda rights, if necessary.

Bill Harrison, the First Man, looked up, showing little surprise. "Good afternoon, detectives," he said, smoothly rising to his feet to greet them. His face was as set and as hard as an ancient ceremonial mask. "Perhaps, this can wait until another time. We're in the middle of a very special luncheon."

"I apologize for this intrusion—" Dawson started to say, but was cut-off in mid-sentence by her partner.

"So, you say, Mr. Harrison, but it really looks like you're just fleecing a bunch of old codgers, if you ask me," Balardi interrupted, loudly taking the lead role. "Maybe they're too busy stuffing their faces to realize that you've got your hands in their pockets, cleaning out every, last dime."

"Now, you just wait a minute, detective," Harrison said.

"Matt, have you lost your mind?" Dawson added.

Balardi ignored them and focused on an older woman at the end of the table. "So, lady, how much did this cost you per plate? $5000? $10,000? $20,000? I know of a good soup kitchen up the street where the food is free. It isn't fancy, mind you, but it is good solid food that will stick to your ribs. Not this cow-palace slop that you'll end up purging in the next hour or so."

The old woman remained seated, exclaiming. "This is an outrage!" She looked like she was about to have a cow.

"Trust me, lady, the food doesn't get any better than this. I'd be outraged, too!"

The others in the room were entirely silent. Nobody moved at the table. It was like a still life, painted by Paul Cezanne. From the main dining hall, Secret Service agents were scrambling through the sliding glass doors, with Harlan Reinhardt bringing up the rear.

President Harrison stood up. "How can I help you, detectives?"

Dawson pushed her partner aside, saying, "Madam President, we're looking for a Secret Service agent named Jones. We were informed that he was a member of your security detail."

"Who informed you that Jones was a member of my detail?" the President asked, maintaining her cool composure.

Dawson hesitated a moment. She was just about ready to reply when she caught a glimpse of movement out of the corner of her eye. Reinhardt pushed his way through a black sea of Secret Service agents into the private dining room. He had his familiar white handkerchief in hand and used it to wipe the sweat from his brow. The intensity of his rage was written all over his blood-red face as he came forward.

"I did, Madam President," he confessed.

President Harrison stared at him, expressionless. "Is the joint task force with the local police closed, or not?"

"The task force is closed. The police have a suspect in custody," he reported, as a matter of fact.

"We still have some unanswered questions, Madam," Dawson said.

"Well, Detective, I doubt seriously if you're going to find your answers here," the President replied, with an edge. "This is a private luncheon for my constituents, and I can assure you that none of the people in this room are connected in any way to your investigation."

"I'm sorry to have troubled you," she said, ever so embarrassed.

Ignoring her completely, President Harrison did not appear to have heard her apology and signaled the head waiter, saying, "Please fill everyone's glass with that Bordeaux we discussed, and you can serve the main course."

"Very good, Madam," he replied.

Harlan Reinhardt put his hand on Dawson's shoulder, which she promptly threw off, and together with his men, they escorted the two detectives from the *Oenos* room. When they were out of site of the First Family, the Secret Service agents hustled Dawson and Balardi out the sliding glass doors, and fast-stepped them out of the restaurant. Out on Jackson Street, they were finally released.

Balardi pushed back at a couple of the agents, but Kate patted him on the shoulder to calm him, whispering, "They'll be another time," which was enough to calm him, temporarily.

Reinhardt squared off with Dawson. "You've got your suspect. This joint task force is closed."

"Yeah, I've got a suspect, all right." She squared her shoulders and stared him down. "A *suspect* who had no motive to kill Meghan Kendrick."

"From what I heard, it was a lover's quarrel. Or at least, that was the headline in today's *San Francisco Chronicle*."

Dawson jutted her chin out. "You know that's bullshit. Ortega's gay. He had no romantic interest in Kendrick. But then, you already know that. You went out of your way to discredit him with that ridiculous personnel file. Were you so worried about your flimsy evidence that you also had to make him out to be a freak?"

"I'm surprised you never heard of the Leathermen," Reinhardt said, taunting her. "They're a pretty violent off-shoot of the BDSM sub-culture. I guess you just never came across them in your investigation of John Monroe."

"You *know* I did." The hairs on her neck bristled at the very thought of the serial killer. "But just because a man gets dressed up in a leather biker outfit for Halloween, it doesn't make him a Leatherman."

"Perception is reality," he responded, savagely.

Dawson acted as if agreeing with him, even though they shared absolutely no point of agreement. "You should have told us that the First Man was having an affair with Meghan Kendrick."

"I don't know anything of the sort," Reinhardt said, visibly annoyed. "I suppose Ortega told you that Bill Harrison was involved with her."

"Yeah, he did."

"And you believed him?"

"Why not? He has no reason to lie."

Harlan Reinhardt hesitated a moment. "Are you aware that Carlos Ortega flunked his last couple of mandatory blood tests? The toxicology screen found cocaine in his system."

"That still doesn't make him a killer."

"But don't you think it's rather strange that we found evidence of cocaine on Meghan Kendrick's body, even though she wasn't using?"

Her features hardened. "You're just trying to muddy the waters, Reinhardt. Who are you really protecting? One of your boys? Or is it someone else who was aboard Air Force One?"

"It's always such a pleasure to talk with you, Inspector Dawson," he said, signaling his agents. "You have such a wonderfully vivid imagination."

Kate Dawson was full of anger and hostility, of incredulity and doubt, as she looked at the Secret Service chief. She managed to keep the rage out of her voice, but not the sense of mistrust. That was interwoven in every word she spoke.

"I'm going to find Agent Jones," she said calmly, but directly, "and I'm going to get to the bottom of this, one way or the other. I really do hope that you're involved, because I'm going to enjoy bringing your ass down."

"Good luck, Inspector," he snarled, following his men back into the restaurant.

Dawson addressed her partner, her eyes flashing. "C'mon, Matt, let's get the fuck out of here."

"I'm with you, boss." He was right behind her.

After sitting in traffic for more than hour, with her partner talking non-stop about their afternoon showdown with the President and the Secret Service, Dawson was relieved to drop Balardi at his sister's house in Noe Valley. She turned on the radio before tuning in a station that was playing lite jazz. Kate then eased back in her bucket seat and let the music carry her all the way home. She was feeling pretty good when she pulled into a parking spot next to Lenny's late-model, two-door Mini Cooper, whose rear hatch was up. It looked like her wayward friend was packing for a trip. She thought a trip was exactly what he needed to put some distance between him and his ex-girlfriend. She waved at him and he stopped loading his car. Dressed in his Obi Wan Kenobi costume from *Star Wars*, which was in desperate need of an iron, he appeared to be upbeat, happy.

"Looks like you're going on a trip," she observed, pointing to the boxes and bags he had loaded into his small car. "I approve. I think a trip would do you a world of good right now."

"Sorry to disappoint you, Kate, but I'm not taking a trip. I've got a Rebel Legion meeting tonight."

"Okay, that sounds like fun. But just remember what I told you, stay away from Rebecca, or you're going to end up back in the slammer."

Lenny Provolone grimaced, as if a sharp pain suddenly erupted in his stomach. "That may be a little hard to do, tonight."

"You didn't make her a member of your club, did you?"

"Not really. She just started showing up at meetings and some of our events. I didn't have the heart to tell her it was just cosplay that my buddies and I did. So, in time, she became an unofficial member."

"You know you can't go to that meeting tonight."

"Why not? It's my club. She doesn't even have a *Star Wars* costume. Why should I be the one to give it up?"

Kate Dawson glowered. She couldn't understand why someone as intelligent as her friend was also so dense. She was determined to reason with him. "Lenny, you've been served with a legal document that orders you to stay away from Rebecca and not to have any contact with her. If you go to that meeting tonight, and she's there, you will be in violation of the protective order. You will be arrested *and* you will go to jail."

"But that's not fair," he retorted, kicking a stone off the lot.

"That's the law."

"She's just doing this to spite me!"

"Lenny, what happened?" Kate asked, lending him what amounted to a caring and compassionate ear. "I thought you had found true love."

Provolone swallowed hard, feeling a different kind of pain. "I thought so, too," he said, all choked up. "But that's the problem. The only women who are interested in me are the mentally insane. The normal ones take one look at me, then run away screaming into the night."

"I did warn you that any woman who crawls into a strange man's bed can't be too tightly wrapped."

"Maybe, you were right," he admitted.

Kate patted him on the back. "Let's face it. I don't know too many sane women who would put a disemboweled skunk on their ex-boyfriend's front porch."

"Yeah, that was pretty extreme."

"She was just too young for you, my friend."

"Rebecca once said something about age," Lenny recalled, a faraway look on his face. "We were sitting in bed, talking, and she said that age was experience. She liked the fact that I was older and had experience."

"Lenny, you are old enough to be her father," Kate chastised him, noting the sixteen-year difference in their ages, "and I really wouldn't keep going on about age and experience. You've got the emotional maturity of a sex-obsessed adolescent, and I'm being very generous here."

Provolone was silent for a moment. "I guess you've got me pegged," he said softly. "Why don't you just call me a pathetic loser? That's what I am, after all. A pathetic loser."

She put out her hand to touch him, to offer him some reassurance if she could, but he refused to be comforted. He liked feeling sorry for himself. He brushed Dawson away and wrapped himself in his Obi Wan cloak, shivering.

"Lenny . . ."

"What's he like?" he asked, eyes to the ground.

"Who?"

"John Prescott. Your boyfriend."

"He's a really decent man, very kind and considerate, and has an enormous heart. He always goes the extra mile to see that I'm happy and to show me that I am well loved. I guess I don't always show him what he truly means to me—and that's a fault I'm always struggling to overcome—but I just cannot imagine what my life would be like without him."

"I met him once on the stairs."

"What?"

"Yeah, I was coming back from Rebecca's place. Early. She had gotten the flu and ruined all our plans for a night out," Lenny said, recalling the details as if they had happened the day before when, in fact, months had passed. "He was on his way out to the store. You were down with the same flu that Rebecca had, and he had gone out to buy you cough medicine and fill your prescription."

"Yeah, I remember that night. It was really cold outside and I didn't want him to go out."

"Well, he and I talked only briefly, but then I watched out my front window for him to return. I suppose I was going to offer to make you some soup or something silly like that," he continued. "But then he returned from the store with a big bouquet of roses, soup from the Bayside Deli, your cough medicine and prescription. He looked so happy to run that errand for you that he radiated warmth and tenderness. I could feel it right through my window."

"Yeah, John is truly an amazing man."

Lenny had a pained look on his face. "I was angry that Rebecca had gotten sick and ruined our plans, and here was your boyfriend thrilled that he could give something of himself to make you feel better."

Dawson reached out for Lenny again, and this time, he didn't brush her away. She rested her arms on his shoulders and looked directly into his eyes. "What happened between you and Rebecca?"

"It's a long story," he said, with a deep sigh.

"Suppose you give me the Reader's Digest Condensed Version. It's late and I have had a long day."

Lenny bobbed his head. "About a month ago, I decided to attend this year's Chiller Theatre and asked Rebecca if she wanted to go with me."

"What's Chiller Theatre?" Kate asked. "It sounds truly bizarre."

"Chiller Theatre was a late-night horror movie program that ran on Saturday nights. Its host Zacherley would run old "B" movies, like *The Night of the Living Dead* or *Attack of the Killer Shrews*, and then interview the actors and actresses who made them," he explained. "When the program finally ended after thirty years, a group of fans got together to honor the host and invited all sorts of celebrities from the world of horror and science fiction to a convention, called Chiller Theatre. The first one was so popular that they've been running them ever since."

"Are you kidding me? It's no wonder why Rebecca is so scared. Zombies and killer shrews. That would give me nightmares, too."

"You've got the wrong idea. Famous people from the movie industry show up and discuss their work and sign autographs."

"Whatever."

"So, when I told her what I had planned, she begged to come

along with me," Lenny said, trying to get back on track with his story. "She said that she had an Elvira costume and wanted to wear it at the convention. I told her that it was likely Cassandra Peterson would be there, signing autographs."

"Who?"

"The actress who plays Elvira on television."

"Okay, whatever you say, Lenny."

Provolone put his hands on his hips and shot her a disapproving look. "A lot of actresses from horror and sci-fi movies attend the convention. They set up dealer tables and sell their autographs."

"Actresses?"

"Yeah, you know, women like Brinke Stevens, Michelle Bauer, Angie Everhart, Sarah Butler, Heather Langenkamp . . ."

"I've never heard of any of them," she said, shaking her head.

"So, I picked up Rebecca at her apartment and, while we were driving downtown to the convention, I stopped into a convenience store and bought a bouquet of red roses."

"She must have been thrilled," Kate commented, putting her hands together and looking wistful.

"The roses weren't for Rebecca," he said abruptly. "I let her carry them, but I bought the roses to give one out to each of my favorite actresses. I figured they would think I was a classy guy when I handed them a rose."

"So, let me guess, she got pissed off and you had this big blow-up."

"No, that's not what happened. Do you want to tell this story or would you like me to finish?"

Dawson glimpsed at her watch. "I'm going to give you another two minutes to finish your story, then I'm going to bed."

"Well, you're partially right. She did get mad at me, but instead of expressing her anger, she got quiet and gave me the silent treatment," he revealed, pursing his lips into a pout. "That's one thing that I really hate: passive-aggressive behavior. The more time I spent hanging out with Brinke or Michelle or Sarah, the quieter she got. She wouldn't even put on her costume because she said she felt uncomfortable."

"I can't say that I blame her. I would have been upset, too."

"At the end of the day, I drove her back home and she slammed the door on me, getting out of my car. Left, without giving me a goodbye kiss or thanking me for taking her to Chiller Theatre."

"You know, I'm really not surprised," Kate groaned.

Lenny shot her a sideways glance. "It wasn't my fault that she didn't have a good time at the convention."

Dawson was astounded; jaw dropped.

"When she wouldn't return any of my calls or emails, I decided to go over to her apartment. At first, she didn't answer the door bell or my knocks, so I had to start pounding on the door. She finally opened it, long enough to tell me she never wanted to see me again, and then slammed the door in my face."

"Understandable."

Provolone smirked. "God, who'd have thought that a nice guy like me would be awakened in the middle of the night by police pounding on my door with a warrant to collect any firearms I might have and a protective court order, restraining me from talking to my girlfriend. The world has gone mad."

"It's all for the best, Lenny. You both need time to decompress."

"I'm telling you that I could resolve this whole misunderstanding with a simple conversation," he said, with determination.

"When she's ready, maybe you'll have that chance."

"Why is it her choice? Why can't I just go up to her at the meeting and talk to her about this?"

"Well, you have to make your own decisions," she said,

turning towards the stairs. "You're an adult and you have to start taking responsibility for your actions. But if you go to that meeting tonight and get arrested, do not call me to bail you out again. I simply won't come."

Lenny stood silently on the parking lot and watched her walk away.

Kate trudged up the steps to the third floor and, in the corridor outside her apartment, she noticed that her door was ajar. She reached under the left arm of her jacket and pulled out her Beretta, clearing the empty chamber. With caution, she approached the partially-open door and pushed it open all the way. Her small, studio apartment had been ransacked. Furniture had been tipped over, her mattress flipped off the box springs, drawers turned out, and personal belongings dumped into a pile in the middle of the floor. Someone had been looking for something and she had a pretty good idea what that was.

She reached for her cell phone and dialed 9-1-1. "This is Inspector Dawson," she spoke into the receiver. "My apartment's been tossed. Please send a forensics team to 3561, Bayside Village Apartments . . . Thank you."

Within the hour, Dawson's apartment had been turned into one of the familiar crime-scene carnivals that were so much a part of her daily existence. She just never thought it would hit so close to home . . . again. Visions, unwelcome memories of the night her daughter was killed with Kate's own service pistol flashed before her eyes.

Members of the forensics team were picking over the main room, searching and probing through her personal things for some clue that would help them establish motive or the identity of the perpetrator. Some of the CSI boys had lent them a hand and were boxing up or bagging damaged items or those too far gone to use again.

Ritchie, the official police photographer, snapped off pictures of the small, studio apartment, but they weren't exactly the kind of photos that would find their way into a memory book. Two uniformed policemen just stood around talking, taking in the sights, while others were out canvassing her neighbors for any information about the break-in.

Clark, Jawara, and Lieutenant Roberts were milling around the front door of the apartment, waiting for Dawson to get off her cell phone. None of the men there had to be told she was talking with her boyfriend, John. The fact that she was involved in a long-distance relationship with a man from the Justice Department was far from being a secret at police headquarters. Often it had become the punch line of a joke or the subject of gossip. Each of them was a bit annoyed, perhaps a little jealous, that she had found someone so devoted to her happiness that the individual relationships they had with her had somehow changed.

"I'll talk to you later, honey," Kate said, bringing her conversation to a close. She pushed the off button on her cell phone and turned back to her co-workers. "I'm really sorry about that. He's very worried about me."

Lieutenant Roberts stated, "That's understandable. So, let's go back over this again, from the top."

"Like I already told you, I dropped Balardi off at his sister's house and drove back here," she explained. "I ran into my neighbor in the parking lot. We talked for a couple of minutes, then I came up here and found my apartment had been tossed. There's really not much more to say."

"Was the door open?" Clark asked, taking notes.

"Yeah, but not really open. More ajar."

"Did you notice any cars in the parking lot that you didn't recognize? Any suspicious characters walking around?" Clark followed up with two more questions.

"No more than usual."

"Were you followed?" Jawara asked.

Dawson scrunched her eyebrows in thought. "No, I don't think so. But honestly, I really wasn't paying that much attention. It had been a long day. The only thing that was on my mind was getting a bite to eat and going to bed early."

"Can you think of anyone who's got it in for you?" Clark asked.

For a moment, Dawson stared at Lieutenant James Roberts, the head of the Homicide Bureau, like he had three heads. She had never really liked her boss and had spent the two years since Frank Miller's death clashing with him over departmental procedures in much the same way her late partner had before her. The Lieutenant had no imagination. He was a slave to the routine of the job and had never bothered to make any effort to learn new techniques of sound investigative work. He was the very model of a pragmatist, a person with all four feet on the ground.

Her eyes never left Roberts' face. "No, but then there may be a handful of religious cultists who are still pissed off that I stopped their plans to trigger World War III. Otherwise, I really can't think of anyone else that I've made enemies with."

Clark and Jawara snickered. Somehow her last big case didn't sound as dramatic as Kate made it out to be.

The Lieutenant ignored them, his gaze fixed on Dawson. "Do you have any idea what they were looking for?" Roberts asked, the big, hulking man towering over her.

"No, sir," she lied.

"No idea at all?" he asked again to make sure she heard him right.

"Take a look around for yourself, sir," Dawson said, like the hostess on a popular game show.

Roberts betrayed none of his suspicion; his face a mask. He was silent for a few seconds, standing in the center of her apartment, examining the bare walls, the few pieces of furniture, the absence of personal touches that often characterized one home from the next. The apartment was as cold and impersonal as any he had seen, including his own.

"My furniture is second-hand. My dishes and stemware are hand-me-downs. I have no jewelry or electronic equipment. My television is used. My clothes have fake labels," she added, pointing several specific items out to him.

He stood there, silently observing.

"What do I have that anyone would want?"

"You should add a couple of potted plants. Maybe a few pictures. That might spruce the place up a bit," he said at last.

Stunned, Dawson asked, "You think that would help?"

"I've never seen a more depressing home. I don't know how you can possibly live here. Maybe, if you gave up the Jack Daniel's, you'd have a few bucks to buy a decent table and chairs."

"I've been cutting back on the booze, sir."

Roberts shot her one of his patented steely looks. "I know you're not telling me the truth. I can always see it in your eyes, even when they're bloodshot. So, don't treat me like some kind of fool."

"I'm not trying to fool anybody. I really *have* been drinking less."

"Good for you! Let's break out the tambourines and have a couple of drinks to your new-found sobriety," he retorted, cruelly.

Dawson folded her arms across her chest and looked down, tapping her foot.

"I don't know what you're hiding," Roberts said, as he reached up to adjust the small, horned-rim glasses on the end of his nose, as if to bring the microscopic image of his detective into focus. "But I know you're hiding something, and I'm going to get to the bottom of it."

"I'm not hiding anything, sir."

"Okay, if that's how you want to play it." The Lieutenant started toward the door, barked out several orders to members of the forensics team and the CSI boys, and summoned the uniformed cops with a wave of his hand. Then to Clark and Jawara, he said, "Pack it up. We're finished here."

"Leaving so soon?"

"Things to do, Kate," Jawara said.

"We'll see you in morning," Clark added, patting her on the shoulder.

Dawson opened the door for her boss and co-workers, her eyes following them down the stairs. When the last two members of the forensics team were out the door, she leaned on the railing, and waved at them. "Thanks, guys," she said warmly.

"No problem, Inspector," one of them yelled back.

"Sorry about the mess," a second one commented, indicating the dusting powder on the door and door knob.

At the bottom of the stairs, Clark and Jawara met Lenny Provolone entering the building. He was fully decked out in his Obi Wan Kenobi costume, carrying his newly-repaired light-saber. When they saw him, both men did a double take so exaggerated that it could have only been real.

"Wow, I never knew Obi Wan lived in Kate's building," Jawara said, breezing past him on the stairs.

"Great costume, man," Clark complimented sarcastically, "but I think you're a little early for trick-or-treating."

With his best Alec Guinness impression, Lenny merely replied, "May the Force be with you. Always."

Kate had been leaning over the railing, staring down the

steps, when the three men who were the closest friends in her life crossed paths for the first time. By the time her one friend had huffed and puffed his way up the three flights, she was waiting for him at the top. "I'm really glad you didn't go to your meeting tonight, Lenny."

"Thanks, Kate," he murmured, so sad and depressed, then continued walking to his apartment and closed the door behind him.

Dawson watched his door a moment, then turned in herself.

In the dark recesses of the corridor, outside her apartment, a shadow moved, with no apparent corporeal form attached.

Kate Dawson awoke with a start to the ringtone of her iPhone. She lunged for it and pressed the button to accept the call. She couldn't put a name to the voice on the other end of the telephone line immediately, but she knew that it would come to her just as soon as she was fully awake. Bleary-eyed, she listened to the woman speak, but the words that she heard did little to cut through the heavy fog that clouded her brain. She told Kate what had happened and where she was. She had even given her an address on Valencia in the Mission District. But within fifteen seconds of ending the call, Dawson's head hit the pillow and she was out cold.

Somewhere in her brain, she played the conversation through again and again, like a sound recording on a reel of tape. Each time Dawson played it through, she picked up on more details. The woman had complained about her office being ransacked and how she was hiding out in a bar. She said that she was afraid to go home; that she needed Kate to pick her up at the Valencia Street address. Rosa Romano was at the Lexington Club and she was in trouble.

A few moments passed before Dawson had the strength and awareness to haul herself upright, throw on some clothes, grab her gun, and get out the door.

The Lexington Club was a gay bar in the Mission District that catered specifically to lesbians and transgendered, even though it seemed to attract more twenty-somethings with their gritty tattoos, tank tops, and boy-cut hair. Straight men and women were certainly welcome, but they were warned to behave, as this was a formidable crowd that didn't put up with any bullshit. Billed as "your friendly neighborhood dyke bar," it was the genuine article with plenty of ambiance. The setting was bohemian fantasy, with vintage woodwork, church pews for benches, and blood red walls which showcased high quality art, plus a pool table and jukebox. The club was high-brow enough to have been featured in an episode of *The L-Word* television series, and yet still raunchy enough to sponsor thumb-wresting contests or host "Good-Girl/Bad-Girl" cocktail hours on Friday nights. For 365 days a year, including Thanksgiving and Christmas Eve, passersby on Valencia Street could hear music and laughter and billiard balls rushing down a pocket on the pool table in the "living room" of the club.

As Kate came through the front door and walked into the club proper, she got the "once over" from several girls sitting at the bar, nursing their drinks. She wasn't quite certain which lesbian type they made her out to be but assumed they had her pegged as "the starry-eyed new girl." She definitely wasn't "the plastic dyke," because she had wisely left her shiny combat boots, bandana, and bomber jacket at home, nor was she the "deceptively sexy faux Butch." While she could easily shotgun two beers at the same time or lift weights better than some of her peers, she didn't have the short hair or tattoos that tended to set them apart. She wasn't "the frat boy prototype" or "the under-ager" or "the lesbian who hated gay bars." That left only "the constantly-pegged-as-straight ultra femme," and she just couldn't see herself in six-inch heels, a skintight mini, a pound of makeup, and two feet of cleavage. She nestled up to the bar between two empty barstools and ordered a Jack Daniel's over ice.

Kate took a sip of her drink, then circled the room looking for Rosa. The air was heavy with the smell of smoke and sweat mingled with perfume. A sea of young, sexy girls on the floor danced to tunes coming from a jukebox, while several older women argued over a game of nine-ball at the pool table. Then, amid the crowd on the dance floor, she spotted a familiar face. Her friend was chicly decked out in a black leather skirt with a frilly blouse that was nearly open to the waist. Rosa wasn't wearing a bra, which showed off her voluptuous breasts.

She was dancing with another woman, her arms clasped around her partner's waist. When Romano saw Kate, standing off to the side with her drink, she leaned over and said something to the girl, who giggled and stripped her with her eyes. They stopped dancing. Arm in arm, they made their way off the dance floor, neatly threading their way through the other dancers.

Rosa Romano sauntered over to Dawson and gave her an exaggerated hug and kiss. Quickly she whispered, "I think I'm being watched. Just go with it and I'll try to explain it all to you later."

"Rosa, sweetheart, I've really missed you," she said, playing along.

Rosa smiled a plastic smile. "Kate, this is my new friend, Twylla," she said, introducing her young dance partner.

"Hi, Twylla. Nice to meet you," Dawson said.

"The pleasure is, like, all mine, Kate," she said, all bubbly. Fresh off the boat from the straight side, Twylla had absolutely no idea what she was doing. Though she had "experimented" with girls in college, she had always envisioned herself ending up with a guy. Now, she labored under the naïve delusion that dating women exclusively would make for deep, fulfilling relationships marked by partnership and mutual understanding. She had a lot to learn. "Are you here, like, to meet someone, or did you just stop in, you know, to have a drink?"

"A drink," Dawson said, holding up her glass.

"I was, like, at home, feeling very lonely, because, like, my boyfriend, you know, just left me. So, like, I didn't feel so good," Twylla explained, running the gamut of emotions with her short story. "I decided, like, to give up on boys, for now to see what it was like to be with, you know, another girl. So then, like, I met your friend, and she's just so awesome. I can't believe, like, I found someone already!"

"She is pretty awesome." Dawson winked and gave Rosa a come-hither look.

As the three of them walked over to an empty table, Rosa pulled her new friend aside, saying, "Girlfriend, I need to have a few private words with Kate. Do you mind terribly if I leave you for a couple minutes? I won't be long. We'll just go powder our noses and come right back."

"I could, like, come with you," the young woman said with a frown, snuggling up to Rosa in a possessive way.

Kate suggested, motioning to the booth with her tumbler, "Why don't you sit down and save the table for us?"

"I really need to speak with her alone," Rosa said, firmly, rubbing her arm.

Twylla pouted, blonde hair swinging to the side. "Okay, sugar. Just don't, like, keep me waiting long. Your baby misses you already, you know."

Rosa kissed her friend sweetly, then took Dawson's hand. As

they walked, she swung it playfully back and forth, and turned briefly to throw a kiss over her shoulder at Twylla. They were headed for the ladies' room, though at the Lexington Club the term "ladies' room" was not as exclusive as Kate might imagine. Transgendered women who were born male, but had decided to become women through various procedures, preferred to use the ladies' room even though they may be in the earlier stages of their transition. Most of them used the stalls rather than pee standing at a urinal in the men's room.

They walked into the dark and shadowy room, the air heavy with the smell of tobacco smoke and weed. Dawson could also make out the odor of crack cocaine being freebased somewhere in one of the stalls. There were several women clustered around the mirror putting on makeup, while a couple of others sat up on the counter with the heads of their kneeling partners between their thighs. Rosa rapped on the doors of several stalls and, when she found one unoccupied, she swung it open and the two of them slipped inside.

"What the hell is going on?" Dawson demanded, in a loud whisper.

That's when Rosa burst into tears, whispering in between sobs, "They're trying to kill me, Kate!" Her eyes were like saucers and she was shaking all over. "I know their secret and now they want to kill me."

Kate gathered her friend tightly into her arms. She held her for a couple of minutes before finally saying, "Rosa, I can't help you unless you tell me what's going on."

"I found the microfilm," she said between sniffles and shedding tears.

"What microfilm?" Dawson asked, incredulous, trying not to be loud.

"Inside the lipstick container." She looked Kate in the eye.

Kate was puzzled. "Are we talking about Meghan Kendrick's lipstick container? I thought it just contained lipstick."

"No, it has a secret compartment, a place for her to carry microfilm without drawing attention to the fact that she has it."

"Give it to me."

"After I dusted it for prints and scraped a DNA sample from the lipstick itself, I decided to break down the mechanism into its various parts," Romano explained, as she began sobering up. She wiped her face with a lace handkerchief from her purse, then handed Dawson the lipstick container. "A special feature of Meghan's brand of lipstick is a shifting mechanism, which forces two threaded tubular elements to telescopically shift the lipstick to its fullest extent with only two turns of the tubular elements in relation to each other."

"You're talking about the round knob at the bottom of the case that you turn to raise or lower the lipstick?" she asked, mimicking the motion with her fingers.

"That's a crude layman's explanation, but yes," she continued, as she wiped away the last of her tears. "When I tried to adjust the cylindrical lower portion of the case to retract the lipstick, it would only go so far and stop. That's when I realized there must be something stuck inside the case."

"The microfilm?" Dawson asked, rhetorically.

"Yes, exactly."

"But why microfilm? That's so old-school. When I think of microfilm, I think of those old spy novels that you could buy for a dime at the local pharmacy. Why not a microdot? Or, better still, a microchip?"

Rosa Romano put it in plain words. "Microfilm is still the safest way to store important documents. It wouldn't be affected by the electromagnetic pulse of an atomic blast or a cyber-attack that would effectively destroy information stored electronically. Microfilm is analog technology, so no manner how things change in the next five hundred years, you'll always be able to scan microfilm into the very latest digital systems, no matter how advanced or primitive they may be."

"I think I understand. Have you had a chance to look at what's on the microfilm?"

"Just briefly. From what I saw, it contains the missing MJ-12 documents. The documents that established Operation Majestic-12 in 1947 under the special classified presidential orders of Harry Truman. The microfilm even has a photographic copy of the letter Truman wrote to Secretary of Defense James Forrestal on September 24, 1947, with Truman's own signature."

"What's so important? Why was she carrying it?" Dawson was attempting to listen to both Rosa and out for snoopers; one ear to the crack in the door and the other for the information.

"They may be the most important and dangerous documents in the entire world. The information on the microfilm dates back to the 1950s, the Cold War, the Military-Industrial Complex, Roswell—" Romano started to say, but was interrupted by a rap at the stall door.

"Hey, lover, are you like almost done in there?" Twylla asked, her voice whinny, almost demanding. She sounded like she was still a kid. A teenager—a hot teenager, at that—who was getting her thrills early in life.

"I'll be out in a minute, sweetheart," Rosa lied, looking desperately towards Kate.

"Okay, but hurry up, will ya? I'm kinda getting lonely."

Kate waited for Twylla to leave, then said, "We've got to get you out of here right now."

Romano put her face in her hands. The self-confidence, the calm assurance and composure that had so defined the

Assistant Medical Examiner had vanished, replaced by doubt and fear. Composing herself, she sniffled and wiped her face, but her hair was a still a tangled mess, her cheeks drawn and hollow, and her face was tearstained. "There's nowhere to run. Secret Service agents are everywhere. I just barely made it out of there alive. You know, I walked in on them ransacking my office and I've been looking over my shoulder ever since. I've changed my clothes twice. I even parked my car at a BART station on the other side of town."

She raked her fingernails through her tousled hair, shaking her head slowly. "I shouldn't have agreed to run those tests on your evidence. I should have turned it over to Brogan. What the fuck was I thinking? I'm going to end up dead and no one's going to weep for me at my funeral. God, I'm so stupid. Just so stupid!"

Kate didn't reply right away. "I'm sorry I got you involved, Rosa, but we're going to figure a way to get out of this."

"Kate, I'm sure they're waiting for us in front of the club."

"Then we'll have to go out the back."

Dawson pushed open the stall door, took Romano by the arm, and steered her toward the restroom window. The other women in the ladies' room were so occupied with themselves or their partners that they didn't notice when Dawson forced open the painted-over latch and pushed the window out. Using the wash basin and an old-style radiator, they climbed out on the window ledge and jumped to the alley below.

Falling flat on her butt in the mud, Romano shot her friend a sidelong glance, as if to ask *What next?* but thought better of it.

Dawson pulled Rosa to her feet and brushed off the mud from her leather skirt. Signaling forward with her head, the two hurried to the end of the alleyway. Even the wildest clubs in the Mission District begin to slow down in the hour just before midnight, especially on a work night. The street was relatively empty of cops and suits making their way home after a late dinner, their places taken by hookers plying their trade, a few street cleaners, and some homeless men looking for a place to crash for the night. The sidewalks were also silent except for the occasional couple or individual leaving a club.

They blended in with the hookers long enough to get to Dawson's car, and with the Secret Service likely focused on the front of the Lexington Club, they slipped away into the night as the fog rolled over the city.

At the InterContinental Hotel, located between Fifth and Howard streets, Harlan Reinhardt walked alone down the corridor to his room. A white handkerchief was perpetually in his hand as he sweated profusely. Approaching the door to his room, he was instantly surrounded by several, very large men in black suits. He did not react with fear or apprehension; in fact, he didn't react at all. He was not the least surprised to see any one of them.

"She wants you," the first agent said.

"Is that so?" Reinhardt spat.

"She demands an update," the second one added.

"You can tell her that I've got everything under control."

"Perhaps you'd better come with us and tell her yourself, Mister Reinhardt," the first suggested.

Reinhardt coughed into his handkerchief. "This recycled air is bad for my asthma."

"Sir?" the second asked.

Reinhardt coughed again. "The chill always gives me a cold."

"We must not keep her waiting," the first said rather adamantly.

Reinhardt looked from the first man to the second, upset they were bothering him at all. "Do you have any idea how late it is?"

"No, sir," first one then the other said.

"It's after midnight. I am not going to knock on the door to the First Family's suite this late at night unless there's a real emergency," he coughed. "I'll have a word with her in the morning."

"Sir, she's not going to like that," the first interjected.

"Now, that's not your problem, is it?"

Reinhardt forced his way through the huddle of very large men in dark suits. He unlocked the door to his room, entered, and closed it behind him.

CHAPTER SIX

Kate Dawson slowed as they approached the Bayside Marketplace and turned into the large, nearly empty parking lot. The festival marketplace served Bayside Village Apartments as well as the whole South Beach area. Built around the original Bayside Market, which was a small twenty-four-hour grocery/deli that specialized in vegan and organic foods, the marketplace had expanded to include vendors selling fresh fruit and vegetables, a few trendy outdoor restaurants and bars, several souvenir shops for tourists, and live entertainment at the Bayside Marina stage. AT&T Park, which was at the south end of the marketplace, was the home field of the San Francisco Giants, and, off-season, played host to concerts and other sporting events. At that hour of the night, only a couple of bars and the Market were still open.

"Any special requests for breakfast?" Kate asked, pulling into a parking spot. "I've already got eggs and whole wheat bread, and I can offer you instant coffee or tea, but if you're going to want pancakes or waffles in the morning, you'd better tell me now."

Rosa Romano shook her head no.

"Well, I'm going to pick up some milk, orange juice, and bacon." She reached into the glove compartment and pulled out the lanyard with her police badge. "They offer a twenty-percent discount to police officers, so I always try to wear my badge when I go in the store."

"Are you sure I'm not going to be a bother?" Romano asked.

"Hell, no. I'll enjoy the company. But if you start to snore, I'm goin' to put you out on the couch."

Romano asked, "I don't suppose you could pick up a small, twelve-ounce cup of Dannon yogurt? Any flavor will do."

Kate looked fondly at her friend. She had been through the gristmill that night with everything that had happened. In fact, they both had. "Sure, whatever you want. In fact, why don't we live it up a little? I'll splurge for a bottle of Jack Daniel's."

"Now you're talking, Kate!"

"Hey, could I borrow a cigarette?" she asked, opening the driver's side door.

"I didn't know you smoked." Romano was truly taken aback.

"I did before I got married. I gave it up when I found out I was pregnant with my daughter. I just have a real craving for one tonight to sort of settle my nerves."

She stared back at her with a stunned look on her face.

"C'mon now, Rosa. You're not my fuckin' confessor. Just give me the damn cigarette."

Romano passed her the pack of cigarettes and the lighter. She took one out and put it in her mouth, cradled the lighter in her hands, striking it several times, and puffed until the cigarette caught fire. Exhaling, she then reached back into the glove compartment and handed Rosa a snub-nosed .38 caliber revolver.

"What's this for, Dawson?"

"Think of it as comfort until I get back, ok?"

Dawson walked towards the twenty-four-hour market. She looked terrible. Clothes torn and dirty, arms and face covered in mud, she might have been mistaken for the walking dead. Yuppie couples, who had been out for a drink, took one look at her and turned the other way.

She paused for an instant, to stop and wave at Rosa, but as she started to turn, she noticed a car driving without any headlights through the parking lot, starting to pick up speed. No sooner had she seen the car, the headlights clicked on. Two pinpoints of light, moving, pointed directly at her.

Kate threw away the cigarette, spun around into a crouch, drew her gun, and held it out in front of her in a modified combat stance. The headlights blinded her, as the car came barreling out of the darkness, bearing down on Dawson at fifty miles an hour. She fired several times. The windshield splintered but didn't shatter as the car kept coming at her. Dawson fired again, then sprinted backwards, against the shops along the Marketplace.

The driver leaned out of the car window with a small handgun and triggered three blasts at Dawson. The first two blasts blew out chunks of the storefront. The third one hit Dawson right in the chest, inches above her heart. The impact threw her backward through the store window. As the glass shattered all around her, she fell through the front display of newspapers and potato chips, and hit the floor in a dead heap.

The late model sedan shrieked off into the night, laying rubber, as Romano scrambled out of Kate's car and returned fire. The echo of gunfire slowly faded away as Romano emptied her six shots and stared off into the distance, watching the red lights vanish.

Several heartbeats later, Rosa Romano turned back to storefront and saw Dawson crumpled in a pool of broken glass. Romano charged to her and threw herself down beside

Dawson's unmoving body. She ripped open her Versace jacket, expecting to find blood, but Dawson's police badge had miraculously taken the brunt of the assassin's bullet.

Kate opened her eyes.

"I'd say you did better than twenty-percent, Kate," she said, unable to contain her happiness.

"Yeah, I guess that'll teach me not to smoke," she joked, feeling the extreme pain in her chest as if she had been struck by a high-speed locomotive. *I'm going to have some kind 'a bruising,* she thought, rubbing herself.

Rosa helped Dawson climb to her feet, gathering her friend tightly in her embrace. "I thought I had lost you, Kate!" she screamed, weeping.

They held each other for a few moments, then exited the convenience store, which was now drawing a crowd.

"Romano, quit looking so damned scared. That bullet was meant for me, not you. They're going to have to try a lot harder than that to kill me. And trust me, they're not gonna get another chance."

"An inch higher, and you would be laying there dead."

Dawson threw off Romano's concern. "Fuck that! You know as well as I do they can't kill someone like me unless they're using silver bullets."

"They weren't using silver bullets, but they were using a caliber I've never seen before," she replied, producing the bullet. "I'd be very interested in knowing what kind of gun fired *that.*"

"I want to bury those assholes," Dawson said, pissed off, holding her chest. "Oh, fuck, that hurts!"

"You just got shot, girlfriend."

"Exactly."

"What do you mean, 'exactly'?"

"It gives us the edge, Romano," she said, wickedly. "I'm a corpse, and as long as we keep this quiet, between the two of us, they're going to be reporting back to Reinhardt that I was shot dead tonight."

"Whatever you say, Kate. Whatever you say."

They heard sirens in the distance.

Within the hour, the police had made quick work of the crime scene. Rosa Romano met privately with the lead investigator and, together, they came up with a plausible explanation for the shooting and its outcome. Gang-related violence rarely rated a full-scale investigation, and on a night when there were plenty of other drive-by shootings, one more was not likely to make a ripple.

Romano soon found herself driving to Bayside Village Apartments in Dawson's BMW, with Kate hiding under a blanket in the back seat. As she came upon the turn into the apartment complex, she said, "You know, I'm afraid we forgot to pick up some milk and orange juice for you."

"And bacon," Dawson reminded her.

"Do you want me to stop by a 7-11 to see what I can find?"

Kate was silent for a moment, then said, "No, that's okay. I'll just raid my neighbor's refrigerator in the morning."

"Is he single?" Romano asked, with her eyebrows raised.

"Yeah, as a matter of fact he is," she replied, wheels turning. "He's also a scientist. Works for Northrop-Grumman in the aerospace industry."

"An egghead, huh?" Rosa queried. "And why haven't you introduced this eligible man to me before? He's not gay, is he?"

"No, he's not gay. He just prefers to date younger women."

Romano smiled, as she pulled into a parking spot near Kate's building. "Listen, girlfriend, one night with Rosa Romano," pointing to herself with pride, "and he'll never even think about another woman."

Rosa waited in the car for a couple of minutes, observing the area, then climbed out and stood next to the car, listening, scanning the shadows, until she was sure they were alone. Satisfied, she hustled Dawson out of the back seat and up the steps.

On the second landing, Kate asked, "How do you feel about *Star Wars*?"

"I love it. I can still remember the first time that I saw it at the local theater, when that Rebel ship flies by overhead, followed by that larger Imperial Star Destroyer that fills the screen. I was hooked, right then and there. Of course, I prefer *The Empire Strikes Back*, which has more of the emotional core of the story with Darth Vader revealing himself to his son Luke, and Han and Leia falling in love. The whole series is magnificent. Why do you ask?"

"My single friend is really involved in the sci-fi conventions," Dawson explained. "He wears a costume from the movie and play-acts with some of his friends. In fact, the first time I ever met him, he was wearing a lightsaber on his belt."

"He sounds a little eccentric, but fun."

"Rosa, you may be just what Lenny needs."

"Lenny? That's his name? He sounds Italian."

"Maybe, I don't know. I never really asked him."

"My parents would certainly be thrilled if I brought home a fellow *paisan*," she said, then quickly corrected herself. "To tell you the truth, they'd be thrilled if I brought home a man who was still living and breathing."

"What about Twylla?"

Rosa Romano shivered. It was hard to tell if it was from the cold night air or the memory of her young dance partner. "I . . . I don't know why I was attracted to her. Maybe it was her youth and vitality, or maybe, like her, I was just feeling lonely. I don't really remember, but at least it sold my cover story."

"That it did, Rosa. That it did." Dawson unlocked the door to her apartment and they retired for the night.

Moments later, the Shadow Man passed by her door, disappearing into the dark recesses of the corridor, where he watched and waited.

In the still, dark, deep of the night, Kate Dawson awoke with a start, swung to the side of the bed and let her legs dangle a moment as she sat, panting, head down, exhausted, her chest throbbing. It hurt to breathe. The raw reality of having been shot jolting her psyche.

Sleeping about two hours, she attributed the respite to her physical and mental exhaustion. Now awake, she couldn't sleep any longer. She looked around and listened. Light from the parking lot glinted through her window and, in turn, reflected on the mirror on her vanity table. Her apartment was silent like a tomb. The only real sound was coming from Rosa Romano who was breathing through her mouth and occasionally snoring. Rosa was curled up like a cat on the left side of the bed, sound asleep. Dawson reached over and pulled the blanket up over her friend's shoulder. *At least* she *can sleep.* Kate pulled her shoulders back, wincing in pain.

The bright fluorescent light in the bathroom hit her squarely between the eyes, like a blow from a prize fighter in the ring. The image in the mirror was unrecognizable. Her face was pale and drawn, the flesh around her eyes dark and brittle like that of a two-day old corpse, and from the neck down she was bluish purple.

"Shit!" she said to her own reflection.

She turned on the cold tap and doused her face with the frosty water. At once her brain cleared. Drying off, she returned to her bedroom and removed her Beretta from her holster hanging at the head of the bed.

In the living room, just beyond the kitchen, Kate slumped in her favorite chair, with her gun in her lap. She had replaced the front door lock and installed deadbolts on the door and all the windows but was still on red alert. Light coming from the court-yard sliced through the slats of the blinds and, occasionally, she made out the shadow of someone walking to one of the other apartment buildings, but no distinct details. Not interested in watching any of the activity, she just wanted to sit there, quietly, and think.

A few hours before, someone tried to kill her, and damned well may have succeeded if she hadn't been wearing her badge. The massive contusion, covering most of her torso, hurt with every movement. She had a pretty good idea of who was respon-sible, and may have even been angry enough to seek some form of revenge if she wasn't so wrapped up in the details of her case. She counted them off on her fingers: *a dead reporter, an illicit affair, microfilm, and a secret that had been kept for seventy years. What did it all add up to?*

As the first rays of the sun crept over the Bay, she was still wrestling with her thoughts. Dawson could not shake the name "Bill Harrison" that kept buzzing through her mind, like a persistent fly on Grandma's shoofly pie cooling on the window sill.

She sat there listening as the early risers hurried to take their dogs for a walk or take a couple of laps around the Embarcadero before they had to go to work. In the distance, she imagined she could also hear the endless waves pummeling the breakers at the beach.

Dawson got up, and pulled on a pair of sweats, sneakers, and a sweatshirt. She scribbled out a note for Rosa, took her cell phone and gun, and closed the door quietly behind her as she headed out to the Embarcadero. She then followed the rocky path down to the beach, and sat in the sand.

"John, I need your help," she said, talking into her cell phone.

Several Secret Service agents in black suits stood vigil near the entrance of a meeting room on the fifth floor of the InterContinental Hotel. The two main corridors that led to the room had been cleared of all hotel guests and personnel, while the rear access hallway had a single man posted.

In a flurry of activity, Harlan Reinhardt exited the fifth-floor elevator and was escorted by several men down the corridor. The dirty, sweat encrusted hanky, forever lodged in his left hand, stood primed for the profuse onslaught of perspiration. He might have resembled a condemned man who was taking his last steps on the way to the gas chamber had it not been for the fact that he was always a step ahead. When he reached the meeting room, his escort released him and joined the others outside. He then walked through the door, completely of his own volition.

For the moment, Reinhardt was alone as the door closed behind him. The small meeting room was not unlike others that he had used in the past to conduct training or disciplinary workshops. There was a large boardroom table, a dozen chairs, a flat panel monitor, and a computer station. He reached for the pitcher of water, and poured himself a glass. Reinhardt then looked up at the air-conditioning duct with disdain. He had an aversion for recycled air. Not only was it toxic for his asthma, but the chill from air-conditioning caused him congestion and a tight chest.

Before he could take a sip, Helen Harrison entered the room through the rear door, flanked by two Secret Service agents. The first female President of the United States was an attractive woman in her early sixties, with medium-length blonde hair. She was stylishly dressed in a black Armani pants-suit accented by a single row of white cultured pearls strung around her neck. She slowly surveyed the room and the Secret Service chief with a cool eye. While she looked like she was out of place, it was hard to imagine where a sixty-three-year-old woman like herself would fit right in. Reinhardt could see that masking her emotions was little more than second nature to her, like breathing.

"Would you leave us, please?" she commanded her escort, and the two Secret Service agents quickly left the room.

"I told you that I had everything under control," Reinhardt said, finally.

"Let's hope so," her quiet voice roared in the small room. "We can't afford to make any mistakes. Both of our reputations are at stake here."

"You don't have to remind me of that. I've served three presidents. I know just how damaging breaches of security can be to the Oval Office," he explained. "In fact, I warned Bill Clinton not to say a word to anyone. I would have handled things much differently, and there never would have been a scandal."

"Yes, but this is my show and my operation," the President said firmly. "If anything goes wrong, it's my neck on the line, not yours."

"I told you I have everything under control. Nothing's going to go wrong."

"I wish I could believe that."

"Well, believe it!" he exclaimed, annoyed. "I've anticipated every possible scenario and made contingency plans for each."

"I expect no less," she said coldly. "You weren't exactly brought into this for your sparkling personality. You were brought in to handle things quietly, expeditiously, and without any problems from the local police."

"I know that."

President Harrison pointed her finger at him. "Well, from the looks of things, you haven't done a very good job. If the joint task force with the SFPD is closed and they have a suspect in custody, then I want to know why there's a police detective out there who's still asking questions."

"She won't be asking questions any longer," Reinhardt said, with a degree of finality. "I asked our friend to—"

"I don't want to know any details," she interrupted him. "The less I know, the better. It's called 'plausible deniability.'"

"Let's just say, her body's now on a slab in the morgue."

Reinhardt and the President exchanged knowing glances. Though they knew each other very well and had worked together for years, both knew there was no love lost between them.

"Madam President, for the sake of security, I don't expect to hear from you again until we're airborne for Andrews," he said firmly.

"It's always such a pleasure to talk with you, Harlan."

Helen Harrison turned to the rear door and disappeared into the hallway where her security detail was waiting. Reinhardt did not move for a few seconds, then he dug the semi-soaked rag from his left pants pocket and staunched the flow of fear beading from his forehead.

Fifty minutes later, when Kate Dawson returned to her apartment, her friend was moving back and forth in the kitchenette, an alcove just adjacent to the front door.

Rosa greeted her happily, "I hope you're hungry, girlfriend," she said, stopping for an instant in the arch of the kitchen, holding a spatula in hand. "I'm making you a real hardy breakfast . . . Hey, how are you feeling? In a lot of pain?" Her eyebrows came together in concern.

"I'll be alright. Bruised and sore as hell. Smells good. What is it?" she asked, removing her jacket, tossing it to the couch, and setting her Barretta on the table.

"An omelet with spinach, cheese, mushrooms, onions, and sliced tomatoes, crispy bacon, and toast."

"Yum! That sounds good, but where did you get the ingredients? I haven't had spinach or mushrooms in this house for months," she commented, sitting down at her small, circular dining room table.

Rosa Romano was silent for a moment, then came forward with a full breakfast plate. She set it down in front of Dawson, and pulled a napkin across her lap. "Your very charming neighbor, Lenny, stopped by to find out how you were doing and offered to help me with breakfast."

"He did?"

Rosa headed back into the kitchen. "I told him that I was very capable of making you breakfast on my own, but that I was short a few ingredients. Well, the darling man went back to his apartment and emptied out his cupboard and freezer for me. I think you'll find that you now have peanut butter and jelly, Oreo cookies, Capt'n Crunch cereal, frozen orange juice, a bag of raw onions, a can of mushrooms, and several packages of frozen spinach."

"Spinach?"

"Well, Popeye the Sailor, he isn't." Romano returned from the kitchen with a couple of glasses of orange juice, and placed one down in front of Dawson. "But he appears to be a very, very sweet man. I told him that I would repay the favor by cooking dinner for him one night this week."

"Rosa, you're really amazing! I just can't get over how you've been able to whip this breakfast up out of nothing."

"Thank you," she said, on the move. "But if you'd prefer cereal, I have a half-eaten box of Capt'n Crunch—"

Kate started to laugh, but put her hand to her chest. *That hurts.* "This is fine."

"Can I get you some coffee, or would you prefer a cup of tea? How about some Advil?"

Without waiting for an answer, Rosa Romano turned around and went back into the kitchen to assemble her breakfast. She scooped a second omelet off the griddle and placed it on the plate, added two pieces of toast on either side, grabbed her mug of freshly-brewed coffee from the Keurig, and headed back to the dining table.

Dawson finally said, "I think the orange juice will do for now."

Rosa sat down with her breakfast, laying a napkin in her lap. "You know, Kate, I've dated really handsome guys who'd stop and primp in every mirror they'd pass. I've dated low-life scum who'd borrow money from me to take me out. I've dated married guys, gay guys, guys that didn't know whether they were straight or gay. Maybe it's time for me to try out a nerd."

"Lenny is a sweetheart," Kate agreed with her.

"No arguments here." She pushed a stray hair behind her ear, with a twinkle in her eye.

"But I can tell you, from my own experience, he can also be a lot to handle."

"Show me a man who isn't." Romano bit into her toast.

Kate held her fork out. "Don't say I didn't warn you about Lenny."

"Girlfriend, you really are pretty clueless when it comes to men," she said, taking a bite of her omelet and swallowing it down with a gulp of coffee. "I'll tell you what a lot to handle is. Picking yourself up off the floor after your boyfriend's hit you again for the third time. That's a lot to handle. Waking up to find the last guy you took to bed has run off with all your cash and credit cards. That's a lot to handle. Finding out the guy you've been dating for three years has been sleeping around on you for three years. That's a lot to handle. Do I have to say anything more?"

"Now I know why I never liked any of the guys you've dated."

Romano didn't look at her. "Can you blame me for wanting to switch teams?"

"No, I guess I can't. Not really."

"Do you have any idea how many losers I've gone out with in the last five years? More than I can count," she added, gnawing on her toast. "Dealing with a guy who likes to dress up and play *Star Wars*. OMG! That's so charming and innocent. I didn't know they still made guys like that!"

"Lenny's had some serious ex-girlfriend issues lately."

"Well, we'll see . . ." Rosa was upbeat. "I only said I'd cook him dinner. If he wants desert, too, then it'll be all about how Lenny handles himself with a sophisticated woman like me."

"I think the real bet is on who cooks breakfast." Kate downed the last of her omelet and drank some orange juice. "And if it's anything like this delicious meal, someone's in for a real treat."

"I can guarantee you, I won't be serving Capt'n Crunch."

Their banter was cut short by the first few cords of "Layla."

"My phone!" Kate said in urgency, her eyes darting around the room until they fixed on the jacket she had worn for her morning stroll. She reached for one of the pockets and pulled the phone checking caller ID. "This is Kate Dawson . . . What-the-hell? . . . Okay, I'll be right there. Thank you."

"What's wrong? Who was that?" Romano asked, sensing a problem.

Dawson could not get over the turn of events. "Remember my suspect, Carlos Ortega? They just found his body in lock-up. Dead. Apparently, he died sometime during the night, but nobody knows anything about it."

"Oh, Kate!" Romano stood and put her arms around her friend. Kate winced. "Look, I'll drive you into work today. Just let me borrow a couple of things from your closet. Somehow, I don't think they'd appreciate me wearing the lace blouse or leather skirt I had on last night."

"Sure, take whatever you want." Kate pushed her away, suddenly overwhelmed with all that had happened.

Rosa took a few steps back, watching as Dawson buried her face in her hands, trembling. She held her, stroking her hair, like a mother calming her infant, very concerned.

"I'm sorry," Kate whispered, after a moment of silence. "I'm really sorry. I don't usually act like this."

Romano looked down at her, shaking her head slowly. "Just let it out, girlfriend. You've had a hell-of-a night and now a terrible shock."

"I want to get those bastards, Rosa," Dawson said, wiping the tears pooling in the corners of her eyes. "I want to get those bastards and make them pay!"

"So, what's your plan?"

"I've been doing a lot of thinking about this, and I've already talked with John this morning. I need to get to the First Man."

"Tell me, you're not going to sleep with him," Rosa said, with a half-smile, trying to lighten things up.

"No, but he's gonna wish it had been a social call."

Rosa Romano was silent for a long moment, then said, "Okay, then. Count me in."

At the Hall of Justice, Kate Dawson walked down several flights of stairs, and when she reached the police lock-up in the basement, she wasn't surprised to find a crime scene right in her own workplace.

Lieutenant Roberts, Clark, Jawara, Balardi, several policemen, and a couple of the guys from Internal Affairs were standing outside the cell where Carlos Ortega had been locked-up under the name "John Doe." Inside the cell, Doctor Brogan was kneeling beside the body, trying to determine the cause of death, while Ritchie snapped off shots of the crime scene. Most of them looked at Dawson like she was a ghost, and after her experience on the previous night, she was not too surprised why they would react to her sudden appearance with some fear and trepidation. The crowd of police officials around the cell parted as Kate approached, as if she was the angel of death come to claim her newest victim.

Dawson crouched over Ortega's body. From her perspective, there were no obvious signs of physical abuse or suicide, no evidence of bruising. It was apparent to her that they had made efforts to resuscitate. His chest was bare and the defibrillator was on the floor next to his cot. She wondered how a perfectly healthy man, like Carlos Ortega, could die in the police lock-up without anyone seeing anything.

She stood up slowly, searching for the duty officer; the same cop who had unlocked the door to Lenny's cell a couple of nights before. "Were you the officer who found him?"

"Yes, Inspector," he replied, respectively. "I noticed that he hadn't moved in a couple of hours. Also, his arm seemed to be hanging off the bunk in a very uncomfortable angle. So, when I listened at his cell and didn't hear him breathing, I immediately went in and checked for a pulse, then called for backup."

"How often do you make your rounds?"

"About every twenty minutes," the duty officer answered.

Dawson added the numbers in her head. "So, you're saying that you did six passes by his cell in two hours' time, and only just noticed in your last pass that he wasn't moving or breathing?"

"We don't look in their cells on every pass," he said, shifting his weight, under scrutiny. "In fact, during the night, when most of the inmates are asleep, we may only look in on them once or twice."

"Well, that's just great!"

"As you can see, Inspector, there's no evidence of a struggle. I saw no sign of injuries on his body other than the bruise on his forehead, and I know for a fact that he sustained that injury when he was taken into custody. If you ask me, he just croaked. Heart attack? Stroke? People die every day."

"Is it possible one of the other guards had it in for him?"

"No, ma'am," he said, without equivocation. "We're not the kind of people who would beat anybody up. At most, if someone is being rowdy, we'll do our best to ignore them, unless they pose a threat to other inmates. Often we'll just let them pound on the bars for an hour until they get tired."

The Medical Examiner removed what looked like a large meat thermometer from Carlos Ortega's abdomen. When it slipped out, it was covered in dark, body fluids that Brogan wiped off with a paper towel.

"Time of death?" Roberts asked, impatiently.

"The skin turns white when I press it. This kind of discoloration is about right for ten to twelve hours." The Medical Examiner kneeled on the floor, registering the dial on the thermometer, and checked his watch. "Eighty-eight degrees would place the time of death around 9:30, plus or minus."

"Can you tell us how he died?" Dawson asked.

"At first, I thought maybe our victim died of a heart attack or a stroke, but there were none of the tell-tale signs that often follow an incident of this sort. So, I examined the victim's neck and arms, parts of the body not covered by clothing, and I found a single puncture wound, no bigger than a pin-prick but enough to leave a tiny, almost microscopic bruise. I think Carlos Ortega was poisoned."

"What? How is that possible?" she demanded.

"It's my guess someone got close enough to Ortega to inject him with a syringe full of poison," Brogan responded. "I'll know more once I run a full toxicology screen back at the lab. I've also asked for a list of all those on duty and who had access to the cells."

Dawson ran her hands through her hair. She was visibly shaken, and everyone around her could see it.

The Lieutenant looked at her. "Are you all right?"

"Damnit!" Dawson yelled, her face pale as a white linen shroud. "We should've done more to protect him. What am I supposed to say to his sister and her two children?"

"There wasn't much more we could do, Kate," Jawara said, putting his hand on her shoulder.

"Jawara's right," Clark chimed in. "We did everything that we could to protect him."

"Keeping a suspect, like Ortega, in protective custody is always the right move," concluded James Roberts, as he scratched the stubble of his day-old beard. "We hid him down here in lock-up under a "John Doe," so no one would know we had him at police headquarters."

"Doesn't look like it fooled anyone," she commented.

"Don't worry, Inspector. We'll get whoever did this. I've already given instructions to Clark and Jawara to go through all the surveillance video from the Hall of Justice. Somewhere, a camera snapped his picture, and when we find it, we'll also find out who he is."

"While you're at it, you might as well have them look for the person responsible for ransacking Doctor Romano's office last night *and* who tried to kill me. I think you'll find it's the same man."

"I'll get a full report from Brogan. It's already in the works," Roberts said, folding his arms across his chest. "You should go home and get some rest. You look like shit."

Dawson's shoulders slumped as fatigue and despair washed over her, like a cold, wet blanket. She struggled to retain her composure, winching from the pain in her chest as she pulled her shoulders back. "I think we both know who got to him."

"The only thing we know for certain is that our number one suspect in a murder investigation is dead." Roberts had been alarmed when he heard what had happened to Carlos Ortega right under his very nose. It was one thing to watch a suspect get killed during an investigation, but then quite another to have it happen in a lock-up he had ordered. The head of the Homicide Bureau wanted answers, too, but he wasn't quite ready to exchange reason for Dawson's wild accusations. "There is no evidence whatsoever that links the Secret Service to this crime scene."

"Well, don't you think it's a little odd that the only person who was there at the crime scene, and talking to us, is now dead?" Kate asked.

"There's never any reasoning with you, Dawson," the Lieutenant said, frustrated. He started to walk calmly from the room, but stopped in mid stride. "Consider yourself on administrative leave. I'll find another detective to pick up your case load."

"Lieutenant!" she screamed, at his back.

Roberts did not seem to hear her or, if he did, care. In silence, he lumbered off down the corridor, heading for the elevator.

"Damn-it-to-hell!" she cursed under her breath.

All at once, Dawson found herself surrounded by her fellow detectives just like a celebrity encircled by paparazzi at a Hollywood premiere. The majority of her colleagues on the SFPD never had the opportunity to fire their guns in the line of duty or, for that matter, was ever mixed up in any kind of "police-involved shooting." Real police work was rather dull and routine, with most officers relying on science and technology to put criminals behind bars instead of their department-issued weapons. So, when they heard that Dawson had taken part in a "police-involved shooting," each one of her fellow detectives vied for her attention, anxious to ask the first question.

Balardi spoke first, "Hey, I heard about that dust-up last night," he said, throwing his shoulders forward, turning the tips of his shirt collar straight up, impersonating the King of Rock-n-Roll. "Convenience store robbery, huh?"

"Yeah, something like that." Dawson refused to commit.

"Are you all right?" Clark asked, putting his notebook away. "I heard that you got caught in the crossfire."

"Yeah, I'm fine. It was really no big deal."

Mikhail Jawara put his hands up in the air, bringing all the speculation to a close. "I got the word directly from the dispatcher," he said, with a high degree of confidence. "You were the target of a drive-by shooting."

"I heard you got hit," Balardi said.

"I just got the wind knocked out of me."

"So, tell us all about it," they said, speaking together as one.

Dawson took a deep breath. She couldn't be angry at Clark and Jawara. They were the only two people on the force who really gave a damn about her. And Balardi, well, he was her partner. "Look, I just don't want to talk about it, right now. Okay? I also don't want to talk with anyone from the Press. Besides, you heard the boss, I'm officially on administrative leave."

"Ah, c'mon, Dawson," Balardi pleaded, wrapping an arm around his partner's shoulders. "We're your pals. We want to hear all about it."

Gasping in pain, she wiggled away. "Later, okay?"

"Sure, if that's how you feel about it."

"I'm just not ready to talk about it yet."

"We're still on for lunch, right?"

"Nah, I don't think so. I've got to go somewhere and think. But I'll take a rain check, if that's okay?" She started to walk away.

"Sure, any time, partner."

Dawson stopped, turning towards him. "Matt, thanks a lot. I know that we don't always see eye-to-eye on things, and maybe that's my fault, but you've turned out to be a good partner."

Balardi shoved his hands in his pockets. "Thanks, Dawson. That means a lot, coming from you."

"I'll call you next week about lunch," she promised.

Jawara butted in between them and handed her a stack of messages he'd been carrying in his coat pocket. "Well, speaking of calls, your serial caller called again yesterday after lunch. He called five times, and once again, this morning. If you're not going to talk to him, would you at least tell him to fuck off?"

"I'll take care of this before I leave."

"You know, I spent more than half of my day, yesterday,

picking up your phone," Jawara continued to make his point.

"I said I'll handle it," she smarted back, then stomped off.

She walked back to her desk, furious. The last thing that Kate had wanted to do was call attention to the shooting and her narrow escape from death the night before. Now she was certain that everyone in the Bureau knew. Angrily, she kicked the waste basket next to her desk, and trash went flying. She mouthed the word "shit," then knelt to pick everything up.

"I hope it wasn't something I said," Rosa Romano joked, as she walked up to her. She crouched down, and together they scooped up the last of the trash, dropping it handily in the basket.

"Oh, Rosa, I've had a hell of a morning already," Kate said, her face flushed red, "and it's not even ten o'clock."

"Yeah, I guess it was quite a shock seeing your number one suspect being measured for a body bag. I'm really sorry."

"Thanks. You're a really good friend."

Romano handed her one of the manila folders she was carrying. "I had a chance to run ballistics on the round that was fired at you last night."

"What happened to seventy-two hours?" Dawson joked, opening the file.

"Let's just say, after finding myself in the crosshairs, 'right away' means 'right away'—today, in fact," she said all serious.

"So, what am I looking at?"

Romano pointed at the photo in the manila folder. "A very rare handgun."

Kate's eyes flickered, as she read the caption: "Makarov, TKB-023."

"The only suitable match as a weapon for the round we found is an experimental variant of the Makarov," the Assistant Medical Examiner explained. "The TKB-023 was first designed in 1965, with a polymer frame to reduce the weight and cost of the weapon. Their first attempt was the Makarov PM, which was essentially a knockoff of the Walther PPK, but it was heavy and most security agents who carried the handgun complained they had to use a takedown lever or some other device to field strip it. Our Russian friends then introduced the TKB-023, their experimental version, with a lighter, all-plastic frame. It passed Soviet military trials, but was never fielded due to concerns about the polymer's capacities for long-term storage and use. Only a handful of these were ever made; most of which went to KGB agents who traveled regularly through security detectors. An unloaded, polymer handgun would appear invisible on the screen because it's made of plastic, not metal."

Dawson felt a cold chill as she digested the new information. "So then, I was shot by a former KGB agent?"

"Nope, you were shot by the Makarov TKB-023. But as you know, guns don't kill people, people kill people. I have no way of knowing who really pulled the trigger. I've dusted it for prints, but found nothing. It's possible the Secret Service may have used the weapon to make us think the Russians are involved."

"I thought you said this handgun was rare?" Kate asked.

"It is rare, alright. Less than a couple dozen was ever made. If one ever came up for auction on the open market, it would likely sell for more than $100,000."

"What did they do? Buy it on eBay?"

"Maybe, or maybe one of them is a collector who has just kept it safe in his collection as a souvenir of the Cold War era."

"That's quite a souvenir," Dawson commented, with an eyebrow raised. "I doubt if one of Reinhardt's young bucks would have owned it. But an old Cold-Warrior like him? That makes perfect sense."

"I agree, but proving it is another thing."

Kate thought a moment. "Rosa, doesn't it strike you as a little coincidental that the minute I come into possession of microfilm, which contains valuable Cold War documents, that I'm shot by someone carrying a pistol that dates back to the Cold War?"

"You said it before, it's like we're caught in the middle of one of those old spy novels."

"Yeah."

"Well, I'm afraid this isn't going to reduce your anxiety level," Rosa said, handing her friend the second of two manila folders she was carrying.

"What's this?" Dawson asked, swallowing hard.

"I wasn't the only one busy running tests this morning. These are the preliminary findings of Brogan's toxicology screen. I'm afraid that Carlos Ortega was killed by a 0.2 milligram dose of the poison ricin."

Dawson fell back into her chair. "Holy shit!"

"Do you recognize the significance of the ricin?"

"Yeah," she replied, scrambling to remember the details. "Didn't it have something to do with an umbrella? And a Communist defector?"

"Right on both counts," Romano said, helping Kate open the folder on her desk. Inside the file, she pointed to a cross-sectional diagram of the umbrella gun, which used a hidden pneumatic mechanism to shoot out a small poisonous pellet containing the ricin. "It was one of the most notorious acts of assassination carried out during the Cold War. Bulgarian dissident Georgi Markov was killed by a jab from an umbrella tip bearing the toxin ricin as he waited for a bus outside his London office in 1978. His KGB assassin was never captured, but a post mortem conducted by germ-war scientists revealed that Markov had been fatally poisoned by the radioactive substance ricin, traces of which were found in his urine."

"I can't believe it," Dawson said, staring out into the room.

"This all goes back to the microfilm and those MJ-12 documents. It seems like everyone who's had contact with that microfilm has ended up dead."

Kate thought of when she first found the lipstick container stuffed under the seat onboard the plane. The Secret Service agents must have searched her purse a dozen times, but being men, didn't notice her lipstick was missing. Only a woman's eye would have noticed.

"Did you hear me? I said—"

"Yeah, I heard what you said, Rosa."

"Do you know what that means? You and I are both on that list, and they tried to get you last night," she said, trying to reason with her. "As long as they think you're dead, they're going to be coming after me next. Understand?"

Dawson tore her eyes from the nearly-empty room to *really* see her friend. "Understand? Yeah, I understand. I know exactly what it means. That's why we've got to get them before they come after us."

At that moment, the phone on her desk rang, and rang again. A bundle of nerves, Dawson fumbled for the receiver and brought it to her ear. She listened for a moment, then said, "Okay, Jawara, I'll talk to him. But you gotta give me a minute before you transfer the call. Thanks."

"I can see that you're busy, girlfriend," Rosa said. "I guess we can table our discussion until later."

Dawson gazed at her intently. "Don't forget where we agreed to meet."

"Two blocks south of the InterContinental Hotel on Howard

Street. I won't forget."

"That's right. Around 12:30."

Rosa Romano glanced down at her watch. "12:30, it is."

The call.

CHAPTER SEVEN

Just after 12:30 P.M., Kate Dawson was sitting in the front seat of a late model Ford van, waiting and watching. She had parked in a metered parking spot about two blocks away from the InterContinental Hotel to avoid detection by the Secret Service agents who maintained a secure perimeter. For all intents and purposes, she was undercover. She was dressed in light green scrubs bearing the corporate logo of the hotel chain, had on a wig, and wore soft-soled tennis shoes. Lenny Provolone was seated in the back, typing commands into his laptop computer.

Rosa Romano approached the vehicle from the passenger side and climbed into the van from the side door. She was attired in a bronze wool blazer, bearing the hotel logo on the left breast pocket. With her hair pulled up in a French twist and wearing fake glasses, she was playing the part.

"Okay, does everyone feel ready?" Dawson checked with both of her side-kicks.

Rosa asked, "Are you sure the First Man is alone?"

"The President and her entourage left the hotel about fifteen minutes ago," Kate reported, glancing at her watch. "They've got stops to make at Golden Gate Park and Sunset, and will most likely not be back for several hours. Bill Harrison is alone in the suite, protected by two Secret Service agents outside the door."

"How did you know he was going to request a massage therapist from the hotel staff?"

"To be honest with you, Rosa, I didn't. But based upon their previous travel plans, in which the First Family has stayed at an InterContinental Hotel or one of its partner hotels, he's requested a massage therapist four out of five times," she replied. "I thought it would be a good bet that he'd order a massage here."

"I've always wanted to know how my tax dollars are spent. Now I really wish that I didn't know."

She stared at Rosa in disbelief. "Whoops, I almost forgot," Dawson said, grabbing a couple of items from the truck's dashboard. She placed a tiny earpiece into Rosa's palm, then tossed Lenny a Walkie-Talkie. "This wireless earpiece is used in much the same way that you would use any other hands-free or Bluetooth device. The difference is that you don't need to connect it to your cell phone. It receives signals from a powerful receiver-transmitter back here at the base station."

"You mean you'll be able to hear everything I say and hear?" she asked.

"Yes, and you'll be able to hear us," Kate reassured.

"Cool."

They held each other's eyes for a moment longer, then Dawson turned around in her seat, surprised to see that Provolone was poised, cool, and in complete command of himself. "Lenny, what about you? Are you ready?"

"I'd be much happier without the intermittent patches of fog," he stated, analyzing the data on his laptop. "They may affect our satellite reception and limit our tracking abilities to thermal and photographic imaging equipment only."

"As much as I would like to wait for a bright, sunny day, we don't have that luxury. It's got to be now or never."

"It just seems like every time you ask me for help with NEMESIS, we're having a less than nominal day."

Dawson tried to console him. "We really couldn't do this without you, Lenny. So, whatever data you provide us with will be better than what we could have gathered on our own."

"Kate," Romano said, rubbing her hands together, "I'm really nervous about this. I can't keep my palms from sweating. Do you think we could go over the plan one more time?"

"Sure, whatever you want."

"How do I get into the locker room?" Rosa asked.

"Almost anyone in Guest Relations has the security credentials you'll need to get into the Spa, and make your way to the locker room. Unfortunately, with security at an all-time high due to the First Family's visit, the only person you'll get close enough to will be the Assistant Concierge," Dawson answered. "Her name is Martina Flores. She's roughly your height and weight, and if anyone asks to see your badge, you'll pass a quick badge check."

"How do you propose I get my hands on her badge?"

Kate Dawson nodded. "Well, now, this is the tricky part," she replied. "The Assistant Concierge takes her lunch break every day at 12:55 P.M. She is a creature of habit and always eats in one of the restaurants that are within walking distance. She never spends more than thirty minutes at lunch."

She looked at Kate, her eyebrows raised, silent question marks. "How are earth did you get all of this information?"

"John Prescott," Dawson acknowledged. "He has friends in low places."

Romano smiled knowingly. "I know the Garth Brooks song. So you're saying, his friends are not corporate presidents and judges and so on, but are rather criminals and drunks and informants?"

"I didn't really say anything," she said, with a thin smile.

"Okay, I understand."

Dawson looked closely at her. "Martina Flores wears her ID badge on the lapel of her hotel blazer. It should be easy enough to unclip it in a standard brush pass. But just remember, you'll only have about thirty minutes. The moment she realizes it's gone, she'll hit the panic button."

"Gee, thanks!" Rosa exclaimed . . .

Dawson opened the door to the van, and Rosa Romano stepped out onto the pavement. She straightened the lines of her jacket, and leaned into the side door of the van with a smile. "Well, wish me luck."

"Good luck, Rosa," she said, finally. "You're going to be just fine."

Romano walked several blocks to the InterContinental Hotel, and then stood on the opposite side of the street, waiting for the Assistant Concierge to exit the double glass doors. When she saw her come out of the building, Romano watched Martina Flores walk towards the Moscone Center along Howard Street.

Without waiting for Flores to commit to one of her three restaurants of choice, she scrambled down the sidewalk towards Fourth Street. She passed by the Yerba Buena Square shopping center and stopped outside Wolf House apartments at the crosswalk. Romano didn't look at her directly, but watched her out of the corner of her eye as she walked the length of the Moscone Center.

At the intersection of Fourth and Howard, she watched Flores lean against the traffic light as she pushed the pedestrian crossing button. She was going to be coming right toward her.

Rosa Romano stepped up to the crosswalk, and when the light changed and the signal indicated that it was safe to cross Howard

Street, she blended into the crowd of pedestrians heading north. Flores was in the crowd of pedestrians heading south. In the manner of a few heartbeats, Rosa aligned herself with Flores, and bumped her as they passed. The bump gave Romano a half of a second to unclip the woman's ID from her blazer, and palm it in her hand. Martina Flores never felt the theft. In fact, as she reached the far side of the street, Flores shook her head, tossing her brown tresses, and raked her fingers through her hair.

At the Moscone Center, Rosa turned briefly, and watched as her mark continued walking down Fourth Street, completing unaware. Romano took a deep breath and sighed. She then thought of Dawson waiting for her ahead. She tore her eyes away from Fourth Street, and headed directly to the hotel . . .

"What about physical security?" Rosa asked.

"There are two Secret Service agents stationed outside that room, armed and mobile. They do a hall sweep every twenty minutes. When they start their patrol at 5-past or 35-past the hour, you'll have ten minutes," Dawson replied, the words sticking in her head . . .

Rosa Romano stopped in front of the Spa and Health Club on the Mezzanine Level of the InterContinental Hotel, and saw the two Secret Service agents standing in the lobby. She took off her sunglasses. Just beyond them, she could make out the twenty-four-hour, state-of-the-art fitness center, indoor, heated lap pool, and spa where several women were enjoying the hotel's Spa experience. She glanced at the watch on her wrist, somewhat inconspicuously. It was 1:05 P.M.

Right on schedule, the two Secret Service agents walked directly out of the Spa and Health Club, and began checking doors on each side of the corridor. They continued their hall sweep until they were out of sight.

Rosa clipped the badge on her blazer, and walked directly into the Spa, heading to the locker room. No one gave her a second look.

Romano gazed at her intently. "Once I reach the locker room . . ."

"You've only got a couple of minutes to locate Olga Komarovski's locker, and remove the lanyard with her hotel ID," Dawson interrupted, without waiting for her to complete her sentence.

"Suppose it's locked?" Rosa asked.

"You'll have to improvise," she replied. "Just remember some of the things that I showed you, and you should be okay."

"What if the ID isn't there? Suppose she's off somewhere else in the hotel giving a massage to another guest?"

Kate Dawson tried not to frown. She said, "We've always accepted that as one of the possible risks behind our plan. We did wait until the last possible moment to cancel the reservation ourselves, but as far as Bill Harrison is concerned, his Masseuse is still scheduled to arrive at 1:15. Someone's got to work out the kink in his shoulder that prevented him from joining the First Family this afternoon on another lunch with Democratic donors. Let's just hope the hotel hasn't double-booked their masseuse, and Olga gets the chance to enjoy the day off."

Rosa Romano was silent for a minute or two, crouching in the back of the van with Kate and Lenny. The interior of the van was cold and impersonal. Other than some of Lenny's scientific equipment, a computer table and folding chair, it completely lacked character of any kind.

"So, once I have Olga's ID, you want me to roll one of the portable massage tables out of the Spa, and place it inside the elevator on the Mezzanine level," Rosa repeated her instructions, in order to get them right.

"I'll be in the elevator, waiting to take it from you," Dawson added.

"Just make sure you've placed some towels, sheets, and oil on the table. I won't have time to stop and gather them myself."

"Right, I won't forget," she replied, still nervous.

Kate Dawson shifted uneasily in the van. "One last thing. Lenny is our eyes in the sky. If he calls 'abort,' we just walk away. No matter what."

"Okay, no matter what . . ."

Rosa Romano opened the door to the locker room, and she skulked around the big, cluttered facility like a cat burglar, scarcely daring to breathe. There was no one in the room and no one in the showers. Immediately she started searching through the lockers for Olga Komarovski's name. The names were not arranged in any kind of an order, so it took time going through each one of them. In the last row, she found the one she was looking for. *Thank God*, it was also unlocked!

She was not careful when she opened the locker, and had to pick up several items that spilled out. She continued to disrupt things, nervous and scared, as she picked through the clothes. While she was digging for the lanyard with Olga's ID, she felt a hand on her shoulder and jumped, nearly out of her skin.

"Jesus Christ!" Rosa screamed.

A Spa guest had emerged from the shadows, and was looking at her with laughter and merriment.

"Did I scare you?" the woman asked, with a bright smile. She knew full well that she had frightened Romano, and somehow that seemed to please her even more. She was young and in her early twenties, and had a mischievous look in her face that came from soft and easy living.

"You should never sneak up on someone," Rosa admonished her, like a mother scolding her child.

"I'm really sorry," she said, still smiling. "I just wanted

to know if I could have an extra towel to keep my hair from getting wet."

"Yes, of course, just help yourself," Romano replied, pointing at the table full of fresh towels.

"Thank you," the young woman said, finally.

Rosa Romano stared at her a moment, without looking. Her heart was still pounding from surprise, and wanted to know if this was what a criminal faced every time they set out to do something wrong. Then her fingers felt the canvas lanyard, and she pulled it into her hand. Quickly, she shoved the rest of the items back into Olga's locker, and grabbed one of the portable tables.

On her way out the door, Rosa picked up several towels, a couple of fresh sheets, and a plastic bottle of oil. She pressed the button for the elevator, and when it arrived on the Mezzanine floor, she pushed the cart into the waiting hands of Kate Dawson. She also placed the lanyard around her friend's neck.

"Thanks, Rosa," Dawson said, speaking through her disguise. "I'll see you back at the van."

"Good hunting, Kate," she replied, and headed for the exit.

Kate Dawson rode the elevator up to the top floor of the InterContinental hotel, and when the elevator doors slid open, she stepped out pushing the massage table in front of her. She saw the two Secret Service agents standing in front of the Presidential Suite, but she made it a point to keep her eyes lowered. She hoped that neither one of them had gotten a good look at her outside the restaurant or on board Air Force One. Even with the clever disguise she was wearing, she reasoned that it would not have taken much for them to recognize her as the "crazy" police inspector.

"Olga Komarovski," Dawson said, affecting a slight Russian

accent. She stopped pushing her cart, and held up her identification card.

One of the Secret Service agents merely nodded, while the other walked up to her and examined her photo ID. "Ms. Komarovski, we are required to conduct a routine pat-down," he said politely. "If you would prefer to have a female agent do this, I can arrange to have one on site in a couple of minutes."

She was quick to brush off any suggestion that would have delayed her getting into the First Family's suite. "There is no need to make special arrangements for me," Dawson said, standing still. "Growing up in Russia as young girl, we learn quickly to accept these personal indignities."

The Secret Service agent patted both legs, one at a time, then moved to her upper torso and back with his pat-down. Finally, he ran his hands along her shoulders and down both arms. "She's clean," he reported.

Without waiting for a response from his partner, Dawson turned and began to push her table forward, but the other Secret Service agent stopped her a few steps from the door. He put his hand on top of the table for balance, just short of her towels and table cloths, and leaned over to look under the cart. He did a routine scan of the undercarriage. "Okay, you can go," the second agent said, straightening back up and opening the door politely for her.

Dawson didn't look at him. "*Spacibo*," 'thank you' in Russia, moving her table forward into the Presidential Suite. Quickly, she closed and double-locked the door behind her. She then tore the wig from her head and gingerly removed her Beretta hidden within the folded massage table, wedged under one of the legs. With gun in hand, Kate crept silently through the suite.

The Presidential Suite at the InterContinental hotel was five-thousand square-feet of luxury. With a panoramic view of San

Francisco's financial district from the 32nd floor, the uniquely decorated suite featured well-appointed touches, such as a marble foyer, gleaming hardwood floors, and oriental carpets throughout. The spectacular living room featured floor-to-ceiling windows, one wide-open deck suitable for Scarlet O'Hara, and a black marble fireplace with a painting of the Prince de Savoy over its hearth. A squad of comfortable Empire chairs, each with an appropriate table and a light, sprouted from the floor in conversation groups. Classic paintings, interesting objects *d'arte*, and unique antiques filled the light space. A corridor to the right led to a media room, a dining room for twelve, and three bedrooms. Each of the bedrooms featured Empire-style furniture, four-poster beds, and amenities set on hardwood floors framed with spectacular red and green striped draperies. The suite offered an opulent yet comfortable living space for the First Family.

Without a sound, she continued moving through the suite, then heard a noise, swiveled around into a crouch, and came face to face with exactly the person she was expecting to find there.

"Freeze!" Dawson yelled, holding the gun out in front her in the combat stance. The muzzle was trained squarely on the First Man's chest.

William Harrison stood still, like an elegant, white marble statue, in the doorframe of the bathroom, a straight razor in his left hand and shaving cream partially covering the right side of his face. He was wearing one of the hotel's plush robes, double-knotted around his waist. Steam bellowed forth from an empty shower and covered all but a small oval in the mirror with a thin layer of moisture.

"Come in," he said, both startled and amused. "Inspector—ah, Dawson, isn't that right? Are you here filling in for my massage therapist, Olga, or is this an official call? Either way, I can assure you the gun won't be necessary."

Dawson kept the gun pointed at him. "I've got two bodies down at the morgue, and a lot of questions that you're going to answer for me."

Harrison did not seem to hear her, and if he did, he dismissed the comment. He slipped back into the bathroom, and stood in front of the marble basin, peering into the small oval he had wiped clear on the mirror. He made another stroke with his razor.

"I said I've got two bodies at—"

"Yes, yes, I heard you," the First Man replied, rinsing the razor in water and following through with another stroke on his day-old beard. "Carlos Ortega, a good, decent man. I really liked him. His death was unfortunate. He was just in the wrong place at the wrong time. If I had had my way, the target would have been Harlan Reinhardt. That stupid, meddling fool."

"'Unfortunate'?" Dawson repeated, incredulously as she watched him shave. "Is that all you've got to say? Unfortunate? We're not talking about some dumb animal that ran out in front of a speeding truck."

Bill Harrison continued shaving, moving the razor across his face with slow, determined strokes, listening, but more concerned with his shave. When he finished, the sixty-four-year-old turned on the water and splashed a handful of water into his face. He straightened up as far as he could, revealing stiffness in his lower back, and reached for a plush red towel.

"He was an unfortunate casualty of war," he said finally. "But then, men die on the battlefield every day to protect the ideals of our way of life."

"How can you possibly justify Ortega's death in that way? What did he die for, other than to protect the identity of the real murderer?"

"You think you got it all figured out, don't you?" he said, staring back at himself in the mirror. "Do you have any idea what it takes to stare down an enemy thousands of miles away who hates you with every fiber of their being? Right now, the leaders in Iran are building weapons of mass destruction to destroy us. They hate everything that we stand for. They hate our democratically-elected government because their leaders are self-appointed. They hate our freedom of religion. They hate our freedom of speech. They hate our freedom to vote and assemble and disagree with each other. They hate everything about us."

"Ortega wasn't killed for any noble reason, like our freedom of speech," she defied him, "or our freedom of religion. He died in the crossfire of our ideals."

She looked at him, her eyebrows raised, silent question marks. "Did I just stumble into some alternate reality?" Dawson asked, her voice full of irony and doubt. "You're not at all like the man I remember. I used to admire the man who stood up for the average guy. I used to listen to your speeches in Congress; how you'd say the one thing that separated us from the terrorist regimes in the Middle East was the value we placed on human life."

"Yes, I do recall saying that," he answered smugly, "but I also remember saying that sometimes the ends justified the means. The fact remains that if we show any kind of weakness now, our constitutional democracy will get plunged into a crisis that will destroy us. We can't afford to be fighting an atomic war with Iran at the same time Congress is divided over a murder and cover-up at the highest level. That would be suicide. So, what we're doing here is a very important and necessary evil—preserving, protecting, and maintaining our way of life—and if a few people must be sacrificed for the greater good, then so be it."

"I doubt seriously if Ortega would have agreed with you."

"Well, then, he never really saw the view from the top."

Dawson's eyes narrowed as she studied his wrinkled features. They were cool and unflappable. "And Meghan Kendrick? Was her death 'unfortunate,' too? Was she also sacrificed for the greater good?"

"Let's just leave her out of this," he said, wiping his face once with the towel, then tossing it carelessly across the room into the shower stall. "The less said about Meghan Kendrick, the better."

"So, there *is* something you care about after all?"

Again, Harrison did not seem to hear her. He was silent for a moment or two, standing in the doorway of the bathroom. He appeared to be lost, deep in thought, a million miles away, but just as quickly, he was back in the present. "I need a drink. Can I offer you one?" he asked, walking to the kitchenette.

Dawson followed him closely, her gun still drawn. "Sure."

"What would you like?"

"Whatever you're having."

"I had nothing but the highest regard for Meghan Kendrick. She was a good reporter; perhaps too ambitious for her career," Bill said, over his shoulder, as he strolled into the small alcove just off the dining room. He rifled through several bottles, mostly wines, soft drinks, and club soda, then produced a full bottle of Jack Daniel's, the black seal unbroken.

"Is that the reason why you had her killed?" Dawson asked.

Harrison paused for a moment. "Jack Daniel's okay? It'll have to be. There isn't much of anything else."

"Fine with me."

"Ice?"

Without waiting for her answer, he took two glasses from the cabinet and placed them on the counter, adding a handful of ice from the freezer compartment of the small hotel refrigerator to each glass. Next, he busied himself with removing the seal on the bottle of bourbon. Harrison poured the clear-brown liquid over ice, and handed her a glass.

"Cheers," he said, clanging her glass with his.

"Cheers," Dawson toasted cordially, drank from the glass, but kept her gun trained on him the whole time.

Harrison didn't look at her. "I didn't have anything to do with Meghan's death," he explained, taking a big gulp. "I loved her. After the mid-term elections, I had planned to ask my wife for a divorce. I was going to marry Meghan, settle down, and raise a family."

"I saw the bruises around her neck," she said, smiling thinly. "It looked like you enjoyed strangling her during sex."

"Not at all. I hated it." He took a moment to sip his drink. "But Meghan got off on forced sex play, so I tried my best to make her happy."

Dawson rejected his objection. "You had sex with her on board Air Force One, then you offed her for the good of the country."

"I won't even dignify that with a response."

"You've got motive and opportunity. Why should I listen to anything else you've got to say?"

"You haven't read me right at all," he said, somewhat disappointed. "I care about my country. I see my life and service to the United States of America with a great deal of clarity and honor."

"As far as I'm concerned, you're a man without honor," she challenged.

Harrison had heard enough. "I think it's about time you left, Inspector, before you get yourself into real trouble."

Dawson's head was whirling. She didn't know who or what to believe anymore. She seemed at a complete loss for words, not that it mattered. She felt like nothing she said made a difference to him. She had come hoping for a confession, or at the very least clarity, now all she had were more questions. She ran across the room and stepped onto the balcony for a breath of fresh air. Dawson leaned over the suite's narrow balcony to take in the view of the City of San Francisco below. The sight was breathtaking, even to someone who had an incredible view of the Bay from her own apartment window. She watched as the cars went up and down on Howard Street, then looked down to see people the size of ants moving along the sidewalk, and the various ramps and platforms of the nearby Moscone Center far beneath her. The warm air from below swept against her face, and, for a moment, she forgot where she was—but only for a moment. She still had a job to do, no matter what the cost.

"I take that back," she said, putting her thumb close to one eye and squinting to remove one of the people below from her line of sight. "Ortega wasn't some dumb animal caught in the headlights. He was an ant, and you stuck your thumb out and squashed him."

Bill Harrison hid his smile and managed a look of disdain. "You just don't understand, do you? The fate of our country is at stake. Perhaps, in time, you'll see things in a different light."

Dawson drew herself together and a determined look settled back on her face. "I want to show you something," she said, returning to the room, pushing her gun into the First Man's ribs. She tugged firmly on Harrison's arm and the sixty-four-year-old reluctantly accompanied her to the balcony. "I want to show you what the view from the top really looks like."

"I don't like heights," Harrison said, struggling to break free.

Dawson maintained her grasp and pressed his upper body to the railing. "Well, then, by all means, you *should* take a look."

"Inspector!"

"Take a really good look," she repeated, forcing him nearly over the edge.

"Dawson, have you lost your mind!"

"Yeah, I'm the crazy woman your people killed last night," she scowled, pushing him closer to his doom. "Think of me as her avenging angel! I can do anything I want and no one can touch me!"

Harrison's legs began to buckle and his breathing was hard and labored.

"Tell me where I can find Agent Jones," she demanded.

"I don't know," he screamed, terrified.

"Tell me where I can find Agent Jones," she repeated, nearly screaming, forcing his head to look down thirty-two stories to the street below.

For several heartbeats, the First Man was gravely silent, then he finally said, "There never was an Agent Jones."

"Then I need to know who called in the murder."

"I did, damnit!" Harrison said, his voice cracking slightly.

"You did?" Dawson asked, surprised. When she realized that she had gotten her answer, she simply loosened her grip and stepped aside.

"I did." Bill Harrison scrambled backwards until he reached the safety of his room, then collapsed to the floor, clutching his chest. His breathing continued to be hard and labored, and sweat was dripping from his forehead. The wrinkles on his face had flattened out into a frightful death's-head, but still managed the smile of a man who had looked into the abyss and had lived to boast about it.

Finally, he said, "Despite what you may think of me, I really did love Meghan Kendrick. Her death hit me hard, yet I couldn't shed a single tear for her publicly without exposing our affair."

"Why didn't you just come forward in the beginning?"

"I couldn't come forward and risk a full-blown scandal." He took a couple of deep breaths, and exhaled normally. "But at the same time, I knew if I didn't do anything, Reinhardt would simply sweep her body under the rug and pin her death on someone, like Ortega, rather than risk a full-blown investigation that might have upset the balance of power between Iran and the United States."

"You called the murder into the SFPD? That was a pretty gutsy thing to do. Suppose Reinhardt had caught you?"

"He still thinks one of his agents called it in. That's when the eponymous 'Agent Jones' came into being." He appeared to be mostly pleased with himself for having duped the Secret Service chief. "But if you'd care to verify my story, I spoke directly to Lieutenant Roberts. I asked him to assign his best detective to the case. I requested that he assign you."

Dawson looked at him for a fleeting moment, engaging his eyes, then looked away. She got the feeling that, right then, Bill Harrison was telling the absolute truth, but he was also still hiding something.

She towered over the sad man on the floor. "Then you do know that Reinhardt ordered his men to sweep Meghan Kendrick's apartment clean less than ten minutes after her body was discovered?" she asked finally. "Other than some furniture, they didn't leave a shred of evidence that she had ever lived there. They took everything that she owned."

"I can't say that I'm surprised." Harrison sat up. "He was probably concerned that she had left something behind that would have exposed our relationship and possibly implicated me in her death."

"You're missing the bigger picture, Bill."

"I am?"

Dawson didn't falter. "Think about it for a moment. If

Meghan's body was found just after nine o'clock on Sunday night, and the Feds raided her apartment ten minutes later, just after midnight in D.C., how could Reinhardt have mobilized his men in such a short period of time?"

"He couldn't have," Harrison said, a surprised look of awareness settling upon his face. "It takes at least fifteen minutes to drive to her apartment from the White House, and that's in perfect traffic. The only way Reinhardt could have done it is if he knew in advance she was going to die."

"Exactly," Dawson said.

"So then, he must have conspired with one or more of his men to have her killed."

"That was my thought also."

"But that doesn't make any sense," Bill Harrison said, puzzled. "Why kill Meghan Kendrick to cover-up the affair she's having with the First Man of the United States? Her death is only going to cause a greater scandal. Why not just try to scare her? Get her to leave of her own accord? Buy her off? There must have been plenty of options."

Dawson got right to the point. "Meghan Kendrick wasn't killed to protect the administration. She was murdered to keep from destroying it."

"What do you mean?"

"This was never about the affair she had with you, although that did provide Harlan Reinhardt with the perfect motive he could sell to a hungry press," she said, piecing the puzzle together. "This was always about the secret she carried in plain view. A rare collection of seventy-year-old documents on microfilm she kept hidden in a lipstick case."

Harrison looked skeptical. "She never mentioned them to me. If they were so important, I'm sure she would have said something about them. What makes you think they even exist?"

Dawson hesitated a moment, as if on the verge of calling his bluff. Then she seemed to think better of it. "I don't," she lied. "But there's been plenty of evidence to suggest they're in play."

"Thanks, Inspector. You've given me a lot to think about," he said, his veneer of polite gentility restored.

With great physical exertion, Bill Harrison struggled to his feet. He was still feeling a bit shaky, but that did not seem to deter him from taking Dawson by the arm and escorting her toward the door of his suite, pausing several times crossing the great expanse of the room.

When they reached the foyer, Dawson plucked her wig off the portable table, and pulled her disguise back on. She then slid her service pistol between the first and second towels, and pushed the table to the door. The wheels rolled smoothly over the polished, hard-wood floors.

Harrison put his hand out, palms up. "That reminds me," he said, mischievously. "You still owe me a massage."

"Next time."

The First Man took her by the arm, leaned in, his eyes boring into hers, saying, "Will there be a next time?"

She was unruffled by the question as he poured on the charm. She could tell that he was attracted to her, and there wasn't a woman in the world that didn't find William Harrison a handsome man. She also knew that it was probably better to play along than to cross him inches away from her getaway. Dawson looked back at him, their eyes locked.

"Sure," Kate replied, playfully. "And I even promise to leave my gun and brass knuckles in the squad car next time."

"What fun would that be?" he asked, putting on the charm.

She reciprocated. "I'd better go."

"Till next time." Harrison opened the door.

Dawson pushed her table past the two Secret Service agents on duty. As soon as she reached the elevator, she punched the "down" button several times, the fingers on her hands a bundle of nerves. Eventually, the elevator doors slid open and she pushed her table inside the car, tentatively waiting for the doors to close.

No sooner had she made her floor selection, Dawson eased back against the wall of the elevator and breathed a deep sigh of relief, watching the doors sweep closed. The elevator car started moving down, slowly, one floor at a time. When it finally reached the Mezzanine level and the doors swept open, she scrambled out, and made her way towards the exit.

Hidden from her in plain sight, the Shadow Man watched Dawson exit the door to the street and bided his time.

Two blocks away from the InterContinental Hotel, Kate Dawson walked down the sidewalk on Howard Street and found the late model Ford van still parked in the metered parking spot where she had left it. She fed the meter another couple of quarters, then went around to the passenger side and climbed into the vehicle from the side door. Lenny was still hunched over his laptop computer, punching commands into the keyboard, while Rosa Romano sat next to him, one hand on his shoulder and the other curling a strand of her hair between two fingers.

"Damn! You were in there for a long time," Romano shouted, nearly jumping out of her seat with surprise.

"Mission accomplished?" Lenny asked, over his shoulder.

"Yeah . . ." She sighed wearily. "Thanks a lot, guys. I really appreciate your help with this."

"Well, did the First Man confess to Meghan's murder?" Romano asked, as her friend pulled off the wig and fluffed her hair.

"No, but I've got a pretty good idea now who arranged to have her killed."

At three o'clock, Kate Dawson stormed into the Homicide Bureau and barged right into the Lieutenant's office, carrying a leather-bound book. James Roberts was sitting behind his desk, drinking stale vending machine coffee from Styrofoam. When he finally acknowledged her, the look on his face said it all: *What the hell are you doing here?*

"We need to talk about Meghan Kendrick," she demanded, walking right up to the edge of his desk.

"I've already said all I'm going to say on the topic," he stated, setting the cup down, sitting up straight in his chair.

"Sir, I think—"

"Ahem," an unidentified stranger in the room cleared her throat.

Startled, Dawson turned around and faced her. She was an attractive Latino in her fifties with long gray hair that had been pulled fashionably into a bun; dressed elegantly in a black pin-striped Armani suit, with a Duria silk sleeveless blouse and Prada shoes. She put her cup of coffee on the side table and crossed her legs uneasily.

"What's going on?" Kate asked, smelling more than the stale coffee.

Roberts peered across his desk. "Inspector Dawson, this is the new Attorney General for the State of California, Alejandra Reyes-Salazar. She's going to be taking over the investigation into Meghan Kendrick's death."

"The Lieutenant has been telling me what a tenacious detective you are," she said, with a very raspy voice. "Like a dog with a bone."

Dawson ignored her, her gaze fixed on her boss. She looked

to him for guidance and leadership, but most of all understanding. It was a first for her. "Sir, may we speak privately about this matter?"

"No, Inspector," he said, staring back at her. "Whatever you have to say to me, you can say it to both of us."

They held each other's eye for a moment longer, then she said, "I need to know what happened on Sunday night, specifically when the call came in about the murder on board Air Force One."

"You've been relieved of that assignment, Dawson." Roberts rose to his full height and came out from behind his desk. "The Attorney General's office is now handling the investigation."

Dawson went on, "You were on-call in the Homicide Bureau that night. How many calls came in? One? Two? Three? A dozen?"

"I told you to forget it," he ordered her.

"Let me refresh your memory, Lieutenant. You received two calls that night: One at 9:02 P.M., then another at 9:19 P.M. The calls were both about Meghan Kendrick and her untimely demise on board Air Force One, but they came from two different callers."

"Who told you that?" Reyes-Salazar asked, suddenly alive.

"It's all right here in the logbook," Kate said, slamming the leather-bound book on the Lieutenant's desk. "But the thing of it is, the actual logbook has been altered. You can see where someone wrote an entry down in pencil, then erased it and wrote another entry right on top of it."

"Where did you get that?"

Dawson shot the Attorney General a sideways glance. "Does it matter?"

"But how were you able to read a log entry that was erased?"

"Spectral imagining," she answered.

Roberts towered over her, a hulk of a man. "Let's not play games then," he bellowed, like a giant in some children's nursery rhyme. "You clearly have some theory, so, let's hear it out."

"I don't have a theory." Dawson garrisoned her resolve and stood her ground. "I have a witness who says that he called the murder in around 9:20 P.M. I wasn't really sure about the veracity of what he told me, but when I checked it against the logbook, his testimony corresponds with last entry I found."

Alejandra Reyes-Salazar shifted uncomfortably. "The one at 9:19?"

"Yes."

"And the other call? The one at 9:02?"

"Meghan Kendrick was still alive at 9:02," Dawson stated, "according to the Medical Examiner's official report."

"Interesting," the Attorney General, said right eyebrow up.

"I think, if you subpoena Harlan Reinhardt's cell phone records, you'll find that he made the call to report Meghan Kendrick's suicide from right here in San Francisco, while the plane was still circling the airport."

"I guess that rules him out as a suspect," Roberts said, at last.

"But not as an accessory after the fact."

Alejandra Reyes-Salazar stood up and walked over to the SFPD inspector. She regarded her like a bug under a micro-scope. "I'd be careful who you go around talking to, Inspector Dawson."

"Are you telling me this, or is he?" Dawson asked, looking from one face to the other.

"Just consider it a word of friendly advice." She took a firm hold of Kate's arm and lead her to the Lieutenant's door. "The only career you should be worrying about right now is your own."

As soon as Reyes-Salazar closed the door on her, Dawson

leaned up against the wall and checked to see that no one was watching her. She then listened at the keyhole. Dawson felt satisfied by the way she had baited her trap and now waited to see what kind of rat she would catch.

"We did the right thing," the new Attorney General reassured him.

"Just not the right way."

"Let me ask you something, Jim," she said bluntly. "Was Inspector Dawson correct? Did you make that change in the logbook?"

"Yes," he said reluctantly, and after a short pause said, "I was originally going to assign Clark and Jawara to follow up on the first call. In fact, I penciled their names down in the last column."

"Was it their turn in the rotation?"

"No, it was hers." The Lieutenant was ticked. "But you don't know her the way that I do. She's a real pain in the ass. If I had my way, I'd bust Dawson down to file clerk and bury her in records."

"But does she get results?" Reyes-Salazar asked.

"Yeah, she gets results, but she busts my balls to get them."

She paused a moment. "What made you change your mind?"

"I got the second call, which came from the First Man. I recognized his voice right off, but he did his damnedest to make me think he was someone else. He told me that Meghan Kendrick had been murdered and asked me to assign my best detective. He specifically requested Dawson."

"Did you ever tell her that?"

"Hell, no!" Roberts said, almost shouting. "She's already got an ego the size of Texas. Why the hell would I want to add to it? I've got enough prima donnas already working in this bureau.

The last thing I'd want to do is tell her the First Man of the United States had asked for her."

"You don't think that would have helped with her investigation?" Reyes-Salazar posed an interesting question.

"No, do you?"

"Probably not." There was a long pause, then, "I've asked around about Inspector Dawson. They've all pretty much said the same thing. They think she's a loose cannon, but all agree she gets results. She could become a very valuable asset to your career, if used properly."

"What do you mean by the word 'used'?" he asked.

"Oh, Jim. You're a very smart man. I think you can figure that one out on your own, without my help."

Roberts laughed, dully. "Thanks, Alejandra."

"When I run for governor next year, I'm going to need trusted allies in law enforcement," she said, in her low, crusty voice. "I want to know that I can count on you to be there for me."

"You can count on me," he responded, like a valued servant.

"Good, then we'll just keep this sidebar to ourselves," Reyes-Salazar stated.

When she thought she'd overheard the last of their private conversation, Dawson gradually straightened up and peered about the Homicide Bureau. She was reasonably certain that no one had seen her listening at the Lieutenant's door. The office was virtually empty, with the exception of one detective. She found Jawara sitting at his desk, typing furiously on his keyboard, trying to figure out some notes he had scrawled on the back of his phone bill next to his computer.

"Hey, how you doing, Mikhail?"

Jawara looked at his fellow detective with an understated sense of suspicion. "How am I doing? I guess I'm doing fine, Kate. It always makes me a little nervous, though, when people ask me how I'm doing, especially when I saw them only a couple of hours ago. Makes me think they want a favor."

"As a matter of fact, I do need a favor," she said, strolling over to Jawara's desk. Sneaking a peak back at Roberts' office, her voice lowered, "Did you and Clark come up with anything on Ortega's killer?"

"You're on leave, Kate," he whispered, looking over his shoulder. "I could get into a lot of trouble sharing that information with you."

"C'mon, Mikhail. I just need a name. Someone who was responsible for my suspect's death."

Jawara shot a look at Roberts' office and then discreetly pulled a folder out of his desk. "Our suspect's name is Anatoly Piotrovskii. He's a former KGB agent who was recruited by none other than Vladimir Putin in 1977, and left the agency to go freelance when it was disbanded in 1991. He has been suspected in several political assassinations, including the umbrella hit that took out the Bulgarian dissident Georgi Markov in 1978, but he's never been captured despite attempts by the British Secret Service and Interpol. Lately, he's been associated with Putin and the new Russian Republic. In fact, some believe that he's Putin's chief hatchet-man, but no one really knows for sure. Basically, the guy's a ghost. We were just lucky to have caught him on one of our security cameras."

"Let me see the picture," she asked, leaning over his desk.

Jawara handed over the print-out. "So, what do you think? Does that guy look like some master assassin?"

Closely, Dawson examined the picture. The low-resolution image depicted a short man in his late fifties, with a sculpted physique, angular facial features, and salt-and-pepper hair. If she didn't know better, Dawson might have mistaken him for a younger version of Jack Lalanne.

"No, but that might be one of the reasons why he's been so successful as an assassin," Kate explained, as she continued to stare at the image. "We always think that super spies should look like James Bond or Jason Bourne. When, in fact, the best secret agents in the world look just like you and me."

"So, you think I'd make a good spy?" Jawara asked, folding his arm across his chest and pretending to support a gun in the other.

"No," she said bluntly, putting the picture down.

"Thanks a lot," he groaned.

Dawson turned and started walking out of the Homicide Bureau. "Thank you, Mikhail. I really owe you one," she said, over her shoulder. She blew him a kiss and headed down the corridor.

CHAPTER EIGHT

At exactly 6:23 P.M., Kate Dawson stood by the pay phone near the intersection of Hyde and Sacramento Streets, waiting for her serial caller to call with directions. He claimed that he had information about Meghan Kendrick's murder, and that he would only share it with her. She wasn't certain if he was a crackpot or someone with real insider information, but with her investigation sidelined by the new Attorney General, Kate understood that she couldn't afford to pass up any possible lead. Even a dead-end was better than nothing.

The fog had returned from earlier that day and the air was thick with patches of grey mist, similar to the vapor that clings to the edges of dreams. All color had been washed away by the tiny water droplets, and what remained suspended in the atmosphere was a monotone of black and white.

When the phone rang, Dawson picked it up on the first ring and held the receiver to her ear.

"Don't talk. Just listen," said a disembodied voice on the other end of the line. "Fisherman's Wharf. Thirty minutes. Pier 39. Buy a bag of Doc Popcorn and be standing in front of the carousel. No cops. If I sense you've been followed, you're all on your own, sweetheart."

"Thanks. I really appreciate it," she started to say, but the line was dead.

Dawson hung up and stood on the curb for a moment, pondering her next move. She needed to know the reason why Meghan Kendrick had been murdered, and she knew where she could possibly get that information. The problem was, Kate didn't know anything about her source. He was just a voice on the other end of the phone. He might have been one of the nutcases who saw the coverage on television and simply decided to seize his fifteen minutes of fame. Or maybe, if she was lucky, he was one of Reinhardt's Secret Service agents who had had an attack of conscience. Either way, time was ticking off the clock, and she had to get moving.

Dawson jumped aboard the Powell-Hyde cable car as it climbed Nob Hill, and "strap-handled" the car down to the end of the line at Aquatic Park. After she had helped the conductor turn the cable car around, along with the eager tourists, Kate scrambled by Ghirardelli Square and headed towards the Wharf. The iconic crab wheel sign, which spelled out Fisherman's Wharf, greeted her as she walked swiftly into the very crowded market place.

As she struggled through the crowd, Dawson checked her watch and realized that she was running out of time. She knew he had given her thirty minutes for a reason, just so she couldn't put together back-up. There was little doubt in her mind that he wanted to meet with her alone, but for what purpose? Was he some whack-job who just wanted to jerk her off? Or was the knowledge he carried so valuable that he was afraid someone would kill him for it? She pushed her way through, mindful of who or what might be lurking in the shadows.

At Pier 39, Dawson spotted the Doc Popcorn counter. There was no one in line, but as she clambered over the wooden dock, she watched helplessly as a large family formed a queue. She ran up to the line, breathless, and quickly looked at her watch. She had about five minutes, and she sweated down each one of those minutes, waiting for the family members to make their selections. When they were finally done, she stepped up to the counter.

"Give me a bag of popcorn," Kate demanded.

"What kind would you like?" the attendant asked, politely, all chipper, with bright white teeth.

"Anything!"

"Well, right now, we're running a special on the 'triple white cheddar with sweet butter.'"

"I don't care."

"We also have the 'all-natural and better-for-you,' if you're watching your caloric intake."

Dawson reached over the counter and grabbed him by the lapels on his Doc Popcorn vest. "Look, I'm in a hurry! Just give me anything!"

"Gosh, all you had to do is tell me," he said, startled.

"I just did."

Nervously, the attendant scooped plain popcorn into Doc Popcorn's distinctive yellow and green bag and handed it across the counter to her. She fumbled in her jeans for a couple of bucks, but came up with only a twenty-dollar bill. Dawson threw it across the counter, and shouted, "Keep the change."

"Thank you. Please come again."

She then hit the ground running with her bag of popcorn, and found the carousel a moment later crowded with lots of children and their parents. She did a three hundred and sixty degree turn, but didn't see a single man standing around with a bag of popcorn. She looked back at her watch. *Did I miss him after all?*

Dawson stood there for a few minutes, angry with herself that she had fallen victim to the serial caller's ploy. Couldn't believe it. But as she turned to the trash receptacle to dispose of her popcorn, Dawson heard a voice behind her. Her first impulse was to turn around and confront the man, but she decided to play it cool and find out what he had to say.

"Excuse me?" Her gaze never left the children on the carousel, yet her senses were on overdrive.

"I said you look like a woman who enjoys her popcorn," he repeated himself, loud enough to be heard over the din of the crowded entertainment complex. "Would you care to try some of mine?"

"Yes, that would be lovely," she responded, turning.

"Don't turn!" he barked, like an angry dog. "Just stand still and keep your eyes forward."

Dawson stopped, froze in place. She kept her eyes straight ahead, but tried to make out him out in the spinning Mylar panels of the carousel. From what she could see, he looked tall and lanky, with thinning grey hair and a mustache. He was wearing a trench coat that was tied, not belted, at the waist, and the collar was turned up to keep his neck warm from the cold night air. His features were weathered and worn, like leather from an old pair of shoes.

He approached her from the side, moving very cautiously, and stuck out his bag of popcorn in front of him as to offer her a handful. He whispered into her ear, "Now, let's take this nice and easy."

"Okay, whatever you say," she took a couple pieces of popcorn in hand and chewed them up.

"You didn't drive here, did you?"

"No, I took the cable car, as instructed."

"You're sure no one followed you?"

"No, I wasn't followed."

With his free hand, he reached around her torso and gently patted her waist and hips and chest. "You're not wearing a wire, are you?"

"No."

"You didn't tell anyone where you were going?"

"No, not a soul," Dawson said, honestly.

The man pretended to drop several pieces of popcorn on the dock, and when he knelt to pick them up, he patted her inner thighs down to the ground. He then hastily repeated the action on the outside of her legs. With slow precision, like a well-oiled machine, he stood back up.

"Look, I've done everything you said." She was growing impatient. "Don't you think this is all a bit—"

"Melodramatic," he said, completing her sentence. "Things are well past that now, sweetheart. The men you're dealing with are very, very dangerous. They're just as likely to slit your throat and bury you in a shallow grave as they are to discredit you with your superiors and ruin your career. They have a switch-blade mentality but manage to disguise themselves beneath the sophisticated veneer of a three-piece, pin-striped suit. They're not your common, low-life criminals. They're the *real* bad guys. They're the ones who run the world as if it were Dodge City."

"I can see why you'd be afraid of them," Dawson commented, disposing of her popcorn in the nearby trash can.

"Afraid?" he snorted, repeating the word in the form of a question. "Lady, I've never been afraid of anything in my life."

She put her hands on her hips. "Then why are you standing behind me?"

After a moment's hesitation, he came up from her left side, walked over to the fence that protected families from the whirling action of the carousel, and turned around to face

Dawson. The man seemed to ignore everyone else around him, his gaze fixed on the female detective as he continued to eat his popcorn. He looked at her with a blank expression on his face, attempting to mask whatever thoughts and feelings that he may have had bottled up inside.

She studied the craggy, weathered lines on his face. "Wait a minute. Haven't I seen you some place before?" Kate asked, trying her best to place him. "*Time* magazine. Right? You're that guy—"

"For the moment, we'll just leave names out of this conversation," he suggested in an even tone. "You never know who might be listening."

They held each other's eye for a moment longer, then Dawson walked right up next to him, and whispered, "I can assure you that no one followed me. Except for all these tourists, it's just the two of us."

"C'mon, I know a place where we can talk more freely."

The man took her by the arm—a gesture that seemed to be very old-fashioned at best—and steered Dawson beyond the carousel to the end of the pier. They walked past the penny arcade where patrons still tossed rings, shot skeet, and tried their best to knock down iron pyramids with baseballs. Towards the back of the arcade, they found classic midway entertainment gave way to Pac-Man, Wheel of Fortune, Deal or No Deal, and The Price is Right. They went by the Player's Sports Grill and the Sea Lion Café. He directed her around the front of Neptune's Seafood Restaurant, and at the first, empty park bench, they sat down together.

Heavy fog rolled in off the Bay, and with it, the sound of bellowing sea lions on the docks. Dawson leaned back on the bench, looking at him. "I thought I recognized you," she said, shaking her finger at him. "You're Colonel Goodine. You've served in the Armed Forces longer than any other man. You're going to be decorated tomorrow by the President."

"Well, don't believe everything you read in the press," he said, guilelessly. He held Dawson's eyes for a second, then looked out across the docks at the marine mammals. "And do try to keep your voice down. At this point, I'm sure only the sea lions have heard you, but we must be extremely careful. They are known for eavesdropping on people's private conversations."

Dawson's senses heightened with suspicion.

"For a cop, you've not very bright," he added.

Dawson ignored his comment. "So, you're the one who gave Meghan Kendrick the microfilm?"

"Yes, she was going to help me stop these bastards from ever killing again."

"But they got to her first?"

"Bingo."

"Why did you pick Meghan Kendrick?" she asked, barely a whisper. "There are plenty of other reporters."

Colonel Goodine leaned back on the bench and looked out to sea. "She was the 'fair-and-balanced' girl at Fox News. Say what you like about the news organization itself, but there was something special about Meghan Kendrick. People trusted her when she went on the air and reported the news. That's a rare quality today, especially when so much of the news is hyped for the sake of ratings. I chose her because I was convinced she would report the facts and let people make up their own minds."

"You must have known they'd try to kill her."

"To be honest, I thought they'd threaten her," he said dourly, "but I never thought they'd kill her. Not without the goods."

"Did you know she was having an affair with Bill Harrison?"

"Yes, and I didn't care. There have been more women in and

out of the Oval office than there have been Presidents. It was never a concern of mine as long as the job got done."

"Is Harlan Reinhardt their leader?"

"No, he's strictly middle management," Goodine described him to a tee. "A thug. A very *effective* thug, but the kind of guy you go to arrange a hit. He didn't kill Meghan Kendrick, but I know he had a hand in setting it up."

"The President?"

He was unruffled by the question. "No, she didn't kill her either, but she okayed the hit on Meghan, and not simply to get even with her husband. She had Ms. Kendrick killed for the secret she carried."

Dawson pressed. "The President of the United States?"

"Sure," he said simply. Even though he was sitting back on the bench, Goodine managed to sneak at glance at her every so often. "But then, who is the President of the United States? Just a man, or in this case, a woman. Someone who outspent the other guy, or had a catchier slogan, and got elected to the office. Do you think they're any different from the rest of us? They're not. They're just people. Some better than others, but each brings their own baggage to the office."

"I never thought of it that way," she said, taking on a different perspective.

Then he leered at her. "But this secret isn't just Helen Harrison's secret. You must know this involves many nations and the legacies that some of their leaders left behind. Eisenhower and Korea. Kennedy, Khrushchev, and the Cuban Missile Crisis. Johnson, Nixon and Vietnam. Reagan, Gorbachev and the fall of the Soviet Union. Sadat, Begin, Carter, and the Camp David Accords. Putin and—"

"But why? What is it all about?"

The Colonel took a deep breath. "To understand that, you

have to go all the way back to the beginning. 1947. Two years earlier, we had just beaten Hitler, Mussolini, and Tojo, and contained the threat of Fascism. But we faced an even greater threat from Stalin and the spread of Communism. We had also unleashed one of the most powerful and destructive weapons ever created by destroying two Japanese cities with a single bomb targeted at each. Our former ally, the Soviet Union, was just two years away from building its own atomic bomb, but that delay didn't prevent Stalin from annexing most of Eastern Europe and drawing an 'iron curtain' around the people who had suffered the most during the war. We may have been riding a crest of prosperity as our soldiers returned home from the war, but at the same time, the seeds for a new war—a Cold War—were being sewn. We didn't trust them, and they didn't trust us. And the only thing that kept them from striking us first was our preparedness to launch a nuclear strike against the heart of Mother Russia."

"Did we have that capability in 1947?"

"Yes, and there were many in the Pentagon who argued in favor of taking out the Russians before they grew strong enough to become a real threat, but Truman opted for a containment plan to stop the spread of Communism," Goodine said, as if he were lecturing a seminar of graduate students at Berkeley. "You have to understand, during the early years of the Cold War, Roswell Army Air Field was the largest base of the Strategic Air Command and housed our nuclear arsenal of about a dozen atomic bombs. The 509th Operations Group, which was head-quartered there, was the unit that had dropped the bombs on Hiroshima and Nagasaki. The unit was considered the only one to have had experience with nuclear weapons, and thus was regarded by many as trained and ready for an atomic bomb mission. All Truman had to do was give the word and our B-29

Superfortress bombers would have taken off from Roswell Army Air Field and bombed the hell out of the Soviets."

She stared at the Colonel with a worried look on her face. "My father was born in 1947."

"A lot of fathers and mothers were born that year." He cleared his throat and swallowed. "They were the beginning of the 'baby-boomers' and will never know how close we came to a nuclear strike."

Dawson had done her homework, too. "That was the year you enlisted in the United States Air Force."

"Yes, but it was still known as the Army Air Corps," he corrected her. "It wasn't until September of 1947 that the Air Force was detached from the Army and became a separate military branch."

"I didn't know that either."

Goodine continued, "I was seventeen-years-old when I enlisted. Of course, I lied and told them I was eighteen. My father had been in the service, and I'd always regretted not being old enough to serve alongside him in World War II. We knew another war was coming, a war with the Soviets. So, just a few weeks shy of my seventeenth birthday, I went right out and signed up to be a pilot. If there was going to be a shooting war, I wanted to be there right on the front lines. But, the Army Air Corps had other ideas. When they learned that I had a flair for writing and knew my way around a typewriter, I was assigned as an adjutant to General Nathan Twining, commander of Air Materiel Command, at Wright Field, later renamed Wright-Patterson, in Dayton, Ohio. That assignment to Twining would have far-reaching consequences that I could not have even begun to grasp at the time."

"Wasn't General Twining appointed Chairman of the Joint Chiefs of Staff by President Eisenhower?"

"Yes, but that didn't happen until ten years later," he again corrected her. "In those early days at Wright Field, Air Materiel Command was concerned mainly with procurement, supply, and maintenance of existing aircraft. The R&D, or Research and Development division, had yet to come into existence. Mostly, the job was routine. We filled procurement requests and shipped supplies."

"Doesn't sound very exciting," she said, standing up and stretching, then strolled to the edge of the pier and looked out. "When I think of the Joint Chiefs of Staff, I think of men like Colin Powell, not procurement officers like Twining. There has to be something more to this."

Colonel Goodine leaned forward on the bench. "There is . . . In fact, the crash at Roswell changed everything."

"Roswell, New Mexico?"

"Yes."

"Roswell, New Mexico," she said, turning around to look directly at him. "Wait a minute. Didn't you just tell me that our nuclear arsenal was stored at Roswell Army Air Field? Coincidence?"

"I doubt it was coincidental," he insinuated. "During World War II, when we learned the Germans were building their own atomic bomb program at Peenemunde, we sent spies and maintained a constant surveillance effort to keep check on their progress. It only makes sense that a foreign power, even an extraterrestrial one, would keep tabs on our nuclear arsenal."

Dawson stared. "But I understood the crash as Roswell was nothing more than a top-secret weather balloon."

"That's what they wanted you to think," Goodine said, leaning back on the bench. "The last thing our government wanted the public to know in 1947 was that the Army Air Corps had captured a downed spacecraft, containing alien bodies, near Roswell, New Mexico. But the fact of the matter is the story became front-page news for the *Roswell Daily Record* on Tuesday, July 8, 1947."

"You're kidding me," she said, doubtful.

"No, I'm not." Colonel Goodine hesitated a moment, like a good storyteller building suspense for his audience. "Walter Haut, the public information officer at Roswell Army Air Field, issued a press release that morning stating that personnel from the field's 509th Operations Group had recovered a 'flying disk' that had crashed on a ranch near Roswell. A few hours later, Commanding General of the Eighth Air Force, Roger Ramey, rescinded the story, issuing a statement that the debris had come from a top-secret surveillance balloon recovered by the RAAF personnel, and not a 'flying disk.' Later that day, at a hastily-arranged press conference, Ramey marched Major Jesse A. Marcel out, the officer who had found the spacecraft, and had him pose with debris (including tinfoil, rubber and wood) said to be from the crashed object, which seemed to confirm its description as nothing more than a weather balloon. Now, you would think that a seasoned Major like Marcel, who was also the intelligence officer, would know the difference between a flying saucer and a weather balloon—and he probably did—but they decided to play him for the fool."

Dawson's eyes were wide. "So, it was a flying saucer?"

"Yes, I saw the wreckage myself, and the bodies," he answered, his mouth suddenly dry. Goodine licked his lips a couple of times. "On Tuesday afternoon, I decoded a telex from Colonel William Blanchard, the commanding officer of the 509th, requesting orders from General Twining. But you see, anything dealing with 'materiel' had to go through Air Materiel Command at Wright Field, so Twining ordered him to sit on the wreckage debris and to keep it secure until we arrived. We boarded a plane for Roswell and arrived shortly after Ramey's press conference. I can tell you that it wasn't debris from a damn weather balloon. I picked up a piece of the lightweight material the ship was made of and crumpled it in my hand, like aluminum foil. Then, when I released it, the material returned instantly and seamlessly to its original state. I had never seen anything like that 'memory metal' before. Other pieces of the foil-like material could not be cut, dented with a sledgehammer, or burned with a blowtorch when put to the test. Several other pieces, which looked like small I-beams, had strange symbols on them resembling hieroglyphics, unlike anything I had ever seen. All of the materials were subsequently packed up and shipped covertly to Wright Field."

Dawson got right to the point. "What about the bodies?"

The Colonel hesitated only a split second before replying. "We were told they found three alien bodies lying outside of the craft and they thought they could see at least one more through a large hole ripped in the side. All the occupants were dead, although rumors still persist to this day that at least one being was still alive. When we finally saw them, they were zippered shut, safe and secure, in child-size body bags. I would describe them as small, approximately three to four-feet tall, with four fingers and no thumbs on their hands. Their skin was gray in color, and their heads were large and misshapen, with huge, almond-shaped eyes. They didn't look at all like the little green men from the sci-fi pulp magazines."

Dawson guffawed. "Flying saucers? Alien bodies? Are you pulling my leg? Now you sound like my friend who's into science fiction."

Goodine didn't think it was a laughing matter, but admonished Kate with a frown. "I assure you that this is all true,

Inspector," he said, in complete sincerity. "In addition to the wreckage and the bodies, we interviewed more than thirty townspeople from Roswell and nearby Socorro and Corona. Mac Brazel who owned the ranch where most of the debris was found, neighbor Floyd Proctor, resident Dan Wilmot and his wife, local newspaperman W.E. Whitman, and Major Marcel. With the exception of Marcel, they all reported seeing mysterious objects flying overhead in the weeks leading up to the Fourth of July weekend. They also remember a horrible electrical storm on the evening of July 4th, a flash in the night sky, and a loud explosion. On Saturday, July 5th, they found debris from the wreckage spread over a thirty-five-mile area."

Dawson stared at him, unblinking. She had never heard such an improbable story in all her life and wanted to attribute the Colonel's whimsical tale to something that was playing on the big screen at the local Cineplex instead of the ramblings of an old army war veteran. *A downed alien spacecraft? Little gray men? Miracle metal?* She wondered what her friend Lenny would have thought, or for that matter, if he believed in the crash at Roswell as fervently as Goodine. She was skeptical. The logical part of her brain just could not accept what he was saying as true.

"We were talking about the MJ-12 documents," she brought him back on topic.

"Operation Majestic-12 was established by President Harry Truman through a special classified presidential order on September 24, 1947 at the recommendation of Secretary of Defense James Forrestal and Dr. Vannevar Bush, Chairman of the Joint Research and Development Board. The goal of the group was to exploit everything they could from recovered alien technology at Roswell and other sites." It was then he decided to put his cards on the table. Taking a cleansing breath, he continued, "On the day before, September 23rd, I typed a memo that General Twining had drafted, and would later sign, suggesting the establishment of a covert group to study the material from Roswell for use in our own aircraft. That memo was sent to General George Schulgen, his superior at the Pentagon, and then forwarded to Truman's office the very next day."

"So, it's true then?" Dawson asked, forcing herself to try to accept it.

Colonel Goodine looked at her disapprovingly, as if beginning to suspect that she was not smart enough, after all, to understand the complexity of his information. "Yes, that's what I've been trying to tell you."

"But it's so incredible," she said, still uncertain. "I don't understand how this could have been covered up all these years."

"Mostly through lies, disinformation, and half-truths," he reflected. "When the public started demanding answers about flying saucers, the Air Force created Project Blue Book in 1952. It collected thousands of credible reports, but dismissed all of them as swamp gas or other natural phenomena. At about the same time, Twining ran another Air Force program called Project Sign. Designated MCIAXO-3, as established under the Technical Analysis division of T-2 (military intelligence) at Wright Field, Project Sign collected, evaluated, and distributed to interested government agencies and contractors all information concerning UFOs and flying saucer technology."

"So, all the while, the public thinks they're being served by Project Blue Book, when, in reality, they're getting screwed."

"Exactly, but this wasn't an isolated incident," the Colonel commented. "For more than seventy years, the U.S. government has made every effort to keep the public in the dark about flying saucers and extraterrestrial intelligence. In 1976, when Jimmy Carter was running for office, he promised his constituents that he would get to the bottom of the cover-up. Shortly after he was elected president, he asked CIA Director George Bush to provide a briefing, but Bush refused, claiming the information was classified on a 'need-to-know' basis. In 2008, Barrack Obama made similar promises, but found himself left out of the intelligence loop as well. In 1995, New Mexico Congressman Steve Schiff claimed that he found documents revealing the Roswell cover-up and the existence of the Majestic-12, but then they were mysteriously shredded by the GAO before he could bring them to light, and he died shortly thereafter. Powerful forces have been working to keep this secret for decades."

Dawson's head was spinning. She needed a good-sized dose of clear thinking as she continued to grasp at straws. "You've mentioned Forrestal, Bush, and Twining. Who else was involved?"

"There were twelve members of the original Majestic-12," Goodine revealed. "They included some of the most powerful men in the military and in the scientific community. The group included Dr. Vannevar Bush, who chaired the Office of Scientific Research and Development; Rear Admiral Roscoe Hillenkoetter, the first director of the Central Intelligence Agency; James Forrestal, Secretary of the Navy and the First Secretary of Defense, who was replaced after his death by General Walter Bedell Smith, the second director of the CIA; General Hoyt Vandenberg, Air Force Chief of Staff; General Robert Montague, the head of the nuclear Armed Forces Special Weapons Center; Dr. Jerome Hunsaker, aeronautical engineer; Gordon Gray, National Security Advisor; Dr. Donald Menzel, Harvard Astronomer; Dr. Detley Bronk, chair of the National Academy of Sciences; Rear Admiral Sidney Souers, National Security Council, Dr. Lloyd, Berkner, physicist, and, of course, General Nathan Twining. Famous scientists, like Robert Oppenheimer, Albert Einstein, Karl Compton, Edward Teller, and Wernher van Braun, also served in an advisory capacity."

"That's quite a list of who's who."

The old man chuckled. "They were trusted, high-ranking officials who were often involved in important government projects. They all possessed diverse skills and high security clearances."

"Let me make sure I get this right," Dawson said. "Members of the Majestic-12 conspired with the military and industrial giants, like Lockheed Martin, Boeing, and Northrump Grumman, to integrate recovered alien technology into our experimental aircraft and weapons systems."

"In a nutshell," he responded, with a tip of his head. "They began research and development at Wright Field as part of the Air Materiel Command under Twining. But they soon realized they needed a more discreet area to test jet aircraft, like the Lockheed U-2, and moved the whole operation to a special section of Nellis Air Force Base in Nevada, known as 'Area 51,' in April 1955."

"So, Area 51 does exist? I always thought it was one of those urban myths," she said, barely able to contain herself.

"The Groom Lake test facility was established by the Central Intelligence Agency working in collaboration with members of the Majestic-12 on land, which was designated 'Area 51' on the map," he reported. "The first tangible result of their partnership was the design and development of a high-level, strategic reconnaissance aircraft, known as the U-2."

"U-2," she repeated. "That sounds vaguely familiar."

"The Lockheed U-2, nicknamed the Dragon Lady, was *the* most successful spy plane in the United States Air Force. After its introduction in 1957, the U-2 flew hundreds of missions over Russia, China, and Southeast Asia, and the plane was only retired from service about ten years ago. You probably remember hearing about Francis Gary Powers? Well, he was shot down in a U-2 spy plane while flying a reconnaissance mission over Soviet airspace in 1960."

Dawson wished she could record all this. "Where did the Majestic-12 get the money for their operation? Surely, research and development funds into the billions of dollars would have been noticed by some government oversight committee?"

"You don't think the government really spent ten thousand dollars for a hammer and thirty thousand dollars for a toilet seat, do you?" he queried. "Clever bookkeeping hid much of the costs associated with the MJ-12, while the Pentagon had the burden of hiding the rest."

"Colonel," she said, trying to sound as tactful as possible, "that's a whole lot for a lay person like me, who slept through most of her history classes, to take in one sitting. How about the Reader's Digest condensed version?"

Goodine sat forward on the bench. "I believe that Harry Truman signed the order that formed Operation Majestic-12 out of necessity. First, to determine if there was an alien threat; second, to exploit their advanced technology in order for us to gain a military, economic, or even a psychological advantage over the Soviets and win the Cold War; and third, to maintain power, authority, and control in a world that teetered on the edge of nuclear annihilation. There were several times when we went to the actual brink, but none of them more critical than the Cuban Missile Crisis. I can just imagine the call that Kennedy made to Khrushchev, warning him to back down or we'd use one of our alien wonder weapons."

"I think I get the picture . . ." Kate's head was whirling.

"I also believe the decision to keep the average citizen in the dark about what really happened at Roswell in 1947 may have spared the world unimaginable turmoil in its socio-economic, political, and religious systems," he added, standing up, "but also created an unnecessary credibility gap. They call it 'plausible deniability,' but we all know now the U.S. Government has been lying to us."

"Will we ever be ready to know?"

"I think it's time for people to start thinking for themselves. I gave the MJ-12 documents to Meghan Kendrick, so that she could share them with her loyal viewers at Fox."

"And they cost Meghan Kendrick her life."

Goodine's nod wasn't an acknowledgement of what she had said, but rather an acceptance of what he knew to be true. "That brings us right back around to where we started."

"Colonel, you should let me take you into police custody. With everything you know, we could break this case wide open."

"I'm not interested in being a hero," he said with utmost integrity.

The two of them were standing alone at the end of Pier 39, embroiled in a private conversation, when Goodine suddenly stopped talking. He stood frozen in place, like a man who had stepped onto a land mine and could not move without killing himself. Dawson saw the look of terror in his face and also stopped talking. They looked around without turning, and listened. The fog was very heavy. They couldn't see a damn thing on the dock. But then, they heard a sound; faint, but distinctive. The sound of someone breathing.

Dawson stood her ground, staring out into the fog. She knew the sea lions were still laying on the docks, gathered into their individual families, but this was something different. She watched and waited for some sign of the interloper. For the first time that evening, she was scared, downright frightened to death. She didn't move for a moment, and then, as she walked directly into the fog, she disappeared from the Colonel's side.

Dawson clambered over the edge of the pier, and dropped

down onto one of the wooden docks that supported the sea lions. She caught up with a man who was leaning against the scaffolding for one of the boat slips. He was shivering from the cold. She could see that he was red-eyed, unshaven, and beaten about the face, where half-formed scabs and cuts were the only recognizable contours of the man's face. He looked, for all the world, like a perpetual drunk who had just finished his last bottle of cheap wine and was looking for a place to sleep it off.

Carefully, she approached him, wondering if the "wino" act was real or just a ploy to sell a master assassin's disguise. But the closer she got, the more she could smell the putrid odor of decay mixed with the cheap aroma of "dago-red" wine that had soaked deeply into his clothes. She watched him as he blinked slowly, his diseased tongue lolling outside his mouth.

Dawson stopped right in front of the drunk and exchanged a fleeting glance as she tried to ascertain his condition. "Who are you?" she asked, engaging his eyes.

The drunk said nothing in reply, but blinked several times, in an apparent attempt to bring her into focus.

"*Who are you*?" she repeated.

The drunk looked at her, but didn't say anything. He blinked his eyes again, then slowly, shivering, he began to slide down the scaffolding of the boat slip. Dawson reached out for him, and held him up, forcing him to his feet.

After a few moments, Dawson sat him down on the boat slip and made sure he wouldn't slip into the Bay and drown. She then managed to dig deep into her skinny jeans and produced a couple of twenty dollar bills. She reached across the void that separated the two of them and stuffed both bills into the drunken man's shirt pocket. The drunk was disgusting, dirty, and needed a good bath, but he was a human being after all, and deserved a modicum of respect.

"Here," she said softly. "This should tide you over for a couple of days."

By the time she returned to Pier 39, Colonel Goodine was pacing back and forth, smoking a cigarette. He was visibly upset, even a little scared. He watched as Dawson came back down the ramp . . . alone.

"I hope you noticed how coolly I behave under fire," he said, with a self-mocking tone of voice. "I'm not a hero."

"I don't believe you, Colonel," she said, taking hold of his arm. "I've read your service record. It's exemplary. You became a flight surgeon at the age of fifty when most of your classmates were retiring from the military and you've served in combat units for the last twenty-five years."

"It's easy to serve others when you're scared shitless." Goodine took another drag or two of his cigarette, then flicked the butt aside. "You focus on their needs and forget that you're frightened. But that's not bravery, that's just basic survival."

"You became a flight surgeon because you wanted to give something back. That's what I'd call a hero."

Goodine didn't wait for her to finish. "Well, if you don't have any further questions for me, I'll be going."

"Does the Justice Department know what we know? The FBI?" she asked, her patience with the Colonel starting to wear thin. "And why the hell haven't they ever done anything about it?"

"They know. They've known for fifty years, or more." His elderly features hardened. "Some of us in the intelligence community had hoped that when Jack Kennedy named his brother Bobby as the Attorney General, the secret would finally come to light and we'd all have a chance to live normal lives again. But the men who ran the corporations that profited from the technology we recovered from Roswell and other sites were not about to let their golden goose get cooked. They backed Kennedy as long as he stood tall against the Cubans and the Soviets, but the minute he started talking about pulling our advisors out of Vietnam and ramping down the sale of arms to other countries, he threatened their livelihood."

"Are you telling me they're the ones who killed Kennedy?"

"Why is that so hard for you to comprehend?" he asked, in the same tone of voice that one shopper might say to another, "Just what detergent do *you* use to get your pots and pans clean?" "I've already told you that these are very powerful, ruthless men. They will stop at nothing to maintain the power and control they wield, including putting a Mannlicher-Carcano rifle in the hands of a fanatic in the Texas Book Depository and ordering him to pull the trigger on a sitting president."

"I can't believe it. I just can't believe it," Dawson repeated.

"Trust me, they're hoping you don't believe it."

Her eyes narrowed, flashing anger like a torch. "But why now? You've known about these men for most of your adult life. Why have you now decided to come forward with what you know?"

"I'm dying," Goodine disclosed, calmly.

"I'm sorry," Kate responded, reaching out tentatively, touching him with her hands, then withdrew them with hesitation.

The Colonel turned away from her. "I don't want your pity," he said, flatly. "When I was told that I had maybe four or five months to live, the first thing that came to mind was balancing the scale."

Dawson listened intently.

"I'm no hero, and I have no delusions about becoming a hero now. Those four or five months are precious to me, and I intend to live them to the fullest, doing everything that I've always wanted to do. I have no intentions of living out my last days in a cell or on the run from an unseen enemy."

"But—"

"You have everything you need to break this case wide open on your own," he said, with a sense of finality. "I've given you the broad strokes on the canvas. You also have everything I gave Meghan Kendrick. So now, you're going to have to do your own research. You're going to have to follow your own leads."

"But this kind of thing is too big for one person!" she proclaimed, feeling overwhelmed.

"I'm glad you realize the significance of the scope," he said, sounding like a mentor. "You shouldn't allow yourself to get bogged down in minor details. It's important that you not miss the grand scheme."

Dawson studied his face. "How grand?"

"This is no longer just about the United States. This has gone global. We're in bed with Russia, Red China, Israel, the Saudis. Everyone's protecting the big secret."

"Is that true?"

"Don't you believe me, after all I have told you?"

"I don't know . . ."

"Did I fail to convince you?"

"I'm not sure."

Colonel Goodine shook his head and walked off, leaving Dawson alone at the end of Pier 39. She watched him disappear into the fog. Only his footsteps were audible as he walked away.

The image of the old soldier in the trench coat disappearing into the fog stayed in Kate Dawson's mind as she made her way through Fisherman's Wharf, back to the cable car station. The fun and merriment that characterized the tourist attraction hours earlier had been replaced by the somber reality that it had all been a façade created to separate patrons from their hard-earned entertainment dollars. What remained were empty stands, penny arcades without players, and restaurants with few, if any, diners eating pizza or shrimp. Maintenance men hosed down the docks, while cleaning crews went to work emptying trash cans and stacking chairs for the next day. She walked past the Doc Popcorn counter, which was now closed, and imagined the bag of popcorn that she had purchased earlier for twenty dollars.

Dawson thought about all what Colonel Goodine had told her, trying to temper the fanciful and fantastic elements of his story against what she knew was true and very real. She would have been the first one to admit that she didn't know that much about the history of the United States. Cold War? Forget it. Kate had spent most of her time chasing boys, and she wasn't the least bit ashamed. She also didn't buy into most of the stuff about flying saucers and little gray men. To her, that all seemed like science fiction. But she did acknowledge there was a group of very powerful men who were determined to maintain their stranglehold on the truth, and it was her duty to stop them.

She came upon the iconic crab wheel sign and gazed at the letters which spelled out Fisherman's Wharf. A few hours earlier, when she first glimpsed the sign, she hadn't a care in the world, now she felt like Atlas, carrying the weight of the entire thing on her shoulders.

CHAPTER NINE

Rather than catching the Powell-Hyde cable car back to where she had parked, Kate Dawson strolled along the Port of San Francisco for a while lost in thought. She didn't know what her next move was, or even if there was a next move, and the smell of the rich, salty sea air helped to refresh her mind.

Feeling the chill of the night air, Dawson pulled her lightweight jacket tight around her as she walked along the boardwalk by the Marina. The fog was cold as it continued to flow in from the Bay. The full moon was fighting to break through the patches of fog and low mist, but it was a losing battle, as even the tall buildings hovering over the Port were steadily being eaten up by its hungry appetite. A couple wrapped up in each other's company would have walked right into Dawson had she not twisted to one side, jostling as the boardwalk became busier with lovers out for evening strolls. A few days earlier, she and John had walked there, arm-in-arm, and as the breeze whipped through her thick brown hair, she paused to think of him.

Without a moment's hesitation, Dawson took her cell phone out to dial Prescott's number. She knew that it was late, particularly on the East Coast, but she just had to talk with him.

"Hello," he answered, groggy, half-asleep.

"Hi, sweetheart," she said. "I'm sorry for calling so late, but I need to ask you for another favor."

"Do you know it's two A.M.?" John asked, sounding like he was standing right next to her.

"Yeah, I'm really sorry for calling so late."

"That's okay, honey. How can I help you?"

"I need to get into that reception tomorrow, but I've been told there aren't any more invitations left. They've all been posted."

Prescott was silent for a moment. "Listen, Kate, we talked about this before," he said finally. "You can't let yourself get pulled into this any further. Your life and your career stand for rationality, not intellectual chaos. You swore an oath to uphold the very same high-minded principles that formed this nation. Those principles are law and order. Keep up this emotional quest for vengeance and you'll lose everything. You'll destroy yourself."

Kate was silent, thinking.

"Did you hear me, Kate?"

"This is not about revenge, John. This is about justice."

"Sweetheart, I understand how you feel," he said, his voice kind and sympathetic. "Beneath that hard-as-nails exterior of yours beats the heart of a woman who's been through a lot this week. You've been shot, suspended, and you've lost your chief witness in a huge murder investigation. I'm truly sorry about Ortega, but you have to let it all go. The Attorney General for the State of California has taken over now, and she will use the resources of her office to prosecute this case."

"So now you're on her side?"

"You know that's not true," John defended. "I will always be on your side. I just wanted to remind you that there will be other murder investigations; other cases to solve. Don't throw your career away, or jeopardize your life any further, with this one."

She thought about it. "No, you're wrong, John. Frank Miller always used to say there was only one investigation, and that was the one you were working on. Nothing else mattered."

"It's a really nice sentiment, Kate, but you and I both know that's not the reality we face daily," he countered, sitting up in bed and turning on the bedside lamp. "We have our caseloads, and most of the cases we're assigned will be closed without a resolution. Occasionally, we get lucky and break the big case. But most of the time we plod along, doing the best job that we can do. I've had months of undercover work go right down the toilet because someone forgot to obtain a judge's signature on a search warrant or one of my investigators failed to read a perpetrator his Miranda rights. Failure and set-backs are regrettably a part of the job we do. No one likes to admit it, but that's the way it is."

"Failure is not an option to me," Dawson said, without equivocation.

"There are few that understand that statement better than me."

"I'm glad you understand," she said, pacing back and forth. "Now are you going to help me, or not?"

There was an awkward pause, then John said, "Let me tell you something that someone much wiser once told me at a similar point in my life. It was my father, and while we never had a close relationship, I did value his advice. He told me to let it go. To turn back from it and go home. It may seem like the hardest thing in the world to do, but it is profoundly easier than what you're contemplating."

"I'm not turning back."

"That's pretty much what I said," he said, laughing through an exhale.

"Good. I'm glad we're on the same page."

"I'll send you the invitation I got. It'll be attached to an email. Just print it out, and you should be good to go."

"Thanks, John. I love you."

"I love you, too," he reciprocated, then hesitated. "Kate, just remember that once you crossover, there are things in the darkness that can keep your heart from ever feeling the light again."

"I need to stop these bastards!" she said, resolutely.

"I know you do," he said in a soft whisper. "Just promise me you'll be careful."

"I will."

A few minutes later, Dawson hopped on the Powell-Hyde cable car heading south away from the Port of San Francisco. She held onto the strap-handle and leaned out of the car, feeling the breeze as it whipped through her hair. She knew exactly what she had to do, and, for the first time all week, she felt focused.

Kate Dawson pulled into a parking spot in front of her apartment building and headed for the stairs. She walked up the first flight at a fast clip, her head down as if lost in thought.

Several heartbeats later, as she passed the second landing, one of the shadows in the stairwell lengthened into the figure of a man who, in turn, followed Dawson up to the third floor and around the corner.

Suddenly, the female detective was no longer there.

Shadow Man turned to the left, then right, looking for her. Gone. Vanished into thin air. He started to turn towards the stairs when Dawson, who had tucked herself into a shadow, grabbed the Shadow Man from behind and shoved him against her door.

"Okay, pal, enough with the hide-and-go-seek!" she exclaimed, pushing Shadow Man's face hard against the numbers on the door; hard enough to create a reverse image of them on his forehead. "You'd better start telling me who you are and why you've been following me . . . and you'd better do it fast."

"It's not what you think, Inspector Dawson."
"Explain it to me then."

Harlan Reinhardt read his watch and made a mental note of the time. 11:43 P.M. He sat alone in the fifth-floor meeting room of the InterContinental Hotel, waiting for the President to arrive. While it was not uncommon for him to meet clandestinely with presidents at any time of day or night, this meeting seemed different somehow. Reinhardt had just met with Helen Harrison earlier in the day and both agreed not to meet again until they were on their way back to Washington D.C. He recalled one final event in the morning—the dedication of the new VA Hospital—and then it was "wheels up" at 12:13 P.M. He poured himself a glass of water from the pitcher on the table and settled into the chair at the table. Just then, the rear door swept open.

Two Secret Service agents ushered President Harrison into the small meeting room, and after a routine sweep, they left the two of them alone. As he had chosen to remain seated, she towered over him, like a schoolmaster at an English boarding school. He wondered if she was going to admonish him with words or simply crack him on the head with a yardstick. Reinhardt wiped the sweat from his brow, then tucked his handkerchief safely away in the pocket of his trousers.

Finally, he summoned the courage to speak. "What's the problem, Helen?"

"Dawson."

"I'll handle her."

"Well, it doesn't look like you've done a very good job," she responded, with a very even tone of voice. "You assured me that she was on a slab in the morgue, but then I learn that she's broken into my private suite and confronted the First Man. I want to know how she got to my husband today."

"She's a very resourceful woman," Reinhardt hissed, extremely agitated, but trying his damndest to keep his cool. "I can see that I've underestimated her."

"Resourceful? That's not the word that I would use. She's a menace, and if she's not dealt with immediately, she'll ruin everything."

"I said I'd handle it, and I will. I've been handling women like her for years. I know what makes them tick."

Helen Harrison exhaled forcefully. "They're pretty upset about this, Harlan. I wouldn't be meeting with you again so soon if they weren't."

"They're just overreacting."

"Well, *they don't think so.*"

"What do they want me to do?" he asked.

"Get rid of her."

"Get rid of Dawson? I can't, not without raising a lot of suspicion. And as it is, we tried that route once already and failed. Now, it's essential that we discredit her and her investigation. I've already initiated the back-up plan we discussed. She's been put on administrative leave."

"Good," the President said, coldly. "And what *exactly* did my office have to promise in return?"

"Reyes-Salazar wants to run for governor next year, but only if she has your full support for her candidacy behind her."

"Fine. Just make sure that Dawson is out of the picture."

"No problem."

"The feeling's very strong about this, Harlan."

Reinhardt and Helen looked at each other with contempt, like two stags locked by their antlers in a life and death struggle for survival. The only thing that he really wanted to do was reach up and smack the smug look off the President's face, but he thought better of it.

"I said that I would take care of it, and I will take care of it," Reinhardt said finally. "Inspector Dawson is ancient history."

"Don't disappoint me on this," she said, pointing at him, waggling her finger. "Because the next time I'm forced to call a meeting, they'll be no pretense of civility, and I won't be talking to you as your employer. I'll be reading you your obituary."

"I'm glad we had this chance to talk."

President Harrison spun on her heels, hair flying, then she vanished through the rear exit door. Reinhardt was visibly relieved as he wiped his brow yet again.

Dawson released Shadow Man from her grasp, took a step or two back, then waited for him to turn around and face her. "So why all the cloak and dagger?" she asked. "Why didn't you just come right out and tell me you were my personal bodyguard?"

Shadow Man straightened up. "When John Prescott first asked me to keep an eye on you, he insisted that I keep a really low profile."

"Low profile? Well, you certainly achieved that objective. I thought I was going crazy every time I saw a shadow move."

"You weren't supposed to see me at all."

Dawson paced back and forth, stroking her chin. For a moment, she was lost deep in thought. "But why? I've lived in San Francisco my entire life. I've never been in any real danger here, and whatever comes out of my police work is just par for the course."

"Really? Well, you're in grave danger now," he said, with a dramatic flair that seemed uncharacteristic of his role as a shadow. "You may not realize it, Inspector, but the moment you were called on Sunday evening to investigate Meghan Kendrick's murder, a big, red target was painted on your back.

They've already tried to kill you once, and believe me, there was absolutely nothing that I could do about that. They will try again, and I fear you may not be as fortunate."

"You keep using the word 'they.' Who exactly are we talking about? NSA? CIA? Homeland Security?"

"It's not an agency, in the traditional sense of the term," Shadow Man explained. "It's a group of very powerful men— some within the government and others who are the presidents and CEOs of the largest American companies—who have conspired with their counterparts in other nations to keep the MJ-12 documents from ever reaching the light of day. Literally, they will stop at nothing, including murder and character assassination, to recover them, or see them destroyed."

Dawson stopped pacing and really looked at Shadow Man. What she saw frightened her, but she didn't draw away. He was tall and lanky, with a pock-marked face that suggested that he had struggled with acne when he was younger. His hair was cut short, ex-military style, and his dark eyes reminded her of the cold, dead eyes of a predator, like a shark.

"Look, I've already had the shit scared out of me by some unknown assassin's bullet, which missed killing me by inches. You're going to have to do a much better job with your threats if you expect to scare me again."

"What do you know about the Military-Industrial Complex?"

"Not much. I think it has something to do with the production of weapons for the Pentagon."

"I suppose in the broadest sense of the term, you're right, but it goes much deeper than that," he almost whispered, constantly scanning the area and listening intently. "In his farewell address in 1961, President Eisenhower used the term for the first time to refer to the unholy relationship that exists between certain legislators, their campaign contributors, the military, and defense contractors. He warned Americans about the growing influence of certain corporations as they built a 'war-based' economy during a time of peace."

"Which corporations?"

"Take your pick of Wall Street's top ten companies. Seven out of ten, including General Dynamics, Boeing, United Technologies, Lockheed Martin, General Electric, Raytheon, and Northrop Grumman, are among the largest producers of military arms and armaments in the world. The economy of the United States and about a dozen other countries around the globe is tied directly into the Military-Industrial Complex. Despite declines in the gross national products of these countries, due to recessionary pressures, the U.S. has continued to increase its market share in global arms sales and is on pace to deliver more than $50 billion in sales to foreign countries this year alone."

"So, that's what this is all about? Money?"

He craned his head and took a defiant stance. "Money *and* power."

"Why hasn't the Justice Department done anything about it? You've had over fifty years to track these people down, flush them out," Dawson demanded, engaging his eyes for a moment, then looked away. "I want to know why you haven't been doing your job."

"It's not as easy as it sounds. The Attorney General of the United States is, after all, an appointed, cabinet-level position. He has to be approved by some of the same legislators he would be investigating, and, ultimately, he does take his orders from the President of the United States."

"Yes, yes, I see."

"But right now, you hold the key to blowing this whole thing wide open," Shadow Man presented the bottom line, sneering.

"With the MJ-12 documents at your fingertips, you control the fate of entire nations; the whole planet, for that matter. You could tip the very balance of power, if you came forward with what you know and shared those documents. Just imagine how everything would change!"

"Like Edward Snowden?" she asked, with a raise of her eyebrows. "He came forward with thousands of classified documents and look at how that all turned out. No, thank you."

"The Justice Department would protect you."

"If what you're saying is true about the Military-Industrial Complex, I doubt if there's a safe house anywhere in the world that would protect me," Dawson said, pulling her hair behind her ear. "And besides, you're making a huge assumption that I have the MJ-12 documents in my possession."

"But I was told you had the microfilm."

"No, I don't," she replied, putting on an innocent face.

Shadow Man focused his gaze on her. "I am not a fool, so please do not play me like one," he said, seeing right through her. "Remember, I have been shadowing your movements since Monday."

"I don't have the documents," Dawson lied, very convincingly. "But I have a pretty good idea where they are."

He avoided her prevarication. "At this moment in time, you are the most powerful woman alive, more powerful than the President of the United States herself, and I feel humbled to serve you. Just say the word, Kate Dawson, and I will do anything for you."

Dawson hesitated, then said, "You're fired."

"Inspector?"

"I don't need protectors or guardians," she said, shooing him away. "I'm a member of the San Francisco Police Department and I can damn well protect myself. I've got a job to do. I'm going to exercise every option at my disposal to see that those who were responsible for Meghan Kendrick's death are brought to justice, no matter what the cost may be to me personally."

"But don't you see, Inspector Dawson?" he asked, raising an objection. "You can also serve humanity by taking on the mantle of leadership and putting an end to the tyranny and oppression these men represent, once and for all time. You could use this power for good."

"End tyranny and oppression by becoming a tyrant?" Dawson mused. "If there's one lesson that I have learned as a public servant, it's the inevitability of the old adage that power corrupts, and absolute power corrupts absolutely. I've watched far too many good, decent people, who get elected to political office, become drunk with power once they see the view from the top."

Shadow Man listened.

"Earlier today, I met with the First Man. He was an individual that I had admired for years because of his concern for the common man. But I must confess, I didn't even recognize him anymore. That's the problem with power. Once you get a taste for it, you become addicted, then you find yourself doing things that you would have never done before just to stay refreshed. The first time you tell yourself you'll only do it once; the next time, you're convinced that it's for the common good, and then, before long, you're compromising every principle you've ever had. I don't want that to ever happen to me."

"I think I understand."

"Good!" Dawson exclaimed, patting him on the back. "Now go back to John Prescott and tell him he'll be looking for a new girlfriend if I find another one of you spooks dogging me. I can take care of myself."

Shadow Man didn't move as Dawson walked toward her apartment, leaving him standing in the shadows of the corridor.

"No, better yet," she said, turning around. "I'll tell him myself. You just crawl back into whatever hole you came out of."

Harlan Reinhardt reached Pioneer Park before his contact had arrived. He waited in the back of his chauffeur-driven limousine, staring up at Coit Tower. Built in 1933, high atop Telegraph Hill, which was already the highest point in the city, Coit Tower was a monument dedicated to San Francisco Firemen. He marveled at the feat of engineering that had gone into its construction.

Less than ten minutes later, Anatoly Piotrovskii pulled his small Toyota Corolla alongside the black limousine. Climbing out of the driver's side, he swiftly crossed to the limo.

Reinhardt leaned over and opened the passenger-side door of the big car. "Get in," he ordered the former KGB operative.

Piotrovskii slid into the limousine next to the Secret Service chief with a big toothy grin. Reinhardt could tell just by the look on Anatoly's face that the former KGB man had something, something pretty big. Anatoly Piotrovskii practically radiated excitement.

"I got something that might interest you," he said, handing the Secret Service chief a manila envelope.

Harlan Reinhardt took the envelope in hand and broke the seal. Inside were a dozen photos the KGB assassin had snapped earlier that night at Fisherman's Wharf. As Reinhardt thumbed through the 4x6 glossy prints, Kate Dawson's clandestine meeting with Colonel Goodine played out in living color.

"I guess it was inevitable." He mopped his face with his ever-present handkerchief.

"Her meeting with Goodine has now compromised the whole operation."

"You had your chance to kill her," Reinhardt reminded him.

"That bitch is like an old alley cat," Piotrovskii said, shaking his head. "She's scrappy, with razor-sharp claws. She's also hard to kill, with those nine lives of hers, and then there's that endless curiosity."

"I thought you didn't make confessions."

He looked away from the Secret Service chief. "I never have. Not before this."

"What happened to you, Anatoly? You used to be the most feared assassin in the whole of Europe. No one could catch you; not Interpol, not the CIA, and not even the British Secret Service, no one," Reinhardt pointed out. "And now look at you! You're weak. You're flabby. You've lost your edge. I guess all that good living and borscht have made you more of a liability than an asset."

In the blink of an eye, Piotrovskii had a long, thin blade at the Secret Service chief's throat. "I still have a few moves left."

Reinhardt pushed the knife away with little concern for his own safety, and coughed into the handkerchief. "I hate the fog in San Francisco. It's bad for my health. The chill always gives me a cold."

The Russian assassin sheathed his blade. "What are my orders?"

Reinhardt stared into his eyes. "Bring her to me."

"I thought you wanted her dead."

"I did."

"You want me to bring her in?" Piotrovskii could not believe it. "Then there's going to be an additional fee. It's going to cost you double, if you want me to bring the alley cat in."

"Oh, and why is that?"

The Russian said seriously, "Because I don't like you."

"The pot meets the kettle at last," Reinhardt said, with a pained look on his face. "Tell you what, Anatoly. For old time's sake, I'll pay you double if you kill her and she stays dead, this time. Okay?"

"Absolutely."

Harlan Reinhardt studied the deadly man's face for a long moment, then focused ahead. "I do hope everything's ready for tomorrow? The President's counting on her stop at the VA hospital to be a 'memorable' one."

"Oh, yeah," Piotrovskii said sinisterly. "Everyone will think it was the Iranians, then she'll have her excuse to go to war."

"No slip-ups or it'll be both our heads."

"No slip-ups."

Reinhardt coughed again into his handkerchief, shivering. "It's getting very chilly here."

"You'd better take care of that cold."

The Secret Service chief refused to regard him, saying, "Get out, Anatoly. I think you'll find Coit Tower interesting. They say it's supposed to be the nozzle to a fire hose, but I find it to be vaguely phallic."

Piotrovskii slid out of the limousine and closed the door. As he looked up at the Tower, the vehicle sped away into the night.

When Kate Dawson opened the door to her apartment, she found her friend Rosa asleep on the couch. Romano appeared to be hovering in that gray area between sleep and wakefulness. She rubbed her body against the back of the couch and reached up instinctively to pull the blanket over her shoulder. Kate thought about waking her to find out how the dinner with Lenny had gone, but then thought better of it, particularly if things had been a total disaster. Kate tiptoed over and laid the comforter over her shoulder, putting it delicately in her hand.

"Katie," she murmured, like a child reassuring herself with her mommy's name, "is that you?"

"Yes, Rosa, it's me," Dawson whispered. "Just go back to sleep. We'll talk about things in the morning."

"No, it's important," Rosa said, starting to sober up. "I've been trying to get a hold of you all night long on your cell phone."

Dawson crouched down next to the couch. "I turned it off. I had a meeting with an informant who's overly cautious about cell phones."

"Lenny's been arrested," she reported.

"What? Not again!" Kate asked, beside herself. "The two of you were going to have dinner and he was going to take you home."

"That was the plan," Rosa explained, sitting up on the couch. "But no sooner had we started cooking dinner together, this crazy woman shows up at his door, forces her way in, and starts throwing things around."

"Rebecca? Was her name Rebecca?"

Romano groggily answered, "I think so."

"Did you call 9-1-1?" Kate asked.

"Never had the chance. The police showed up just after she did. They put the handcuffs on Lenny and dragged him out of there before I could call you or anyone else."

Dawson slammed her hand on the coffee table. "Son-of-a-bitch!"

"Would you mind telling me what's going on?" Rosa asked, confused.

"Remember when I told you he was having problems with an ex-girlfriend? Well, Rebecca broke up with him a couple of weeks ago and swore out a protective order against Lenny, claiming he was abusive. She said that he had threatened to kill her unless she agreed to continue having sex with him."

"Are you kidding me?"

"No, I'm not," Kate said, with a tired look on her face.

"What a fuckin' drama queen."

"You know, the more I think about it, the more I'm beginning to think that he's the one who needs protection from *her*."

"Yeah, after what I saw tonight, I think you're right. That bitch is a real piece of work!"

Dawson took her cell phone out. "Do you know if they were going to book him at the Hall of Justice or one of the other precincts?"

"I'll do you one better," Rosa said, producing her own iPhone. Quickly, she scrolled through several numbers, finally landing on one. "When I couldn't reach you on your phone, I tried calling down to the precinct. I spoke with Lieutenant Ramos who verified that he had Lenny in custody."

"Oh, shit! That asshole?" Kate's shoulders slumped and head fell forward.

"You know him?"

"Yeah, I know him," she said disgusted. "He's convinced that Lenny's some kind of sexual deviant who needs to be put away behind bars."

"Well, that's who's got him."

As Romano confirmed her worst fears, Dawson checked her gun to make sure it was fully loaded and slipped it into the waist of her jeans. She then tucked her police badge in the breast pocket of her jacket, with the badge facing out.

"Do you want me to go with you?" Rosa asked.

Dawson patted her on the shoulder. "No, this is strictly between Ramos and me. But do me a favor, lock up before you leave."

"Good hunting, girlfriend."

By the time she reached the Hall of Justice, Kate Dawson had broken most of the city's traffic violations. She pulled to the curb and darted across the street at the crosswalk to the old brick building. But she didn't head directly to Lock-Up, which was in the basement, she clambered up two flights of stairs to the Special Victim's Unit (SVU) on the second floor. Once there, Dawson was forced to wait in the Lieutenant's outer office.

"Give me five minutes, then show her in," Lieutenant Emmanuel Ramos said, putting the telephone receiver down slowly. He sat back in a large, leather chair behind his desk, mesmerized by the steam rising from his hot cup. Ramos debated whether he should drink the chamomile tea or simply inject it into his veins. When his doctor had warned him about drinking too much coffee on the job, he had reluctantly agreed to substitute tea as his stimulant of choice. No matter what tea he tried, however, it never really took the place of coffee, and it certainly did not improve on the flavor. Every tea still tasted bitter to him and only served to remind him how much he missed his coffee.

He took a couple of sips of the hot tea, frowned, then pulled Provolone's file closer to him. He had just completed the first eight hours of a double-shift and he was already feeling edgy.

There was a curt knock at the door, and one of his men escorted Dawson into his office. He did not acknowledge her in any way but appeared to be thoroughly engrossed in the file he was reading. So, she just stood there in front of his desk, staring.

Impatiently, Ramos rifled through the contents, then closed the folder shut. The beige folder had a diagonal black stripe across it which meant that Provolone was a potential "sex offender." He hated sex offenders worse than drug dealers and perverts, and if he had had his way, he would have had them all castrated and exiled to some deserted island where they could no longer hurt anyone. He looked down at the folder with weary-eyes. Taking another couple of sips from his tea, which had grown cold, he regarded Dawson. "Why don't you take a seat, Inspector," Ramos said, finally.

"Great idea!" Kate answered with a hint of sarcasm. "I'm glad you thought of that, Lieutenant Ramos. It never would have occurred to me."

"Dawson, I got a real problem here."

"Is that right?"

"I understand you're here to sign Mister Provolone out of lock-up again," he said, sitting back in his chair. "You signed him out a couple of nights ago, making yourself legally responsible for his actions. I want you to explain to me why I shouldn't be locking you up in a cell right next to him. You were supposed to be keeping him out of trouble, not making the problem worse."

"The altercation that happened tonight between Lenny and his ex-girlfriend was not his fault," she defended her friend. "He was at home, minding his own business, having dinner with a mutual friend when Rebecca stormed into his apartment and started throwing things around like a crazy person. She's the one who should be locked up, not Mister Provolone."

"No, I don't think so." He sat back smugly, fingers interlocked before him. "I spoke with Miss Thompson earlier this evening by phone. She was still very upset. Apparently, Lenny had provoked her by sending an unwanted and unsolicited email which suggested she seek professional help for her 'psychotic behavior.' He then went on to say how he had met a woman who was normal, and how he never wanted to deal with psychos like her ever again. Can you imagine receiving an email like that? This just goes beyond the pale."

"I don't know anything about that," Dawson said, face drooping.

"That's exactly what I expected you to say!" Ramos barked.

"Most friends of sex offenders say the same thing. They just bury their heads in the sand, pretending there's nothing wrong with their friend."

"I'll admit that Lenny's a bit odd, perhaps even socially immature, but I can assure you that he doesn't represent a threat to anyone."

The Lieutenant stared at her, unblinking. "Next, you're going to be telling me what a nice boy he is. How he helps little old ladies cross the street. How he wouldn't even hurt a fly."

"What gives with you, Ramos?" Dawson's boiling point was coming soon. "You've had it in for my friend since day one. What happened? Did you know each other in college? Did he steal your girl? Beat you in the science fair? I want to know why you've been such a hard ass with Lenny."

"I've got a problem with sex offenders," he said flatly.

"Lenny's not like that at all!"

"Your friend is a sexual predator!" Ramos bellowed, cutting her off. He picked up the folder on his desk and hurled it across to her.

Dawson caught it mid-air, brought it down to her lap, and opened it, thumbing through the first couple of pages. She was shocked to see he had a police record. As she read through his rap sheet, Dawson noted that his criminal history had been divided between actual convictions, where he had plead guilty to rape and *nolo contendere* to several counts of indecent exposure and solicitation for prostitution, and arrests, where numerous charges for indecent exposure, solicitation, and sexual assault had been dismissed. Most of the charges against him were misdemeanors, which carried monetary fines and community service requirements but no real jail time. Perhaps the most egregious of all the charges was the one for rape. But as Kate breezed through the case file, she realized that he had been convicted of statutory rape of a minor when he was barely eighteen-years-old. While the charge had resulted in a felony conviction, Provolone did not spend a single day in jail. Alternatively, he was released on probation and given three hundred hours of community service to discharge. Since all his convictions had taken place before 1997, he was not registered as a sex offender in the National Sex Offender Registry. To her mind, Lenny seemed like a poor, troubled soul.

"Your friend has quite a criminal record," Lieutenant Ramos commented, glaring at her. "Statutory rape, indecent exposure, sexual assault, solicitation for prostitution . . . These are all sex crimes in my book."

"Mostly misdemeanors and no convictions in the last twenty years."

"Oh, he's been arrested plenty of times in the last twenty years, Inspector. In fact, the most recent arrest was just three months ago for indecent exposure at a peep show in the Tenderloin. He's just gotten very clever with his excuses. The charges didn't stick, but I promise you the next time, they will."

"Sounds like you've got your work cut out for you," she said, giving him her full attention.

"Let's just cut through the bullshit, shall we? I don't like creeps like Lenny who prey on little girls half his age. They should be locked up with the other perverts and wackos out there, and we should throw away the key. In my book, only a loser would prey on a younger woman. They haven't got the balls to go out with someone their own age, so they skulk about the playgrounds and school yards until they find some innocent who doesn't know any better."

Dawson looked at the Bureau Chief of the Special Victims Unit for a full half minute, thirty seconds of rage and disbelief. She managed to keep the anger out of her voice, but not the incredulity. "If I didn't know better, Lieutenant, I'd say you're taking this personally. And the one lesson that I remember from my academy days was to leave my personal feelings out of my police work."

"Well, I guess, you've caught me." He paused and took a deep breath before continuing. "I created the Special Victims Unit within the SFPD six years ago to handle crimes against the city's most vulnerable residents. We brought together units that investigated child and elderly abuse, domestic violence, sex crimes, human trafficking, missing persons, and financial crimes into one special unit. But I must confess that I established the unit as a tribute to my eight-year-old sister Maria Ramos who was raped and murdered by Jesse Rojas, an unregistered sex offender who had been previously convicted of sex crimes and lived on the same block. He killed Maria after luring her to his house under the pretext of showing off a new puppy. Not a day goes by when I don't remember her happy, smiling face, and the reason why I've put everything on the line for her."

"I'm really sorry about your loss," Kate said sincerely. "My daughter was killed in a violent act, but not due to a sex offender."

"Then you understand. Catching these sexual predators and putting them behind bars is more than just a job to me. It's my life. It's what motivates me to get up every morning and come to work."

"I do understand." And Dawson truly did.

"Then why do you insist on protecting men like Provolone?" Ramos asked.

"I don't know any other men like him. I just know Lenny," she said directly. "He's troubled, and he needs our help. But from what I've seen over the years, he just wants to be loved, like the rest of us. He's spent so much of his life, groping around in the darkness looking for love, that he really doesn't know what it is. He thinks it's all about a perfect body, bright, white teeth, no sags or wrinkles. He doesn't realize that it's about deep feelings that come from within a person. Feelings like compassion, caring, sacrifice, selflessness, commitment, and intimacy. He's not likely to learn those feelings in prison, but from people who care about him and love him. I guess that's the reason why I've been his friend all these years."

Lieutenant Ramos closed his eyes and lowered his head. "It goes against my better judgment, but if you think he's better off with you than in prison, then I won't stand in your way."

"Thanks, Lieutenant, for your understanding," Kate said, smiling.

"Just do me one favor," he said, reaching for the telephone.

"What's that?"

"Keep him out of trouble."

"I'll try my best." She stood and returned the folder. "I think it's only fair that you warn Rebecca to stay away from Lenny. I'd say that he has more than enough to file a restraining order of his own against her."

Dawson shook his hand on the way out the door, and collected Lenny Provolone at the Lock-Up on her way out of the building.

They had driven a good ten blocks back towards the apartment complex before one of them spoke. Dawson asked, "Why didn't you ever tell me that you were arrested for having sex with a minor?"

"I didn't know she was underage," Lenny replied, defensively. "We met at a sci-fi convention and she seemed old enough. But that happened over twenty years ago. What has that got to do with my arrest tonight?"

"And sexual assault?"

"Damn it to hell! You saw my rap sheet!" he exclaimed, curling into a protective ball on the bucket seat, much like a turtle retreating into its shell.

"Yeah, Lieutenant Ramos shared it with me." She made the turn at the next street and drove another couple of blocks before adding, "Statutory rape, indecent exposure, sexual assault, and solicitation for prostitution, you've got an extensive criminal record, Lenny. You're lucky you haven't been required to register as a sex offender in the National Sex Offender Registry."

"I'm so embarrassed." Lenny stared out the window, wishing he was anywhere but there.

"Let's drop the pretense, will you? Try to imagine my embarrassment walking into Ramos' office, insisting you were innocent when he had a rap sheet on you a mile long. I'd like to know why you never told me."

"I don't know what to say, Kate. I always intended to tell you, but it never seemed like the right time."

"You should have *made* the time," she insisted.

"Yeah, you're right," he said, hanging his head.

Dawson shot him a sideways glance. "Now, what am I going to do with you? You've not only broken my trust, but you've also made a fool of me in front of one of my superiors on the Force. You've lied to me. You've manipulated me. You've had me put my job on the line for you. And to make matters worse, you've now involved one of my closest friends, Rosa Romano."

"I know, Kate. I'm a big disappointment to you."

"You don't know shit, Lenny! You've been so focused on yourself that you really don't have a clue about other people's feelings. Everything's always about you and what you're feeling. Not once have you ever considered the impact that you have on other people's lives."

Provolone was close to tears. "Maybe you should just shoot me and put me out of everyone's misery."

"You've had worse ideas, lately."

They rode in silence for another couple of blocks, all the while Lenny thinking that Dawson was going to take her service pistol out and shoot him in the head. But, of course, she had no such intention. Reaching the light at Delancey, she came to a full stop before making a right turn on red. She looked at him as if he was nothing more than an acquaintance, someone she knew only casually. Her heart started to soften when she saw that he was silently crying.

Quickly, Kate pulled out a couple of tissues from the box she kept in the car and passed them over to her friend. "Stop that sniveling," she demanded. "You're a grown man. You should start acting like one."

"You're right. You're always right," he said, snorting back the tears.

Dawson pulled directly into a parking spot near their building and turned off the engine. They both sat there in silence for another couple of minutes, then Kate turned to face him. "Let me ask you something, Lenny."

"Sure. Anything," he responded, wondering, *What next?*

"Did you send Rebecca an email today?"

Provolone hesitated for a moment. *Shit!* "Yes, I just wanted to let her know that we were through."

"Lenny, why did you do that?" Kate asked, pounding her hand on the dashboard in frustration. "Don't you know that was like throwing kerosene on a fire? Why couldn't you have just let things be?"

"I felt like we both needed some kind of closure," he explained.

"Rebecca had the closure she wanted when she filed the protective order against you," Dawson said, trying to reason with him. "I think this was more about you trying to get even with her for breaking your heart. You wanted to shove your newfound friend, Rosa Romano, in her face, in much the same way that you wanted to make her jealous by inviting me to attend that sci-fi convention last year. You were the one who provoked that altercation tonight, not Rebecca."

"Am I facing any jail time?"

Dawson cringed. "There you go again, thinking all about yourself. Do you have any idea how upset Rosa has been? I found her camped out on my couch tonight, all worried sick about you."

"I didn't know."

"How could you have known? You've spent the last hour so concerned about yourself that you never once asked about her."

Dawson left Lenny in her car, brooding; waited by the trunk a good two minutes before walking around to the passenger's side door and opening it wide for him. He fumbled with the seatbelt, then struggled to get to his feet with her help.

He shot her a worried glance. "Do you think I'm gonna go to jail?"

"No, Lenny, I don't think so."

"I'm terrified with the thought of going to prison. Do you have any idea what they do to sex offenders?"

"I do, and you should be afraid, very afraid." Kate gave him a stern look. "But don't lose too much sleep worrying about it. I plan to stand right next to you when you have your court hearing with the judge."

"Really?"

"Sure, Lenny. I'm not about to let you walk into that court-room alone. I'm your friend."

Provolone started tearing up again. "You mean, after all this, you still want to be my friend?"

She put her hand on his arm. "Yes, Lenny. That's what friendship is all about. Learning all about another person, including those deep, dark hidden parts that no one ever sees, and still caring enough about them to be their friend."

"I thought you'd never want to speak to me again."

"No, I'm afraid you're stuck with me."

Lenny Provolone put his arms around her, hugging her for dear life. Tears ran down his cheeks. Kate hugged him back, pressed him closer, held him tightly. At that moment in time, she couldn't have felt more wanted and alive.

CHAPTER TEN

Just before 10 A.M. on Thursday morning, Kate Dawson pushed her way through a crowd of several hundred people that had gathered outside the new Veteran's Hospital on the grounds of the Presidio in northwest San Francisco. She made her way toward the entrance of its newly-constructed Atrium disguised as "Miss Lonelyhearts," a fifty-five-year-old spinster. Dawson was also mindful of the fact that she could also be arrested for malicious trespass if any one of her fellow officers from the SFPD spotted her. She tiptoed past Balardi, Clark, and Jawara at the main entrance and vanished into the crowd as just another anxious fan wanting to get a look at the new female president.

Members of the Press began snapping pictures and rolling their cameras as the Presidential motorcade slowed down in front of the hospital. Everyone was cheering, waving flags, and clapping when President Harrison climbed out of the limousine with her administrative aide and several Secret Service agents. Flashbulbs exploded in her face and reporters from several networks struggled in vain to have a brief word with her, but the President's detail kept her moving. All she could do was acknowledge and wave at familiar faces as she approached the entrance.

Secret Service agents led President Harrison through a large stone archway, and once inside the shade of the glass-covered Atrium, they slowed long enough to give her time to shake hands and converse with some of those who had been waiting patiently for over an hour to meet her. Miss Lonelyhearts was among the first group of people she met face to face, and the fifty-five-year-old spinster made a point of telling her how proud she was to have a female president as a role model. For Helen Harrison, it was like walking into the middle of a gladiatorial arena as the multitude of people and the media pressed forward, against the makeshift barriers, to try to get a piece of her. Awash in a sea of humanity, the President continued moving forward struggling to maintain a good sense of humor. The podium, which must have seemed so close only a few minutes ago, now felt like it was a world away. Agent Smith, her lead escort, was ordered by a voice in his ear to step it up a bit, so he and two of his fellow agents began clearing a path for the President, shoveling people out of the way, like granules of snow, while additional agents kept others from trailing behind.

Miss Lonelyhearts was one of those who had been discouraged from following her idol, so she broke off from the rest of the pack and moved anonymously through the horde of people, looking for their ring leader. She stumbled upon the Secret Service chief, moving, like her, through the crowd, and tucked herself neatly behind him, reduced to nothing more than a shadow.

With sweat glistening off his brow, Harlan Reinhardt looked around, trying very hard to mask his discomfort as crowds of people surged forward to get their one-and-only glimpse of the Commander-in-chief. Flash bulbs fired off like gunfire and reporters from each of the major networks jockeyed with their camera crews for just the right angle to scoop the other networks with the best story. As he continued to circulate through the crowd, Reinhardt saw hands sliding into pockets, parasols raised in the sunlight, eyes shifting . . . Every movement was a potential threat and every shadow hid an assassin. He took a deep breath and checked the time. Less than ten minutes to zero hour.

Reinhardt tapped on the little receiver in his ear, then barked into the microphone on his wrist, "All right, boys, let's go for the count off."

"East Annex . . . clear," the first agent reported in his ear.

"North Tower . . . clear," the second agent said, with a Texas accent.

The third agent sounded off, "West entrance is clear, sir."

Overwhelmed by the sheer volume of the crowd, Reinhardt spun around in each direction as reports came in from his men. He couldn't help but notice there were windows everywhere in the Atrium. He swallowed down hard. It was a Secret Service nightmare!

"South Tower report!" he shouted into his microphone.

"We're clear, sir. Sorry for the delay," the agent apologized.

Reinhardt fumbled for a clean, white handkerchief in his pocket, and when in hand, drew it across his profusely-sweating forehead. His hand was shaking as he returned it to the pocket of his suit jacket.

"Garage . . . we're good," another agent reported.

"Ground cover . . . good. Twenty-four . . . clear. Thirteen has blue skies. Eleven is a go," the last of his agents reported in, all at once.

Reinhardt was just about ready to clear the President's detail for the podium when he felt something or someone gnawing at the back of his head, like an inch he couldn't scratch. He spun around and, for an instant, thought he saw Dawson. She was wearing a cockamamie disguise, but it was her okay. He searched the Atrium for some sign of her, looking for reflections in the glass, then scanned the perimeter, finding the entrance clear; noting where the two exits were located. Searching the second floor, he saw that one of the curtains had moved.

"Rear annex," he barked into his mic, still searching for Dawson. "That building should have been cleared over an hour ago."

"Copy. It's clear," the agent reported.

"I've got a flutter on the second floor," he snarled. "Third window from the right. That room's supposed to be empty."

"Roger. We'll check it again," the agent replied.

Harlan Reinhardt pulled out a small pair of binoculars from his jacket and zeroed in on the room with a couple of twists of the lens. At the window, he saw his agent come into frame and pull the curtain free.

"Sir, a breeze must've blown the curtain," the agent said, talking into his mic. "We've got it now."

Reinhardt said softly, "Okay, let's bring POTUS on in."

Agent Smith, with the help of the other two Secret Service agents, escorted the President through the huge crowd and helped her climb up two short steps to the podium stage. At the top, Helen Harrison was greeted warmly by Mayor De Soto and the other dignitaries. The two leaders smiled and posed for photos, shaking hands. Once the President had shaken hands with De Soto, she turned to greet the other city and state leaders, Alejandra Reyes-Salazar and Colonel Goodine among them, working the photo-ops with her official press photographer. Eventually, President Harrison found her seat and sat down in the front row. As the mayor moved slowly to the podium, he was a bundle of nervous energy.

The cheers, clapping, and exaltation from the people drowned out everything else, making it almost impossible to hear in the large atrium. It continued unabated for another moment or two, until Mayor De Soto finally raised his hands in the air and stepped up to the microphone. The crowd of well-wishers gradually quieted down and everyone returned to their seats in an orderly fashion. The Atrium soon fell silent, except for the occasional cough or whisper.

"*Buenos tardes*, and welcome," De Soto said, speaking into the microphone, like a seasoned politician. "Thank you so much for being here on this momentous day. It gives me great pleasure to introduce the Forty-Fifth President of the United States from the great state of Arkansas . . . Helen Harrison."

As the President stood up amidst another round of cheers and applause, she seized the opportunity to shake several hands of those nearest her, including Reyes-Salazar. She waved again at the crowd and took her place at the podium. They continued to cheer and applaud her as she adjusted the microphone for her height, waiting for the crowd to settle down.

"Distinguished guests, ladies and gentlemen, members of the press," she began her speech, "I want to thank you for the warm show of support you've given me during this very difficult and trying time in our Nation's history. While we are here today to dedicate this brand-new Veteran's Hospital, we are also here to rededicate ourselves to the mission of peace that we so desperately desire from—"

BOOM!

Suddenly, there was a blinding flash, followed almost instantaneously by a large explosion that rocked the very foundation of the hospital. Fire and debris shot into the air, and then came raining down on the crowd. The lights in the Atrium and the adjacent towers flickered off and on, then permanently off. In the milliseconds between the flash and the explosion,

Dawson thought the flash itself looked like a super nova in the brilliantly-lit Atrium, and as the circle of light radiated outward, she saw the leading-edge turn from blue-white to red-orange. Reds and oranges mixed with yellows at the center of the blast as the ball of fire gained intensity and strength. From where she was standing, the scene had an eerie sense of unreality about it. Time stood still, as she turned in slow motion to watch the President fall from the podium and Reinhardt's agents reach out in vain to keep her from falling. Some people were thrown into the air, while others were tossed aside, like rag dolls.

The leading edge of the shock wave radiated outward in all directions, like the blast wave of a nuclear explosion. She saw that the shock wave was going to hit the windows that made up the glass-covered Atrium, but there was nothing she could do, except tuck herself into a crouch and cover her head with the jacket she was wearing. Shards of glass came raining down on the few survivors who had managed to get to their feet and were bolting for the exits. Some managed to get out safely, while others fell victim to the thousands of razor-sharp glass spikes that fell.

Dawson tried to scream, to warn people away, but she couldn't hear herself. She couldn't hear anything. The blast had deafened her. People from the crowd ran wild screaming, but she couldn't hear a thing.

"Oh, my God!" she screamed in terror.

BOOM!

Just then, another bomb exploded, and the entire Atrium floor shuddered from the impact of the explosion. The shock wave, accompanied by the incredible blast of light that flooded the large room with blinding shafts of blue and white, catapulted her across thirty feet of floor before she even realized what had hit her. Overhead, the fluorescent lights recessed in the ceiling exploded into a shower of sparks, as several sections of the lighting conduit broke loose and came crashing to the floor. Without a moment's hesitation, she rolled under one of the few tables in the room and put her hands over her head. Seconds later, the rest of the ceiling that wasn't made of glass collapsed inches away from where she had just been laying.

When she dared to look up, Reinhardt and several of his agents were forcing the President to her feet, then fast-stepped her, sometimes dragging, sometimes carrying, to safety.

Dawson crawled out from beneath one of the tables; nothing but death and destruction, total devastation. Near her, a Secret Service agent lay dead. She quickly patted him down, searching for his gun and comlink. She found his Sig Sauer P229 and shoved it in her waistband at the small of her back. Kate then made fast work of stripping away the earpiece and plugging herself into the comlink. She listened to the chatter, but only for a moment.

"Master Command, I need a twenty on POTUS," the first agent demanded.

"Eagle's down. Repeat. Eagle's down," the second agent shouted into his mic, panic rising in his voice. "Does anyone copy?"

"Is she dead? Over," the first one responded.

"No, but we need to move Eagle now," the second agent emphasized. "We may still be under attack. Unknown number of assailants."

"Copy that. We'll start clearing a path so we can get her out of there!" the first one said, excitedly.

Reinhardt broke into the conversation. "I want a perimeter set up, starting at a block out from the hospital complex. Let's get the local authorities to sweep through all the buildings along the rear annex, starting with the annex itself. No one goes in or out without our say."

"Yes, sir. We're on it," the first one acknowledged.

"You lock it down, and you lock it down right now!" the chief ordered, with his commanding voice. "I don't want a single one of those bastards to get away. You're authorized to shoot first, and ask questions later!"

"Copy that," the first agent said finally.

As Dawson scrambled to her feet, she took the Sig Sauer pistol in hand, slipped out the magazine, put it back in, and worked the slide. KA-CHINK. "I'm ready for you, boys," she said, running after them.

Out on the street, against the clear, blue, morning sky, the explosions' subsequent smoke and fire at the brand-new Veteran's Hospital were now visible to south-bound commuters on the Golden Gate Bridge and as far away as the Financial District and offices in Potrero Hill. It was a devastating yet somewhat attention-grabbing sight to behold as fire licked out of the windows and blast holes and danced into the cloudless, blue sky. The roof on both the North and South towers started to give off a hellish, red-orange glow as smoke billowed into the air. Bypassers below were crowded on the streets and sidewalks in the Presidio, looking up helplessly, chatting and shouting in fear and despair. The sirens of the city police and fire departments could be heard wailing across the streets, and a wave of communal panic was spreading as people quietly used the words "terrorist" and "attack" in the same sentence. No one noticed Harlan Reinhardt and his small team of Secret Service agents, with the President in tow, leaving the hospital grounds and piling into plain, unmarked sedans, ready for their perfect getaway amongst the commotion.

Within minutes, the first engine companies of the San

Francisco Fire Department arrived at the scene and began deploying men and equipment to tackle the blaze, under the command of Battalion Chief Robert O'Hara. He was one of the most outspoken critics in the city of tall high-rise buildings; his firefighters couldn't easily fight a fire above seven floors. So, when he rolled out of his command car and first glimpsed the Veteran's Hospital, he spit out the chewing tobacco that was wedged in his gums, and shouted, "Son-of-a-bitch!"

"Bob, she's throwing a lot of smoke," one of his lieutenants reported, running up to him from the hospital entrance.

"An explosion in the Atrium, right?" O'Hara asked, putting on his gear.

The lieutenant stood awaiting orders. "It's bad. We've got a lot of casualties, but the smoke's so thick, we can't tell how far in it's spread."

"Exhaust system?"

"Yeah, I know. It should've kicked in and reversed automatically. It must have blown with the blast."

"Sprinklers?"

"They're not working either."

O'Hara stared at him a moment, disbelieving. "Why not?"

"I don't know. The explosion?" the junior officer replied.

"Okay, this is what we're going to do," the Battalion Chief said calmly, pulling the heavy oxygen tank onto his back. "I want you to set up our forward command post in the lobby, then go in and get a good look around for me. I'm going to get on the horn and call the third alarm in."

"Affirmative, Chief."

By now, fires were breaking out all over the building, and smoke was choking off the last of the escape routes to safety.

On the far side of the Atrium, Colonel Goodine lay sprawled

out on the floor, his face flattened against the linoleum floor. Shards of glass were scattered all around him, but he was fortunate enough not to have had a direct strike by one of the larger ones. He exhaled heavily, relieved that he was still alive. As he felt the life coming back into his limbs, his right hand twitched, then his left, then he moved his arm. Gradually, he rocked himself into a seating position. His head was pounding as if someone had hit him hard from behind.

Goodine looked across the smoke-filled room and saw the bright-red exit sign beckoning to him. It seemed to call out his name. For a split second, images of what he had planned to do during his last four or five months flashed through his head. Fly-fishing in Montana. A sunset cruise along the Seine. Parasailing over Iguaçu Falls. Scuba-diving off the Barrier Reef. No-limit Texas Hold'em in Las Vegas. He reached his hand up and tried to grasp each one as they floated by, to gather them into him somehow. What he did not know was that they were already far behind him.

He forcefully pushed those thoughts to the far recesses of his mind as he climbed to his feet in pain. He then pointed at two Secret Service agents who were slowly coming around. "You're now, orderlies," Goodine commanded, his deep military voice. "Follow me." They looked at each other with surprise, got to their feet, and followed him, staggering out of the Atrium, down the corridor to the emergency room.

In the North Tower, the Veteran's Hospital was flooded with fear and panic as the doctors, nurses, administrative staff, and patients struggled to get to safety before the tower collapsed inward on itself and plummeted to the ground. In one section, people streamed down the narrow corridors like ants to the central bank of elevators, pushing and shoving to get the last car down. In another, panicking people were hurled against the outer walls or trampled each other to the floor as several aftershocks erupted and buffeted the tower wildly. In yet another section, a woman cowered in a dark corner, holding one of her children in her arms and shielding the other with her body. Her two children were crying aloud in terror, but their cries were muffled by the screams of those racing wildly by. And in the boiler room, where the great turbines continued to turn and supply power to the elevators, hospital workers scrambled to keep the power on, but were suddenly overrun by people racing to be the first to escape.

Just outside the administrative suites on the third floor, Matt Balardi and several uniformed cops stood as beacons in the corridor directing people to the one set of stairs that hadn't already been consumed by fire or flooded with deadly smoke. He was sobbing and tears had stained his middle-aged features. He tried to maintain order with his well-rehearsed use of hand signs and traffic signals, but he was fighting a losing battle. The fear and panic of mob rule had overtaken all manner of reason as people clawed and scraped to reach a place of safety. Finally, he found himself swept up in the flood of humanity and pulled down the corridor.

Four engine companies and two ladder companies had now responded to the call, and with help from his lieutenants, O'Hara deployed his men strategically around the grounds, like a battlefield general commanding his troops. The proud red San Francisco fire engines erected two large ladders from two of the trucks, reaching to the roof and the windows of the North tower. Firefighters with oxygen tanks and protective masks climbed several stories straight up. Other equipped firefighters entered the building from the South Entrance as jets of cold water from fire hoses sprayed into the affected areas of the hospital complex. Fire bellowed as it was struck by water, producing clouds of black smoke that spiraled up into the sky; smoke signals that ordered passersby to keep away.

Kate Dawson had two of Reinhardt's agents in her sights. She powered along the corridor of the hospital after them, with her gun drawn, hoping they would lead her right to the Secret Service Chief himself. As she took the fork in the corridor, Dawson saw where parts of the floor had collapsed into the floor below. She flattened herself against the wall, and side-stepped carefully around the edges. The fresh, cooling air from below refreshed her as she continued to fight her way through the smoke and fiercely-burning fires. Once clear, she started to keep to the shadows, blending into them herself, sensing she was getting closer.

At once, an older man with a knife lunged out at Dawson through one of the open doors. Scrambling backwards, she lost her footing and fell through the gap to the floor below. She hit the linoleum floor hard, knocking the wind out her and dislodging the gun she carried. She lay there dazed, unmoving, covered in the debris that had fallen with her.

Her assailant stood on a small outcrop of the floor above her, looking down at the fallen detective, trying to decide whether she was dead or if he was going to have to go down there and finish her off. Impatient, he started to pace back and forth, like a wild animal waiting for its prey to die.

After a few long moments, Dawson exhaled heavily, her face contorted with pain. She sat up, pulling her legs back under her.

The assassin peered down in anger at Dawson's persistence; his hate-filled eyes boring into her. He jumped carefully down from the higher plain onto the unstable floor below, brandishing his knife, right when an enormous plume of smoke roared up from the fire below. Feeling a rush of danger with so much aggression, savoring the kill, he quickly maneuvered the small fires that had burst to life in his path, making his way towards her.

Dawson didn't hesitate in quickly pulling herself up and balancing on the floor that seemed to move and bend under her weight. Getting her footing correct was the key to staying alive; only the most stable of them would survive the rolling movement of the building that seemed to be collapsing in on itself, right below their feet. Her assailant was suddenly upon her, ready for the kill.

Driven by what appeared to be manic rage, the assassin struck out with his knife, slicing downwards as if to cut Dawson in two. Ready for the attack, she ducked right, letting the knife swipe through the air to strike a nearby fire extinguisher, sparking against the metal. Dawson was ready for him after that strike and reached out for the knife, grabbing the hilt with both hands as her assailant fought to pull it back.

The two, locked in a treacherous balancing act, fought to get the upper hand and push the other one away. Feeling the sheer brutal strength from the assassin's rage, Dawson jabbed out with her fist into his chest, hitting his ribs with a dull thump. The punch didn't seem to faze him in any way. He just retaliated with a sharp twist of his body, sending his right knee into her lower abdomen. The blow was brief, but enough to knock the air out of her, weakened temporarily, giving her assailant the upper hand he needed. She was forced down onto the floor near the edge, her head hanging precipitously over the side, as he pressed his advantage. The assassin gritted his teeth, pushing the knife down, seeking flesh, as she struggled to maintain her grip on his wrists. Dawson was near the breaking point, losing the battle for the knife.

The assassin's face was red from exertion; his crisp black suit torn from the fight; his gray, wavy hair blew in the updraft of smoke and fire. Dawson could no longer hold her breath, exhaled, gasped, in desperate need of oxygen, then held it again, pushing with all her might. He snarled in rage, spitting out saliva as the wild animal inside him escaped. Sensing death mere seconds away, he continued to press his advantage.

With her assailant totally focused on plunging the blade deep into her chest, he didn't see Dawson's next move until it was too late. She brought her knee up as hard as she could, socking him in the groin. The blow was just enough so Kate could push him off. The assassin kept hold of the blade as he stumbled back, but she used his backward momentum to pull herself up to her feet. Heartbeats later, he lunged at her again, but Dawson ducked back, throwing her arms out in a frenzied attempt to keep her balance on the ledge.

BOOM!

Another blast sounded and echoed through the empty halls of the hospital. The shockwaves from the blast, now much closer to them, shook Dawson and her assailant from the floor itself. They let out a cry of despair as they both plummeted helplessly through the floors. Dawson tried hugging the wall as she fell, but the assassin was not as fortunate. He came down hard, landing directly on his left heel, splintering the bone on impact.

"AAAAAAAAAAAHHHHHHHHHH!!!!!!" he screamed in agony.

Dawson reached across to the assassin to check his condition, but he lunged at her again, slashing her arm as he struggled to his feet. Dawson was momentarily stunned from the sting and burn and the blood on her hands. She parried his next thrust, then clambered to her feet and started running to keep ahead of him.

Relentlessly, her assailant pursued her with a broken ankle; the shattered bone like a thousand knives jabbing him all at once.

Alejandra Reyes-Salazar climbed to her feet, using the dead bodies of Mayor De Soto and his wife on the podium as her ladder. She was covered in superficial cuts and bruises, but as she staggered through the smoke and flames on one shoe, she started coughing uncontrollably. Beyond the Atrium, she managed to reach the Fire Department's forward command post where an EMT caught her and sat her down on a gurney. He placed an oxygen mask over her nose and mouth, dabbed away blood from the injuries to her face with a 4x4, and applied several small bandages. She had considered staying within the safe confines of the forward command post, but when the fourth explosion rang out loudly in her ears, she threw the oxygen bottle into a dead woman's canvas bag, slung it over her shoulder, and headed for the exit. Outside, she stumbled along, swept up in the stream of fleeing hordes running for their lives.

In the emergency room, Colonel Goodine, a couple of doctors, a handful of nurses, and several medical technicians administered the wounds of those who had been injured in the Atrium explosion.

Like a battlefield surgeon, Goodine triaged the injured as quickly as possible, moving from one patient to another, assessing their situation. Patients with non-life-threatening injuries, like broken bones, burns or smoke-inhalation, were marked as low priority and placed in one section of the ER. Those patients with light injuries, such as minor scrapes or bruises, were marked as the "walking wounded" and immediately pressed into service assisting others with basic first aid. Patients who would not survive without immediate medical attention were given the highest priority. Those with severe bleeding from wounds, amputation, or internal injuries fell into this category. The Colonel knew that basic first aid was not enough to save these patients. They would require immediate surgery. For those badly injured patients who only had a slight chance of survival, he gave the nurses instructions to make them comfortable with a morphine drip, but to focus on the others.

One woman, a Latino who had been very close to the blast, floated upright in a vertical position inside the hyperbaric chamber, with a set of electrodes attached to key spots on her chest. The medical technician who had pulled her body from the podium monitored her heartbeat and breathing, while two nurses gradually increased the air pressure one atmosphere at a time. They hoped that by increasing the partial pressure of oxygen her blood would gradually be oxygenated. For a while it appeared as if she were trying to resist the urge to breathe normally, preferring short, irregular breaths. Though unconscious, her body still thrashed about in delirium.

Nearby, one of the nurses comforted a lost child by holding him close to her and stroking his hair. He was crying his eyes out, and with each new explosion, he shuddered in fear and cried louder.

On the top floor of the South Tower, William Clark and another policeman had taken over a breeches buoy from several firefighters, and were struggling to maintain order with the unruly mob. A volunteer, who had spent most of his time in the Navy, had rigged it crudely to a nearby high-rise apartment building to transfer people from one location to the other. The principle was simple enough: a single-person harness was attached to a zip-line between the two buildings and, one-at-a-time, people climbed into the harness and glided down the line from the burning building to safety. With the elevators out and smoke billowing up the stairs, this was the only way to get safely down from the tower.

But each time they managed to maneuver the harness back into place, a mass of people raced up the ramp, pushing and shoving to be first to climb in, under a hail of explosions and blinding sparks. Clark tried to hold them back, but he was knocked to the ground and trampled underfoot.

Just then, as if nothing else could go wrong, the South Tower began to rock back and forth, like a top spinning out of control.

Bloodied and battered, Clark crawled to one side and collapsed to the floor. One of the firefighters, a paramedic, came to his aid before moving on to the next victim.

For an instant, the Veteran's Hospital shuddered from yet another explosion. People and equipment were knocked to the ground. A part of the overhead conduit broke loose and sparks from the emergency lights rained down from the ceiling. It seemed like the whole building was going to collapse.

A few seconds later, the shuddering began to subside, then stopped.

One by one, the doctors and nurses and their surviving patients started to pick themselves up, peering at the overhead ceiling as if God was somehow embodied in the remaining ceiling tiles. The reality was that they had survived yet another blast—perhaps the final blast—and a sense of relief spread collectively on their faces. Among them, Balardi released a deep breath as he continued to search through the rubble for signs of life. A victim was lying on the floor, a few feet away from him.

They acknowledged one another, for there was nothing more to say or do.

Each second that passed seemed like an eternity.

A police siren wailed behind the crowd that had gathered on nearby sidewalks; people shouting and pointing at the blaze. The police car left the lights flashing as two officers got out to keep the crowd at bay. The Chief of Police got out and fixed his hat square on his head, his uniform jacket buttoned up tight. He was a big man with a grey mop of visible hair under the hat and had a short mustache that made his face appear larger than it was. He pushed through the crowd, followed closely by Lieutenant Roberts, who climbed out right behind him.

"Get that TV crew out of here!" Roberts shouted to one of his officers across the top of the crowd as he struggled to get through. "C'mon! Get out of my way! This isn't *Candid Camera*, damnit!" He then reported to his Chief. "I've got detectives in there."

"What the hell were they doing here?" he asked.

"The Meghan Kendrick murder."

The Chief of Police bulldozed his way to the front steps of the hospital entrance, ushering back a couple of photographers and journalists reporting to their cameras. "Let us through!" his anger rose with his voice.

"Oh, my God! I don't believe it!" the reporter shouted.

The exclamation of the nearby TV reporter and the cry of the crowd shifted the Chief's attention to the roof of the North Tower where he and Lieutenant Roberts spotted a rescue at hand. A figure of a man carrying a young woman dressed in white over his shoulder appeared at the edge of the roof, their silhouettes highlighted against the black smoke that poured from the building. He carried her over to a waiting ladder from one of the fire engines, stood at the top for a moment, testing his balance and grip against the ladder, then slowly turned and backed onto the ladder. The crowd below gasped in shock at what they were witnessing, while the photographers snapped their pictures and the men with television cameras cranked their film. The police and firemen stood by helplessly watching.

Taking it slow and easy, the man came down the ladder, climbing hand over hand, one rung at a time. He seemed to lose his balance a couple of times as he rocked unsteadily on his feet with the weight of the girl on his shoulder. Each time he wavered, the crowd screamed in horror. The climb down took several minutes, but as he reached the fire engine and the waiting arms of firefighters below, the crowd erupted into cheers and applause, smiling and hooting at a true hero. The firemen took the girl into their arms and set her down on the edge of the curb, plying her with oxygen and a towel for her shoulders. The man came all the way down, and when he reached the curb, he turned around to more cheers and applause. Though covered in soot and dirt, Mikhail Jawara was the man of the hour.

"Give her some room," the first fireman ordered, pushing the people back and away from her.

"Get a doctor over here someone!" the second fireman shouted.

"You're safe now, miss," Jawara said, kneeling down and holding the girl's trembling hand softly.

"How can I ever repay you?" she asked, lifting the mask away from her face. "You're my hero."

Jawara just peered up to where they had been; relived and thankful to be alive. The firm hand of the Police Chief pulled him up to his feet. As Jawara spun around, his face contorted from anger and rage to resentment and finally acceptance when he spotted the police badge on his uniform jacket. The Chief stood directly opposite Jawara, matched for height and imposing stare.

"I wanna know what you were doing here, detective," the Chief snarled.

"My partner and I were following up on a lead, sir," he replied.

The Chief of Police said, "No, the Meghan Kendrick murder case has been turned over to the Attorney General."

"I was not aware of that, sir," Jawara lied.

"You get your ass out of here, detective, before I have you put up on charges," the Chief shouted, right in his face.

"Yes, sir," he answered, moving away.

The Chief of Police pulled his Lieutenant to the side. "Damnit-to-hell, Roberts, if you can't keep your people in line, then maybe you'd better start looking for a new job. Never, in my whole life, have I seen a sloppier bureau!" He fixed James Roberts with one final look, then stormed away.

The dimly lit corridor outside the emergency room had grown quiet. A single medical technician moved past one of the windows carrying supplies, struggling through the smoke and debris.

Just then, movement outside the window caught his eye. The reflection of the emergency lights in the glass obscured his view for an instant, but as he drew nearer the window, a body hurtled by, followed by another, and then another. They smashed to the concrete parking lot below. People on the higher floors were preferring to jump to their deaths rather than be consumed by the smoke or fire. Then a huge chunk of the hospital's newly-completed helipad plummeted by the window, crashing into emergency vehicles below.

Startled, the medical technician dropped his supplies and raced around the corner towards the ER.

Battalion Chief O'Hara came up behind two of his firemen who were using a fire hose to push some of the flames back from the ceiling.

"Work it around. Up there," he said to the firefighters.

They complied with his instructions and started moving the hose around in a circular fashion, spreading the water around.

One of his other lieutenants shot him a worried look. "The fire's spreading. We don't have enough personnel to contain it."

O'Hara yelled back, "I got a fifth alarm in."

"What about the ceiling?" the lieutenant asked.

"I don't like the looks of it," the Battalion Chief said, evaluating honestly. "It looks like the fire is running the length of the ceiling."

"We'll have to pull it down."

"Agreed," he said. Quickly, O'Hara tapped the two firefighters with the hose and pointed at the segmented drop-ceiling overhead. "Pull the ceiling down before it falls down on our heads."

Together, with their probes in hand, the three firemen reached up, took hold of the aluminum grid, and pulled down hard. All at once, the wire that held the grid in place snapped. Ceiling tiles started collapsing, one right after the other, like dominos in a row. Water that had been collecting in the rafters and, at various junctures, sloshed back and forth, then came raining down, quenching the flames.

"Good job," O'Hara shouted, patting his men on the back.

The dull lights in the emergency room went bright for a second, then flickered out, and came back on, brighter than ever, and finally went out again. Each time the lights went out, there was a collective gasp as the doctors, nurses, technicians and patients took a deep breath seemingly at the same time, then released it in an audible sigh when the lights came back on.

Goodine regarded the ceiling lights. "What-the-hell?"

The frightened med tech rushed into the operating theater just as Goodine was about to return to his patient.

"People are jumping to their deaths," the tech said, nearly out of breath.

"What?" Goodine asked, with skepticism.

"I saw it. Through the corridor window."

"That's impossible!"

"No, I'm telling you it's happening."

Suddenly, the station was rocked by an impact, and every single electrical system in the sickbay snapped to life with a spike of energy. Everyone in the ER reacted in their own individual ways, but the general consensus among the doctors, nurses, and patients was that they were all living on borrowed time. At any moment, they expected the end.

"We're going to die!" the med tech cried.

Near the door, among those who had just been delivered to the ER, William Clark looked up from his gurney and moaned. "I've got to get to my post," he said, nearly delirious.

Goodine raced over to his side and held him down. "You're not going anywhere," he ordered. "Whatever this is, we can't be any worse off than we already are."

"But—"

Before Clark could utter another word, Goodine grabbed a syringe and pumped a sedative directly into his vein. He paused only briefly to ponder their predicament; his reverie cut short by his medical technician screaming hysterically.

Goodine slapped him across his face. "Pull yourself together, man!" he ordered. "We've got patients who need our help!"

"What difference does it make? We're all going to die anyway."

"No one dies," Goodine shouted at the top of his lungs so that everyone could hear him, "unless I say they do!"

All the medical personnel and a few of the patients lying on gurneys were stunned by his outburst and stopped what they were doing. As several seconds ticked off the clock, the tension in the room was so thick that you could cut it with a scalpel. No one moved or even dared to breathe. Goodine looked sternly around the room at each one of his people and eased the tension with a nod of confidence. Almost at once, they were back to work.

"I sent you out of here for supplies," Goodine scowled at the med tech. "Where are they?"

"I dropped them in the hall, sir," he said, in a terrified whisper.

"Well, go get them! And fast!"

Colonel Goodine watched the tech race out of ER, then turned his gaze back at the ceiling. If people were jumping to their death, then he didn't hold out too much hope for his own survival. For the first time in his life, he wasn't scared about dying and faced his mortality head-on.

Kate Dawson wasted little time in putting some distance between her and her assailant. She took the main corridor, which stretched the length of the hospital, avoiding any of the hot spots where there was smoke or fire, fearing they might cut off her route to safety. Not stopping to think for a second, she thundered along. When she reached another spot where the floor had collapsed upon the floor below, she jumped from the plateau and caught one of the metal girders with the blistered, raw edges of her hands, swinging her feet out in front of her to take full advantage from the momentum of the jump. She then released the girder, tucked herself into a roll, and landed on the other side of the chasm. Fighting exhaustion, she pulled herself upright, listening intently—muffled screaming from others trapped in the building. Dawson knew she had to keep moving.

With the smoke from several fires starting to close in, she raced to the end of the corridor, searching for the "exit" sign. The stairwell at the end of the hall had apparently collapsed into itself, and was now a twisted mess of concrete and metal. She had reached a dead end. Seeing no way to get out through the exit, she ambled up and down the short hall, pacing. *There is no way out. I'm trapped.* Dawson realized that she had to go back the way she came, and that meant running right into the assassin who was still in hot pursuit.

Barging into an empty room, she dashed to the window. She was several flights up—too far to jump, even if she could get one of the windows open.

Dawson decided to wait for her assailant in the smoke-filled corridor. She had made up her mind to use his own weight against him. She knelt as close to the floor as she could, to capture whatever fresh air there was left, held her breath, listening, and when she heard his very distinctive limp along the corridor, she braced herself. As he charged forward, limping, she reached out and grabbed him by the lapels on his jacket, rolled onto her back with her feet planted in his abdomen, and hurled him across the room with whatever strength she still had. The man thudded against the wall, then slid heavily to the floor on his left foot.

She gritted her teeth as once more she rose to attack, this time managing to grip hold of his shirt collar and pinning him to the floor with her knee planted firmly on his chest. She looked down at him, with her arm coiled into a spring and the fist of her right hand ready to strike.

"Who are you?" she demanded, breathing heavily, looming over him like a prize fighter in the ring.

"You know who I am. Goodine told you," he replied, sucking air into his lungs, wracked with pain.

"Anatoly Piotrovskii! You're a former KGB agent, recruited by Putin himself. It doesn't make sense that you'd go to work for Reinhardt unless you're the one who's pulling all the strings."

"I've got nothing to say to you," he said defiantly.

"Why are you doing this?"

Piotrovskii was silent; looked straight through her as if in a trance. He appeared to be a man with a singular mission who would stop at nothing to complete it. He tried to get up, but she rammed her knee in deeper, smashing the assassin across the bridge of his nose with the full fury of her fist. The man's head snapped back hitting the deck, blood splattering everywhere.

"Okay. Now, I want some answers," Dawson insisted, completely out of patience.

"You're not going to get anything out of me."

"We'll see about that," she said determinately, as she stood up.

With flawless precision, the assassin executed a drop swipe at Dawson's ankles and, as the female detective fell forward, Piotrovskii wrapped his legs around her neck and tried to snap it, his ankle dangling uselessly. Dawson struggled, thrashing underneath him as he started to close the loop. She grunted and hissed, pushing and straining to break free of his chokehold. Her assailant had the upper hand, and he knew it. Taking his time, he slowly began to squeeze his legs together, ignoring her feeble attempts to pry his legs apart. It was then she saw an opening for her only counterattack. With both hands clasped together, like she was getting ready to pray, she hammered down on his groin. The maneuver stunned her assailant for several heartbeats, enabling her enough time to roll free and scramble to her feet, coughing and gagging.

Dawson charged down the narrow hallway, frantically

seeking an exit, covered in blood; the assassin close behind, hobbling, grunting in pain, and struggling for air.

Then one of the shadows came alive. The Shadow Man stepped out of the darkness and struck Dawson's assailant across the back of his neck with a karate chop. The assassin reacted by turning around quickly with the blade of his knife out, but he was far too slow for Shadow Man's cat-like reflexes. Shadow Man pivoted in place and struck a second, disabling blow to the assailant's upper chest cavity. The assassin went down hard, his eyes folding back into his head.

With sweat pouring off her face, Dawson looked at Shadow Man with relief. "Thanks!" she said, breathless. "I thought he had me."

"Not a chance, Inspector Dawson," Shadow Man said. "I've been following your every movement for the last several hours. I should have anticipated the ambush at the hospital. Sorry."

"Didn't I fire you?"

"Yes, but under the circumstances—"

"Well, consider yourself back on the payroll."

"Thank you, ma'am."

"No, I'm the one who should be thanking you." Kate fumbled with Shadow Man's first name. "Just what the hell is your name, anyway?"

"Joe," he said simply.

"Joe. . . ?"

"Just Joe."

"Well, okay, 'Just Joe,'" Dawson said, pun intended. "I'd like you to give me a hand with our Russian comrade over there."

"Yes, ma'am."

By the time Kate Dawson reached the forward command post, the fire was mostly out, and members of the San Francisco

Fire Department were mopping up their operation under the watchful eyes of Chief O'Hara. The lobby of the Veteran's Hospital looked like a twisted mess of drywall, metal, plywood, wires, and equipment, but facility maintenance crews and other hospital personnel were already hard at work helping to evacuate the building for safety. They were worried that the rest of it would collapse and injure others. People with minor cuts and bruises or smoke inhalation were moved outside the building, and were sitting or lying around the parking lot being cared for by paramedics or staff doctors and nurses. She was not surprised by the fact that Reinhardt, the President, and her Secret Service detail were nowhere to be found. She reasoned that they had already made good their escape.

One by one, Dawson and the others were helped by maintenance men wearing orange fatigues over the chunks of debris, which separated the lobby from the rest of the hospital. Joe and Dawson drug the assassin forward, a dog on a very short leash. Reaching firm ground, they dropped him to the pavement and gulped air. Dawson's wounds, which were largely superficial, had already stopped bleeding, but she looked like bloody hell. Shadow Man stood vigil over the assassin.

Matt Balardi was among those helping in the parking lot just outside the lobby. Seeing Dawson emerge from the building, he wasn't surprised. For some unknown reason, it seemed inevitable. She walked up to him, smiling, so choked up to see him, she didn't quite know what to say; just kept staring at his wonderful face.

Balardi broke the silence, "I might have guessed you were the one behind all the trouble."

"And you would have been right," she coughed.

Balardi patted Dawson on the shoulder and whispered, "I was wrong about you, partner. I guess you just can't tell about some people, can you? Even the ones you think you know inside out."

"Thanks, Matt. I appreciate it." She bent over gasping for air, her whole body racked in pain.

"Well done, Kate." Jawara walked over and warmly embraced her. "I'm really glad you made it out of there alive. But next time you plan to do something crazy like this, give us a chance to talk you out of it."

Dawson sputtered, "Okay, next time."

"The body count is mercifully low," Balardi stated. "If it hadn't been for Colonel Goodine pitching in to help, we might have been looking at a lot more casualties."

"What happened to you?" she asked Jawara.

"It's just a scratch, Kate," he said. Battered, his head and hands were bandaged, but thankfully, the detective's injuries were not life-threatening. He'd be back to normal in no time at all. "I already feel like I'm getting my second wind."

Dawson pointed to the assassin, saying, "Gentlemen, I think you'll find that Mister Anatoly Piotrovskii is our perp. He was the extra Secret Service agent that boarded the plane at Andrews Air Force base, no doubt with forged documents provided by Reinhardt, *and* he was the one who went into the rear restroom and strangled Meghan after the First Man left her nearly dead. He made it look like someone else did it; had us chasing our tails looking for some younger man who never really existed. He got away with it because no one paid him any mind. They may have seen a Secret Service agent in a black suit, but just assumed that he was doing a routine check prior to landing. He also killed Carlos Ortega. Again, no one paid him any mind because he was the officer who took Ortega to the cell after questioning. He also orchestrated this 'terrorist attack,' working covertly with members of the President's Secret Service detail. I don't think he meant to get caught in the building after the bombs started going off, but then maybe that was something Reinhardt had arranged with a couple of his men to wipe the slate clean. The first rule in assassination is to kill the assassins."

Balardi signaled to two of the uniformed SFPD officers who were standing nearby to take charge of Piotrovskii. Relieved, Joe released the prisoner and stepped back as they snapped cuffs on him. "Take this man down to interrogation and call a medic to look at his injuries," Balardi said, pointing at Piotrovskii.

"You'll never make me talk," Piotrovskii spit out through excruciating pain.

Balardi swung around, grabbed Piotrovskii by the lapels of his jacket, and shoved him against the nearest cruiser, raising him several inches. He then got right in his face and barked, "We'll just see about that, scumbag. Because when I get through with you, you're goin' to be down on your knees begging me to listen to you."

"Never," Piotrovskii said defiantly, chin up.

Matt Balardi loosened his rigid grip on Piotrovskii's lapels, letting him crumple to the pavement. He couldn't begin to explain what had just come over him, and made no effort whatsoever to apologize to him. "Take him away, boys," Balardi said to the cops, "and lock him up in the deepest, darkest hole you can find."

Dawson, lost in thought and probably in shock, had seen what transpired but did not appear to have heard his orders. Seeing them lead the Russian away, she shouted, "Stop!" Running over to him, she started turning out his pockets, not quite sure what she was looking for. But as Kate patted him down, from head to foot, she found it. A roll of film. That wasn't what she expected to find, but it was enough. She tossed the roll of film in the air, caught it with her right hand, then shoved it in her pocket.

With one officer on either side, they shoved him into their patrol car.

"So, he's the Iranian terrorist?" Jawara asked.

"No, he's a paid political assassin," Dawson corrected him. "The Iranians had nothing to do with this so-called "terrorist attack." It was orchestrated by a handful of rich, old men who profit by us going to war with Iran."

"What?" Balardi was stupefied.

"Are you sure about this?" Jawara asked. He could not wrap his mind around it.

"That's crazy!" Balardi exclaimed.

"I know it sounds insane, but I can back up everything that I've said with proof."

"Someone had better tell the President," Jawara said. "She's scheduled to hold a press conference in about an hour aboard Air Force One, and I got a feeling it ain't going to be pretty. She's likely to drop the hammer on Iran."

Dawson was visibly shaken by the news that the President had intended to hold a carefully-scripted news conference later that day to use the incident at the Veteran's Hospital as a pretense to go to war with Iran. The news disturbed her greatly, and yet at the same time, she couldn't help but feel a sense of release, much like a mistreated slave who had just learned that his master was dead. She had to think of something.

"I've got to get to the President, right now," she said, resolutely.

And with all due haste, Balardi, and Jawara fell right into place. They were prepared to follow her to hell and back, if necessary.

Joe, who'd been silent the whole time, was anxious to join them. "So, what's your plan?"

The other two looked at him, wondering just who-the-hell this guy was, but if Dawson trusted him, he was good to go.

"I don't know," Dawson threw her hands up. "I'm making this up as I go."

The President's office onboard Air Force One was large, approximately three-hundred square feet or roughly the size of a modern boardroom. A naturally, well-lit space, the soothing pastel colors of tan and light green made the office feel comfortable, even luxurious, by cosmopolitan standards. An exquisite, hand-crafted cinnamon oak desk dominated the room, with a great brown leather chair behind it, and the seal of office bolted to the wall at eye level right next to the desk. Some of the finest technologies, such as video-conferencing, motorized shades and screens, and touch-screen controllers were incorporated in the room and easily accessed through a remote-control unit built right into the desk telephone. Next to the phone, a laptop computer with Internet access sat on one side of the desk. Set up in front of the desk were a set of studio lights and a single, high-definition television camera, its lens fixed like the barrel of a gun on the great, brown leather chair.

With the press conference mere minutes away, President Helen Harrison, dressed in an elegant but reserved Versace pants suit, accessorized by a single strand pearl necklace, sat in a tall director's chair, having her make-up applied by a professional stylist. Extra attention was directed to cover a few flaws from that morning's blast. She'd been cleared by Air Force One's physician after the attack, only a few minor cuts and bruises, and gotten herself cleaned up. Still somewhat shaken, she was reading through a prepared speech that a speechwriter back in Washington had faxed to her. Every so often she'd pause to make a correction with a red marking pen.

Her husband was sitting behind her, observing the transformation, worry from the events of only a few hours prior etched on his handsome face. He'd not attended the dedication but had met the entourage at the airport upon hearing of the bombing.

Dawson entered the room, flanked by Harlan Reinhardt on one side and a Secret Service agent on the other. She looked like she had been through a battle. Mostly covered in soot, her face was bloody and bruised, her clothes torn in tatters. She walked unsteadily into the room, surveying everyone with a cool eye, but tried her best to mask her true emotions. If Dawson felt nervous, she didn't want to show it, at least not to them. She knew that it was important to project her best poker face, if her plan was to succeed. She sucked up the pain that had spread to nearly every limb in her body, struggling for an image of strength.

With a small movement of her hand, the President dismissed her stylist and she removed the paper bib as she got up from the chair. The stylist's eyes were as big as saucers taking in Dawson's appearance as she walked from the room.

The First Man jumped to his feet as she came in and thrust out his hand, cool as a cucumber. "I don't think we had a chance to be formally introduced before," he said, lying through his teeth. "I'm Bill Harrison, First Man and advisor to the President. I understand you're the police detective who's solved the murder of Meghan Kendrick." He put on a good show, even though he knew the President knew, and bet Reinhardt did, too.

"Inspector Dawson," she said, shaking his hand, playing along. "I didn't break the case solely on my own. I had a lot of help, including some from your security chief, here." She cocked her thumb in Reinhardt's direction. "But overall, I'd say forensics played a big role."

"Ah, forensics, the science of criminal investigation," Bill added. "I've always been interested in that subject. Perhaps you'll tell me how forensics played such an important role in your investigation?"

"I'd be happy to explain it to you, sir, but it's imperative that I have a word or two with the President first."

"Oh, I understand. Let me see what I can do for you, Inspector."

Harlan Reinhardt had done his best to hide his dislike for the detective. Annoyed that she had survived his best efforts to have her eliminated, he figured that his hired assassin was probably lying dead somewhere in a grave meant for her. He shoved his way past the First Man and Dawson, who were embroiled in their own conversation, and approached the President on her right side. She was anxious to get his report.

"She's clean, Madam President," Reinhardt reported, with a snarl. Then he reached into the pocket of his black suit jacket and produced an elegant, shiny black lipstick container with a pretty silver collar. "Besides her police badge, she was carrying only this. We thought that you'd probably want to get it back."

"And the film?" she asked, almost a whisper.

Reinhardt leaned over, and whispered in the President's ear, "I checked inside. The roll of film is there."

"Excellent," she replied, taking the item from him. She held it up the air, marveling at how the shiny case reflected the light with little shards of black and silver, then slapped it down on her desk, making everyone jump.

"Sweetheart," Bill Harrison said, interrupting his wife's discrete visit with her security chief, "Inspector Dawson would like a brief word with you."

"Certainly, Dear," the President said, in a normal tone of voice. She regarded Dawson as if there was no one else in the room. "That was very thoughtful of you, Inspector, to return my lipstick container. You just can't imagine how long I've been missing this."

Kate Dawson walked up and looked her straight in the eye,

then bowed her head slightly as if before royalty. "Madam President, I was just wrapping up the last few details of my investigation and I realized that I had something in the evidence lock-up that belonged to you."

"Do you have a suspect in custody, Inspector?" she asked, genuinely curious.

"Oh, yes, ma'am," Dawson replied.

"What's his name?" Bill Harrison asked, also curious.

"Anatoly Piotrovskii," she answered, acknowledging the First Man's question but addressing the President. She cut her eyes quickly to Reinhardt, who had a pained look on his face. "He's a former KGB agent who was recruited into the Secret Police by Vladimir Putin in 1977, but later left the agency to go freelance in 1991. He's been suspected in a number of political assassinations, including the infamous umbrella hit that took out a Bulgarian defector in the late seventies. Interpol, the French Deuxième Bureau, the British Secret Service, and our CIA have all been after him for years."

"But *you* caught him," Bill said, a twinkle of admiration in his eye.

"Yes, sir."

Helen Harrison came from around the desk to stand mere inches from Dawson, who stood to her full height, and stared into her eyes. "You've been described to me as a bull dog that just won't let go. I admire tenacity, particularly in a woman. You'd be a huge asset in my administration. Would you ever consider coming to work for me?"

Dawson considered her offer for about thirty seconds, never blinking, mostly out of courtesy but never as a real consideration. "I'm honored, Madam President, but I've got a six-month backlog of cases that need my attention."

"Inspector," Bill broke in, quickly changing the subject,

waving his hand at everyone, "I'm sure we'd all like to know how you apprehended Piotrovskii."

"Yes, do tell us how you caught this master assassin." Helen sat back against the desk.

"Well, I attended the dedication ceremony at the new Veteran's Hospital this morning incognito," Dawson explained. "I had hoped to use the event to flush him out into the open. You know, beat the bushes and see what came out. But then when all the commotion started, I hunkered down and waited. I was fortunate enough to catch him red-handed in the act of lining up his next target. He's been in police custody even since, singing like a bird. He's already confessed to killing Meghan Kendrick and Carlos Ortega, *and, yeah,* trying to kill me."

Bill Harrison blanched. "Do you suppose he was working with the Iranians who perpetrated the terrorist strike?"

"No, sir, he was strictly working alone." She directed her attention to the President. "And for the record, I never saw a single Iranian terrorist."

"But that's what the press is reporting," Bill said, with a raised eyebrow.

"When did facts ever get in the way of a good news story?" Dawson asked.

Helen Harrison was flabbergasted. "This morning! I was there this morning to dedicate the new hospital!" she exclaimed, gulping down the surprise in her throat, looking at the others, in particular Harlan Reinhardt. She asked the question that they all wanted answered. "Dare I ask the question? Who was his intended target?"

Dawson frowned. "You were, Madam President."

There was a long moment of silence, as everyone in the room, except Kate, caught their breath. Dawson stared at the President expressionlessly, probing for a chink in the armor that she may have missed. The woman appeared to be visibly shaken by the revelation, which had been perfectly obvious.

"I want to thank you," Helen said, trying to compose herself. "Anything you want, Inspector, just name it."

"I just need a moment of your time . . . Alone."

Anxiously, President Harrison glanced around her office. She was looking for the man who was going to direct her press conference. When she didn't see him, she shouted, "Tony, how much time do I have before the broadcast?"

"Twenty minutes," he yelled back from the outer office.

She turned to Dawson and said, "You've got twelve minutes."

After the First Man, the President's security detail, and Harlan Reinhardt had vacated the room, Helen Harrison closed the door behind them and sat down at her desk. She reached into one of the drawers and produced a small metal tray which bore the Presidential seal, a pack of Virginia Slims, and an Alfred Dunhill lighter. She then took the lipstick container in hand, and with a couple of twists on its case, she shook out the microfilm. "I have a confession to make," she said, positioning the film in the center of the tray directly in front of her, while she grasped the lighter in her right hand.

Dawson took the chair next to her, listening carefully.

"I still smoke," she stated, as if it was a big deal. "I just can't beat the nicotine habit. And to be honest with you, it calms my nerves, particularly after shocking news. I am aware that the previous occupant of this office used to smoke like a chimney, and not just cigarettes. In fact, I used to criticize him for not setting a better example for our youth, then I found myself in exactly the same situation. So, we do keep my smoking on the down low."

Dawson said seriously, "Your secret is safe with me."

The President picked up the pack of cigarettes, and leaned forward, offering her one. "Would you like a cigarette?"

"I quit."

"Congratulations, but you know it will never last." She sat back in her great leather chair. A moment later, she put a cigarette to her lips and lit it, exhaling luxuriantly. The smoke circled around her head, rose, and dissipated in the air. "Well, Inspector, I owe you a real debt of gratitude. In fact, the country owes you a lot for returning the stolen film of the MJ-12 documents," Harrison said, looking down at the roll of film. She flicked the ash from her cigarette in the tray and some of the gray matter spilled onto the film, igniting little pin-points of flame, burning little holes through the celluloid. "I had the chance to review some of the actual documents when I was sworn into office a few months ago. Fascinating material! A rare insight into the Cold War. Colonel Goodine has done a truly excellent job in putting it all together. I suppose I'll have to destroy it now. What a pity, I've always had a soft spot in my heart for historical documents, particularly if they are genuine. But you and I both know that information must never reach the public. Once it's destroyed, I don't expect it'll pose a threat to me anymore."

"Why must the public be kept in the dark about Roswell?" Dawson asked. "What is your administration afraid of?"

"Fear. Panic. Rioting in the streets. Mass suicide on a scale that would make Jonestown look like a Sunday picnic," she stated as she drew heavily on her cigarette. "People would be literally frightened out of their minds if they learned aliens and flying saucers were real. Nations would fall, our religious institutions would crumble, and the value of our currency would plummet. It would change everything. Not only that, but an announcement about extraterrestrials would be front page news for months, maybe even years. It would stymie and dominate the government's every action and not allow us to carry out any of our planned business. Think about how the Monica Lewinsky scandal dominated the news cycle for more than a year, then multiply that by a thousand. That should give you a sense of how truly devastating it would be."

"That may have been true in Truman's day, but not now," Kate disagreed. "The public's a great deal more sophisticated and knowledgeable than you give them credit for."

"Really?" asked Harrison, eyebrows raised. She snuffed out her cigarette in the metal tray. "How well do you remember the attack on the U.S. consulate in Benghazi, Libya in 2012?"

"Not a whole lot."

"Well, I was in the Oval Office meeting with the President when we got the news that our compound had been overrun by Libyan protestors and four of our people were killed."

She looked at the detective for a fleeting moment, engaging her eyes. Turning to the roll of film, diffidently, she took it in hand, and held it over the flame from her lighter. The film caught fire instantly, and she was forced to discard it into the metal tray to keep from burning her fingers.

"Yeah, that's right. Now I remember," Dawson replied.

"According to reports from our intelligence community, the Libyans rioted and killed our courageous ambassador and three members of his staff as the direct result of some video that was posted on YouTube, titled 'The Innocence of Muslims,'" she continued, "and that was just a stupid video. Could you imagine what would happen if those same people learned that aliens were real and Mohammad was not? They'd tear apart the whole world and burn it down to the ground."

"That's a rather cynical view of humanity."

"Not cynical, truthful," the President corrected her, without looking up. She was too busy watching the celluloid burn itself to a crisp to maintain eye contact. "Let's face it, Inspector, most people don't really care what goes on in the world. As long as they have a roof over their head, beer in the refrigerator, someone to fuck now-and-again, and cable television tuned to ESPN, they're happy. The Romans discovered the secret to controlling the masses and instigated Bread and Circuses to pacify their people and avoid civil unrest. How are we any different? But instead of gladiatorial contests, we give them *Survivor*, March Madness, and the Superbowl. We keep them fat and happy and not asking a whole lot of questions, so that those of us in the ruling class can maintain the status quo."

"Ruling class?" Dawson was aghast with raised eyebrows.

"Maybe you'd prefer a different name? Like the Elite? It's really all the same. Every great society has its leaders and its followers. In this country, we've got political dynasties that lead the masses. The Kennedys, the Bushes, the Clintons, all great families that have been pre-ordained, like Caesars, to rule. After all, someone has to run things, while the masses plug in and tune out."

Dawson was trying to take it all in. "I guess Meghan Kendrick threatened all of that?"

"No, not really," she said stoically.

Once the roll of film had stopped burning, Helen Harrison poked at the ashes with a pencil to make sure there were no scraps left unburned. She looked up from the ashes, saying, "Good, that's done. Now where was I? Oh yes, Meghan Kendrick . . ." She cleared her throat. "As long as Miss Kendrick reported the news over at Fox, nobody really cared, except for maybe the Tea Partiers. And nobody really cared what they said anyway. But the minute she started listening to Goodine and his wild theories, she posed a real threat."

Dawson's eyes never left her face. "So, you didn't mind that she was sleeping with your husband?"

"Hell, no." Harrison was blasé, brushing off the query. "As

long as she was having an affair with Bill, I could control her, and him."

"Was it you or was it your security chief, Harland Reinhardt, who decided to have Meghan Kendrick killed?"

"What do you think?" she asked the detective.

There was a knock at the door. "Five minutes," the voice said.

"Well, when I questioned Piotrovskii, he told me that the decision had come from the top," Dawson said seriously, standing tall. "That left me with two possibilities: either you're in charge of the Executive Branch of the government and made the decision to take out Meghan Kendrick or Reinhardt did and you're nothing more than a figurehead. So, who's calling the shots, Madam President?"

Harrison's eyes flashed with anger. "Now you listen here, detective. I'm the President of the United States, and, therefore, any decisions that are made for the good of the country are made by me, not some flunky security chief."

"Then you admit that you made the decision to have Meghan Kendrick killed?"

"No, I don't admit to anything!" she shouted. "This interview is over. I'm going to have to ask you to leave."

Dawson hesitated a moment. "One of your predecessors, Harry Truman, had a sign on his desk which read 'The Buck Stops Here.' In one of his most famous speeches, he explained what that meant, and I'm just paraphrasing here, 'You know, it's easy for the Monday morning quarterback to say what the coach should have done, after the game is over. But when the decision is up before you . . .'"

"'. . . the decision has to be made,'" she completed the quote.

All at once, the door to the Presidential office swung open and Bill Harrison walked into the room. He looked at the gulf that had widened between the two women and said,

"Inspector Dawson is right, Helen. The President—whoever he or she is—has to decide. The buck can't pass to anybody. No one else can do the deciding. That's the President's job. That was your job."

"Bill, I'm glad you're here," Helen said, relaxing a tad. "She's been trying to trick me into admitting that I ordered the hit on Miss Kendrick. But you know that couldn't be further from the truth."

"Well, if you didn't give the order, then who did?" he asked, demanding an answer.

The President held her hands out in front of her. "You know as well as I do, Bill, that some decisions are made, while others just sort of happen. You know, someone brings a problem up at a meeting, no official decisions are made, then a week later, the problem is solved. We call it 'plausible deniability.' She has no real evidence that I was involved in Meghan's death, so we can just pass this off to a lower-ranking official, like Reinhardt, and no one will ever know the truth."

"I'll know," Bill said simply, honestly, pointing to his chest, red in the face.

"Well, then, I guess you and I will just have to trade sins," she scowled, "because I clearly know about the heated affair you were having with her right underneath my nose."

"It wasn't some tawdry affair, Helen. *I loved her*. In fact, after the mid-term elections, I was going to marry her."

The President glared at him, disbelieving. "You would've never been happy with her, Bill. I know that for a fact. You would've found yourself banished by the Party to some no-name, flyover state, in Middle America; forced to live in suburbia, out of the limelight, in a middle-class house with a mortgage you couldn't afford; shopping at Costco and Wal-Mart on the weekends, and living out the rest of your pitiful existence pitching horseshoes and having backyard cookouts. Tell me what part of that night-mare sounds the least bit appealing to you, my love."

Bill Harrison gave no sign of having heard, just stared at her, searching her face for a sign, some symbol of remorse or repen-tance. She just stood there in defiance of the mounting evidence against her.

"She doesn't have anything on me," she said, heading for the door.

"I hate to burst your bubble, Madam President, but I have the one indisputable piece of evidence that links you to Meghan's murder. I still possess the microfilm with the MJ-12 docu-ments," Dawson said to her back. "The roll of film that you just torched was a phony. But considering you didn't know that when you destroyed the evidence, that makes you an accessory to murder, after the fact."

"You'll never make that stick," Helen fired back, eyes flaming.

Dawson touched the small earpiece receiver-transmitter that was in her left ear, saying, "Joe, did you get that?"

"Loud and clear, Inspector," he replied into her ear.

"Time to send in the cavalry," she told him.

"Affirmative," Joe returned. "Agents from the Department of Justice are on their way up."

Dawson took a deep breath, then turned to face the President head-on. "Madam President, you're under arrest—"

"You can't arrest me. I'm the President of the United States!" Helen declared, turning from Dawson to her husband.

". . . for conspiracy in the murders of Meghan Kendrick and Carlos Ortega. You have the right to remain silent. Anything you say can and will be used against you in a court of law. You have the right to an attorney, and to have the attorney present while you are being questioned. If you cannot afford one, an attorney will be appointed for you. Do you understand these rights as I have explained them to you?" Dawson asked the President.

"We won't give you any trouble, Inspector," Bill Harrison reassured her.

"To hell with that!" Helen protested, loudly. "You'll never be able to make any of these charges stick. When my attorneys get through with you, you'll be lucky to have a job as a school-crossing!"

Kate Dawson said calmly, apologetically, "I'm afraid you're going to miss your press conference, Madam President."

"Do you have any idea what your actions will do to this country?" she sneered.

"I hope I've just saved it," Dawson replied, as she seized Helen Harrison by her arm and took her into custody. She led her out of the President's office and into the nearby corridor, with Bill in tow. "By the way, I'm sure you'll be relieved to know that the Vice President is already en route to the White House and will likely be sworn into office by the time you've been booked for murder."

"You bitch!" the President shouted.

"I'm sure that's just what the Iranians will think of you," Kate said, "once the Secretary of State has delivered his olive branch and explained to the Ayatollah just how you set them up to take the fall for the VA bombing. Maybe this is just what we need to start fresh and work out our differences?"

At the far end of the corridor, a slight commotion was beginning. Secret Service agents and others who were on board Air Force One were putting their hands in the air, murmuring in protest, while agents from the Department of Justice, with their weapons drawn, moved in to arrest them.

Dawson paused with her prisoner for a few seconds as the commotion continued to spread her way. Then she noticed that someone very large was moving through the crowd, with his head lowered and his fingers intertwined behind his head. He was moving very fast. Dawson recognized him first; actually, gasped as Reinhardt came into her view. He was being escorted to the front hatch of the aircraft by two Justice Department agents.

As Harlan Reinhardt walked by her, Kate said to one of the agents, "Be sure to find him a nice dry cell away from the air conditioning ducts. He has terrible allergies and I would hate to see his asthma get triggered by a cold, damp room."

"We'll see what we can do, Inspector," the agent said with a wink.

"Thanks," Dawson said, smiling. "After all, Mister Reinhardt is going to be there for a very, very long time."

Reinhardt's eyes narrowed at her as they led him away, perspiring profusely.

EPILOGUE

Kate Dawson opened the door to her apartment and stumbled over the two baskets of folded laundry she had dropped near the entrance the day before. She was more tired than she realized and quickly changed her mind about raiding the refrigerator for a bowl of Breyers Rocky-Road ice cream. Instead, she decided to get some sleep and surveyed her rather Spartan-like studio apartment for something that resembled a bed. She blinked twice, stood motionless in the room, waiting for her eyes to adjust to the darkness. *Ah, there it is*, she sighed, putting her gun, badge, and assorted items from her pocket down on the kitchen table.

From out of the darkness, a pair of hands reached for Dawson, just as a vague, indeterminate form crept noiselessly to embrace her shadow on the far wall of the apartment. Kate did not see the shadows on the wall, nor did she sense the presence of another person. Her only thoughts were focused on reaching the bed and hitting the pillow. But as she proceeded to unbutton her blouse, the pair of hands continued to reach for her, closing in, like a noiseless spider and its prey.

Just then, out of the corner of her eye, she glimpsed the

shadow and felt the tiny hairs rise on the back of her neck. Suddenly, every nerve ending in her body crackled to life, as if she had just gotten a full jolt of 110 volts of electricity from touching a faulty extension cord. The terror that burned and sizzled through her mind was real enough, but she couldn't determine if the threat was a real one or just the play of light on the wall and her very active imagination. She turned around very slowly, to give the bad feeling plenty of time to go away, but she had no such luck. Her sensory information registered in nanoseconds, each one progressively worse than the last, until she had turned completely around.

Dawson's eyes came down to lock on the face of her shadowy assailant and they shared a moment of mutual paralysis and recognition . . . then John Prescott embraced and kissed her intensely.

"I thought you'd never get home," he whispered, kissing her again, nuzzling her neck.

Dawson slipped out of John's embrace and staggered backwards against the door. She stood in the entrance, breathing heavily, trying to catch her breath. Her body was still reeling from the shock of her surprise visitor, but she didn't want him to know that. She had spent far too many hours during the last week trying to stay one step ahead of the bad guys; to not show a single ounce of weakness to him or anyone else. Slowly she felt herself regaining control and composure.

So much for things that go bump in the night, she thought, turning to bolt the security lock on her apartment door. "You were quite literally the last person in the world I expected." She caught her breath and swallowed. "You gave me quite a start."

"I'm sorry."

"You should be," Dawson said, pointing her finger at him. "Don't you know that you should never sneak up on someone you know carries a sidearm? That's how accidents happen. I warned you about this before."

"Yeah, and I'm really sorry, Kate."

"What are you doing here? In San Francisco?"

"Well, after all the trouble you've caused this last week, you must have known that Justice would assign someone to come out and pick up the pieces," John said, grinning, engaging her eyes with his.

"And you were the lucky one who got the assignment?"

He held her eyes. "I'm not sure how lucky I am, Kate. It's really quite a mess. The OIC has appointed an Independent Council. A Tea-Party Republican, and she's very focused on getting to the bottom of all the double-dealings that the Harrisons have been involved in, going all the way back to their days in Arkansas. The House Judiciary Committee has already drafted articles of impeachment and the House is set to vote on them Monday. The stock market hit an all-time low today as allegations about the top companies came to light. Russia, under Putin's leadership, is rattling its saber again, and Iran continues to build its nuclear arsenal."

"I was just doing my job."

"I know, sweetheart, and I'm really proud of you for that," John said, reaching for her hand. "Things will eventually sort themselves out. But right now, I haven't seen a mess like this since the Monica Lewinsky scandal."

"I'm really glad you're here." She moved closer to him. "I'm just sorry it has to be under these trying circumstances."

"No worries."

Dawson put her arms around him and kissed him slowly. The heat of the kiss shimmered on his lips. John felt a sudden surge of arousal pulsate through his body, and he held her tight and kissed her back deeply. His robe open, he rubbed his manhood against her as they embraced. While they continued kissing, he reached out and unbuttoned the rest of the buttons on her blouse, slipped the blouse over her shoulders, and let it fall to the floor; reached down, unfastened her belt, and unzipped the fly to her slacks. They slipped to the floor at her feet and she stepped out from them, without thought or hesitation. Finally, he reached behind her back and unfastened her bra, allowing it to fall to the floor. She moaned and curled around him; he held her tight, her breasts pressed sweetly against his rugged chest.

After a moment or two, Kate tried to pull away from his embrace, but John held onto her tightly, with a passion that was nearly overwhelming. She wanted him unlike any other man she had ever met, but at the same time she needed a moment for herself.

"Oh, darlin'," he said, breathlessly. "I love you . . . I need you."

But Dawson pushed gently back, put a finger to his lips, then rushed past him to the bathroom.

"Hold that thought," she exhaled. "I'll be right back."

"I'll be waiting for you right here," John reassured her, breathing heavily as he walked confidently to her bed and stripped off the black-and-white comforter that covered it. He then took off his robe and slipped naked between the sheets. As he adjusted the pillows behind his head, his eyes glimpsed a roll of film sitting on the kitchen table, next to her badge and gun. He climbed out of bed and snatched the film right up. The seal from the lab with Rosa Romano's initials hadn't been broken, and it was obvious to him that Dawson had never even opened the roll. For an instant, he was tempted to break the seal and hold it up against the light, but he thought better of it.

"So, do you still have the microfilm in your possession?" he asked fingering the film.

"Yeah, as a matter of fact, it's been in my safety deposit box, but I did pick it up on my way home tonight."

"It's here in the apartment?"

"Sure."

"Did you ever get a chance to look it over? You know, read some of the documents?"

"No, I've been so busy with my case that I never really got the chance to sit down and read them."

"Pity."

Dawson stuck her head out of the bathroom. "Did you come here to make love to me, or to talk about those damned MJ-12 documents? I'm so sick of them."

John waited for her to go back into the bathroom, then raced back across the room to return the roll of film to the kitchen table. "Well, to tell you the truth," he said, "I thought we'd fuck, then while you're in the throes of passion, I'd read them to you, one document at a time."

"In your dreams, Romeo."

Prescott was silent for a few seconds, then said, "You know, that was a pretty clever trick you pulled."

"What's that?"

"Switching the rolls of film."

She grumbled aloud. "Are we back on that subject again?"

"How did you know Piotrovskii had a roll of film on him?"

"I didn't," she admitted for the first time. "I just remembered that he carried a blade, and I thought that he might have another one concealed on his person that I could sneak into the President's office. I just got lucky with the film."

Dawson flushed the toilet and came out of the bathroom, bare-ass naked. She stopped for a moment to check herself in the mirror—*The bruises will fade, the cuts will heal*—fluffed her hair, and approached the bed.

"You took an awfully big risk, sweetheart," he remarked, looking up at her, touching a couple of the worse injuries.

"What else could I do? I had to stop her from going on network television and declaring war on Iran. What would you have done?"

"I'm not sure." John really did not know what he would have done.

"Well, all I can say is that I put it all out on the line and I got lucky."

John Prescott sat up in bed and took her by hand. She followed his lead and took his hand into hers. As she leaned down to kiss him, he turned his face up to hers with his eyes already closed.

"I'm so glad that you're here, John," she said, her lips momentarily disengaging from his.

"So am I."

He pulled her down onto the bed; kissed her again deeply, gingerly pulling the covers back with one hand and leading her between the sheets with the other. Dawson smelled sweet, like fresh orchids, and as he buried his face between her thighs, her hips undulated up and down. Her breasts, full and heavy, responded to his fondling; her nipples became hard as thimbles. Her belly was firm and quivering, and she responded to his wet lower kisses by clawing at the sheets. Kate closed her eyes and settled deeply into the mattress as his tongue found the inner recesses of her body, and bliss . . .

In the morning when she awoke, John Prescott was gone . . . and so was the microfilm.

ACKNOWLEDGMENTS

By their very nature, books are rarely the product of a single hand. They are often collaborative affairs that involve many other people in the process, like editors, agents, researchers, friends, and relatives, besides the author who gets to have his name proudly displayed on the cover. I would also like to acknowledge several people who helped steady my hand or inspire me while I was writing *Murder on Air Force One*. First and foremost, I want to thank my early readers, Claudine Biggs and Pamela F. Peay, who had the opportunity to read the manuscript early, and offer valuable suggestions about its content. Next, I want to thank my friends and family who know what a flawed and imperfect man I am, and yet still find a place in their hearts for me. During the writing of this book, my cousin John passed away. He was only sixty-seven. Born the same weekend as the Roswell crash in 1947, he always kidded everyone that he was an alien, but John was, in fact, an extraordinary man with this incredible gift for love and hope. When I attended his funeral in Atlanta, I got to witness first-hand the extent of my family's unconditional love for me as the prodigal son who had not been home for more than thirty years. It was a truly wonderful feeling, made bitter-sweet by the loss of a man who meant the world to me. I lost my cousin Debbie, age 50, shortly after John's funeral; a former Miss

ACKNOWLEDGMENTS

USA runner-up, she also represented the embodiment of love and kindness. The world was diminished by the loss of these two, loving people, and we will not likely see their kind again. I want to thank my agent, Jeanie Loiacono, for her support, and helping find venues for my work. And finally, I want to thank the City of San Francisco and my late father John Johnson who still resides there in spirit.

ABOUT THE AUTHOR

Born in Chicago, Illinois, in the 1950s, Dr. John L. Flynn is a three-time Hugo Award–nominated author, psychologist, teacher, and college dean. In 1977, he received the M. Carolyn Parker Award from the University of South Florida for excellence in creative writing. He received his Bachelor's and Master's degrees in English from the University of South Florida and worked as an English teacher in Baltimore, Maryland. He published his first book *Future Threads* in 1985. In 1998, he earned his PhD as a clinical psychologist from the University of Southern California. He has published nearly twenty books and dozens of articles. He currently resides in Lake Worth, Florida.

THE KATE DAWSON MYSTERIES

FROM OPEN ROAD MEDIA

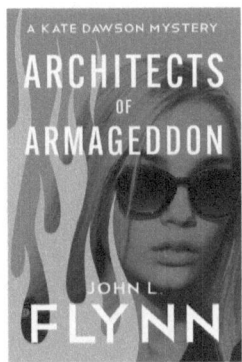
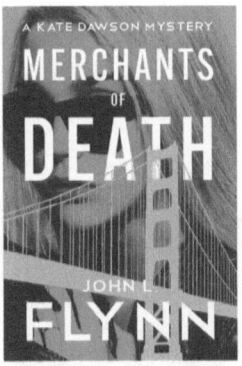

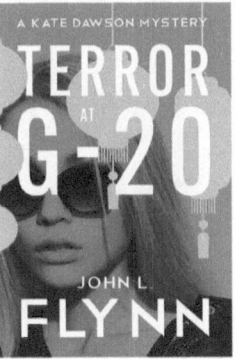